Unyielding

D W Macleod

Grateful thank you to:

Alexander for his tireless work and insightful suggestions. If this is any good, it is in large part due to you.

My wife and children for humouring and encouraging me in this endeavour.

Robert, Marianne and Mum for their unstinting encouragement.

Remembering Dad, who loved a good book.

Kitty Walker for her guidance after the first draft.

My brothers on session.

Mark 12 vs 1-12

&

Mark 10 vs 42-45

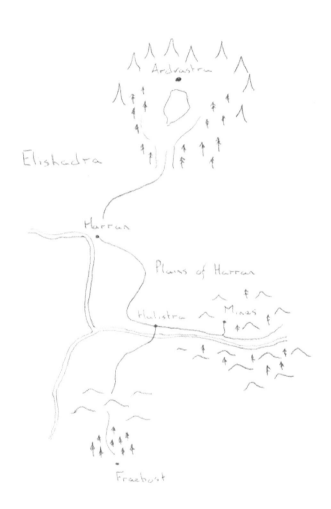

Prologue

Nehlo looked down at the man kneeling on the smooth stone floor. He was unsure and this made him irritable. The man was shackled and his arms wavered as they struggled to keep his body off the floor and away from the blood dripping onto the hard, impassive stone beneath him. His face, which bore a slightly unkempt beard, was swollen and bruised, the greying hair on his downturned head matted with blood and sweat. He was obviously weakened but Nehlo was sure, from the report he had just heard and the man's build, that he had been strong and a skilled fighter. He had no actual power though and it was this that made Nehlo unsure; without it how could this man have hoped to best him? Was it possible that he was being tricked, that there was a threat that he could not detect? These questions nagged at him, as did the only words the man had uttered since being half carried in.

"You came here to help me?" Nehlo mused, half to himself. He turned away and walked to the fire which always burned in this room. Holding out his hands he felt the warmth turn to pain in his fingers but he still felt chilled inside. He always felt cold inside. Stopping that train of thought he turned back to the man, who had not moved.

"Why would I need your help? What help could you hope to give me?"

The man did not answer, his eyes still fixed on the floor where a small pool of blood was forming from the drops falling from his brow. The hands which were cracked and weathered but strong strove for purchase to hold him up. Feeling a sudden surge of anger, Nehlo stepped forward and swept the hands away with his foot, watching as the man toppled forward, unable to protect his face from crashing onto the hard floor. The man gasped and almost choked as blood came from his mouth and nose and ran, unchecked, down his face. He drew his arms up and struggled back into a kneeling position. The eyes that now rose to meet Nehlo were wet but strangely clear and he read in them not fear or anger but something that stung him and made him want to look away. Nettled, he held the gaze, his

1

anger growing again though he was not sure why. He turned away again purposefully, looking at his attendants who stood ready to act on his smallest whim and felt the power that bound them to him, relishing again his ascendency. He looked again at the man, forcing himself to meet his questioning but defiant gaze. The man tried to speak, his lips moving noiselessly for a few seconds, and the voice when it came was hoarse and so soft that Nehlo instinctively leaned forward to hear it.

"How has it come to this? What has become of you?"

Startled, Nehlo for a second did not know how to answer. His initial response was to rebuke, to dismiss him with the violence his impudence deserved. The question, though, cut him deep, supposing, as it did, some knowledge of his prior self. He looked closely at the man again, trying to see past the lines, the matted beard, the bruising and swelling, and the pain that marred his face to see if he knew him. Something stirred in his memory of a friend, a life of lightness but no consequence, of loyalty amidst adversity, of being accepted; and he wondered. But that was impossible; it had been many years and his friend had been powerful. He delved again, searching carefully for any sign of power but again found none. He forced himself to be calm, to consider. When he spoke his voice was quiet, smooth again.

"Who are you? Why have you really come here?"

The man ignored the first question. "I have told you the truth. I am here to try to right some of the wrongs that you have done and to help you."

"I have done nothing wrong. And what help can you offer me? You cannot even help yourself."

"I can offer you a way back. It is not too late."

"A way back?"

"To a meaningful life, to acceptance once again, to healing rather than harm. To a right and good way of life before our maker. You would have to renounce your power, but it has only brought you misery and loneliness. Harm and suffering follow in your wake, but judgement stalks you."

A little spark of desire flitted through Nehlo, a yearning to be part of something, to be known and accepted, that briefly flared but uncomfortably so, like a gnawing pain as if he hungered. He forced himself to remember that the world he had renounced had never wanted him, never accepted him and only sought him out now because he had power that threatened it. A great wave of darkness and bitterness rolled over him, flooding through him, drowning out any desires.

"Renounce power? Only the weak and powerless think of this as a good thing. I don't believe in your god. I can do what I will, without any fear of the judgement you speak of."

He stopped again. He had not meant to engage with this man. He tried to master his thoughts again, to focus on determining what to do. This man had reached through to his inner circle and, if reports were correct, had undermined the power that he had built over many years. He did not fear for himself, he had spent years ensuring that his power was unmatched. It did raise questions though about how this man had unravelled so much and this uncertainty would not be quelled. There was silence, broken only by the crackle of the fire and the laboured breathing of the man before him who shifted on his hands to try to keep his

2

balance. He consciously stilled himself, relishing the coldness, the lack of emotion, knowing that in this state he was capable of anything. He spoke softly.

"There is no meaning to life without power. I have no desire to give that up for the paltry things you have spoken of."

The man raised his head again and looked at him directly. "You understand little of what is happening and even less of the judgement that awaits you. You have abused the power the creator gave you and trampled on the laws he wove into the world. You cannot be allowed to carry on as you are; you have caused too much harm and suffering." The man's words came quickly but he had to stop to regain his breath. He spoke more slowly, effortfully, on restarting. "Whatever happens here, your power will be broken but it does not have to be this way. I offer you again the chance to come with me, to leave this country to let it heal before it is too late for you. There is still mercy for you."

Mercy! The word stung Nehlo. He loathed this above all things. Only the weak and broken sought mercy, those who had no other option but to beg from people in whose power they lay. He knew no master, recognized no authority and lived as he chose, without recourse to any other or thought of consequence. He glanced at his attendants, standing around him with their heads lowered but hearing all that was said. They were lined against each wall, their faces hidden in the shadow cast by the flickering lamps behind them, but he was sure he had seen one of them watching him. Once the thought had arisen he could not shake it. What was the look he had seen in their eye? Had it been scorn, or pity? He felt acid rise in his throat but swallowed it down impatiently. He knew they could not speak of anything they saw or heard but the thought that they might interpret these moments as weakness grew in his mind, bringing images of them smiling derisively. He glared at them in turn, willing them to betray some hint of disdain, but their heads were downcast. Except that same one man; had he been slower than the others? Surely he had meant to meet his gaze. The thought that this wretch, bound as he was, might think him weak provoked a savage anger. It overtook him before he was able to quell it, sweeping away his awareness, power channelling into shaping, compressing, forging. He surged towards his attendant, driving his rage through his hands which cut down savagely, blood pouring from the deep gash left in their wake. His attendant fell, hands clutching feebly at his neck. The man could not cry out but Nehlo saw his terror as he died and this doused his anger. He felt the familiar emptiness taking its place and welcomed the control it afforded.

Breathing heavily, he looked around, taking in the sparseness of the room, the darkness of the window recesses, from which little of the moonlight penetrated, and the stillness. He felt calmer as he turned back to the man who even in that short time looked more frail, old and pathetic. He resolved to end this pointless discussion, to be done with him and with him to finally end any lingering feelings about his past life and be stronger for it.

"I have no need of mercy."

Hearing those words, the man's head bowed and he dropped his gaze to the floor. His shoulders sagged and his arms shook as they lost what little strength remained in them. Nehlo feared no one now, not even his past masters and cared nothing for the laws they upheld and lived by; he had surpassed them long ago. He felt nothing but contempt for the man in front of him but even now, with the

3

man broken and barely able to kneel, he continued to feel this uncertainty that was alien to him. He chastened himself and banished the doubts from his mind. He moved purposefully forward and raised his arms once more. The man offered no resistance or plea, no movement at all except the ragged motion of his chest as he breathed in gasps. All Nehlo could see now was a pathetic, broken shadow of a man.

Chapter 1

Tam stopped just at the turning of the track where the town came into view. He adjusted the straps on the horse walking beside him, but his attention was on the wooden walls and gate ahead of him. There was not much activity – it being the middle of the afternoon; those working the fields had yet to return and what merchants visited were inside. Two guards stood nonchalantly at the gate with their spears laid against the wall their swords on their hips. There was almost certainly a small garrison inside a town this size but neither they nor the guards concerned him.

Having finished his scrutiny Tam picked up the reins again and walked along the track to the town, his horse by his side. The guards looked up as he approached but saw nothing to concern or interest them. He was of spare build and unarmed, carrying the necessary pack and dust from the road of someone who had travelled some distance that day. His hair, which was closely cut, was sandy brown but now greying, his face was lean but not hard and though there were some lines on his face, it was a little difficult to age him. His clothing was plain and though clearly well worn was well kept and looked to be of good quality. He kept his gaze downward and did not meet their eyes which raked over him before dismissing him and allowing him through.

Tam led his horse through the gate and up what appeared to be the main street in the town. The buildings on either side were built of wood and rose two stories, though some leaned in towards each other creating a closed-in atmosphere. He looked around but was careful not to attract anyone's notice. Everyone walked in the same manner, heads bent down, moving fast and not paying overt attention to the people around them. He threaded his way through the people, moving toward an inn that he had spied. There was nothing outwardly to distinguish this inn from any other but he could sense a difference, a slight but noticeable reduction in the darkness that he could feel all around him. It would be enough. He tied his horse at the front and went in the door, stopping momentarily, just inside, to adjust his sight to the loss of light. He continued in and leant forward at the bar to catch the attention of the landlord. What few people were there resumed their conversations as the landlord moved toward him. Tam was aware of the landlord measuring him before, having decided he was no threat, beckoning him to take a seat.

"I don't recognize you sir and I know most people in Fraebost."

Tam acknowledged this with a slight nod. "No, I have just travelled for two days and am in need of shelter and warm food for me and my horse."

"Those you will find here," the landlord replied with a smile. Tam looked up at him and caught his eye for a few seconds before looking away again. The eyes that met him were alert and watchful but also frank and open.

"I would appreciate a room and a meal but first I must see to my horse." The landlord nodded and told him where the stables could be found out behind the inn, adding that he would have some hot food ready for him on his return.

Tam walked his horse round to the rear of the inn. He found an empty stall and, taking his time, rubbed down his horse, talking to it in soft whispers. It was a fine animal, built for endurance and speed rather than show and he had grown fond of it over the last few months, it becoming a companion of sorts. Ensuring it had food and water, he left and returned to the inn to find the landlord as good as his word and hot food on the table waiting for him.

The room was sizable, though the ceiling was low and the windows small. Pleasant smells of cooking lingered, mixing with the remnants of smoke from the oil lamps hung in the corners that would be lit in the evenings. As he ate he watched the people around him. They were clustered together in close-knit groups, hunched over tables with tankards in the middle and some breads and cheese. They spoke in quiet tones, their heads leaning in, so it was difficult to pick up anything of their conversations. A few people sat alone or silently with a companion, tiredness etched into their faces. He noticed some glances being directed surreptitiously in his direction, but he feigned ignorance. He heard the door open and turning saw some guards walk in, a woman at their head. The room went quiet and just then the landlord bustled back into the room before stopping abruptly, his face turning pale.

Tam felt the tension in the room and he reflexively lowered his head while keeping his gaze roving carefully between the people. He could feel a slight darkness emanating from the woman; it was nothing he could see, just a sense that something was off kilter, that the air was heavier with a tang that was mildly sickening. She was of slight build with dark brown hair that gave her a youthful appearance though her face was thin, the skin stretched tightly across sharp cheek bones. Her eyes constantly darted from place to place, at odds with her movements, which were slow and deliberate, careful in the way big cats were when stalking their prey. She walked to the middle of the room while her men stayed behind her with hands on their sword hilts, feet spread apart in readiness, their eyes searching for movement. There was none, however, except a further lowering of heads to avoid attention. The sound of movement and passers-by outside, previously unnoticed, drifted in to mock the silence that had enveloped the room.

The woman surveyed everyone, seemingly unmoved by the reaction she and her men had caused. She pointed at a man who was sitting at one of the tables and two of her men moved forward swiftly followed by two more who drew their swords but stood a little back, the final two remaining at the door, their hands ready over their weapons. The man scrabbled back, his seat toppling over behind him as he struggled to get up. Before he could move any further the guards reached him and pushed him heavily in the chest causing him to crash backward over the fallen chair. He landed awkwardly, the arm trapped beneath him twisting with a horrible crack that Tam could hear, sitting ten paces away. The man yelped in pain but tried to rise, his eyes casting around for support. Tam sensed movement in the tables nearest as if some considered rising but with looks and gestures from others they stayed in their places, their faces blank.

The woman had noticed though. She stepped forward and spoke with a strong authoritative voice. "The mayor has commanded that he be taken. It will go better for everyone if you do not intervene." The man on the ground whimpered slightly, but no one else moved and they kept their eyes assiduously fixed on the tables in front of them.

The guards pulled the man to his feet, ignoring his cry of pain as they gripped his arms tightly. He looked around desperately, hoping for someone to come to his aid but his appeal foundered on hunched backs that tensely averted themselves from him. His body went limp and he had to be half carried, half dragged from the room, his face registering a despair and betrayal that struck Tam forcefully, almost causing him to rise from his seat before he remembered that he could not afford to reveal anything of himself. The remaining guards fanned out around the prisoner, their eyes roving across everyone, watchful and challenging. The woman nodded and gestured for them to leave. Her eyes met Tam's for a second and she studied him appraisingly before he looked away, not wanting to seem to challenge her, though he felt a mix of shame and anger at doing so. She turned away, beckoning her men to follow. The landlord stepped forward as if he wanted to remonstrate with her but before she saw him he stopped and turned away with a pained and shameful look on his face.

Silence wrapped the room long after the guards had left with their prisoner. Tam took a deep breath, consciously relaxing the tension that had built in his jaw. He did not feel scared, just angry that he had been unable to intervene. He wondered for a second whether he should have but then what effect might that have on the task that lay ahead of him? He would witness worse he was sure; he mentally added this incident to the tally building in his head by way of some recompense. He did not know whether the man's arrest had been justified but the nature and suddenness of it, as well as the lack of given reason, made him doubt it. Glancing cautiously around, he saw shock on most faces and some anger, but not as much as he had expected. The overwhelming sense he got was of resignation; most of the men looked down, their hands fingering cups that remained undrunk, their eyes staring but not focusing. Tam knew from their responses that other people had been taken in a similar way; maybe they had once protested or resisted but they had clearly learned not to. He could understand that; when things started to turn bad, as he knew they had here, you just had to look after yourself and your nearest. Finally, the landlord bustled forward, the sudden movement jarring with the lassitude that had threatened to settle over everyone. He saw that Tam had pushed the remains of his meal away and came toward him, his manner falsely jovial though his tall broad frame was stooped and a sheen of sweat lay across his face, which was still pale. He rubbed his hands on the cloth at his waist, leaving them there for a moment before picking up the plates.

"I am sorry for that disturbance. Not right, but there you go. Is there anything else I can get for you?"

Tam shook his head slightly, but the landlord remained standing, his pained gaze on the table where the man had sat.

"Do you know him?" Tam asked quietly.

7

The landlord did not seem to hear for a second before responding mechanically, "Oh, yes. All of us do." He then caught himself and stopped, suddenly alert and suspicious. Tam raised his hands slightly and looked at the landlord steadily.

"I am a stranger here. I just want to understand what happened. The man had no look of a criminal."

The landlord held his gaze before looking down and continuing quietly. "He was no criminal. I have known him many a year. He just talks too loudly."

"What will happen to him?"

The landlord sighed. "I don't know." He paused again, his slightly lined face suddenly sagging. Around them people were starting to rise and leave. He turned and murmured his goodbyes, clasping some by the hand as they passed. Before long only a few others remained. The landlord turned back to Tam.

"What are you in town for if you don't mind me asking? We don't get that many visitors."

Tam thought before answering. "I am just passing through really. I am on my way to Ardvastra, where I have some business to finish."

The landlord looked surprised for a second. "The capital. That is some way yet and from what I hear it is not the friendliest place to be as a visitor. Still, I am sure you know what you are doing."

Tam shrugged his shoulders slightly but did not want to dwell on his destination just now or draw further attention to it, so he changed tack. "Have you been here a while?"

"Coming on twenty years."

"The leader of the guards, she spoke of a mayor. I take it he is in charge here?"

"Yes, though we rarely see him now. The captain of the guard, the lady you mention, she does his bidding and reports back to him. She marked you as new here, so unless you want some unwelcome attention I would move on quickly."

Tam nodded and then asked quietly, "Have you met the mayor? What is he like?"

The landlord started back and looked around quickly before turning back to him with an angry look. "No, I have not met him, nor could I hope to. What he is like is none of my business. I just look after my own affairs."

Tam held up his hands again. "Sorry, I did not mean to pry. I just like to get an idea of the places I am traveling through."

"Okay, but a piece of advice," he said quietly as he leaned in to pick up a knife that had fallen from the plates. "It does not pay to ask those kind of questions around here, or anywhere. There are many who would cause you trouble for even thinking them."

With that he motioned for Tam to follow him and led him upstairs to a room containing a bed, a chair and a bowl of water for washing. It was clean if a little shabby.

"Thank you for the food and the room," Tam said, holding out a small silver coin in payment. The landlord took it and paused for a moment.

"Can I ask your name?"

Tam paused briefly before giving it.

The landlord reached out and took Tam's hand in a strong grip. "Well Tam, I am John. I hope you rest well." With that he turned to leave but stopped at the door with one hand on the latch. He paused before saying in a slightly forced voice, "My apologies for my terseness downstairs. It is not the welcome I wish to give visitors but these are difficult times as you saw and loose talk to strangers is foolish."

Tam thought quickly. He needed to know more but did not want to raise more suspicion than necessary. Maybe though, John was willing to say more? He decided to take the risk. "Did things begin to change when the mayor arrived?"

He saw John stiffen but he did not immediately respond. When he did it was quietly and hesitantly. "Aye, or soon after. But the real blow was the change in the guard who were there for everyone before, but who now solely act for him and his interests." Tam could sense the bitterness and anger in his words, but John remained still. "But the worst of it is we do nothing about it. We are like foxes living off scraps yet fearful of the boot above us."

Tam wanted to reach out to him, give some sort of encouragement, but knew that it would be meaningless from him. He felt his own anger rise at what this big, seemingly decent man had been reduced to and had to accept.

John cleared his throat suddenly and ran his hand across his brow. "Don't mind me. I can get melancholy at times. If you need anything I will be down in the bar area." And with that, he opened the door and quickly left, pulling it tight after him,

Tam sat heavily on the bed, thinking about everything he had seen and heard in the short time he had been there. The enormity of the task ahead of him pressed down on him but the need for action or change goaded him on. He went to the window which overlooked the main road in front of the inn. The road was fairly busy with people, some on foot, others leading horses hitched to carts carrying household goods or produce for sale, as well as the occasional horse-drawn carriage. There was, however, none of the hustle and bustle of a normal street. What conversations occurred were in low tones. Those with things to sell were calling out their wares, but even they did so with care rather than striving to outdo those next to them. No one lingered; everyone conducted their business and moved on. Someone passed in a carriage and all the people averted their gaze in obvious submission. Tam pulled himself away from the window and lay on the bed, his thoughts busy but unsettled. He thought how easy it was to destroy a community, to seed division and mistrust and how hard it was to build it again. He knew he had been marked out by the captain of the guard as being new and therefore meriting attention that he did not want. He had to move fast now as it was imperative that he stayed ahead of any word reaching Nehlo, but he must also do what he could for the people of this town.

Chapter 2

Seth put his glass on the table, listening to the arguments around him which were expressed in urgent, quiet voices. Around him were ten or so men and women, ranging in years from his own, the age of completion of an apprenticeship, to some older men who were about to lay down their trade and enter retirement. He knew them all, either personally or through someone close to him; they had to be able to trust each other. All looked serious and he knew all would be armed, though covertly as carrying arms in Harran was forbidden unless you were one of the guard.

"This can't work. He has too many people around him." That was Thomas, who looked worried, unable to sit at ease.

"But we have to do something because no one else is," Kayla countered. She was always outspoken, something Seth liked about her.

"With just us?"

"No, we know some other folks who we think would join us if they felt it had any chance of success." Alec answered Thomas this time, with his easy confidence.

One of the older men, Neil, gave Alec a keen look. "That is the problem though, isn't it? Folks did try a year or so back but they disappeared before anything came of it and that has scared a lot of people. And why would this be any different?"

"It has to be, that's all." Seth felt Kayla's frustration rising as she spoke. "Every day things get worse, ordinary folk either get more angry or worse more beaten down, and the others rub our noses in it. If we don't do something soon and harness the remaining anger there will be no resistance left."

"I don't disagree with you lass," Neil replied, "but how do you approach people with this? How do you know who to trust? There is a lot of fear and uncertainty out there."

Suddenly the candles on the table flickered, and the flames pulled toward the door and windows. Within seconds they all went out, plunging the room into darkness before their eyes adjusted to the little light coming in the windows from the bright moon outside and the streetlamps. Everyone stood, pushing chairs back, which toppled over and created noise that masked any sign of potential threat. Seth stood too, suddenly uncertain, and his hand went automatically to his sword. He backed toward the nearest exit, pulling Kayla and Neil with him.

He felt something grasp him. He tried to shake his arms free but they moved slowly and with great effort. His breathing became laboured with pressure building on his chest and throat. He sought to quell the rising panic inside of him, but still he felt as if he could not get enough air in. Blackness started to crowd his vision, and he swayed just as his hand reached the door handle and wrenched it open. He gulped the cold air from outside that rushed in on them but then felt a rough hand push him down. Stumbling, he turned in time to see Neil, arm outstretched, gasp as a blade sank into his chest, blood leaking all around it. Looking up, Seth grabbed his own short sword and stabbed upward, feeling it catch in the man above him who grunted but raised his own sword again. Kayla was past him now though, and she pushed their attacker away, her own short knife cutting across his arm. Seth turned to help Neil, but he was on his knees, his breathing laboured. He pushed Seth away, urging him to go with the last of his strength as he fell prostrate on the ground.

Alec was out of the door now and Seth could hear him breathing heavily behind him as he turned and ran. From inside he could hear the sounds of metal crashing off metal and the cries of their friends as they were cut down. Two more figures loomed out of the shadows, their swords cutting arcs through the air. Seth ducked and stabbed clumsily as he ran, somehow finding unprotected flesh. Wrenching his blade free he ran a few steps before remembering that Alec was behind him and that the other assailant was uninjured. He turned and saw Alec swiftly draw up close, parry the first blows before returning them with smooth arcs, moving forward as his attacker desperately defended himself. Alec moved too fast though and twisting reached under the struggling blade of his opponent and thrust forward, piercing him just below the ribs. The man dropped his sword and fell to the ground, hands seeking to stem the flow of blood. Seth turned and ran, once more hearing Alec's footsteps close behind him.

Seth followed Kayla as they left the sounds of battle behind them and kept running, moving through the city streets at random until the sound of pursuit had fallen far behind them. Seth leaned between Kayla and Alec, against a wall in the short lane, and struggled to get his breath back and stop his heart from pounding with painful force. There was silence for a long moment. Seth tried to take in what had just happened and the awful thought of the people they had left behind, who were almost certainly now dead. In the darkness of the lane a heaviness seemed to sink in and around him. His chest felt constricted making his breathing somehow difficult for a few moments. His eyes moistening, he saw again Neil, slumping down clutching the bleeding wound that by rights should have been his. Suddenly, he felt weak and cold, and he gripped the sides of his legs hard to stop his hands from shaking. An acid taste filled his mouth, and he thought for a second he might be sick.

He felt an arm round his shoulders causing him to straighten and meet Kayla's concerned gaze. She looked pale and shaken but also angry. Alec had moved from the wall, his face hard but his agitation showing in his constant pacing the short width of the alley. Seth took some deep breaths, trying to calm the whirl of thoughts and emotions that had seemed to be carrying him away. The slight pressure of touch and the sight of his friends gave him a small sense of connection to his surroundings again and enabled him to think more clearly.

11

What had happened? Surely he had not imagined the feeling of suffocating, of fighting for the very air he breathed? Had he panicked? But then, everyone had reacted the same; everyone had experienced the same. Something had happened to them all, and it had led directly to the slaughter of everyone but those who stood with him now. He could not imagine anyone else making it out of there alive. He could not understand or really remember how they had made it, except for that moment when he had felt Neil's hand pushing him down, out of harm's way. Fear clutched him again. What were they facing? Who could do these things? How could they fight back against such a thing? And then he felt ashamed of his fear. He had lived where others had not been so fortunate. He felt an alien desire to feel some physical pain, as if that would ease some of the mental pain and somehow connect him to those who had died so suddenly. He let out a long breath which almost turned to a groan and broke the silence. He wanted to say something, to express what he felt.

"I feel awful about Neil." He paused, looking for the words. "He was always good to me and was as honest as they come. He saved me back there or it would have been me lying on the ground." Seth felt tears spring up again and his voice catch as he spoke his name.

The others did not speak for a moment, but Alec stopped his pacing and looked at him and Kayla in turn. "He was a good man. They were all good people." His voice was hoarse and forced but he looked angry now, his mouth set.

"Someone must have told them. And what makes it even more sickening is it must have been someone we know." Kayla sounded drained but there was a hint of anger there too that Seth just could not muster.

Alec nodded grimly. "Someone we knew. Whoever told them, they may well have died back there. It did not save them."

Seth heard these last words but did not have the energy to respond. For the moment he just wanted to forget, to slip into the unfeeling of sleep in the safety of his home. He grasped their hands briefly, agreeing when they would next meet before walking homeward, his steps wooden, his mind blank. Despite this and his weariness he somehow knew that sleep would elude him.

Back outside the building a woman stood watching as men carried away the bodies. She had lost four men, but that did not concern her. Her informant was also likely dead, but that was a small price to pay and there would be others, happy to betray for money or influence. It had been a year now since a similar group had sprung up. She had no thoughts about them being a threat to her, but they could cause trouble, and she had worked hard to create an order of sorts in this city, order that kept her at the helm and everyone else in their place. At least two people had escaped, judging from the bodies of her men at the rear entrance way. They would need to be found and dealt with.

She felt the pulse of the bond in her mind. This subjection angered her; a part of her longed to throw it off and to act on her own, for herself, but she knew she never would. It was too big a risk and she had more than she had ever thought to have. Nehlo always found out when she went her own way with what latitude she had. She was not certain of it, but she suspected he had spies everywhere, feeding back to him alone. Powerful as she was, she was fully aware that she was at his mercy, that her power came from him and could be taken away again. What would she have then? Her influence? What was that without power or fear to support it? It would fade quickly. No, she had made her choice and would accept her place as others had to accept theirs. Turning she ordered her men to dispose of the bodies carefully. She left then, walking swiftly through the dark streets, looking straight ahead her hooded cloak hiding her features.

Chapter 3

Tam stood on the roof of one of the taller buildings in Fraebost. He carried nothing and was dressed in the clothes he had travelled in. From here he could see the large house on the top of the slight hill at the centre of the town. It was the darkest period of the night, but he could see the outline of the building due to the lights flickering at different points around it. He could see the shadowy figures of people clustered round the lights, some standing looking outward, others hunched around small stoves, where likely some tea was brewing. Everything else was quiet and still, unusual for a town this size where there were often some people out, even if they were generally not up to any good. There must be some sort of curfew, Tam thought to himself, but now that it was enforced the security had obviously relaxed, which helped him this night. Tam counted the figures, numbering about ten in total and then doubled that to avoid any nasty surprises. He then mapped his route into the building; once he started speed was his ally. He did not want to fight his way through to the mayor who, long experience had told him, was going to be in the highest point of the building. Either way, he would know where to find him when he got nearer. There was a wall surrounding the house, about eight feet in height, Tam estimated; high enough for a normal residence but not really a defence against concerted attack. Beyond the wall was a garden with trees and then the house, rising three stories. A balcony on the third floor, safe from normal thieves and burglars, was his entry point.

Decisions made, Tam moved. Running lightly over the roof he jumped and as he did so summoned the air beneath him to lift him up and carry him, noting momentarily the wind as it rushed in to fill the space he had created. He felt energy fizz through him, the wonderfully familiar lurch as he was propelled forward. The noise of the sudden wind caught the attention of the guard whose gaze was drawn to it and therefore did not see his approach. He skirted over the remaining houses and controlled his speed to land somewhat heavily on the wall. Releasing the air it whistled back, causing some of the loose shutters of the nearby houses to bang. The guards on his side of the building, already on alert, now started and rose to their feet, looking outward, weapons ready. Tam, above them on the wall and over to one side saw this but did not hesitate to wait for their next reaction. He lowered himself down off the wall and ran lightly through the garden, shielded from view by the trees. He stopped, listening and feeling for any movement of approaching people but nothing came. He moved forward and jumped, once again summoning the air to lift him up to the balcony wall thirty feet above him, which, having grasped with both hands, he pulled himself over and dropped lightly onto the rough stone. Crouching with his back to the wall he heard and felt the air move back again, rustling through the branches and leaves of the trees he had just run through. He paused for a second, stilling his heart and breathing.

Tam now scanned the window in front of him and felt through to the room beyond. He did not trust the window to be silent, so he carefully channelled tendrils of air into the cracks and crevices, removing the grime and rust and loosening it in its holdings. He then moved the air beneath the window and lifted it up smoothly before slipping inside and closing it again. Once inside he stopped again. He could not hear any disturbance outside or in, sensing with satisfaction that the guards had not raised any alarm. The easy bit done, he now moved further into the house, casting his senses ahead of him to feel for anyone there but questing mainly for the mayor, whom he knew would be obvious to him, tainted as he was. He sensed him, close by but also someone else walking between them. He moved now silently, air cushioning his footfalls, so that he disturbed nothing as he crossed the room and moved out into the hallway.

He saw her immediately on coming into the hallway, but she was walking away from him. Her hand lay upon her sword, which sat easily on her hip. He could not see her face, but he guessed that she was the leader of the guards he had seen earlier at the inn. He would need to be careful. She was almost certainly bonded to the mayor's will. He ran lightly toward her, flicking some air ahead of him to attract her attention away from his coming advance. She spun round as he reached her, which surprised him but by that point he was too near. He compressed the air around her face into a small bung, suffocating her before weaving it into a line which he wrapped around her hands and legs. He sensed her consciousness leave her and lowered her gently on the lines of air to the floor, her face still showing the shock of his attack.

Still there was no noise, though he expected the mayor to have been alerted now to his presence; his master would have given him enough talent to subdue most threats, so he would be dangerous. He crept quietly to the door and pushed it open. The slight compression of the air ahead of him alerted him and he ducked and rolled, feeling the blade pass over him and glance off the door. He was on his feet and turning in one movement. The man before him was bigger than him and strong with a sword held loosely in both hands. He showed obvious surprise at Tam being unarmed but came in again, thrusting his sword forward in a quick movement before at the last second anticipating Tam's defensive move and flicking his blade to the side. Tam saw and felt both movements as well as the intent to kill him. He deflected the strike with a band of air, pushing the blade further than it was meant to go, the mayor tilting slightly as he over-reached. In the same instant, Tam gathered the air on that side, compressing it tightly till it was solid, the lights flickering out as he created a brief vacuum in the room before more air seeped under the doors and windows with a howl. He pushed off the wall he had created and using the momentum moved swiftly to the side of the mayor now left undefended, refining the air he had just projected himself from into a razor-sharp blade. Almost gently, his blade stroked across the mayor, beneath his sword, and sliced through his jerkin and skin, blood following its path.

15

The mayor staggered at the blow but did not collapse. Tam reshaped the air he held again and now forced it toward the man, seeking to bind him. The mayor fought back but this was not a battle of physical strength and Tam had years of training and skill. The mayor sagged, the air pressing in on him, stopping his breathing and binding his arms to his side. He stared now with panicked eyes at Tam as he struggled for oxygen, the invisible band tightening around his limbs and throat. Tam watched him closely and then relaxed his hold, just before he sensed the man about to lose consciousness. He released the bond of air around his throat but kept his arms tightly bound. At this, the man looked at Tam, calculating, then started to speak, his voice initially coming out in a rasping noise before becoming stronger, though it remained a low hiss throughout.

"You are a fool to meddle here. If you kill me, my master will know it, and he will find you. You cannot hide from him any more than I, and your power is nothing compared to his."

Tam focused on him, willing him with the intensity of his gaze to listen. He spoke clearly but quietly.

"I have no intention of killing you, but you must face justice for what you have done here. I cannot, and do not want, to save you from that. What I offer you is freedom from your master. A chance to make amends, to pay the price for what you have done and start again."

The man looked at him with confusion mixed with anger in his eyes. Tam knew that he had willingly given himself to Nehlo, allowed himself to be bonded in exchange for the talents and skills he had been given and the promise of rule and power. It was possible though that he had come to realize the horror of what that bargain had meant. He spoke again.

"I ask you to give up your bond to me. You will lose your power to bond others and what skill you have been given, but you have lost it already this night. If you don't, I will take the bond from you, but I warn you, doing it forcefully will leave you damaged in ways that I can't protect you from."

Tam watched him closely for his response. He saw in the man's eyes suspicion that he wanted the power for himself, to use in his place. To be able to give up the bond he would need to want to with every fibre of his being, to renounce utterly and completely his previous master and all that he had been offered. Tam thought there was little hope of that, but he offered him one last chance.

"Choose now, as I cannot wait for others to find me here. Give it to me willingly and take your chances with the people here. Plead what you will about being forced to act as you have. If you choose not to give it to me, then I will take it. I cannot leave you to cause more harm."

The man's face contorted into an ugly leer, the lips twitching upward, the eyes narrowing. "You cannot know what you face, or you would not dare to attack me in this way. Your offer is meaningless as you have neither the power to do what you must or what you suggest. You should turn now and flee while you have this chance. I will give you till morning to be gone before I hunt you down."

The man waited for a second before lashing out with all his strength, his arms straining against the bonds that held them, his head pitching forwards with his teeth bared and a growl-like noise ripping through. Tam felt the power of the mayor's hatred and anger as he sought to control the air around him to rip it from Tam and attack him with it. Tam forced him back with steely determination, building the pressure again until it pressed down with too great a weight onto the mayor, his muscles still straining ineffectually against it, his breathing coming in short, limited gasps. Tam reached forward and took the man's head in both hands. He delved, seeking the most tainted part of the man's mind. Finding it, he mentally focused on it and drew it into himself, feeling it resist but then rip away as he continued to pull.

Tam recoiled in disgust as it settled into his own mind and immediately started to reach out to ensnare him. He could feel it trying to taint his thoughts, as if a creeping plant tried to grow through the crevices of his mind, leaving a sickening decay in its wake. But it was active, searching for weakness, for areas it could reside and grow, feeding off his own impurity, his anger, his ambition, his cowardice and greed, the many parts of himself that he alone saw and tried to face down every day. Parts that rationally he knew were common to all, but if the bonding held sway would be amplified, controlling him and leaving him prey to its master's will. Breathing deeply to counter the nausea and anxiety that threatened to well up, he focused again and imprisoned it with layer upon layer of his own defences, his own conscious will, till its effect was muted, but still he could feel it, pulsing in the periphery of his mind.

The man sagged now, powerless. His lips drooped on one side and his strength gave way. He fell forward, groping with his hands which Tam now released. He could not speak though, his voice coming in gasps. He would improve but Tam did not know what long lasting effects there would be. He felt a moment of sympathy for this man now as he had nothing left and would not be the last to fall for what his master offered.

Tam sensed movement around him as the enforced bonding that the mayor had put upon the captain and the guard was released. Looking once more at the mayor who lay prostate on the floor, he left the room. He released the weaves of air that held the captain and checked quickly as he passed that she was breathing steadily. Returning to the window he vaulted over the balcony wall, drawing air around him to break his fall to the ground, the rustle through the trees going unnoticed. At the guard posts he could see movement as they moved uncertainly toward the house in a large group, obviously seeking the man who had held them enslaved, yet unsure of what lay before them. In their anger he was not sure what they would do so reaching out he slammed the door to the mayor's room using tendrils of air to lock it. He hoped that would slow their advance long enough for their anger to cool and others to arrive. He had no wish for anarchy to be the result of this night.

Turning Tam sprang over the wall and gently down the other side. He walked now through the town, not caring which direction he took. He needed time to consider everything that had happened in those brief moments. He had started on a path that he could not return from. He would either succeed or die and he knew that as surely as he felt the taint now that was present in his mind.

Chapter 4

Zoe paced the hallway, her stride languid but senses alert. She felt exhausted, but she could not rest. He would not let her rest, not while he did. Her hand rested on the sword and moved with the handle as she walked, the movement giving a sense of rhythm, an order that she latched onto and which let her drift from her task for a moment. Then her mind darkened again, and she once again became his sentry, guarding him against any foe while he slept. He filled her thoughts; his command directed her will, and she knew no other.

A little sliver of something slanted into the darkness. What was that? A memory? She grasped it for a second, hungry. Her walking continued, back and fore, as she grappled to focus on the something. A younger woman, proud, standing in front of a group of people, mainly men. Two people were at the front, with proud faces. Something was being attached to her shoulder; the two people were clapping and smiling. Turning she could see a smaller group, dressed as she was now, but standing to attention as she walked among them. She tried to look back to those two people, to see their faces, to feel the strange warmth of their presence like the sun breaking momentarily through dark winter clouds. But the darkness was returning, the will that crowded out all thought of self or others. She had been commanded to guard while he slept and suddenly her senses were sharp again, straining to listen for the sound of someone approaching, her hand twitching at her sword, loosening it in its scabbard to make it ready. The walking made it easier, fending off the tiredness.

She stiffened slightly. What was that faint noise? She kept walking, but her focus was behind her, listening, appraising. Whoever they were, they would not get to her master; she would not, could not let them. Another slight noise caught her attention, this time in front, as if someone had kicked a stone by accident. But she knew the original noise had been behind her. A part of her liked her cunning, seeing through such ruses easily. Spinning round suddenly she started to draw her sword, ready to strike without warning.

For a second she could not work out what was happening, but then she realized she could not breath. She tried again to suck air in but nothing came; her chest heaved as her heart hammered on it. She tried to lift her hands, but they were tied to her sides though she could see nothing. She broke into a sweat, fear flooding through the darkness. What was happening to her? Focusing, she saw a man approaching, someone she recognized but could not immediately place. He looked surprised. No, disappointed. She felt herself falling backward but strangely slowly. She tried to reach out to grab something but could not with her arms pinioned to her sides. Her vision closed in and the man's face, looking intently at her, faded from view.

Zoe opened her eyes slowly, carefully. She did not immediately know where she was. Something was different. She was lying on something hard, her hands by her sides. Turning, she saw a shut door near her before she realized she was on the floor.

Suddenly the memory of what happened flooded in. She gasped, panicked, but air flowed in, filling her lungs beautifully, and she sucked it in greedily. She lifted her hands to her face and stared at them as they moved freely. Slowly she stood, flexing every muscle in turn, enjoying the movement and strength. But this was not what was different, wonderful as it was when only moments ago, it seemed, she had been powerless. What was it?

She looked around her, taking in the hallway and the stairway beyond with its elaborate banister. She looked at the pictures on the walls, enjoying the different colours and use of light. One was of woodland, and it triggered a memory of swinging from branches as a young girl before leaping down and resting against the rough bark. She could almost feel it. As she enjoyed the memory, she was almost fearful she would lose it. They had always been fleeting intrusions into the darkness. But this time the darkness did not flood back, no voice filled her head but her own, no alien commands demanded her attention. She fought to concentrate, to focus on her thoughts, to filter them for any sign of him, but she could not find any. A feeling of lightness in her chest arose as if she were unshackled and could float free. A thought appeared that she could just leave this place, walk down the stairs and out the door, leave the town behind and find these woods. She delighted in this idea, almost tempting something to come in and take if from her. But nothing did. She allowed herself to believe for a second that she might be free, but suddenly scared, she pushed it away. She lifted the picture down and stared at it more closely, seeing all the detail, her gaze following the trails and branches.

She heard a clamour of noise outside that was unusual at this hour. Was there a gathering happening? Maybe she could join in? Then she realized where she stood and at whose door. It remained shut. Maybe the mayor was under attack? She should do something. But then, shockingly, a stronger thought barged its way into her head. Why not join the attackers? The mayor was nothing to her. Worse, he had been her tormentor. Anger filled her, like the fire that rose from her belly after taking a strong spirit. It made her vision clear and her muscles tingle with a vitality that she did not think she had felt before. Drawing her sword, she stepped forward confidently, pulling on the door. It was locked, which was strange. Taking a key from her belt, she opened the door and pushed it wide with a smooth strong movement. She stalked into the room, wishing him to be awake so she could strike him.

Initially she saw nothing, but as her eyes adjusted, she saw a figure lying on the bed. She raised her sword, but something stilled her, and pausing, she gave it attention. The same memory of her parents, of her parade, where she had been promoted to lead the guard. Her pride, almost bursting out of her, at their love and at the respect of her people. And she knew that she was not someone who killed anyone in their sleep. Even this man who had enslaved her.

How had he done that? How had she changed from that woman to become an extension of his will? She could not remember clearly. A fog existed between memories that she knew to be her own and those the last years had spawned. Had it been a touch, a word? Had she? She could barely think it, the sickness of shame rising quickly. Had she wanted it? Had he offered her something? She did not think so. She had never wanted power or men in that way, but maybe he had found some weakness? She forced herself to look at him again, meaning to wake him, but then she realized that he had changed as well. He looked weak, pathetic even. His face drooped, his eyes were glazed, saliva dripped from his slack mouth. He was alive but severely weakened. She knew with certainty that he would not be able to harm her ever again. Pity tinged her loathing. He could not defend himself. She would not lower herself further. Turning, she walked from the room, closing and locking the door behind her.

She slumped on the floor, resting her sword across her knees. She touched the blade, feeling its sharpness, enjoying its definition. Her mind buzzed with activity that threatened to overwhelm her. Every thought her own. That thought was suddenly tinged with bitterness, however, as she realized her first meaningful action on becoming herself again had been to spare the one who had caused, to her and through her, such harm. She felt tears stream down her cheeks. Bowing her head, she surrendered to them and wept.

Chapter 5

Tam woke in his room in the inn about midday. He had slept deeply, having returned just before the stirring of shopkeepers and trades folk at daybreak. Until then he had walked in the streets seeking to quell a simmering tension that he knew would rob him of rest. He had not expected the bonding to be like this. So insistent, so sickening. It wanted to control but to do so by exacerbating all the baser inclinations that he sought to minimize. Even now he could feel it, like a taint that was waiting at the corner of his mind. He had spent a portion of the night training himself to ignore it, to barricade it in but even now he could feel it, pulsing slightly, waiting to infect. He had learned, however, that to control it well he must not fear the bonding, as that gave it too much of his focus, but he still had to be wary of it. He had eventually walled it off sufficiently to be able to rest well and now felt clear minded. He rose and washed, enjoying the fresh cold water. As he was putting on a clean under-tunic he became aware of commotion in the street outside.

Tam finished dressing and walked to the window. In the street below he could see some men talking animatedly but could not make out what they said. After a few moments they moved away up the street. As he stood watching them, Tam became aware of more people moving in the same direction, from where a swell of noise arose. He considered for a moment whether to slip away from the town and continue his journey but curiosity, and a sense that he was partially responsible for what may be unfolding, caused him to walk down the stairs and into the street to join them. He walked at the pace of the crowd up the slope to the square in the town centre. Along the way he caught snippets of angry conversation mentioning the mayor and the captain and a few times was jostled by those around him who glared at him, clearly itching for confrontation. He kept his head down, though, avoiding their challenging stares.

In the town square a small dais had been erected upon which three men and a woman sat at a table while the captain stood, partially facing them and the crowd that had gathered, her head bowed and her hands hanging limply at her sides. The crowd, which was growing, was quiet though Tam could sense their agitation. He focused on the lady who sat with the men on either side. She sat upright, and her angular face and eyes looked stern as she swept them over the people before returning to the captain. She spoke loudly and with authority.

"We have heard your version of what happened last night. It sounds, frankly, implausible, but I can see that you stand by it. We will come to the truth of that another time. What we must decide here today is what blame you carry, as captain of the guard, for some of the atrocities that have taken place here over the last years. Your role, as their captain, was to ensure the guard acted honourably and to maintain the rule of law, but it is clear you and they have acted not only in grievous dereliction of this duty but may also have done wrong both to the people and fabric of this town. What is your response to this charge?"

The captain was silent for a moment, which felt like a long time to Tam, who could feel the tension building in those around him. Eventually, she lifted her head and looked quickly over the crowd before fixing her gaze on the lady. "I cannot deny these things but," she answered softly before her voice was drowned out by an angry shout from the crowd.

"Enough. We all heard her confession. She is guilty and should be punished."

A loud roar of agreement followed this.

A woman's voice could be heard above the clamour, almost rising to a shriek. "She took my husband away in front of my children. He was returned to me a broken man and my children still cry at night. She betrayed us all by siding with the mayor and doing his bidding."

Angry shouting followed from different parts of the crowd, their voices drowning each other out.

"My business was ruined by her and her men, turning people away, favouring another. How was I meant to survive?"

"My son! Where is he? My wife and I have not seen him since she and her men took him away!"

"They ransacked my store. Where could we go for help?"

Each shout struck the captain afresh as she flinched and seemed to shrink in size, tears streaming down her face. The angular-faced lady stood and raised her hand. Eventually, quiet was restored, but on glancing around Tam could see the intensity of the anger and grief, the strain so visible in their faces. Anger built up over years of struggle and compounded by the impotence of being unable to make any change. He felt it too, though directed not at the captain but at Nehlo. This was what people like he and Nehlo were meant to protect against, not cause. How could he have betrayed their trust so completely? But then his doubts arose again; what if he had done more for Nehlo? Could these wrongs have been averted? Tam was relieved to have the lady break through his thoughts.

"Many of you have suffered and while we cannot bring back what you have lost, we can look for justice. But we must hear what the captain has to say. She must be given a chance to account for what has happened."

She turned again to the captain, who was shaking visibly. This time when she looked up her gaze was haunted, almost fearful as it roved the crowd, searching for any sympathy. When she saw Tam, he saw her start in surprise, and when she spoke she kept her eyes on him. She started hesitantly. "I cannot deny these things that I am accused of. I have done terrible things and for each I am sorry and beg the forgiveness of you all." Her voice broke and she had to stop, her breathing deep, her hands clasping and unclasping. Around him, Tam could sense people about to speak, their bodies tense, ready. They held their silence though their faces remained hard. Tam felt a clutch of tension too, fearing what may be ahead for the captain.

After a few more deep breaths, she started again. "I do not know how to explain what has happened to me. I can only describe it to you and ask you to believe me. It is as if I have been in slavery while visibly walking free. My mind has been enslaved, though the chains that bound me were unseen. The mayor did this to me. I have come to see that in the hours since I was set free. I was foolish. I spoke to him when he became mayor and he took me into his confidence, speaking to me of his plans. I was flattered; he was wealthy and powerful but seemed to need my help. At that moment, I think I wanted to please him. It did not seem wrong at the time, but when I first did his bidding in a small matter it led to more. I do not know how, but somehow he took control; every thought, every action, was his, and I could no more go against his will than your plough could choose to move against its horse. All the time, his thoughts and will were present, forcing me to act, even though a part of me knew what I did was wrong and caused harm. You could not see but with every strike my heart bled a little more; I only know this now when I feel so broken and wretched, now that my mind is clear, and I can see what I was." She bowed her head again and wept, silently, though each sob racked her slender frame.

There was silence after she finished speaking as the crowd absorbed what she had said. Tam could see the hatred in some faces had softened a little but others remained hard, unmoved. The angular-faced lady spoke into the momentary silence.

"What you describe is impossible. How could someone control you to this extent? I have never heard of such a thing. And it is convenient for you to blame the mayor, who cannot now refute or confirm what you say. How can you prove such a thing? How can we believe you?"

On hearing this many jeered at the captain, shouting that she was a liar and not to be trusted. Tam felt suddenly protective of her. He alone knew that what she said was true. But it would be near impossible for others to understand and believe her. She did not try to speak but only listened, her face pale and drawn. The angular-faced lady, clearly the leader, raised her hand again to ask for calm.

After a few moments, the captain tried to speak but her voice broke, and she paused in an attempt to regain control. She tried again, her voice husky and strained. "I cannot prove what I say, how can I? I can only ask you to believe me and to speak to my men who will vouch for what I say as they were afflicted in the same way. None of us were free to choose what we did."

"Ask her men. See what they say. Their lies will find them out," someone shouted from the crowd.

"They are all together in this. All culpable. Why should we trust any of them?" shouted another to harsh cheers of support.

The captain looked around desperately, looking for someone to support her, to speak for her. Her eyes again fell on Tam and lingered there. "There is someone else who could speak for me. The one I spoke of earlier, who defeated the mayor and somehow freed me. Ask him."

All heads swivelled round, following her gaze and settling on Tam. He saw people move away from him, not willing to be caught in what was unfolding. Tam felt his heart suddenly race within him as he thought feverishly about what he could say that would exonerate the captain and not inflame the crowd any further. He toyed with the idea of pushing his thoughts onto everyone; he thought he could just about do it, would be strong enough. At this, the bond in his mind seemed to rise up. Tam could feel it being strengthened and empowered by his entertainment of this idea. Distracted for a moment, he consciously turned his mind to a different way, driving back the bonding. As he did so, he became aware of the crowd around him becoming more restive.

Tam looked at the leader on the dais. He tried to make his voice strong and certain. "I am a stranger to you all and know that my word carries little weight here, but I give it nonetheless. I can vouch for your captain of the guard. I know she speaks the truth. I know of people who are able to enslave just as she has described, and once they have done so, the poor enslaved wretch is completely in their control. She may have been foolish initially and guilty of favouring the mayor but once in his grip she had no capacity to decide her actions. She is no more guilty of much of what she has been accused than the knife is that causes the wound. Her wrong was to be enamoured by his power. The guilt, though, is the mayor's. He directed her actions. He has abused her trust and loyalty and led her and this town close to ruin."

The leader looked at him fixedly, weighing him up. Around him he could feel people wanting to argue, to shout him down, but they were unsure.

A harsh female voice broke through, startling everyone. "He is a stranger and cannot be trusted. We know what happened here. All this talk makes no sense We have all seen what the captain has done over the years. She should be strung up!"

A roar of approval met her words. Tam saw someone bend down, and before he could react, they straightened up and threw a stone, catching the captain on her face, drawing blood from her cheek. She cried out, her hand reaching up to the wound, her eyes searching for more attacks. Tam saw others reach down, scrabbling for something to hurl, ignoring the pleas for calm from the dais. Another stone flew from the other side, catching the captain on her side, causing her to spin round, wincing in pain. The people on the dais stood and quickly moved away, leaving her there, alone. Tam strode forward, ignoring hands around him that sought to hold him, pushing roughly through those ahead. He did not think. He just felt consumed with a heated desire to protect the poor woman who stood, friendless and bereft. As he approached, he felt more missiles split the air around him. Reaching out, he drew the air from all around, exulting again in the energy it contained, and formed it into an invisible wall, sufficient to shield himself and the captain. Standing by her, he wielded it, blocking all the stones arcing toward them. A gasp of wonder and fear ran through the crowd who fell back, their remaining stones falling from their hands.

Tam looked round at them all. He almost felt too emotional to speak, his heart full of anger at what these people had suffered mixed with a heaviness at the injustices they had endured, but both fuelled his words and his determination that there should be no more. "Is this who you are? Who you want to be? A mob attacking a woman before her guilt has been determined? You are rightly angry, but would you now add this woman's blood to all that has happened? Do you want that guilt on your heads? I ask you, before you condemn her, which of us has never been tempted by power, never been drawn to wealth and influence, never wanted to be part of the inner circle? Which of us would have been immune in her

24

position?" He stood on the dais, talking loudly, almost without thinking, his words pouring out on the torrent of his emotions. Around him he could see heads being lowered, eyes not wanting to meet his own or their neighbour's. He released his hold on the air and in doing so felt suddenly tired. His voice softening, he continued. "Some of you will be scared, many angry, some confused by what you have seen. I ask that you look beyond all of that and listen to what you have heard. Sometimes what seems most strange is true. How could she have made this up? Why would I vouch for her? I have nothing to gain. Ask her men. And I ask those of you who have been in this town the longest, you who have known this woman for many years. Do her words ring true? Did she change unaccountably when the mayor came? Does she seem more her true self now? I do not know her, but I know that she is more herself now than she has ever been these last years. And she hurts, possibly as much as any of you."

There was a long silence as his words struck through. He could see that their initial anger was dying away. They would wonder at his words, at what had stopped their stones from reaching their mark. There was a chance now, but it needed someone to speak into it. A strong voice rang out.

"You all know me. I have lived here these last twenty years. What this man says rings true. We knew Zoe before. She had always been one of us, had served this town well until the mayor came. Why would she throw that all away? And she does seem now to be the woman I remember. I for one, am willing to accept what she says." Tam saw a movement in the crowd and John, the innkeeper moved through, his strong presence adding weight to his words. He climbed onto the dais and stood beside them. Tam did not look at him, keeping his gaze on the crowd. He could see some heads begin to nod, some faces to soften, though many remained disbelieving and angry. He became aware of the town leader taking her seat again, flanked by her associates. She looked worried and Tam could understand; she faced an impossible decision. Exonerate the captain and she risked a riot, but the alternative was to condemn a woman who was not innocent but who was not ultimately culpable for all the wrong that had been done. The weight of the decision also pressed down on Tam with the sudden realization that it had to be faced in every town and city across the land where Nehlo had placed his people; Tam's success meant potential chaos everywhere. Would that be welcome? He could maybe remove the oppressors but what would follow? If there was disorder or recriminations would some, possibly many, resent the change and even wish for a return of Nehlo's yoke as it carried a measure of stability even amidst the wrong?

The lady raised her hand again. "We must deliberate on these matters. Awful things have happened, but we must not compound them. This must be a new beginning where the rule of law matters, and each person can expect justice." She rose and moved away with her associates.

Tam turned to John and Zoe. He looked at her closely for a few seconds; she looked tired, her skin pale and tight, but her eyes were settled and focused, not jumping from object to object as they had before. She could not hold his gaze, however, but looked down, ashamed.

"You are hurting and your guilt will feel unbearable just now. You are not, though, ultimately responsible for what has been done these last few years. You need to realize that," Tam said, softly but insistently.

25

Her lips trembled and a small tear ran down her face. "I want to believe that but how can you know that for certain? I have done awful things. I deserve all their anger and more."

"You could not have done otherwise. You were not to know the extent of the mayor's power when you were tempted to follow him. Once you were under his control you could not fight it; no one could have. You did not choose to be so. It was done to you."

"Are you sure?" Zoe looked up at him, suddenly hopeful.

"I am sure. I don't know everything about this but this I am sure about. The mayor chose to accept Nehlo's bond, to accept his absolute rule, no doubt for the promise of power and influence himself. For that he was given the capacity to bond others against their will, just like Nehlo can. Once you had put yourself under his influence any further choice was taken from you. A great evil has been done to you."

"But I still remember what I have done, though my memories are clouded. I hate myself and cannot imagine feeling anything different. I feel filthy and fear I will never feel clean again."

"In time the memories will fade, though I am afraid in my experience they do not leave you and there will be times when they will rise again to torture you, often when you are least able to defend yourself against them. At those times, you will face a battle anew to remember that you are not that person anymore. You are free from that now; you have a new start, a new life to forge. You need to live out this new life, not the old one. Learn from what has happened, what you have done and what has been done to you and live a new life in that light"

She continued to hold his gaze. "I hope you are right," she answered quietly, "as I can't really carry on while feeling the way I do at the moment."

"You need to. The town leaders will need you and your men to help get order back to this town. You can help right the wrongs that the mayor did here. Part of the route back is recognizing you are free now, free to serve the way the creator intended for us all. With him, I believe, there is always a new start for those who seek it."

She nodded slowly, uncertainly, though he could see her considering and weighing up what he had said. He had not meant to speak of his own beliefs and did not know whether thinking of a creator above all things would be a help or a hindrance to her; sometimes in his experience it gave the solace of ultimate purpose and justice, but often it gave rise to more bitterness and questions.

John moved to her side and put an arm around her shoulder, pulling her in tightly. "We will support you as best we can. You will have shelter under our roof should you ever need it. Me and my wife can be friends to you if you will have us."

She gave a little cry of laughter mixed with tears. "I would love that, though I'm scared you may come to regret it."

The crowd around them had been talking and murmuring but suddenly grew quiet. Tam saw the town leaders approach again. The men took their seats, but the lady remained standing. She stood for a moment and looked at each of them. They nodded to her to proceed.

Turning to the crowd she spoke loudly and clearly. "This is a difficult moment and it may yet define how we move forward as a town." She paused, considering. "Whatever we decide here, there will be some who remain angry, who feel that an injustice has been done to them personally. I ask all of us to try to turn aside from our hurt and anger and look to what can rebuild our community. We have discussed what has been said and, not without misgivings and doubts, have decided to trust what the captain has said, and you," she added, looking at Tam. "Indeed, I am not sure that we have any other option or explanation for what has happened."

A few cries arose in response to this but not as many as Tam had feared. The lady looked relieved too. She raised her hand, seeking silence again. "We do not think, however, that things can just go back to how they were. Too much hurt has been endured, too much trust broken. We, therefore, have decided to strip the captain of her rank and position. She may remain a guard but will have no authority in this town. She may yet have the chance to earn back the trust that requires."

Tam saw Zoe slump a little. She had received a glimmer of hope but now felt the shame and guilt return. One of the men at the table stood and walked purposefully toward them. Slowly, he reached up to Zoe's shoulders and removed the stripes of office from her. She stared ahead, but Tam could see the hurt in her eyes. He recognized the necessity of such a move but felt saddened. Now Zoe had to start to build her life again, in the face of distrust and uncertainty.

"We will appoint a new captain in due time. For now, the guard will remain under our direct command." Tam could see most accepting of the situation, though some still bore pained and angry expressions. The town leader now turned to Tam. "We do not, however, feel able to condone your actions, which have been taken without consulting anyone and may have caused and may yet cause great harm." He returned her gaze steadily but did not reply, though his stomach clenched, as he felt the truth of her words. "We recognize that you have done what we could not, and we also recognize the wrongs the mayor has done but that cannot condone such reckless action, taken as someone who is not one of us and without our sanction. We do not feel, however, that we can spend time and effort now in sorting out what to do about you with so much else needing doing, so we want your assurance that you will leave Fraebost and not return."

Someone gasped in the crowd, but most murmured in agreement. John and Zoe moved to speak but Tam motioned them to be silent. He felt a sense of sadness, almost weariness. He wondered at how the removal of such blatant evil at the heart of the town could cause such suspicion, but he also saw now that they may not have seen it as such and had become used to living under a shadow, possibly even some had benefited. He sighed.

"You have my word. I will go and not return."

The council members looked relieved. He was obviously one less problem for them to think about. Their leader nodded brusquely. "Then the business of this meet is done. Please," she added, turning to the crowd, "go to your homes, make sure that your family and neighbours are safe and provided for. We will work tirelessly to keep order and build back our community."

Slowly the crowd started to disperse. The town leaders stepped down and disappeared into a nearby building. Before long, only Tam, John and Zoe remained. Tam felt weighed down by what had just happened. He had never intended to stay, indeed had planned to slip away without anyone noticing, but that was different to being told to leave, ignominiously, and not to come back, as

27

if he were somehow polluting the town. The taint in his mind pulsed more strongly as if sensing his emotions, but he pushed back against it and sought to control his thoughts. He felt now his weakness and for the first time doubted his ability to carry through his plan, which surprised him. This stab of uncertainty was not due to the foes he faced, or the risk to himself, but to the thought that no one would care or, worse, people would actually resent him for it. And yet, was that why he had come, leaving everything behind to help these people? To be known as some sort of saviour?

John turned to him. "I am sorry how that worked out Tam. I don't know you well, but I am sure you have done us a good turn and did not deserve that. Where will you go?"

Tam focused on him, welcoming the distraction. "I will continue on my way to Ardvastra. I will head in that direction just as soon as I can get ready, though a bite to eat would not go amiss."

John smiled broadly. "That I can get for you. And if you ever need my help, just get word to me here." Zoe nodded in support, her face still pale, but Tam wondered whether he saw a slight sense of peace beginning to dawn in her eyes.

They walked the short distance to the inn and Tam climbed the stairs to gather his small pack. A short while later saw him leave the town by the same gate he had entered only the day before, leading his horse and turning to follow the road round the walls before entering a wood and the town was lost to sight.

Chapter 6

Nightfall found Tam in the hills to the north of Fraebost. He had travelled through woodland after leaving the town and had enjoyed the shade and gentle movement of the trees, which quietened his thoughts and mind. He had then come upon a small village surrounded by well-tilled fields of fertile land, which had been cleared from the surrounding wood, but he had skirted round it to avoid any people who may have contact with the town he had just left. The road subsequently climbed into some low hills and then moved into scrubland with small, stunted trees, which were buffeted by a wind that came in lively gusts. His thoughts kept turning forward; he had started on a more offensive tack he knew, and it would attract the attention of the capital, so he had to move more swiftly now.

Stopping when it became too dark to see the ground ahead easily, he ensured his horse was tied up to a tree near what grass and foliage there was. He poured some water in a bowl and, though he was tired and hungry, forced himself to take the time to rub her down, talking gently to her all the time, as he had hardly spoken all day. He then put down his small pack, which contained his blanket and a change of clothes as well as his cooking gear should he need it. He scoured the land for some branches which he gathered up and used to form a small fire, lighting it with flints and protecting it from snuffing out when it was still weak by erecting a small shield of air. Once done, he boiled some water, sprinkling some tea leaves into it. While it brewed he ate the food that John had prepared for him and then sat, facing the fire, the cup of hot tea warming both hands. He wondered what his wife and sons would be doing just now; he imagined them just finishing up the tidying after their evening meal, the easy joking and discussion. Would they stay up, maybe play at cards, or read together? They might go to bed early, his sons needing to help out at home with him being absent and also get to their own work as apprentices. He knew they would look after their mother well. He looked out beyond the fire at the hills darkening around him and felt suddenly lonely, the desire to be with them in the warmth of their companionship causing a swell of emotion that almost felt like an ache in his chest. He shifted uncomfortably, before drawing his saddle up and leaning back against it, his eyes now unfocused on the ground before him.

He started awake, feeling a slight flow of air followed by pressure on his neck. His heart suddenly hammering, he rolled instinctively away, pulling in air to create a blade. A peel of laughter surprised him as he struggled to focus in the low light of the fire. He released the air, squatting on his heels, his breathing still slightly fast.

"Got you that time Tam"

He grimaced at his sister who was still smiling. "Got me? The shock almost finished me!"

"Sorry, I could not resist it. Not often I catch you napping."

He got up and hugged her warmly. Aside from his wife and children there was no one he would rather see at that moment. "Fair play. I owe you one though. My heart still hasn't settled."

"No worries. You will never get me so easily. I can sense you coming a mile off." She punched his arm affectionately.

"You are pretty amazing at shielding your gift now. I had no awareness of you at all."

She smiled. "I am not sure you would have sensed a horse and cart coming; you were fast asleep."

He grimaced. "Busy couple of days."

He stretched his back to ease the tension that had built up there and bent to stoke the fire whilst she tended to her horse. He brewed more tea and handed her a cup with some of the food once she had finished. He watched her while she ate; he was told they looked alike but he had never been able to see it. Her face was straighter and softer, her shoulder length hair, which was always tied back, a darker brown. She looked well but a little tired though her eyes remained watchful. She had always been aware of everything around her, able to read situations at a glance. He rested back again feeling more settled for her being there, with him. He would sleep more easily too.

Marrea woke slowly, enjoying the warmth of the new morning, wrapped up in her cloak with Tam's makeshift windbreak over top; a sheet tied to one of the small trees that dotted this region, the other ends pinned to the ground. From where she lay she could see her brother kneeling over their small fire. They had both been too tired for much discussion the night before and had quickly gone to sleep. He straightened and looked over at her, seeing that she was awake.

"Good sleep Mar?"

She nodded and smiled before rising. "Pretty good really, in the absence of a proper bed." She stretched her arms above her head, easing the slight pain in her back that had developed through the night. She drew her cloak around herself and sat on a small hillock, accepting the cup of hot tea and piece of bread and cheese that he offered her.

While she ate she took the chance to study her brother. There was something about him that she could not quite grasp, a change that she could not describe. She put her cup down and looked more closely at him before moving forward and lifting her hands. He flinched a little, starting to move away from her but then relented and allowed her hands to rest on his head. She focused for a second before sensing the strange pulsing evil that was so incongruent. Her mind recoiled immediately from it, and yet even then it left a residue that she felt somehow lingered within her. A slight gasp escaped from her mouth before her hands dropped to her side. She kept her gaze on Tam, blinking away a slight misting of her eyes.

"Why?" was all she could think to ask.

"I had to. I realized that it was ultimately not enough to defeat the mayor. This bonding would have gone back to Nehlo and alerted him but I also wonder whether he is weaker without it somehow. This way, me holding it, may be a help to us when we have to finally face him; we may need any advantage we can gain."

"I saw it in you though; you just looked slightly strained. It is contained but still very much alive. Are you sure you can keep it under control?"

"For now," he replied gruffly. "My slight concern is what to do next time."

Marrea felt worry tinged with frustration bubbling inside her but she kept her voice neutral as she knew it would only annoy him to hear her concern. "You can't keep doing this. Even you can't fight this as well as everything else ahead of you. It is only going to get harder."

Tam looked at her though this time with less certainty. "I know Mar but I can't really see any other option. To undo what Nehlo has done, we need to remove his influence and that means removing his bondings and those that carry them. Otherwise, even if we succeed with Nehlo, we leave behind people similar to him and achieve nothing lasting for the people here. I think it has to be this way."

She nodded slowly, her heart full. She held his gaze for a moment trying to read him and convey her support. They had discussed this as soon as they had realized what Nehlo had done in placing his bonded servants to extend his control through the whole country. She had just not realized fully, tangibly, what that would mean for Tam, and she was not sure he had either. The time stretched out, neither speaking until Tam looked away and busied himself with his pack.

"Did you find out anything of interest in Fraebost?"

"Definitely the biggest town we have come across so far and the only one to have someone so obviously placed by Nehlo. It used to be more prosperous but now has a feeling of decay. There was a lot of anger too; I fear for what may come in some ways. Though as you found there are some good people who could take it forward."

Tam's normally serious face looked somehow heavier for a few moments before he nodded. "I hope so. The town leaders do, I think, want to do the right thing but are fearful. If there are more like my inn keeper then they should be okay. We cannot help now though."

"What of the mayor? Was he strong?"

"Strong in bonding and a good enough swordsman. Enough ability to bond twenty people, none of them weak, and he could sense the use of my skill and for all other purposes manipulate air around him well enough. He really struggled to keep his bond to Nehlo; I had to do more damage than I had intended to remove it."

Marrea felt a flash of anger. "Don't you dare feel guilty for any harm done to that man. He deserved worse than you gave him or what he will get from the townsfolk."

"It is certainly not the worst thing that I will probably have to do before this is finished."

31

Tam's slight smile, which was somehow tinged with sadness, quelled her anger in an instant. "Then let's not go any further. We can still go back home. I know you think this is your fight, and I am here to help you fight it, but is it really?" She could hear the plea in her voice but did not try to hide it this time, hoping he would respond. "These people have made choices that have set them down this path and we are not responsible for everything that Nehlo does here."

"You hold no blame Mar. You were always a friend to him. But I have to take some responsibility for what he has done, for what he has become." Tam spoke quietly, his face turned away from her, so she could not see his expression, but he had stopped what he was doing and was still and tense, obviously trying to get his thoughts together. "I could and should have been there, have supported him but I chose the college, the order, the old ways and beliefs that I thought were so important." She felt her old resistance to his beliefs stir, but she quashed them. Tam after a brief pause continued. "I don't regret that but often wonder whether a choice had to be made or whether I was being too strict, too sure of myself, too committed to seeing things in only one way that excluded him rather than seeing that maybe we could have compromised or moved more slowly." His voice tailed away. "For the sake of friendship and more."

"But would that have changed his mind? When I look back, I see him diverging from us all long before that day. That was just the point that the inevitable became apparent, and there was nothing you could do. He was set on his path."

"As I was on mine. That was the problem maybe and it has led to this."

"You don't owe him anything now. Surely the ties we had, which were strong once I know, surely they cannot hold us to this course? And is it our role to try to solve the problems here? Surely the college should decide what is best to be done."

"You know he never trusted them and is less likely to now. And even though much has changed, they will not seek to bring him back, only stop him by whatever means they can. They will see only what he has done, what he has become, not who he was, what he meant to us. Maybe we can heal some of the harm he has caused and bring him back to us?" Marrea heard the hope in his question but she could not share it.

"At what cost?"

Tam grimaced. "Not too much I hope. But I don't have a clear idea what is ahead of us, only that it is right that we try, and taking this wretched bonding on to myself felt like the only thing I could do at the time. It somehow felt like a step towards a healing for Elishadra. Maybe for Nehlo too somehow."

Tam was silent for a while, twisting the ropes of his pack in his hands. Marrea wanted to argue but remained quiet, watching him. She could not fully share her brother's beliefs, though she agreed with the principles tied to them that he had been working toward since Nehlo's departure. She saw the familiar resolve in him as he set the ropes down, lifted his head and straightened, firm once again in his mind and purpose. She sighed inwardly.

"Onward?"

"Yes, onward. If that is okay? I don't want you to feel you have to be here with me in this, though it seems an easier path with you beside me."

Marrea felt a small stab of surprise. It was unlike her brother to be so open about his wishes or needs. She grasped his arms, squeezing tightly. "Of course it is okay. Someone has to watch your back. And as for Nehlo, he is as much my concern as yours though we might differ in what is due to him now. He saved my life too, way back when we were kids, remember?" She gave him a quick hug before stepping back.

Tam nodded and drew his hand across his eyes before suddenly becoming brusque. "Let's get packed up and moving."

She smiled to herself, half amused at his inability, even with her, to be openly emotional. She had joked with his wife many times about it without his knowing. Turning she joined him as they packed what they had and walked on together, leading their horses.

Chapter 7

Tam knelt behind the tree, trying to ignore the moisture from the soft mossy ground as it seeped into his trousers. He took a moment to catch his breath while looking around for the others. The widely spaced trees provided plenty of cover, but he did not think anyone was nearby. He focused on listening past the creaking and rustling of the branches above and the shrill sound of the birds as they chattered among the foliage. Nothing caught his attention, so he edged forward a little to see round the tree.

Ahead of him was a clearing which looked bright and warm compared to the cool shade in the trees. He could see Nehlo standing next to the rusty bucket hanging from a post they had driven into the ground in the centre, while Ben patrolled on the far side. He watched them both for a few minutes, tracking Ben's movements and checking to see how often he looked round; clearly, he expected Tam to be coming from the other side. Somewhere out there, though, the others were searching, and they would return soon.

Tam lay on the ground and pulled himself forward on his elbows and knees. When nearer the clearing edge he stopped again and lay still for a few moments listening carefully. This close he could hear Nehlo scuffing around, clearly fed up; Ben too appeared to be losing interest in his task and had taken to swiping at the branches above him with his sword. Tam slowly rose and grasping his own sword tight crept forward till clear of the tree line and then broke into a run. Nehlo spotted him instantly but knew better than to make any noise; had Ben been paying attention he would have noticed that Nehlo had stopped pacing, but he was too intent on attacking a foe above him. Tam raced forward and swinging his sword in a wide arc smashed it against the bucket, sending it flying to the other side of the clearing with a loud clang as the wood resounded off the metal. Ben swirled round, cursing and yelling for the others to join him. Tam and Nehlo smiled widely at him before raising a hand in mock salute and running into the trees again, knowing they had the time he would take to return the bucket to its home before he could chase after them.

Tam followed Nehlo as they weaved between the trees, grimacing slightly at the noise and trail he was making as he crashed through branches and tripped over roots. He stopped suddenly, causing Tam to almost run into him. They could hear shouting behind them as Ben called out to the others the direction in which they had run. Crouching down they moved more slowly now, tracking back to circle round the clearing. They found a tree with low hanging branches and crawled under them to rest against the base of the trunk.

Nehlo took a cookie out from his pocket, which had been inadequately protected in a piece of linen. It had been crushed by their escape, but they both took it in turns to pinch some crumbs and eat them, Nehlo emptying the last fragments into his mouth before stuffing the linen back into his pocket.

"You took your time. I was about to call it in when you sprang out of the trees like a harried deer."

Tam leaned his head back against the tree and grinned up at the dense foliage above.

"I could see you getting a bit testy. I was just biding my time, coming up quietly, unlike you with your stamping around, leading them right to you."

"Not that easy for people built bigger than a fox to run around these woods."

Tam didn't reply to the well-worn jibe. Nehlo had always been bigger and stronger than him, despite being the same age, which he rarely failed to point out. He let his focus drift, blurring the leaves above together into different shapes in the shifting light that filtered down. Nehlo too was quiet for a while before nudging Tam, waking him from his revery.

"That has got to be Ben roaming around. Why don't we take him and the bucket and let them come and rescue him?"

Tam nodded, hearing too the sound of rustling and muttering from close by. They separated and crept out from behind the tree from different directions. Tam could see Ben now, walking toward him, looking around warily but obviously not having spotted him. He remained where he was, watching, until he saw a movement behind Ben that he guessed was Nehlo. Tam stood up and moved forward toward Ben, who saw him and was about to shout when Nehlo bundled into the back of him, knocking him to the ground and the wind from his lungs. Before he had a chance to move Nehlo was kneeling on his back with one hand pressing his face down. Ben scrabbled frantically, his breathing coming in gulps as he sought to regain control of it with Nehlo's weight above him. Tam picked up the sword that Ben had dropped and pointed it at him.

"I think you are squashing him Nehlo."

Nehlo started and looked down at Ben struggling beneath him before rising to his feet.

"Really?" gasped Ben, lying still for a few moments before sitting up and glaring at Nehlo. "You big oaf. You could have suffocated me."

Nehlo looked sheepish for a second before shrugging. "Sorry Ben. I was just holding you till Tam got here to make sure you couldn't escape."

"Right, you know the rules. We could gag you so no calling out or attracting attention or we can exact punishment. Let's go and get the bucket. I am starving and Mum is making bramble pie for pudding, so I am heading home once Nehlo and I claim the bucket."

Ben, obviously still nettled, nodded and rose to his feet. Tam led the way this time, threading carefully through the small paths between the trees till they made it back to the clearing. There had been no sight of the others, but they had to come when the bucket was struck to say a hostage had been taken. Ben sat next to the post while Tam and Nehlo took up position on either side of him, swords drawn, eyes darting around.

Tam felt a prickle of anticipation run through him, bringing a faint tremor to his hands and stomach, as he gazed out, waiting for the others to attack as they must now that he and Nehlo held the base. He quickly wiped the sweat that had sprung up on each hand on his trousers before grasping the wooden hilt tightly again. He glanced at Nehlo, who appeared completely relaxed, his sword held loosely by his side. Tam lowered his own sword and attempted the same nonchalance. For all his size and apparent heaviness, Nehlo was surprisingly adept with his hands and easily outfought Tam and the others when they met. He always said Tam was too tense and that this slowed him down, and certainly Tam had none of the flexibility he saw in his friend when facing him. He struggled to relax now as he knew the others would view him as the weaker party and likely come for him first, and though not real, the swords could still prove painful if caught in the wrong place.

35

Tam relaxed his grip on the sword, trying to focus instead on the arc of trees around him. Nothing happened for a little, but then he heard a slight crack that made his heart race a little and caused him to tighten up again. Swivelling to where the noise came from, he was just in time to see Ryan and Maj creep through the trees into the opening. Seeing him turn, they both broke into a run, separating slightly to attack him from either side. Tam raised his sword, crouching slightly to balance himself and calling on Nehlo to help him. The two boys rushed toward him, but just before they struck, Tam felt rather than saw a movement ahead of him, pushing toward him as if the air itself was attacking him. Instinctively, he raised his blade to meet it but encountering nothing his arms were carried by his momentum up over his head. Tam only had time to see the look of surprise in Maj's face before his sword rushed underneath his raised arm, catching him heavily on his ribs with a sickening crack. A sharp pain reverberated through his chest, catching his breath as he curled his arms around it and sank to his knees. He could only kneel there, gasping on the ground and watch as Maj and Ryan circled round Nehlo, probing and attacking before, good as he was, darting through his defence with a quick jab that caught him in the stomach causing him to double over and drop his sword in submission.

Minutes later they were both sitting under the bucket, back-to-back, watching while their three combatants took the spoils of a slightly grimy flag, their swords and the requisite copper penny, and then sauntered with annoying bravado from the clearing. Tam and Nehlo would both have to wait now to allow them to get well ahead before carrying the post and bucket home as a sign of their defeat.

"Nice one," grunted Nehlo. "What happened to you to make you jerk your arm around like that? Did something sting you or bite you?"

"Thanks for your concern. My side hurts as if a herd of cattle trampled over it," grumbled Tam in return. "I don't know what happened. I thought I felt something coming and reacted to it but clearly it was nothing." He lapsed into silence. He could not understand what had happened. The sensation of something coming toward him had been so real and it was just before Maj's blade had swung round. Maybe he had just imagined it, but whatever had happened, he had an already impressive bruise to show for it.

"Come on, let's get the bucket and go home."

Nehlo nodded and rising pulled the post from the ground, tossing the bucket to Tam to carry. Bouncing it off his thigh with one hand while the other hugged his aching side protectively, he followed Nehlo out of the clearing and along the main path out of the wood to his home.

Nehlo pushed his plate away with a contented sigh. The stew had been good, but Tam's mother was famous for her deserts and the bramble pie with cream had not disappointed. She was up now bustling around, clearing plates. Glancing at him, she held out the last portion of desert.

Nehlo smiled at her. "I can't move as it is. You know I would have thirds of your amazing pies if I could."

She smiled happily before disappearing out the back of the house to the pump that they used for washing all the clothes and dishes. The room was almost as familiar to him as his own home. He gazed around at the hams hanging on hooks to one side and at the tapestry on the other wall, faded a little by time and sun, above the solid wood chest that had always been there. The smell of leather, which somehow made its way past what remained of the fragrant stew, was also always there. He liked the sameness of it all.

Nehlo started as something bounced off the side of his head. Turning, he saw Tam aim another pellet of paper at his sister, who ducked away, pulling a face at him before skipping away *after her mother. Tam's father looked up from the book he had been studying, causing Tam to desist straight away and assume an innocent look.*

"What are you boys going to do now?" Tam's father asked, his eyes, made slightly stern by the heavy brows, swivelling between them.

"I thought we might go up to the show. There is a juggler who they say can do amazing leaps and turn head over heels at the same time."

"Can I go Daddy?" piped up Marrea, who had come in to pick up the last plates in time to hear Tam speak. Nehlo saw a flash of annoyance cross Tam's face, which his father did not see. He could not really understand Tam's dislike of his sister tagging along. He found her easy to talk to and enjoyed making her laugh. He missed their company when back in his own home.

"As long as you stay with Tam and Nehlo that sounds fine. And you all need to be back home before sundown. You too Nehlo."

Nehlo nodded. He would not normally need to be, but Tam's father was stricter than his own and he did not want to go against him. Tam nodded too, giving his sister a grimace as she walked past him, which she returned with a triumphant smile.

Chores done and with a penny in his pocket from Tam's father, Nehlo walked beside Tam with Marrea just behind. It was cool but with a warmth to the light, the way it could be after a sunny clear day. They walked along the dusty track from Tam's homestead. From the slightly raised ground they could see the other houses in a neat line along the main road, with their tended land neatly laid out front and back on the slight slope. Most contained cattle, as this was rich ground for grazing. The milk went to the main town about half a day's ride over the steep hill beyond the woods they had been playing in earlier. Their target though was the other side of the river beneath them, where there was an open area of land that was shared between all the villagers and used for gatherings, markets and fairs. Beyond it densely packed trees stretched out as far as they could see, most of which was out of bounds to them.

"Marrea, can you stop dawdling and keep up!" Tam's voice sounded irritated.

"Okay," she replied, a little crossly, but as far as Nehlo could see she made no discernible increase in her speed. He grinned at her, and she smiled back, a little dimple showing on one cheek.

"We have time enough Tam. It will just be getting going and the stalls will be out for the whole evening." Nehlo barged against Tam with his shoulder causing him to trip on a rut on the road and almost fall. Tam regained his balance and twisting, caught him round the waist and Nehlo felt himself toppling over under the weight. They rolled in the dust for a few moments, but despite Nehlo's strength advantage, Tam managed to pin him down and resist any attempts to be dislodged.

"Okay, you have me." Nehlo laughed, tapping the ground.

Tam got up and extending his hand, pulled Nehlo up after him.

"It's been a while since I got one over on you." Tam's good humour, which was never far away, had returned. His sister had been watching with a bemused look on her face but now looked with mild concern at a tear in her brother's trousers and a graze which leaked a little blood on his knee.

"That's nothing," Tam said to her, noting her look.

"I was more concerned about your trousers. I will be the one stitching and cleaning those tomorrow."

Tam laughed. "So you will. I will get you something at the show then to make amends."

Mollified she turned and walked on with them. The track lead down the slight slope, and in a few moments, they were standing looking over the river. It was faster and deeper than normal after the recent rains, the water swirling round the inset stones that forded it. Marrea looked a little nervous.

"Can we go round the long way?"

Nehlo looked at Tam, who was considering the strength of the surging water.

"I don't think there is time now to go back up and round the other way. We would miss most of the show. You will be okay; you have done this countless times."

Marrea did not look up from the river, but Nehlo could see she was nervous and had gone a little pale. Tam looked at him questioningly, but he shrugged, unwilling to make the decision either way.

"Right. You go between us, and we can help if you get stuck, but just take your time and it will be fine."

Tam stepped out lightly onto the first stone and continued confidently to the second before turning and beckoning Marrea to follow. She hesitated for a few moments, and Nehlo could see she was torn between not wanting to lose face in front of him and her brother and her fear of the water. She tentatively stepped out and reached the first stone easily enough despite a slight tremor in her legs. Tam smiled at her confidently and moved on a couple of stones into the middle, where he stopped and waited for her. She seemed to gain confidence from him and stepped easily onto the next stone, before stopping and saying something that Nehlo did not hear. Tam nodded and held out his hand to her.

Nehlo watched as Marrea reached out tentatively, leaning forward. Suddenly, Tam's arm shot forward, before Marrea had fully reached him, just as it had that morning. Nehlo saw with a lurch in his stomach the surprise and fear on Tam's face as he tried to correct his movement, but he was off balance and all he could do was cry out as Marrea's hand missed his and she toppled forward into the water. Nehlo tried to move forward to help her, but his movements seemed sluggish and heavy compared to the speed with which she pitched forward and entered the water, disappearing in an instant in the heavy flow. Before he could react further, he saw Tam frantically searching and then diving in after her. Nehlo watched, his heart hammering painfully, unsure what to do, his eyes scanning back and forth where he thought they could be. After what seemed far too long, he saw them, Tam struggling to keep them both afloat with Marrea clinging to him, terrified.

Nehlo forced his numb thoughts to react more quickly, to focus on what he could do. He broke into a run along the water's edge, tripping on roots and scrambling up again in a mad dash to get ahead of them. He scooped up a broken branch on the way and continued to race them down the river. Tripping again, he forced himself up and to keep moving forward, trying to keep his eyes on the bobbing heads that were beside him now but still out of reach. He yelled out and pointed ahead to where the bank cut in and there were some overhanging trees. It was flatter there, and he pelted along, gaining ground on them before skidding to a halt in front of the tree. Grabbing one of the branches, he swung out over the river, reaching as far as he could with the branch that he had carried with him.

Calling out as loud as he could, he waved the branch, but it was heavy, and he was doing all he could to keep his grip on it and the tree on which he clung. Almost too fast, Tam was beneath him, and for a horrible second, Nehlo thought that Tam would not be able to reach far enough as the current dragged him down. Nehlo saw a look of fierce determination and desperation on Tam's face as he pulled back against the flow and flung out his hand and grasped the wood, holding on as tightly as he could as the water pulled at him, greedily urging him to release his hold and succumb. Nehlo yelled at him to hold on and gritting his teeth pulled as hard as he could on both arms to bring them closer to the bank. Marrea, her arms clamped around Tam, kicked out with her legs, and with the extra momentum, they reached the shallower waters, and Tam was able to stand and half lift, half pull her out of the water. They collapsed on the side, utterly spent, as Nehlo swung back and rested near them.

No one spoke for some time. Tam looked up at Nehlo, his face white and his eyes still showing their sense of what could have happened. He held Nehlo's gaze for a few moments, looking hard and intently into his eyes, and in that look, Nehlo read his unspoken gratitude. Marrea did not look up but hugged her brother tightly, and he in turn held her to him, his hands gently stroking her back.

In that moment of relief, Nehlo felt a strange sense of isolation and distance as he saw the strength of a bond that he could not have and that was independent of anything he could do. For a brief second, he resented Marrea's love for her brother, which seemed to have no room for thought of him at this moment of crisis. He looked away, letting the river draw away his gaze and willing it to take away his thoughts. Before long, he became aware of them both stirring next to him. Marrea was standing, supported by her brother, but was pale with cold. Cursing himself for not thinking of it sooner, he took off his own jacket and covered her. She gave him a weak smile, which made him feel ashamed of his previous thoughts. Together they supported her back up the track, back to their home. Nehlo watched as their mother engulfed Marrea in a hug and hurried her inside. Tam turned and gave a brief, worried wave before following them, leaving Nehlo to walk the short distance home on his own.

Chapter 8

Seth paused over the table leg that he was working on. He wiped some sweat from his forehead and then resumed sanding it down, the repetitive movement helping him martial the swirl of thoughts in his head. It was a few days since the disastrous meeting that had led to the deaths of eight people, three of whom he had known personally. He still struggled to direct his thoughts away from what had happened and how quickly men and women had died. The movement of his hands kept a slight tremor at bay as he thought of it again and with a great effort focused himself on the task in front of him. It did not help that he was tired, the result of nights of disturbed and restless sleep. He had anticipated some risk to what they had proposed, but the suddenness of the violence and the worthless and pointless loss of life before they had even started still left him shaken. He had been in his fair share of fights growing up but only with fists, and he had never killed anyone. The vision of Neil lying on the ground and the feeling of his own blade piercing their attacker stayed with him. What training he had had with sword was from Alec, who said he was pretty fair, but he was no soldier. What he knew was wood, its grain, and how to shape it to make things that were useful and beautiful. He ran his finger down the table leg, satisfied that it was ready, before attaching it to his lathe. He slowly rotated the wood, focusing now with his sharp gouge as it took fine strips of wood away. He leaned in, his concentration growing, and soon his concerns were gone as the small but complex movements shaped the wood in front of him, bringing out the natural grain and features of the wood itself. After an hour or so he straightened, stretched his back, and surveyed his work with satisfaction. Some further gentle sanding and it was done. He would never be rich as he took his time, but he found it satisfying to form something useful and beautiful.

He had not spoken to Kayla and Alec since that night, but he had seen them in the streets as he was going on essential errands. Since that night, he felt scared anywhere but his home and his workshop. He was fairly sure that no one apart from Kayla and Alec knew he had been at the meeting, as everyone else present had died, but that did not stop a nagging feeling that he was being watched, that at any moment someone would recognize him on the street and denounce him as a rebel, or men would descend on him to arrest him. He knew that others had disappeared with little or no warning.

He had little contact now with Alec in a normal sense. The last few years had led to a large change in their fortunes. His was one of the families that had come down on the right side of the line separating those that fitted in with the new system and those that did not. It was hard to be clear exactly how it had happened that some families had risen and others fallen by the wayside, but now there was an invisible but real dividing line between the two groups. To attempt to interact with the favoured ones, except when asked to serve some function, would earn someone like him at the very least an embarrassing brush off and, more often than not, a bloodied nose or worse for his trouble. Subsequently, Alec moved in different circles, and to all but his closest friends, he seemed to fit in pretty well and was hated accordingly. These divisions between groups were becoming more entrenched and bitter; soon there would be little common ground, only enmity as some felt a growing sense of injustice and impoverishment at the others' hands. Seth pondered this for a second; how such change could happen, how difficult it was to work out why and at what point the changes had come about, and how difficult it would be to reset them. It could not be as simple as removing the person in power, but it had to start there; he could see no other way.

He stood and took a long drink of water from a flask that hang on a hook on the wall. Then he stepped over to a pair of chairs that he had recently finished; they had been commissioned by a local trader for one of the wealthier merchants and were due today. He inspected them carefully, running his hand down the slight curve of the back before looking with a little pride at his signature mark on the base of the seat. He scanned his workshop quickly to ensure his tools were all away; it was small, so everything had to be neat, and despite the low roof, there was a reasonable amount of light coming in through the small window and from the doorway, which was usually open unless it was too cold outside. He picked up the chairs and carefully negotiated the door, turning to lock it with a large key.

It was getting late in the afternoon and lots of people were out, either returning from work or hurrying through the last tasks of their day. He threaded carefully through the narrow street where his workshop lay, nodding at a few people that he knew well. He paused for a second at the junction before entering the main street. A carriage passed, moving quickly, splashing through the mud from the previous night's rain. Seth cursed under his breath and wiped the mud from one of the chairs with his tunic. He walked swiftly on, keeping his head down, but his gaze vigilant, ensuring that he did not bump into any of the people around him. He felt a tension in his shoulders, and the more he tried to walk normally, the more he felt it was obvious that he had something to hide. A sudden shout behind him caused him to jump and set his heart racing. He turned quickly, half expecting to see people bearing down on him, but everything looked normal and he could not make out who had shouted. Resuming his quick stride, he narrowly avoided hitting a well-dressed man with one of the chairs, getting an angry rebuke. He apologized hastily, the man turning away again with a dismissive gesture. It was not worth getting into an argument, so Seth moved quickly on and was glad to turn into the trader's shop.

Inside, there was a couple of chairs and a large counter. Very little was sold directly here; Marek had built up a profitable business taking orders and then commissioning tradesmen of skill to complete them. He bustled out from the room at the back when he heard Seth enter. He was a thin man with small eyes and a quick way of moving that Seth found disconcerting, but he could not choose who to work with these days.

"Ah Seth, I was expecting you earlier, but I see you have what we agreed." His eyes roved quickly and expertly over the chairs.

Seth placed the chairs carefully on the surface. "My apologies. My understanding was that the end of business today was what we had agreed."

Marek ignored him while he studied the chairs, his eyes looking for any defect, his hands darting in quick movements to assess the joints and lines. Satisfied he looked up at Seth.

"Your work is satisfactory. I will take these as we agreed." Seth felt a slight annoyance at his tone and words; he knew his work was exemplary, but he had also learned not to expect any compliments. "I am afraid, however, that my buyer has changed the price. They are now willing to pay ten pieces of coin."

Seth could only look at him in astonishment. That was half what they had agreed and only just covered the cost of the wood and materials he had used. There would be nothing for his labour or skill. He swallowed down anger that he knew would not help him.

"We had agreed twenty pieces and even that only covers my costs and half my time. I cannot be expected to work for nothing." He tried to keep his voice neutral and calm, but he spoke quickly and his breathing seemed unnaturally difficult.

Marek showed no sympathy. Maybe he couldn't. Maybe he had no option and was struggling himself, but Seth doubted that and felt a sudden hatred for this dry little man. "Nevertheless, that is what they are offering. They have advised me to tell you that if you do not wish to accept their price, they will not purchase your work. I am afraid I have no other buyers at present for these."

His tone made it clear that there was no room for negotiation. Seth wrestled with a desire to just pick up his chairs and leave rather than accept such an insulting offer, but he needed even this small amount to cover his costs. He nodded dumbly but felt empty, the signature mark that he could just see on the chairs seeming to mock him. Marek lifted the chairs off the surface and disappeared into the back room before returning with a note of purchase and the coin. Seth pocketed both and walked out without another word, ignoring the farewell that was offered. Once outside, he leaned on the wall, not caring that people had to step round him. How could he build his business, hope to establish himself, maybe earn enough to support a wife and children, if this was the reward for his labours? How could anyone? But there was nowhere to turn. He knew there was no point going to the authorities; they were part of the problem. He wanted to lash out in frustration but instead pushed himself off the wall and walked numbly back the way he had come.

That evening Seth sat in the room he rented at the top of a terraced house. His hands rested on the small table, upon which sat his empty plate, with his gaze fixed on the cold hearth. It was always cold in his room, even in summer, the little heat there was coming up from the rooms below, and what was generated when he had enough money for a fire, disappearing into the draughty ceiling above him. The only other furniture, apart from some shelving, was his single bed with a thick blanket. Back then he had been able to overlook the room's darkness and cold as he felt he was just starting his trade, that he would be able to afford something better soon. Now he felt trapped, barely able to pay the rent let alone save any money. He still felt angry and aggrieved at what had happened earlier, and his mind kept churning out things he should have done and said instead of meekly accepting such meagre payment. He also felt humiliated, not valued for his skill and impotent to change what had happened. He thought of his parents, how proud they had been when he became a master tradesman, how worried they would be now if he told them how near he was to becoming destitute. He could not face disappointing them and the thought of doing so swirled around, exacerbating his worsening mood. He was glad when he heard the slight rattle on his window as some gravel from below bounced off it; looking out through the grime that threatened to block out any light, he could just see Kayla below. He waved and, picking up his jacket, headed for the stairs. As he went down, he could hear voices from each of the rented rooms, some murmured, others loud in argument. He did not pause to listen. Hurrying to leave the dark enclosure and enter the relative openness of the street below, he greeted his friend with a clasp of her hand. He would have been happy to keep a hold of her hand, but as ever the touch was brief, and he let it drop before stepping into stride alongside her.

She broke the silence as they walked along together.

"How have you been doing?" she asked, tentatively.

Seth paused for a second, unsure how to respond. "Okay, I guess. Nothing's changed and everything's changed."

She nodded at that and again was silent for a moment. "Night-time is the worst. I keep seeing it all again." Seth felt a yearning for her but kept his face neutral. She lived alone and had done so since her father died young, about two years ago after a short illness. She had had at least one offer of a home that Seth knew of but up till now she had preferred to keep to herself and with her work in the school had enough to get by.

"I know what you mean. I do too. Work helps though."

She nodded. "Yes, it is good to have something to focus on."

Seth hesitated for a second, unwilling to voice his thoughts or his fear. "Do you think anyone is looking for us?" he asked quietly.

She turned her head, and he could feel rather than see her appraising look. "I don't know. Sometimes I think so, but surely something would have happened by now? And we were careful not to tell anyone else of our intentions. No one knew we were going to be there for certain till the night itself. I think we must be okay."

Seth nodded, though he did not feel completely reassured. They walked on again in silence for a few minutes till, rounding a corner, Seth saw someone walk out of the shadows to meet them. It took a few seconds for him to recognize Alec in the poor light, but when he did so, he gave him a warm smile and clapped him on the arm. They both followed Kayla, who obviously had a destination in mind. A few minutes later she stopped next to a door in a terraced house. She knocked gently on the door a few times and it opened slightly. Seth was aware of someone looking out at them before the door opened wider and they were ushered in by a man he had never seen before. He was old and a little stooped, but his eye was still bright and keen. He patted Kayla on the arm as she held his hand for a moment and then turned to introduce Seth and Alec.

"This is Simeon, a friend of my parents from way back."

"Friend to you too Kayla," Simeon replied gruffly but warmly.

"I know," she replied, giving him a smile, which Seth noticed suddenly he had not seen from her this evening.

Simeon turned and led them along a corridor before opening another door and going down some stairs. Seth hesitated, but Kayla encouraged him on with a slight nod. At the bottom of the stairs, they entered a warm room with no windows. The smoke, from the few candles that lit the room with a low light, drifted up and disappeared somewhere through vents in the ceiling, though incompletely as what remained hung in the air giving a pleasant scent. A woman played a violin in the corner while a man sat next to her and beat softly on a drum on his knee. Small groups of people sat around tables talking quietly with pitchers of ale in front of them. Another woman, who Seth took to be Simeon's wife, moved briskly about with a jug, filling glasses that were half empty. Kayla led Seth and Alec to the back of the room, where a low bench sat behind a table. She slipped into it with her back to the wall, and Alec took the chair opposite, leaving Seth with a slightly awkward decision. After hesitating for a second, he sat on the bench next to Kayla and Simeon's wife came up.

"Welcome Kayla. We have not seen you here for a while, but you are always welcome, as are your friends."

"Hello, Anna. I know, I have been a bit remiss, but I have been busy."

"No excuses needed. We are just glad to see you and to see that you are well. Let me fill your glasses." And with that she was off again, leaving them with their drinks.

Kayla took a long drink and leaned back against the wall. Seth sat forward, holding his drink, a little anxiety flitting through him about whether he had enough money to pay for it. He looked around at the different people, some of whom nodded in a friendly manner before turning back to their own tables. Alec sat back in his chair, stretching his legs, immediately looking at home as he always did. Seth decided to follow suit and rested back against the wall next to Kayla.

"I just felt like being among people, and then I thought of here. My dad used to take me sometimes, though towards the end he was not really able to come. It has always felt a bit like a safe haven for me, a bit out of the way of everything."

"It's nice. You would never know it is here."

"That's part of its beauty. You never do find out unless someone who knows takes you, particularly now that there is so much suspicion about. Everyone here has been coming for ages or is known personally and vouched for."

Seth felt and appreciated the compliment. He drank some of his ale, which was cool and light. Simeon and his wife joined them and asked Kayla a few questions about how she had been over the last while. Seth's thoughts wandered back to the afternoon, and he felt his mood darken.

He felt a touch on his arm and turned to see a questioning look from Kayla. He realized his fist was closed and that he was leaning forward. He consciously forced himself to relax and sit back. Simeon had clearly asked him something, but he had not heard.

"My apologies, I was daydreaming. What did you ask me?"

Simeon gave him a keen look before replying. "Just who your parents were, as I may know them."

Seth smiled. "I doubt that sir as they keep themselves pretty quiet. My father is a clerk for a clothing merchant, and my mother works as a seamstress. They have always lived in the eastern part of town, where I grew up."

Simeon nodded. "You are probably right." He looked thoughtful for a second before standing. "Right, we must be about our own business," and motioning to his wife he moved away to fill the jug that he carried to replenish the drinks of his guests. Kayla held out some money for their drinks to his wife, but she pushed it back and murmured, "You need it more than we do," before moving off to help her husband.

"They are good people," she said, half to herself and half to Seth and Alec.

Seth nodded but said nothing. He didn't seem to have anything to say. Alec gave him a light kick under the table.

"Anything the matter? You look like your ale is sour."

Seth considered saying something light to divert the question, but he could not think of anything. He grimaced. "The ale is great. I just had a hard day, that is all."

"How so?"

"I had done some work making some dining chairs for Marek, but he has reneged on the price we agreed. Said his buyer would only pay half which is barely enough to cover my costs."

"I hope you told him to keep his money?"

Alec had a hard look on his face. "How could I? I need the money. And I may need the business he can send my way, though it pains me to be dependent on him."

"There must be other work for you. A man like him should not be able to commandeer all the work."

Alec's voice had started to rise, and Seth became aware of a couple of heads turning to listen. He motioned for his friend to be quiet. He did not have the energy to argue about it, particularly with Alec who, with his relative wealth, did not face the same difficult decisions.

Kayla had been sitting listening quietly but now had a thoughtful but sad look on her face. "I am sorry to hear this Seth. You work hard and don't deserve to be rewarded like this. Listening to you has brought back memories too. About my dad." She paused and looked down at her ale before continuing. "I always wondered why his business disappeared. And when it did, he seemed to lose heart, and then, when the illness came, there was no fight in him. By that time, he had few friends left, except for folks like these." She nodded in the direction of Simeon. "Were it not for me, sometimes I think he was glad to be done with life."

Seth gave Alec a quick look. She rarely spoke about her parents, though he had heard from his own many years ago that her mother had died soon after she was born. Alec looked uncharacteristically serious.

"Do you think something similar happened?" Seth asked gently.

"I don't know as he never said or complained in my hearing. But I never heard from anyone else either why things had changed. In the last couple of years, as I hear about how things work here and how easy it is to fall foul of someone and be ruined, the more certain I have become that it happened to him. And the more I see it, the more I am reminded of it and the more angry and resolute I become."

Her look had changed from sadness to bitterness and then anger. She looked hard at them both, almost challenging them to doubt her.

45

Alec held his hands up and smiled grimly. "No arguments from me about that." Seth nodded too though, despite what had happened to him, he felt conflicted. He thought of his own parents, both still alive, working, their main aim to live quietly and to worry about what was in front of them and leave the bigger decisions and issues to others. They wanted the city to be different, he knew, but would never think to take things into their own hands, even if they had the means. And they would struggle to understand if he did.

"Things will change. It is only a matter of time," Alec said rapping his hand on the table for emphasis. Kayla nodded, but her gaze was now down at her drink, her anger settling. They were quiet for a spell, as around them the quiet hum of conversation continued, broken occasionally by a loud laugh or jest.

"He was a good man your dad," Alec said.

Seth nodded in agreement and Kayla smiled sadly, a slight moistness to her eyes. They all lapsed into silence again for a while, Seth thinking through what Kayla had said; worryingly, he could imagine feeling broken by the loss of his trade, which would bring not only the loss of his source of income but also the loss of his identity. Alec spoke again, a little more brightly, clearly trying to raise everyone's spirits.

"Mind the time he caught us all skipping school and ready to hike out for the day with nothing but a bottle we had somehow come across."

"And we thought he was going to roast us and march us back to school to be humiliated by old Levett," Seth said, attempting to join in, a smile starting to grow.

"As my parents would have."

"But instead, he packed up some bread, made sure we had something warm and just ensured that no one saw us leave."

Kayla smiled. "He confiscated the bottle though."

Seth chuckled. "Probably for the best. There could have been anything in that bottle. I think we got it from Wardle, and mind he was found a little later, pretty unwell from something he had brewed up."

Alec and Kayla laughed. "So he did. I had forgotten that. Maybe your dad did us a bigger favour after all."

"We had a good day though, just camping out in the bend of the river, imagining everyone else sweating away and trying to evade old Levett's attention."

Seth and Alec both nodded. Seth took a drink and relaxed further as the conversation drifted on, staying on the reassuring ground of their growing years. He was not sure how long they sat there, but when he returned home the combination of the late hour, the last few restless nights and the memory of sitting back doing nothing much with friends meant it was little time before he fell into a deep sleep, untroubled by memory, anger or fear.

Chapter 9

Tam sat on a rock on the side of a hill looking down over Halistra, which lay ahead of him. It was a large town, set on a crossroads, from which a road snaked up into the hills to his right following a river that ran between him and the town before continuing its path out of sight. The main road took a different direction along the flatter ground on either side of the town. He had just come along its southern portion before striking off up the hill. Some distance from there, the road then crossed the river on a stone-built bridge, which was the first he had seen in the region, and which he felt marked the increasing prosperity of the area. North lay the fertile plains of Harran, which provided much of the grain and fruit for Elishadra, and beyond that Ardvastra. The area around him was known for its trade, with other towns and cities, of the stone quarried from the nearby hills and the fine wool from the hill tribes. Halistra had a much busier appearance than the towns he had been in so far. Barge-like boats were moored at a dock a few hundred paces from the edge of the town, and a steady stream of carts pulled by large strong horses made their way between the two. Guards stood at each gate and manned the docks; even from this distance they looked alert and attentive. The men and women at the docks guiding the horses worked quickly, using pulleys to lift the cargo from the barges before loading it onto the carts. Now and again a better dressed man or woman, whom Tam assumed to be merchants, appeared from a building at the docks to remonstrate with the guards or the workers. The town itself as far as he could see was a mass of brick-built houses with little space for gardens except in the centre, where there was more order and the houses were larger and more spread out. Outside the town, there was a thin line of smaller houses leaning up against the town walls and each other, and from these, children ran to and fro, largely ignored by the guards.

Marrea had gone ahead of him into the town. She was adept at finding things out, like the atmosphere in a place, where power lay, and who was behind it. She also went unnoticed, something he put down to her gifting and also her inbuilt lack of desire for attention, which he could remember about her even as a child, many years ago. She had always been content in her own space, not needing others or their good opinion, something that he was still learning. She would listen to the conversations in the streets, talk to some of the tradespeople or barmen, buy the odd drink for someone here or there, and quickly get a feel for a place. She would be at least a few more hours, so Tam turned from his viewpoint and climbed back up to a more sheltered spot, where he could no longer see the town and was hidden from view. He did not fear being spotted, but he did not want to deal with the questions and furthermore just wanted to be on his own.

He undid the pack on his horse and let it roam a few feet away to a patch of grass. He then took out some bread and cheese that they had picked up on the way. The simple process of preparing and eating a meal in this sheltered peaceful spot gave some relief from the heavier thoughts weighing on his mind. He was tired; the night before last he had confronted another of Nehlo's servants, a woman this time. She had resisted, and again he had been forced to remove her bonding. It resided now in the walled-off area of his mind, but he could feel it there, stronger now, pushing and questing all the time to invade and control. He had not been seen at all this time and had left before any questions were asked of him, but disquiet lingered in him about the effect of ripping the bond from someone, even one who had done much harm with it, as well as the potential for chaos and that could arise from the sudden loss of leadership. He gazed out over the countryside, allowing the green spaces and solitude to quieten his mind.

Tam woke some hours later to find Marrea busy around him. She smiled and held out some fruit and meat that she had brought from the town. Tam accepted it gratefully. She also had a small flagon of ale, only slightly warm, which was a welcome change to water. She was silent for a while.

"It was good to see you resting. You look the better for it."

Tam nodded. "I feel better. How was your day?"

"Interesting, but let's finish this first and then I can fill you in."

They sat for a while, eating as the daylight around them faded and the sounds of the town closing up for the night drifted up to them. Once finished, they sat with their backs to the slope of the hill and looked outward. From here they could not see the town but only the hills to the side and then land disappearing off in the distance, already smudged by the coming night.

"This place feels different," Marrea began. Tam nodded to show his attention, though he continued to look outward. "From what I can tell there is a man who nominally leads but no one ever sees him, and some say he is unwell or possibly even dead. There is, though, many more soldiers than I would expect for a town this size and they keep everything in check."

"What was the feeling about the soldiers?"

"Mixed I think. Most people just keep out of their way and don't question their presence. A lot of the soldiers are not from the town, so are not really known and don't really go out of their way to become known. They seem to change a lot too which is unusual, rotating through from other places, mainly Ardvastra. Most people said that they were fair but hard and not to be crossed without good reason. They seem well drilled from what I could tell."

Tam nodded again. Having a strong garrison here would make sense in some respects. The town was an important crossing point for trade and other industry.

"Who is the man in charge?" he asked.

"A man called Tomaz, but I am not sure how much influence he still holds."

"Is there anyone else who may be above him that we need to consider instead?"

"Not that I could discover. The captains of the soldiers come and go with their men, and there is no other focal point beyond that. There is a council of

48

merchants that meets regularly, but they stick strictly to business and don't seem to concern themselves with the affairs of the town."

"Okay, Tomaz it is."

Marrea nodded her agreement. "But I would take care. We know little about him, and there may be much more to him than his lack of visibility would suggest."

Tam continued to look out over the view ahead of him. "Any obvious contenders to take over the reins? I imagine the council of merchants will step up to keep business running? Or maybe the current captain?"

"Possibly though it is impossible to say for certain. There is more order here than in most places. That might not hold though. I also think that word is going to make it back to Nehlo more quickly from here. It is a town of greater consequence." Tam saw Marrea look at him quickly to gauge his reaction, but he only shrugged.

"It is going to happen sooner or later. I don't expect him to react to the reports though. He will sense that all his bondings are still out there, in place. I don't think it will occur to him that someone would take them on to themselves."

"But he might well be more on the alert than otherwise. Shouldn't we just face him now while he does not expect us?"

Tam thought for a while. Would it be better to just face him? But then, what would become of all these towns and cities where his influence was so palpable? And if he failed when meeting Nehlo, then no one would be better off. A thought had been developing with each encounter that there was maybe a way of ensuring some degree of success if he kept doing what he was, even if he failed when they met.

"I think we need to keep doing what we are Mar; it seems the right way forward for now. What do you think?"

Marrea looked at him closely for a few moments before answering. "I don't know Tam. Either way there is risk, to you, to the people here, to me even. I am willing to take your lead with this. Your instincts are usually right. There is something else though. There is talk of a mining town up in the hills. That is where some of the boats come from, bringing minerals and precious stone to be processed and sent back to the capital. That is partly why there are so many soldiers. But the talk is of people, prisoners, being brought through here in great numbers." She paused for a second. "And not returning. No one really talks about it, but you hear bits and pieces here and there and putting it together there is something here that no one wants to acknowledge."

Tam felt the weariness come on him again, and Marrea, alert to any signs of weakness in him, was quick to respond. "I could go and look and see if there is anything in it?"

Tam smiled, sensing her concern. "No, it is probably best that you go on ahead to Harran as we planned. I can investigate the mine and then I will find you there."

"Okay," she assented but he could hear her uncertainty. In many ways it mirrored his own. He felt a sense of anxiety at not having a clear plan that he could pursue, instead having to make difficult decisions at each turn, for good or ill.

Chapter 10

Tam lay on the ground under the small scrubby trees, ignoring the dampness soaking into his jacket and trousers. He watched the guards move around the building in front of him. Getting to this spot had been easy enough. Once darkness had fallen and the hour had moved onto the deepest part of the night, he had moved through the encampment outside the town looking for the least-guarded area. Walking lightly, he had not even disturbed the dogs that lay at the doors of the makeshift houses. He had then simply climbed over the wall and dropped to the other side. Threading his way through the streets, he had searched for the area where there was the highest number of soldiers, assuming this to be where the man he sought would be, though he was still unsure what he expected to find. He was patient though, having learned through long experience the value of watching and studying to mitigate the chance of surprises, though there were still always some. That too he had learned.

He watched the movement of the guards to see if there was any pattern to it. They were well trained and alert, largely focusing outward along the three roads that led up to this point though some scanned the area where Tam lay out of sight. The house itself was not large but was well-built with an open stretch of grass between it and the iron fence that surrounded it. He tried to sense whether there was anyone of power inside, but so far he could sense very little. He mapped out his route of entry and noted the position of all the windows and doors, using those to form a rough impression of the inside of the building.

A commotion on the far side of the building caught the attention of the guards, most of whom moved in that direction. Some stayed at their position, however, showing Tam how well trained they were. He hesitated long enough to note how many they were and rose smoothly, drawing his scarf up over the lower part of his face as he ran forward. Summoning air as he ran, he jumped and used the air to lift him up and over the fence landing softly on the far side. The guards started, turning in his direction, their attention caught by the sound of the wind rustling through the fence and trees as Tam drew it to himself. Tam did not release the air but wove it into bonds, which he wrapped around each of them as they turned, pinning their arms to their sides and closing their mouths tight. They fell and stared up at him with frightened eyes as he approached. He sensed other guards coming round the corner, so he moved to the side of the house and through the door that was ahead of him. The guards would quickly realize that the slight disturbance that Marrea had created was no threat and resume their patrol. They would soon find their comrades.

Tam cushioned his steps beneath him, almost floating on the raft of air he kept around him. He channelled it ahead of him, testing floorboards and seeping it around doors to loosen them if needed. He concentrated though on seeking out the bonding that he could now feel, above him and to the right. He looked at the stairs that led up to the dark hallway above, which was narrow and would leave him exposed. He could feel the movement of one, possibly two people up there, so after a quick assessment of the other areas, he gathered the air he had been searching with and prepared himself. With one fluid movement, he jumped and in two bounds was at the top of the stairs, rolling as he landed to avoid any potential attack. There were two men there, but they had not heard him approach and he had bound them with air before they had even drawn their swords. Tam paused and listened. He could not hear movement from within, and so far no alarm had been raised outside. Slowly, he moved forward and eased the door open. Within, he saw a moderate sized bed chamber with a man sleeping soundly, though not peacefully. He was thin and unkempt, the clothes that he wore from the daytime still on him but crushed and shapeless. He moved a little as if in pain or distress and a slight sheen of sweat was upon his face, which looked pale, almost grey in the slight light filtering in through the shutters from the moon and lamps outside. Tam could sense the bonding within the man, those in his own mind reacting to his disgust by clawing at his defences.   He hesitated here, not sure about what his next steps should be. The man stirred though, forcing Tam to move forward and pin him to the bed with a cushion of air and a smaller one to gag his mouth. He woke properly now and stared at Tam with frightened but strangely pleading eyes.

Tam looked at him for a long second before speaking. He sensed a difference here from the last of Nehlo's people, as if this man was fighting the bond, seeking to assert his own control again. Maybe that was why he had been unable to sense it until he was inside the house.

"I am not here to hurt you. Do you know what is in you, what binds you?"

The man nodded in short, quick movements.

"I can take it away from you if you wish, but you will lose whatever influence you have here."

A sudden hope seemed to stir in the man, and he motioned with his eyes down to his mouth. Tam released the gag from him slightly to allow him to whisper.

"Please, I don't know what you can do but please help me or kill me," the man pleaded. "I hate every minute of this life, this bondage. I have from the moment that I accepted it, but I have been unable to turn away. It sickens me yet controls me, no matter how I resist. I hate what it has made me do, though now I resist at every turn. I would rather die than carry on as I am, hating myself and hurting others."

Tam thought quickly over all that had happened recently. He knew that he was not meant to interfere with due process, that once released this man should be left to the justice of the people of this town. He also knew though that this could be merciless on a man who had caused such harm, and there would be no understanding or even knowledge of any mitigating circumstances. He had, from what he said, but also from what Tam could ascertain of him now and his lack of appearance in this town, regretted his decision whenever that had been made.

51

Should he answer now for crimes relating to a decision taken possibly years ago and striven against ever since? He wanted to trust that this man would start again, would make it worth his risk and live a life striving to recompense for the harm he had been party to.

"You will have nothing once it is removed. All your power and influence will be gone. You may become an outcast."

"That would be no more than I deserve for what I have become, what I have done. I may have chance at living my life again. I would take that chance, to try and make amends."

"I can take it from you, but I do not know what effect that will have on you. It may damage you or change you because it is deep inside. You will have to trust me and give it up and push it away with every fibre of your being and will."

The man nodded, this time vigorously. Tam thought for a second before taking the man's head in his hands. He reached out with his mind and located the bonding deep within, feeling its extent and the attachments it had made deep into the man's consciousness. Tam looked at him, holding his gaze and imparting his own strength and certainty, and then he nodded and mouthed "Now."

As Tam pulled at the living, writhing mass with his mind he could feel the man pushing, rejecting, cutting at the evil within, desperately seeking to scrape it off every last thought, motive and desire within. Tam aided him and guided him with his own thoughts, searching out every area of blackness and pulling it into himself. Once again, he felt the sickening clawing at his own mind as it came to rest in him, and he walled it off, quickly and thoroughly before it could seek to control him. He slumped, for a second defenceless against any attack, before rallying himself to find the man looking at him in wonder.

"Why?" he gasped.

Tam did not answer his question but instead listened for sound outside the room. "We must move quickly. You must leave this town tonight and never return. You have done or been part of doing great harm here, and though I see the change in you, there must be some payment for what has happened."

The man nodded again. "Anything. All I want is to live simply. I was tempted by power once and now I want nothing to do with it. I want to start again, doing anything that people will let me do where I am not known. If I can have that chance I ask for no other."

Tam looked at him carefully; he was already more alert, the sheen of sweat had lifted and he saw new life returning to his body. Tam moved to the window and saw now the evidence of soldiers coming together toward the house. They had not raised an alarm, seeking not to alert their intruder but had organized themselves to move into the house. Tam worked threads of air into the window, loosening it, and eased it open. The cool of the night flooded in, providing a welcome relief and the promise of a new start to the man beside him. He moved forward eagerly, but Tam held him back for a second.

"There are guards outside. You need to keep trusting me if you can."

The man looked at him for a brief moment before again nodding.

"Then follow me."

With that, Tam climbed to the window and without hesitating jumped, hearing only an astonished intake of breath behind him as he fell. Drawing air to break his fall he landed softly and looked quickly around him. Sensing the man falling above

52

him, he broke his fall with the air beneath him before releasing it quickly. The man staggered forward and fell before quickly scrambling to his feet. Tam pulled him forward now, moving quickly through the garden. Two guards rushed at them, but Tam motioned his arm, sweeping the men away with a compressed gust of air. They flew back and landed heavily on the ground, the breath and strength knocked out of them. Tam felt rather than saw the approach of arrows from the house, and releasing the wind, he redirected it back, catching the arrows and whipping them away from him to dig aimlessly into the trees. More quickly now, he ran toward the fence and jumped, summoning the air to lift him and his companion high over the fence and onto the small pathway on the other side. He caught the man as he fell forwards but immediately pulled him away into the path's secluded darkness. As they ran, Tam heard the commotion behind him as the soldiers gathered together in pursuit. Soon the man beside him was flagging, breath coming in gasps as he fought to keep up the pace. Tam forced him on, almost carrying him with buffeting air behind and beneath him. They ran on, between the sleeping homes to the walls, which they clambered over before disappearing into the darkness of the outer encampment and the hills beyond.

Tam slowed to a fast walk but did not relent on the pace till they were high up in the hills, with the town and any noise of pursuit far away. He looked back and could not see any sign of their pursuers or of disturbance in the town. The soldiers were obviously looking carefully but quietly, and he wondered whether they did not want it to become known what had happened. Maybe this man would not be replaced and things would continue as before; after all he had been rarely seen and folk questioned his ongoing existence. Maybe the memory of him was enough to keep the established order in charge, in which case he may not have achieved anything. Then he turned and looked again at the man beside him. Despite the exertion, he looked more alive than he had, taller, straighter and with purpose now. He stood and looked down at the town with something of regret in his gaze but also with intent. He turned and saw Tam watching him.

"Words are not enough, but I am forever in your debt." He reached out and grasped Tam's hand before kneeling on the ground and pressing his forehead onto the hand he held tightly in his own. Tam pulled him up and set him on his feet again.

"You owe me nothing except to make good on what you promised and start to make amends in whatever small way you can."

The man nodded thoughtfully. Tam felt for him. He would have nothing and would have to make his way without friend or family to aid him. He would find it hard, particularly with the suspicion that governed much of people's response to strangers after years of betrayal and violence at the hands of rulers like him. He had more than he deserved though, and that would have to be enough.

"I would head south from here," Tam added, pointing down the way that he had recently come. "You may find shelter and acceptance there. If you come to the town of Fraebost, there is an innkeeper there by the name of John. He was a friend to me, and I am sure he would be to you too." The man turned to look where he pointed and gazed into the darkness.

"How can you do these things? Control the air around you, jump so far, defend yourself in that way?" he asked, without turning.

"Could you not? Did your previous master not give you this ability?"

53

"No. But then, I never tried to develop his gifts." He almost spat the last word out. "I could bind people to my will once they had initially trusted me if I focused enough, but once I realized how awful it was to be bound to Nehlo, I resisted forcing that on someone else, though he made me do it often enough regardless. He sent me here, to run things for him, though really the soldiers that rotate through from the capital do that."

Tam was silent for a few moments. "Manipulating air is a gift, I suppose. One that I have been taught to develop. Manipulating others, like Nehlo, is a perversion of that gift that has been used for the wrong ends here." He paused before continuing. "Can you tell me something?"

The man nodded, turning to face him

"The town up the river from here. I heard some rumours about people going there, prisoners, but not returning?"

The man turned away again, looking uncomfortable. Tam waited for him to speak, which he did after a visible struggle.

"It is a mining town," he answered slowly. "It is from there that much of the metals and precious stones come that get sent to the capital, Ardvastra. The barges transport them down, and then the teams of soldiers return with them to the capital. My previous master controls it all, which is really why I was here."

"And the prisoners?" Tam prompted.

"They come from all over the country, sent from all the main towns. Some are criminals, properly convicted. Some, though, are here for the crime of standing up to what is happening or against some of the corruption they were seeing around them. They come through the town and then up to the mines. After that I don't know what happens to them."

"But they don't come back."

He looked down at the ground. "No, they don't come back. And more keep coming. I suppose I have never allowed myself to think beyond that."

Tam allowed the silence to fill the space. Words, at this moment, would only make more difficult the process the man had to go through to find freedom from his guilt. Tam was also angry. He could imagine Zoe or John being lead away in chains, to work till they died, exhausted, hopeless. Worse, his wife or sons suffering the same fate, separated from all they loved, safe from this fate only because they lived in a different country. And it could only happen if people looked the other way or in some way were complicit. He unclenched fists that were tightly closed and took some deep breaths, thankful that his wife and children were far from here. He looked more closely at the man beside him and saw his struggle, his regret and self-loathing and also the fight that he had undergone to be better, without anything to guide or help him. Suddenly his anger died away, and he was filled again with a rush of emotion for him and all the people in this land, bent under the weight of a great evil. He reached out a hand and grasped the man's arm.

"I will do what I can. You know what you have to do."

The man looked up and inclined his head a little in response.

"One last thing, your name? It is Tomaz, is it not?"

"It was, but I think I will go by Tom now." He smiled weakly.

Tam returned the smile more warmly. "Mine is Tam."

The man held his arm for a moment longer, gazing intently at him before nodding and turning to walk down the far side of the hill into the ever so slight lightening that came with the dawn. Tam turned the other way and skirted round the hill to find his horse and small camp nestled into the side of the hill. He yearned for rest but instead packed his belongings onto his horse and led it in the direction of the river, keeping to the high ground out of sight of the town below.

Chapter 11

The road that Seth stood on was eerily quiet at this time of night. Terraced houses lined both sides; all the windows were shuttered. It was a cold, dreary night. The rain had fallen in a slight haze ever since he had taken up position. The doorway he leaned into only slightly protected him, so he was nearly soaked through and was aware of his clothes sticking to him and the water running down the back of his neck from his hair. From where he stood, he could see along the road as it sloped down the hill toward the docks on the river. He tried to stay alert and to listen for any sound of what was happening down there, but either because of the rain or the distance, he could not hear anything. He had kept this post for what seemed like hours but in reality was probably only an hour, and more than once he had wished that he had not stumbled into this.

The night before he had followed Kayla again but this time to a very different meeting house. She had been quiet the whole way. They had walked to a part of the town that he was not familiar with, and Kayla had stopped at a doorway to a house that looked like any other. She had knocked quietly on the door and then spoken to someone in quick terse sentences before the door had opened to allow them both in. The man at the door stayed in the shadows as they passed, so Seth had not been able to see him, but he could feel the scrutinizing and appraising look the man gave him before closing and bolting the door behind them.

They had walked to the end of the hallway before turning into another room where they were asked to wait. Kayla had sat down immediately, clearly expecting this, so Seth had done likewise. He had not wanted to ask any questions, the atmosphere seeming to forbid it, so they just waited in silence while some men and women walked through to an adjoining room from which voices could be heard. The room itself was dull and dark, lit only by a single candle, and by the time the woman came to speak to them, he had started to feel restless and cold. She had not given her name and had spoken mainly to Kayla, whom she seemed to know, which Seth wondered about as he had never seen her before. They did not talk for long and, as far as Seth could tell, it was only to confirm a time and an address. Kayla nodded and then motioned for Seth to follow her back out of the house without anyone saying anything else. She had been quiet for some time after that as they walked a different way back to her home.

Once inside her own home, she had explained that the people they had met were planning things in the city, things that would destabilize the leaders and allow those to take control who would end the oppression and extortion of ordinary folk. She did not want to say where she had heard about them but reassured him her source was reliable. She also did not know much about their plans but said that they had been allowed to help on this occasion and would be allowed to do more once they had shown they could be trusted. That had led to him standing in this cold doorway, having been left here by Kayla what seemed like weeks ago with instructions to keep watch and report on any soldiers or anyone suspicious moving toward the docks. If he spotted anything he was to allow them to pass but then climb to the rooftop and light the torch that was held under his coat, in the lee of the rain. This had all seemed simple when he had been first told about it, but since then it had rained continuously, and he seriously doubted if he would be able to light the torch. With the cold seeping into his arms and legs, he was even unsure if he would be able to climb up the rough, pitted wall. He fervently hoped that nothing would happen, and so far his hopes had been met.

Peering through the night, he could just about make out the buildings at the docks that were lit by some basic lamps. He could not see any movement there at all and was starting to think that he had been forgotten. Once he had looked more closely, however, he could see that there were some soldiers down there, standing close to the buildings. As he watched, more people emerged from the shadows outside the lamps reach and approached the buildings. They came from both sides of the perimeter and circled in, moving with obvious care. When they were almost up to the area that was lit they broke into a run, converging on the buildings. Seth watched, unaware that he was holding his breath, as they reached the guards, who were caught completely unaware by the speed and ferocity of the attack. The guards were cut down, their bodies falling where they stood. Seth felt suddenly faint and leaned against the doorway, letting his breath out in a gasp. He could not look away though as the figures moved into the main building. He could not see now what happened but heard some shouts and cries as men fought. Then there was silence again and a pause. Eventually, Seth saw figures come out of the building, this time carrying what looked like bags over their shoulders. They ran now, scattering in different directions away from the docks and back into the shadows of the surrounding houses. The whole episode had lasted just moments but for long minutes afterwards Seth felt the nervous energy pumping around him and struggled to control his breathing. He continued to wait, but his mind now was leaping between ideas and possibilities. He started when he felt a tug on his sleeve and turned to find Kayla beckoning him.

They walked quickly together away from the docks, winding their way through the narrow streets of the older part of town toward Kayla's home. They did not speak until the warm safety of her kitchen had infused into both of them. Seth broke the silence.

"What just happened?"

Kayla paused for a moment before answering. "I was only told that there would be an attack on the docks. Precious metals get shipped in from a mine up country, and the group wanted to stop them getting through. They think that the metals go from here to the capital and are then used by Nehlo to buy the allegiance that he does not already own."

Seth involuntarily shuddered when Nehlo's name was mentioned. That was a name that was never spoken in public for fear of being noted as an enemy; people

57

had disappeared for less. He had not thought beyond his own city to the rot that had set in throughout the country, but he was now faced with being part of a rebellion against the power behind it all.

"Will it not make things worse? If he does not get his supply, will he not come to find out why?"

Kayla shrugged. "Probably. But we either face up to him eventually or things just carry on as they are. No one knows who took the shipment tonight, and no one will find out until the group is ready. They are hoping initially to cause a rift between him and Malzorn."

Seth thought about that for a second. He did not know how this all linked together. The man who led the city was not often seen, but he was feared by everyone Seth knew, including himself. It was his men that had likely killed his friends and many others who had tried to stand against him. He seemed to command absolute authority and people said that he knew about everything that went on, something Seth had always put down to the sort of rumours that circulate about a powerful and callous person whom people know very little about. Now this group had struck directly at him and his link to Nehlo. There was no going back from this without further bloodshed. The question for him was whether he would watch from the side-lines and not get involved and maybe avoid harm, or whether he risked everything and threw his lot in with this shadowy group. He did not know who they were and his only link to them was through Kayla.

"How involved are you? Do you know who these people are?"

Kayla again considered her answer. "I know some of them. One you have met, and you know another one. They try to ensure that identities remain hidden as much as possible, to avoid detection and infiltration from Malzorn's cronies. I have done little jobs for them but have not been involved in anything big." Seth looked the question at her. "No, I was not at the docks tonight. I was keeping watch, just like you."

"Did they kill those guards?"

"Yes."

Seth absorbed that for a second. "Did they have to? They could just be normal people like you and me."

"There is no normal anymore." Her sudden anger surprised him. She saw this and visibly controlled herself. "They made their choice when they became guards. They were not forced into doing that. And they have chosen to side with everything that is wrong with this city. I don't like it, but I don't see another way."

Seth looked at her for a long moment. She held his gaze before looking away. She had always been decisive, but there was a new hardness to her that he had not seen before. He wanted to reach out and take her hand, but something held him back, so he just sat in silence not really knowing what to think or do. Kayla was the first to speak, though she did not look at him.

"What are you going to do?"

"I don't know. I want things to change as much as you do, but I am not sure this is the right way. Though maybe you are right, and it is the only way."

"What have you been training for with the sword, if not for this? And how are we to avenge Neil and the others, if not by fighting?"

Seth had no answers. He supposed he had always known that it might come to this but seeing people being killed so quickly and without pause had unsettled him and made him question whether he was strong enough or willing enough to do the same. He trusted Kayla though. It ran deeper than that, but he had tried not to give space to those thoughts. He could, though, see a gulf opening between them if they went down different paths, and he did not want that, almost feared that. He also realized that he agreed with her that waiting and not doing anything would never bring about change, and what other option was left to them?

"I suppose I just never really thought that I would have to kill anyone," he began before tailing away, realizing how weak that was going to sound. "I want to help," he added, forcing his voice to sound firmer.

She looked up at him and smiled. Taking his hand, she clasped it tightly. "You have already passed their first test, and I will vouch for you. You can stay in the background if you wish, but I am glad you are with me in this."

Seth looked at her intently, knowing that the decision he had just taken was the only one possible to him.

Chapter 12

"I had no idea rebellions were so dull."

Kayla turned to look at Seth and grimaced before turning back to peer out of the small window she was crouched next to. He was sitting, leaning back against the wall with a short sword across his knees.

"I think the biggest threat to my life at the moment is dying of boredom or starvation because of losing what is left of my clients." She did not turn round this time though nodded her head in assent.

He was only partially joking about the last bit. He had struggled to keep up with what work he had because of sometimes being out most of the night. Due to that, people had started to go elsewhere. He knew there was precious little work to go round and it would be difficult to rebuild. Trade in the city was being affected by their activities. Those with money didn't want to draw attention to themselves and were becoming insular and secretive, suspicious of any who spent freely.

Seth knew very little about what they had been doing, however. Most of his time had been spent in rooms like this or alleyways, ostensibly protecting an escape route or watching for approaching guards. He had not been told what the targets were in advance and often only found out afterwards by listening to the gossip on the street. He knew that they had struck at businesses owned by the powerful, usually ransacking them or redistributing the goods, as they were jokingly referring to it now. It was always at night, always in different parts of the city, and if there was a pattern to it, Seth could not make it out. It was having an effect though as more soldiers were on the streets and the richer families now employed their own men to protect their homes.

It was having an effect on normal people too. His parents had been discussing it when he had last visited them. They were quiet folks, keen to earn enough for a decent life and for years that was what they had done. For the first time in his life, Seth heard them worrying about where they were going to get the money for their rent after meeting the rising cost of food and other essentials. They had no love for the authorities, but they had always got by. Now, they were faced with the possibility of eviction. Seth had not known what to say to them. He knew that they wondered about him, about the hours he kept and his loss of focus on his trade. Ever since he had become a master of his trade they had respected his privacy, and they did not invade it now though he could tell that they sorely wished to. He said nothing but made sure some of the money he did make made it into their pot. This all gave him some disquiet about what they were doing and whether they were achieving anything.

And then there was Kayla. He had absolutely no idea what to think about her. He could not tell whether things had changed or not. That night, when he had agreed to join with her in this cause, he thought that some connection had been made beyond the friendship they had always shared, but now he was not so sure, and he could not think how he would bring it up with her. They had not spoken at all about each other despite spending a fair amount of time in rooms like this, though often with one or two others. He was pretty sure that he loved her, but much as he looked, he could not ascertain whether she felt the same about him. It was frustrating, more frustrating even than the frequent boredom and lack of certainty about what he was doing. He mulled it over again in his own mind, trying to figure out a casual way of introducing the topic and was just about to venture something when he saw Kayla stiffen and hold her hand out behind her as if to quieten him, though she could not have known he was about to speak. He stayed silent and focused on listening to the sounds coming from the square outside, but he could hear nothing untoward. He watched Kayla for a second, but she did not move, intent only on looking through the window at something. He edged forward as quietly as he could until he was next to her and then carefully lifted himself up to look out.

It took him a second to familiarize himself with the buildings around the square, which were only dimly lit at this time of night by the weak light coming from the lamps placed at intervals on the outer aspect of the square. The houses here were large, and some even had balconies, though no one used those now. He refocused on the shadows, trying to see what Kayla had seen and then drew in a sharp breath, a small fear clutching at him. He saw men, soldiers almost certainly, positioned in various points around the square, and looking round, he saw that they were focused on the north aspect. He was not sure how many there were, but he counted about twenty. They were alert and all held weapons ready as if they were expecting immediate action.

Seth looked across at Kayla and saw some of his own worry sketched on her face. They both sunk down beneath the window and leaned in so that they could whisper.

"What is going on?" Seth asked.

"They must know something. This isn't a routine patrol. They are here for a reason, and they are expecting trouble."

Seth nodded. He could make that out.

"But how?"

Kayla did not answer him. That was a question for later, if there was a later.

"How are we going to get out?"

"I don't think we can, not easily without being seen anyway. But I don't think they are looking for us; they have not searched at all. They are waiting, which means they must know that the others will be coming through here." She tailed off, obviously thinking hard. Seth swallowed, trying to keep his rising fear at bay. They were meant to be here to protect the returning party from isolated patrols, not from an organized force. He silently cursed; the boredom he had been moaning about seemed suddenly appealing.

"We have to help the others, or this is all over," Kayla whispered to him.

Seth nodded. "But how?"

"They should be coming from the north. That is where the job is and that is why the soldiers are focusing that way. I don't think that we can get to them to warn them to go another way, but we can maybe stop it becoming a disaster."

Seth nodded again but did not say anything, waiting for her to finish her thoughts.

"I think the only way is to get as close as we can so that we are ready when they come." She turned to him as she said it, and he could see the resolution in her eyes. "I think all we can do is help them by attacking from behind, and maybe, with surprise on our side, we can cause enough disturbance to allow our friends to get away."

Seth looked away for a second, thinking quickly. He knew that he would do this, but his heart rebelled against it. There was every likelihood that they would not even get close to the soldiers before being spotted and cut down. Did he really want to die for this cause? What on earth was it going to achieve anyway? Despite these thoughts he had given his word that he would do what was asked of him and that would have to be enough reason for now. He nodded quickly, before looking back at her. She was staring at him intently, measuring.

"For now, though, we wait as we should not expect them for a little yet."

She leaned back against the wall and beckoned for him to lean against her. The rough edge to the wall dug into his back but he stayed still, scared to move unless it upset this moment with her leaning against him, her head against his shoulder. Tentatively, he lifted his arm and placed it round her, and finding that it was not rejected, tightened it round her. They sat like that for the remaining time, not talking.

Eventually, Kayla stirred and lifted herself up gingerly to look out again. "The soldiers have not moved, and the others must be close now, though there is no way to know for sure. I think we have to move now."

Seth looked out the window and studied the square. He mapped it out in his head and saw routes they could take to approach the soldiers in the shadows. He leaned closer to her again.

"I think we should separate and each circle round the square to attack from either side. If we make enough noise, they might think that there is a lot of us. It all depends on getting there unseen, which will take some luck."

She nodded and motioned that she would take the longer route. Seth silently shook his head and intimated that he was going to do that. She looked at him again, waiting for a second before nodding.

They both gripped their swords tightly and Kayla lifted the latch on the door, which swung open silently. Seth moved past her, lightly brushing her back with his hand as he passed and moved out into the night, keeping next to the walls and in the shadows. He looked back briefly to see Kayla move in the other direction before he turned and half crouching moved as quickly as he dared along the buildings, stooping under any windows. He could feel and hear his heart hammering in his chest, and every breath sounded laboured and loud, try as he might to still it. The sword hilt felt clammy in his hand and alien to him as if at any moment it might betray him by crashing off something. Somehow, he made it round two sides and was now approaching the north aspect. So far he had been unchallenged. He wondered briefly to himself whether the soldiers had become less alert with waiting or whether they were now so focused on where they thought the threat would come that they neglected to focus elsewhere. Either way, he was not going to question it but fervently hoped that his luck would hold. He could not see Kayla, but she must be in position already, and the fact that everything was still quiet meant she was safe for now.

Seth almost trod on the man before seeing him, but he had the advantage, the soldier's attention only being half on his watch, half on the men behind him. He didn't stop to think but rushed forward, his blade held out in front of him. He almost lost control of it when it struck, but he saw the shock and pain on the man's face as the blade struck deep into his throat. He reached up to clutch the gash, unable to make a sound, seeking to stem the flow of blood. Seth pulled the blade free, only just managing to keep hold of it, its weight suddenly feeling too much for his trembling hands. He reached forward to try and help, unable to take his eyes off the face before him, which had gone pale and was etched with fear. The blood was sticky in Seth's hands, and he could feel the breath bubbling out of the wound. The man could do nothing to stop the blood flowing out, and he slipped to his knees his head falling forward. Seth caught him and lowered him to the ground gently, leaning over him and holding his head as his eyes clouded over and he saw the life leave him. Seth continued to stare, unwilling to believe that he had just taken a life and stunned at how quickly it had happened. The fragility of life shocked him deeply. The man was young, about his own age, and he did not recognize him, but he could imagine knowing him, talking to him. Even in death he looked pleasant. Seth looked for a long moment before dragging himself away, remembering suddenly what he needed to do.

His head felt foggy and unsteady as he stood up. His arms were weak, and he hated the feel of the sword in his hands. He willed his legs to move forward again, knowing that any moment the others would walk into a trap and Kayla would come out of the shadows. For her to have any chance, he needed to be there. All his limbs felt heavy, and his mind was numb, struggling to fathom the depths of what he had just done, what he might yet have to do. He shook his head, trying to focus and looked around. Amazingly, only a few moments had passed and nothing had changed in the square; the soldiers were still there, unaware that one of their number was dead. And Kayla was somewhere out there, about to risk her life.

He crouched down in the shadows again, trying to hear anything above the noise of his breathing and the blood pumping in his ears. He wanted to drop his sword to wipe his hands and brow but didn't dare in case it brought attention. Peering ahead he could see movement as the waiting men shifted quietly, but no words were spoken. In the seeming calm, the tension in Seth increased until it was almost pounding in his head. He blinked to try to clear his head and steady himself, feeling that his body was swaying. He flinched as he heard the faintest noise, or maybe he just sensed people stiffening, readying themselves ahead of him. Two people slipped into the square, moving quietly, looking around them but obviously not seeing the ambush waiting in the shadows. The main body of men followed, numbering a dozen Seth thought. He held his breath. For a second nothing happened, and he hoped fervently that they would somehow be allowed to pass. Then he saw sudden movement as soldiers charged forward, weapons drawn, catching those at the side and the rear before they had a chance to respond. The others turned quickly and desperately sought to defend themselves.

At the edge of his vision, he saw movement as Kayla moved forward a little. Seth forced his limbs to move so that she could see him. They both raised their swords and almost as one started to run forward. Seth heard Kayla scream out and saw the soldiers start and turn around. He drew in his breath and forced himself to yell out as fierce a noise as he could, trying to be heard over the clash of steel and cries of men. Some of the soldiers turned toward him, uncertain of what they faced and their formation loosened. Seth raised his sword ahead of him and ran as hard as he could, focusing on moving his legs and looking ahead rather than letting his thoughts take over and steal his strength. He dipped his shoulder and rammed into the first man just as he raised his sword, forcing him backward and into the men behind him. Not stopping, Seth swung his sword in a wide arc, feeling it shatter off steel so hard that it sent a jolting pain up his arm, his hand almost loosening from its hilt in response. He kept moving, not really seeing what was in front of him but darting back and fore, swinging his sword up and down, sometimes connecting with stone, sometimes with blade. His breathing became ragged, and his throat was aching from shouting. It was only seconds but already he was slowing, and his movements were weaker. He felt a dull blow to his leg, which suddenly sagged beneath him, the movement actually saving him as another blade punched the air where his chest had been. He dropped to his knee, struggling to hold his blade up, unseeing now from confusion and from the sweat trickling into his eyes, mixed with some tears at the finality of this moment. He had no idea where Kayla was or what had happened to her, and he struggled to focus so that he could see her and maybe reach her.

The expected blow never came. He heard shouts that seemed to come from a distance, and the soldiers turned, leaving him kneeling in the dust of the square, his leg throbbing and his mind exhausted and empty. He was dimly aware of men engaged in fierce struggle around him, but in his confused state he struggled to tell who was friend or foe. Looking around, he saw Kayla, lying on the ground a few feet away from him. He dragged himself over to her, willing her to be alive. She looked pale and was unconscious but breathing, a large gash on her head the most obvious sign of injury. He knelt over her, offering what protection he could as the battle swirled around them.

Soon it was all over and an eerie calm fell on the square. Seth looked up from where he knelt to see men and women in dark clothing moving around between bodies on the ground. Now and again they knelt to check a body and some they picked up and carried between them. Seth could not see any soldiers standing. One lying near him was alive; he could hear him softly moaning in pain, almost whimpering, clutching at his stomach. A man moved toward the solder to check him before lifting his sword and stabbing down into his chest, twisting the blade as he forced it down. The soldier spasmed in pain and shock, his whole body shaking before becoming limp. Seth turned away in horror, feeling sick. He could almost feel the blade, hear the sound and see the man as he died, and he screamed internally to make it stop. Rough hands gripped his shoulders and pulled him up. Turning, he found himself looking at Alec, whose eyes were serious, but his mouth almost twisted into a smile. He heard Alec give some orders, and two other men came and half lifted him under their arms. Others came and lifted Kayla and together they moved swiftly from the square. Seth stumbled along with them, not caring where they took him. He turned back as they left the square, but he could not make out anything, the site of all the bloodshed already hidden from him. He looked up for some reason and started. He wiped his eyes and looked again, but this time he saw nothing. He could have sworn, though, that there had been a figure, a woman he thought, standing on a balcony, watching them as they left.

He reached out and grabbed Alec's arm, who turned sharply to face him.

"Why? That man?" He was unable to say any more than that.

Alec looked puzzled for a second before realizing what Seth was asking.

"We expect no mercy from them, so we show none. They sprang their trap too early, leaving our rear guard free to attack but even so had it not been for you and Kayla we would all have been cut down. As it was, we lost seven good men and women and others injured, some severely."

His look and tone did not invite any challenge to this, so Seth offered none. He just could not see things with this starkness and was not sure he wanted to. He felt spent, emotionally and physically, and it was all he could do to keep up with the group, even with the support of the men either side of him. They moved swiftly but quietly through the narrow streets. Every few streets a few of the group separated and moved away without a word. The two men carrying Kayla turned off into a side street after a nod from Alec. Seth sought to protest, but before he could do so, they hurried on, the group now only consisting of Alec and the two men who half carried him along. Eventually, when he felt he could not move another step, they stopped. Alec knocked softly on a door, which was immediately opened, and they all walked in. Seth saw Alec speak briefly to an older lady who met them before nodding and walking back toward him.

"You have done well tonight. You helped us avoid a disaster that would maybe have finished us." He grasped Seth's arm as he spoke.

Seth looked up at him, seeking to get his thoughts in order and to determine what was most important to say. He settled on the woman he had seen.

"There was a woman on the balcony, above where we were. I saw her just as we left the square. I am sure she was watching."

Alec looked at him sharply. "What did she look like?"

"I really don't know. I only caught a glimpse; her face was in the shadow."

"How do you know it was a woman?"

Seth shrugged. "She just looked like one. More by shape and size than anything about her face. I could not tell whether she was friend or foe."

"Whoever she was, she was unlikely to be on our side. Nothing we can do about that now though." He gripped Seth's arm again. "You will be safe here tonight. This lady is a friend who will help your leg to heal."

Seth became aware of his leg again and looked down. He was amazed to see a deep gash in his thigh where a sword had obviously pierced him. A bandage was wound tightly round it, stopping the bleeding. He wondered distantly why it had not hurt more at the time. He wobbled a bit, feeling faint. Hands caught him again and guided him to a pallet that the lady pointed to. Someone placed a cup to his lips, and he drank deeply the cool water that was offered. He fell asleep almost immediately and was not aware of the men leaving or of the lady removing his trousers, cleaning his wound with gentle care and then bandaging it up again with clean linen.

Chapter 13

Tam sat just off the road watching the convoy of carts move slowly by. The soldiers looked him over suspiciously but did not challenge him. The road was well maintained, and he wondered at the work that had gone into creating this, felling trees and creating bridges over deep ravines. Some of it would have required Nehlo's skill to have been possible, so he had obviously taken a personal interest in whatever lay up ahead. He had also not seen a single person except for another convoy of carts like this one.

Despite the loneliness he had enjoyed the journey. He had stayed in the hills, following the river until he came to another port area, which was really just a wooden structure built out into the river so the barges could stay in the slightly deeper water. It was built at a junction between the road he was on, which continued to follow the river, and another one that wove between the trees away from it. He had watched for a while as a convoy had come down that road and the men had unloaded crates and carried them onto the barge, which had then quietly slipped downstream. He had chosen to follow this new road and had thought about staying above it in the trees, but as the landscape had become more arduous and particularly treacherous for his horse, he had moved down onto the road. The trees were turning a multitude of colours and he was pretty sure he had seen a wildcat in the woods to the side. Despite his hurry he had revelled in the beauty of these old trees rising high above him, creating a mixture of shade and shafts of light that caught the greens and reds of the foliage underneath. He had been traveling now for two days since leaving Tom behind and felt reinvigorated by the journey, if a little hungry after only eating what he could forage from the woods.

He rose when the convoy had gone past and led his horse back up onto the road. He looked around him as he walked, his mind and thoughts still and absorbed in what he could see around him. He could feel the pulse of Nehlo's bonding in the background but out here, where he was most happy, it was easy to quell it almost to the point of him being unaware of it. He had not really thought at all about what he might find ahead of him or what he had left behind him. He was becoming more certain of his ultimate path but out here that seemed a long way ahead and less difficult.

A few hours later he rounded a turn in the road and stopped as ahead of him there was a clearing in the trees, beyond which was a tall, well-maintained wooden fence, easily twice his height. He studied it carefully, realizing that it was designed to keep people in as well as out. A heavy gate covered the only entrance that he could see, and it was through this that the road led, though he could not see beyond it at present. He did not think that anyone had seen him, so he retreated back round the bend in the road again and climbed up among the trees. He let his horse roam a few feet away from him and sat with his back to a tree that had moss growing around its base and was warm and dry to the touch.

He thought over his options. Getting in should not pose any problems, but he would need to do it at nightfall unless he wanted to alert the whole encampment. He wanted, though, to find out what was happening, and he was more likely to find that out during the day. From what he could see, though, he did not expect that they were just going to let him saunter in and have a look around. Still, that might be the quickest option. He had no skill in making up stories, and he knew from experience that he was a hopeless liar, deception not coming easily to his tongue. Smiling at his dilemma, he decided on the straightforward approach. He called to his horse and reached into the saddle bag to pull out the remaining apples and berries that he had picked as well as some shrubs that were bitter but more filling. He ate them slowly, tossing the cores and some of the berries to his horse in response to a nudge from its nose. Then he leaned his head back into a nook in the trunk and gently fell asleep.

It was dark when he awoke. Rising he found a small stream, and he drank deeply of the cold water before splashing some on his face and neck. Fully awake now he called quietly to his horse, which had wandered off a little into the trees. He spoke a few words to it before tying it loosely to the trees within easy reach of plenty of grass and the small stream. He then moved down to the road and followed it toward the fence, staying just within the trees. Everything ahead of him remained quiet, the fence visible only as a dark smudge at the end of the road.

When he neared the fence he circled around, away from the gate. He walked for some time before turning to face the fence again. It was made of trunks of wood, fashioned into points at the top, sharp enough to cause him some harm if he were to get this wrong. He looked around him and listened carefully, but he could not sense any people close to him. He moved quietly to the edge of the fence, and then summoning air slowly so that it made only a slight rustle in the trees, he channelled it beneath him to raise him slowly up to the top. Grasping the tips of the trunk with his hands, he peered between them to survey what was on the other side.

Directly beneath him there was a space and then some long wooden cabins with small openings for windows that were shuttered against the cold night air. There were a number of these in a line, and then further toward the centre he could see similar cabins, but as far as he could tell there were no windows and whatever doors there were must have been in the side facing away from him. All these cabins were arranged in a circular fashion and orientated toward the centre, where he could just about make out some larger buildings. Everything was quiet, and he was not aware of any guards. Pulling himself up he squeezed between the points of the fence and lowered himself down on the other side before dropping gently to the ground. He paused again, listening carefully, but could not hear anything.

He crouched and ran quickly to the nearest building. Pulling himself up he peered in. There was a small stove in the centre, which cast a little light, and by

67

this he could see what looked like a barracks for soldiers. There were neat bunks with sleeping figures, each separated by a small space for the storage of clothes and goods. Swords were carefully arranged beside the bunks in grasping distance. Tam counted six figures in all. Lowering himself down he moved further in toward the centre. He moved quietly round the cabin in front of him, confirming to himself that there were no windows, only a small hole in the roof from which a little smoke could be seen when standing this close. Moving round to the side nearest the centre, he became aware of another figure standing, leaning against the door post. Staying in the shadow he looked around carefully and thought he could see a similar figure at each of the inner cabins. He was not going to get any further tonight without being spotted, so he retreated and slid under a space in the cabin and lay back on the damp ground to wait till morning.

The sound of tramping feet above roused him from the near sleep that he had been in. Peering out he saw that it was almost dawn, the first rays from the rising sun coming through the trees and creating long shadows against the cabins. Soldiers stood at the entrance to each cabin, talking to each other. One reached over and banged heavily on the door, which opened soon after and some men and women shuffled out to form a group. They were largely ignored by the waiting soldier, who clearly did not expect any trouble. Once the group had formed, they moved out to the centre of a clear space in between, where groups from the other cabins were also gathering. Tam counted about ten cabins in all, each holding eight to ten people. They joined into one large group, and the soldiers with harsh shouts and shoves forced them into a line about five people abreast.

Tam drew air and pushed it quickly away from himself, causing the doors on the far side to slam shut in unison and drawing the attention of all the guards but not the prisoners, who barely glanced up. Tam rolled out from under the cabin and pushed his way into the group, the prisoners making way for him dumbly and without question. The ones closest to him looked up, but their eyes did not register any surprise or question. The soldiers brought their attention back to the group, and when more prisoners were added, more soldiers brought up the rear. Slowly the group shuffled forward, Tam imitating the hunched, tired shuffle of those around him. With his head down he stole glances around him. He had rarely seen a more abject group. It was hard to tell who was male and who was female, they were so formless and thin. Their clothing was thick with grime, and he could see sores in their skin. Their faces were thin and gaunt with no hint of motivation or purpose, just dull acceptance. Their movements were stiff and slow and for many painful. More than one stumbled and was caught up by their companions as the group wound its way out the other side of the encampment through a gate and then shuffled down a short road to a clearing in which a gaping hole in the hillside led down into what Tam supposed was the mine.

The group barely paused as it moved forward into the mine. Immediately, it was cold and wet, but the hole that had been dug was high enough to walk upright and wide enough to walk four abreast. It was periodically lit by lamps, their light glinting off the walls. As they moved further in, some of their number peeled away down side-tunnels without any prompting from the soldiers, and Tam in his turn followed those nearest him, trusting to the poor light and the soldier's sense that everything was the same as every other day to ensure that he was not spotted. On they went until the tunnel became narrower, and eventually they stopped at a dead end, where tools lay piled on the ground. Here, the tunnel roof above them was lower, so they had to walk stooped over. The prisoners each picked up a small pickaxe and hammer and shambled forward to the rock in front of them and started to pick away at it dully. Tam did the same and found that what had appeared a mat, featureless surface was studded with occasional bright, flashing stones that caught the eye, even in the dull light of the lamps. He followed those around him and started chipping away at the rock, finding that after a while the brighter stone was release. Picking it up he turned it over in his hand, feeling the weight and sharpness of it as well as noting the deep luster. It felt hard, and although the axe bit deeply into the rock surface, it did not even mark these stones. He felt a hand nudge him and turning saw the person next to him nod down behind him. Tam followed his gaze and dropped the stone into the barrow at his feet before turning back to the task in from of him.

He had no idea how long he stood at that wall. Periodically, different prisoners came and removed the rock, taking it back to the surface. At one point they stopped and from somewhere a small amount of water was portioned out and some bread and dry cheese. Hungry and thirsty as he was, he ate both quickly, noting that the others did the same and did not ask for more. At a rough word from the guards at the end of the tunnel, they all rose and started again. He developed a thoughtless rhythm with his arms picking, scraping, picking, scraping, trying to ignore the aching fatigue leaching into his muscles and the cramping pain developing in his low back. He squatted at times to relieve the pain in his back and to provide a different position for his legs. Sweat rolled off him, adding to his deep thirst, despite the damp cool of the tunnel. The men and women to his side and those that came to take away the rock did not pay him any attention, focused on their own tasks as he was on his. The hours rolled by in the monotonous chipping at the impassive rock face in front of them. Eventually, however, a shout from the entrance caused those around him to turn wordlessly, move to the mouth of the area that they were in, drop their tools in a pile on the ground and move toward the surface in the same, slow, bent-over posture that they had worked in throughout the long day. Tam followed, dropping his tools with the others and stretching his tired arms and back. He no longer wondered at the behaviour of those around him; instead, he wondered how they survived at all.

Blinking they all moved into the daylight, which, although fast waning, was bright in comparison to the tunnels. Instead of moving back into the compound, however, they stayed in their groups outside the tunnel and waited. Tam waited along with them, keeping his head down, though there was little chance of being picked out now that his clothing was filthy and his face darkened by the dust and sweat of hours of labour. After a delay some of the soldiers came out, and Tam saw that they carried the barrows of each section with them, which they then deposited in front of each group. He wondered for a second how they knew which barrow belonged with which group as they all looked the same to him, but then he realized that they didn't care; the barrows were just apportioned randomly. Each was then inspected, and one group singled out, which had obviously secured less stones than the others. They were pushed forward by the soldiers and forced onto their knees. Tired as they were, many sank down almost gratefully. At a shout from the soldier in charge, the soldiers behind each prisoner raised their hands holding rough and knotted sticks and brought them down sharply on the withered, shrunken backs before them, drawing gasps of pain and causing some to fall forward onto their faces. They were roughly dragged up and a further blow given, and then a further, until even the strongest were lying in the dirt, their breathing ragged and shallow, welts already appearing on their backs, where the sticks had easily pierced their tattered clothing.

Tam watched, horrified. He realized this must happen regularly as those around him just watched in resignation with neither pity nor fear on their faces. The soldiers checked the group and lifted some to their feet roughly. They motioned to some of the other prisoners, who stepped forward and supported them though they were barely conscious. Some though, they left on the ground where they lay, those too far gone to be thought worth the effort or dead already. He thought back with anger to all he had heard about this place, but he could not believe the wanton waste of life. He watched the soldiers through it all, marking those who watched and those who turned away, those who pitied and those who revelled in it.

At another shout from the lead soldier, the group slowly shuffled into line again and walked slowly back along the road, through the gate, which closed shut behind them, and back to the clearing in front of the cabins. Once there the soldiers monitored them all as they moved toward their cabin, obviously checking each one in. Finally, only Tam stood in the clearing, having made no attempt to move with the others. He stood, erect now, all the pain banished from him in his anger. In its place he could feel all the energy of his kind coursing through him and connecting with everything around him. The lead soldier approached him in anger, but also with an air of uncertainty and a strange fear on his face.

"Who are you and what are you doing here?" he barked.

Tam did not answer but continued to look at him.

"How did you get here?"

Still Tam did not answer. The man approached him with his fist raised, but Tam looked at him with such contempt and fury that even in his anger the man stopped and took a step back. He motioned with his arm instead. Tam felt the movement prior to the pain and could have stopped it but instead allowed the stick to crack across his back and behind his knees, forcing him down. A further strike whipped across his shoulders with a lancing pain. He looked up again at the leader. He could sense his uncertainty, the fear of making the wrong choice about what to do with him. Tam reached out with his mind and, reaching into that uncertainty, commanded the leader to take him to his superior. The man paused and looked confused for a second before ordering that Tam's hands be bound tightly with rough cord. He was then dragged to his feet and pushed through the clearing to the large house at its centre. He was forced to wait there for some moments while the leader went inside, and then he was pushed forward into a hallway. Looking around him, he saw evidence of wealth and care everywhere, not least in the large room where he was finally stopped. The floor was cool smooth marble, the furniture dark and heavy with cushions and on the table enough food to feed the prisoners for a week. On the couch a man was seated, half lying, on the cushions. He was older, the hair on the side of his head showing grey where it was closely cropped. He looked like he had once been physically strong, but now he was just large, though there was still hardness in the fleshly face. The leader of the soldiers spoke softly to him and then was quieted by an impatient wave. Cowed, he stepped back, his head down. The man turned his attention to Tam.

Chapter 14

The man looked at Tam from where he sat without saying a word or making any outward display of emotion. Tam returned his gaze evenly, waiting for him to take the lead. He was aware of soldiers in a loose circle around him, but he was also aware of some power emanating from the man. He tried to read him facially but did not probe him, conscious that would reveal more of himself than he wished to disclose. The man was obviously puzzled though by Tam's presence as he maintained his silence for some time, considering whether he presented a threat or an opportunity.

Eventually he spoke in a hoarse, slightly rough voice.

"My men tell me that you were found in the work party?"

Tam inclined his head by way of answer. He generally found saying little was the quickest way for people to reveal their truer selves.

"Why were you there?"

Tam still stayed silent but kept his gaze closely on the man. He motioned with his hand and once again Tam felt the approach of a blow, which he allowed to strike across his back, flinching as it landed, but with effort he kept his gaze level. The man motioned for another strike to be delivered, but Tam turned and looked at the advancing soldier, willing him to hold his ground, which he did, confusion spreading across his face.

"Who are you and what are you doing here?" The man was visibly angry at being obstructed in front of his men.

"I am here to offer you a choice. You preside over this prison camp, and you are responsible for all the crimes that are committed here. It ends today. Your only choice is how it will end for you."

The man sneered at him openly. "No crimes are committed here. These men and women are criminals and sent here for punishment. They are worthless and as such get what they deserve."

"And you?"

"I am here, as you say, to manage this place and these people as I see fit, until such time as I am called back to the capital when my work here is done."

"And what is that work? What are the stones for?"

The man was about to answer and then realized from the stares of his men that he was talking too much. He flushed and anger flashed over him.

"Enough. I do not know why you are here and do not care. You have made a foolish error by coming to this place."

He motioned to his men, who advanced in a circle upon Tam. Tam maintained his gaze on the man but reached deep down into himself and drew heavily on the air all around him. The atmosphere of the room was suddenly transformed as air rushed in and open windows shattered as they slammed shut under the force of the movement. With the air now gathered to him, Tam flung wide his arms. The air slammed into the men. They flew back against the walls, as if hit by a heavy weight, and slumped to the ground, unmoving. The man looked shocked for a second before lifting his arms and seeking to draw air to himself. Tam could feel it and was surprised by the man's strength. Without moving he reached out at the same time and battled him for control, will against will. He did not move his gaze from the man's eyes and saw them turn from anger and pride to desperation and fear as he slowly weakened and the sweat started to roll across his face. Eventually, he slumped as Tam forced the air down onto him, compressing his chest and limbs and suffocating him. His knees buckled under him, and he fell to the floor, gasping.

Tam moved forward now and stood over him. He lifted the man's head, so he could look at him as he spoke.

"I know what is inside of you, and I know who gave it to you. I have seen the evil that you have done with it. Whatever happens after this, you will lose that power and with it whatever hold you have over these people."

He paused, waiting for some sort of response. He could feel the man striving against the greater will that held him. Suddenly, he felt a shift in focus from the man, who reached out to the bonds trapped within Tam's own mind. Tam felt his barricades loosen and the bondings begin to scrabble out, and a wave of revulsion and fear swept over him, causing him to momentarily loosen his control. He fought now like he had never had to before, exerting his will to rebuild the walls in his mind while battling the will of the man before him. He saw a malign look cross the man's eyes as he felt his ascendency. Tam saw this and felt his own anger grow. He refocused with all his might and bound the bonds more tightly than they had ever been before, walling them off with such ferocity that they became barely sensible within him. He lashed out at the man in front of him with such unrestrained power that he immediately broke through. He continued pushing down, suffocating him, feeling the life draining away but not wanting to stop till he had got rid of this evil. Suddenly though he saw the man's eyes wide with fear, and Tam realized that he was the cause. Shame crept in and broke through his fury and the swirl of power that he was channelling. The anger drained away, and he lessened his grip on the man but did not release it. He saw his breathing come in gasps and realized how close he had come to killing him. Tam waited for him to regain sufficient strength and for clarity again to reach his mind.

"You have a chance now to start again, little as you deserve it. I am going to take the bonding from you. If you give it to me willingly, it will go better with you, both now, and in the future, as I will try to mitigate the judgement against you. If you decide to keep it, I will take it from you by force, but I warn you I cannot tell what the effect on you will be. It may be worse than death if the bonding has wormed its way throughout your mind as I worry it has."

Tam watched the man carefully to ensure that his words had sunk in. He saw the indecision, the calculation of weighing up the loss of power against the risk of worse. Tam saw him harden and with an inward sigh prepared himself. The backlash was powerful, but this time Tam was ready and maintained his control. He reached out with his hands and gripped the man's head. Delving deep with his thoughts he mapped out the bonding, seeking its margins and its core, and then he pulled with focused determination. He almost felt the ripping as he tore it free and scoured the man's mind with what he could only understand as a white-hot heat to burn out any remaining taint. He pulled it all into himself and again walled it off with layer upon layer of his own mind till it receded into the distance. The man in front of him fell forward, his face slack and empty, drool falling from his lips and his eyes dull. He was alive but the trauma to his mind was extensive, the taint having spread widely. He would improve but Tam doubted he would ever be whole again.

Tam released his hold on the man and lifted him onto the couch again with a pillow under his head. His eyes looked around without comprehension, and Tam felt again a spasm of guilt at what he had done or been forced to do. He knew now, though, that there was no other way if he was to fulfil what he was here to do. He stood heavily and looked around him. The soldiers had not moved in the minutes the conflict had taken. Outside he could hear some movement and shouting as some of the soldiers who had been bonded were released. Tam moved to one of the windows that stretched down to the floor of the room and opened out onto a small balcony. He paused for a second and then projected his thoughts, searching and sifting the minds of all the soldiers and prisoners beneath.

Taking a breath, he then focused all his power outward, and channelled his will to the people below in such a way as to be impossible to ignore. To the prisoners he spoke words to cause them to rise and stumble out of their cabins to face the world anew. To the soldiers he commanded that they take the prisoners in, feed them, heal their sores and build them back to health and strength. To them all he commanded no revenge or harm to fall on the other. To some of the soldiers though, the ones in whom he had only seen evil intent, his command was for them to leave and seek life where they could find it, to go their separate ways but not to return. Each person felt his command settle on their minds and become their own will, a strengthening of the part of them that longed for that command. The prisoners stumbled out to be met by hands that drew them in in welcome instead of harsh rebuke and, weak as they were, they were enabled to stand and accept it where before they would have recoiled in fear and suspicion. Seeing this, Tam withdrew his power, and, turning, walked slowly back into the room.

Chapter 15

Tam felt exhausted. Going over to the tables, he picked up some cold meat, bread and fruit. Not wanting to stay in the same room as the man, who still lay where he had left him, he explored the house till he found a large bedroom which was obviously intended for the head of the household. There was a washstand with a jug of water next to it. He washed his face and neck, feeling better as the refreshing coolness removed some of the evidence of his toil through the day. He then ate some of the food before undressing and putting on the newly laid out night clothes. For the first time in some weeks, he lay down in a bed and was soon asleep.

When he woke, he found that his clothes were washed and dried and waiting for him in a neat pile on the chair by his bed. A fresh jug of water with a towel had also been laid out. He had not been aware of anyone in the room, which surprised him. He looked out the window and found that it was nearly midday, judging by the position of the sun. He figured he must have slept soundly from early the previous evening. Whatever had happened, he felt rested and full of purpose again. Pouring the water, he cleaned himself thoroughly before placing his old clothes back on. Newly cleaned they looked fresh and the material had returned to its original softness that belied how hard wearing it was. He then realized how hungry he was and went in search of some food.

He passed a few people as he wandered round the house. Some were obviously servants, but he also passed a few soldiers. He made it back to the room where he had been brought to the man, but it was now empty. A woman appeared quietly through another door and announced her presence with a quiet cough.

"I am Anisa, head of the household servants. Can I get you anything?"

Tam was about to decline but then thought better of it. "Some food would be great. Just something simple. And a mug of tea."

She smiled and turned away swiftly causing Tam to realize he would have insulted her by not allowing her to serve him. As he waited, he looked out of the window. There were not many people in the open, but those he could see, although not happy, at least looked to have more purpose. Soldiers still manned the gates, and some were clearly alert, which he was glad to see. This place needed protecting for some time to come to allow the necessary healing of the one-time prisoners. Particularly once he was gone.

Anisa reappeared with some hot porridge and bread as well as some fruit and a mug of steaming hot tea. He ate it all quickly and after finishing he stood again and walked down to the front entrance of the house. There he was met by a heavyset soldier, who stiffened and saluted him.

"I am Finn, sergeant of the guard. Sorry, I mean captain." He paused, embarrassed. "The old captain left after what happened yesterday. The soldiers said I needed to step up so," he tailed off and shrugged.

"Thank you, captain," Tam replied with a smile. "You look to be doing an excellent job so far."

Finn smiled in response, looking gratified. "Is there anything that you would like to see?"

Tam thought for a second before replying. "Can I speak to some of the prisoners? Any of those who were here for dissent." Finn furrowed his brow in consideration.

"I don't rightly know what each of the prisoners was here for, but I think the one that is called Will would fit that description. The other prisoners all look up to him and most of the soldiers do too, though they would not admit it. I will go and look for him."

"Thank you. Can you also show me where the stones that are taken from the mine are kept before they are shipped out?"

"Sure. Figure they are yours now anyway." Finn smiled, his rough face looking suddenly kind and more youthful.

He walked ahead, motioning for Tam to follow him. After a few minutes they came to a small building with a heavy door. Finn took a key from his belt and opened the lock before swinging the door open. Inside there were shelves with boxes. Taking two down, he opened them to reveal a number of stones in each. He nodded at Tam and then walked away to find Will.

Tam looked into the box with interest. There were about eight stones of differing sizes and shapes ranging from a fingertip across through to larger ones maybe double that. They were differing colours of amber, green and brown, but when they caught the light, the colours changed and shifted, becoming richer and clearer. They were rough, but Tam could imagine with a bit of work and skill they could make distinctive and attractive jewellery. Stones of value, no doubt, but not equal to the price in lives that had been paid for them.

While he was looking at them, Finn returned with a brown-haired man. He looked to be well into midlife but was probably younger, the lines around his eyes and his sallow cheeks and skin ageing him considerably. He was thin but stood straight and tall, and there was still clarity in his gaze. He looked at Tam with obvious respect but also questioning. He reached out and took Tam's offered hand with a surprising grip.

"You are Will? My name is Tam. Thank you for coming to talk with me."

Will smiled a short, bemused smile. "The honour is mine. My life, all our lives, is in your debt and your service. So if you ask me to come, I come willingly."

Tam inclined his head. "Thank you, but I do not expect or want any thought of debt or repayment. I would appreciate though if you could tell me what you did that led to you being here?"

A flash of anger crossed Will's face. "I was, am, a teacher in Ardvastra. I ran a school there for children of the more influential, though I also ran an evening

76

school for the kids from the poorer parts of town who were working through the day."

"Anything else?"

He hesitated before replying. "I attended a few meetings where people spoke out against the authorities. I may have been spotted, or someone may have told the authorities I was there. I don't know. I did not do anything apart from listen, as I felt that what they were proposing would likely have led to harm to the poorer kids I taught."

"How long have you been here?"

"About two years I think, but it is hard to keep track."

"How have you survived?"

"Luck mainly, I think. I have not fared as badly as some and was pretty healthy when I came. And I have a lot to live for and go back to."

"Family?"

"Wife and two kids, though I have not heard sight nor sound from them since coming here. They will have waited for me though, if they were able to."

Tam nodded and was silent for a while. "And what will you now you are free?"

"Try and keep my head down and get to know my kids again."

Tam shifted his gaze down to the box in front of him.

"What do you know of these stones?"

"They are bloody hard to get out of the ground, and I wouldn't care if I never saw another one," ventured Will.

Finn stepped closer and had a look. "I have been on some of the convoys. Most go to Ardvastra and sell for a lot to those with wealth. The King himself controls what happens to them I think, particularly these rarer ones."

Tam grimaced at the title given to Nehlo; in some ways it showed how far he had erred from the path of service they had sworn to. He picked up one of the stones Finn had pointed at. It was different, heavier in his hand than the others. The stone was clearer, with little intrinsic colour, but when the light shone on it directly, it blazed with different hues. He ran his fingers over it, feeling the texture, which was strangely smooth. He had read about these before starting on his journey to Elishadra.

"Your country was famous for these once. They were sought after, but then the supply ran dry. Nehlo must have known this and searched for new sources."

Finn and Will flinched at the use of his name but looked at the stones with renewed interest. "What were they used for?"

"They are much harder than these others; not many materials can even scratch their surface. They are used to mould and fashion other rocks and metals into different shapes. Some were even used to sharpen weapons or fashioned into armour for wealthy kings of the past."

Picking up an axe he laid the stone down on a wooden post and swung at it with all his might. The axe slid off the stone before embedding deep into the post, the stone flying off some distance. Both men watched him with interest as he picked up the stone again and examined it. There was not a mark on it. Finn picked up the axe and ran his finger along the edge which had a mark scored out of it where it had struck the stone.

"They used to be a source of wealth for the people of Elishadra; your people."

"And now they all go to the King to build his own wealth and power?" Will asked, his voice bitter.

"I think so. Nehlo is powerful in lots of ways, but even he needs to have ways of securing people's loyalty. To some he can offer power, others status and wealth. But something like this should be for the benefit of all." Tam's voice hardened as he spoke; he thought back to the hovels up against the walls of Halistra with the barely clothed children running around and the people of Fraebost speaking of their suffering at the loss of livelihoods and loved ones. He was silent for a few moments, considering. "Is this the only mine?"

Finn nodded. "As far as I know."

"Before you leave here, it is important that the entrance is sealed and only opened and worked again if better times come."

Finn nodded again, though his face betrayed his uncertainty at what the future might hold for them all.

Tam nodded, satisfied for the moment. "What do you know of Nehlo?"

Both men looked uncomfortable, diverting their eyes. Will eventually spoke up.

"Only what is common knowledge really. He first came as an advisor of sorts to the old King, but there were rumours even before the King died that he was the one really making the decisions. When the King died, he assumed the throne and no one challenged him."

He paused, reluctant to continue, but then started to speak again, though in a lowered and hushed voice.

"People used to say that he could read people's minds and make them do things, bad things. And that he couldn't be killed. Back in the old days I heard that a few people tried to kill him but did not get close."

Tam, deep in his own thoughts, did not immediately respond. He struggled to relate the stories he continued to hear with his childhood friend. Part of him thought they must be exaggerated, that he would track Nehlo down and be able to appeal to him as a friend and find something of that friend he had grown up with still there. But then he remembered the bindings walled off in his own mind, threatening and frightening in what they could do to him, had done to others, and he knew that they came from Nehlo. He also remembered the suffering he had already seen, brought about through Nehlo's influence if not his direct action. Finn and Will remained quiet for a few moments, allowing him the time to think. Finn then cleared his throat, causing Tam to look up.

"I don't know how to ask this, but with all that has happened here and all that you can do…" He trailed off, unable to find the words to ask his question.

"You are wondering if Nehlo and I are similar in some way?"

Finn nodded. "Folk are talking. No one is questioning, mind. Not after what you have done."

"How did you do that?" Will broke in. "Command us like that, make us listen."

Tam looked down, unsure what to say before meeting Will's questioning gaze. "I can't force you to do things, at least that is not what I am seeking to do." He paused again, looking for the words to explain what he did not fully comprehend himself. "If I focus intently, I can sense some of the stronger emotions or desires that people have and bring one forward in their mind so that it becomes dominant…"

He couldn't finish; as he spoke, his voice sounded so arrogant, so utilitarian and cold. He did not mean it like that. It was a power he rarely used because he knew how invasive it was, how potentially dangerous. As such, he was not a master of it in the way that Nehlo had become. He was conscious of Finn and Will watching, weighing. He tried again.

"I reach out to the thoughts, emotions, motivations that are there in people, and I amplify them. That is all. I don't make people do what they do not want, at least in part, to do. And I rarely do even that, except in great need."

Tam was silent for a second. Talking about this made his thoughts turn to the man who's binding he had removed. "Where is the man who used to lead here?"

Finn looked startled for a moment before answering. "Stannon is being looked after, little though he deserves it. He does not speak but is eating a little and starting to move more easily. What did you do to him?"

Tam sighed. "Only what I had to. He had given himself to be bonded by Nehlo in return for power and the ability to bond others. I removed the bonding when he would not release it, and I warned him of what might happen."

"You don't need to find excuses for what happened to him," said Will heatedly. "The bastard deserved that and much more."

"What do you mean by bonded?" Finn asked.

"It is difficult to explain, as I have no direct experience of it. Imagine what I did to you all but this time it is amplified so that you cannot resist, and it is permanent. My command was transient, though its influence will linger for a little, and could not go completely against your will. Nehlo has focused on becoming more and more powerful at binding others to his will permanently. That protects him but also spreads his influence. It has become almost a physical presence within their minds, influencing and permeating everything they do or think. And with it they have in some way the same powers as their master, though more limited in scope. That is what I removed as I want all of Nehlo's influence removed."

Finn and Will both nodded though they looked far from understanding it all. Tam changed tack, not wanting to linger on this area. "What do you plan to do now, Finn?"

"I think we must stay here for some days to allow folks to regain their strength, and then we need to move on. There is nothing for us here, and people are already talking about returning to their families. I think we need to stick together though, to see everyone safely home."

Tam nodded his appreciation of this. "How many soldiers have stayed in the camp?"

"I have thirty-two men and women, all of whom are well trained. There are also a number of cooks and support people. All told about fifty."

And turning to Will, Tam asked, "How many of the people who used to be prisoners?"

Will considered the question. "I am not sure, but I would say around ninety. Most are weak and will not be able to walk far in a day, never mind fight."

Tam nodded. They had a hard road ahead of them. His influence would wane over the next few days though he hoped by then that they would be bound by duty or even friendship. They had a better chance if they stuck together, at least till the weakest were able to make their own way.

"These stones, you say they are worth something? They should be shared out among you all and used to aid you on your way. You will need something to buy food and other supplies as you go."

They both looked at the store, Will with some distaste. Eventually Finn answered. "They have been a cause of much hurt and suffering, but we can maybe take them and make good use of them. There should be enough here to get everyone home and then some." He looked at Will, who nodded though it clearly caused him some pain.

"These other stones, the harder ones. I think you should leave those here, hidden for now? Their trade will be useful to help rebuild what has been broken. You could perhaps lead whoever comes after Nehlo to them?"

Finn nodded. Tam read the pensive look on his face and felt his uncertainty. He had found himself with the responsibility of getting everyone to their homes and now Tam had possibly linked him to his country's future. It was a lot for him to process, but Tam knew that he would just take one step at a time, deal with what was in front of him, the way good soldiers always did.

Later in the evening, Tam lay on the bed thinking through his conversation with Will and Finn. How different was he from Nehlo? They had been as close as brothers when young and, though they had different temperaments, they had always supported each other. They also had the same gifts and training, but Nehlo's actions had led to distrust of anyone like them.

When had their paths diverged? Looking back, he remembered the day they had been told that everything they knew about Morgan had been false. It had felt like part of their childhood had been a lie, but Nehlo's response at the time had startled Tam, revealing a side to his friend that he had not seen before. After that, and the humiliating beating they had endured, Nehlo had changed. But he himself had changed too, by degrees.

He could almost smell the library where he had spent many hours, hoping to discover that Morgan had been the hero he had envisaged but instead finding evidence scattered through the texts to lead him to believe he had been as bad, if not worse, than Nehlo had become. In this time of research, he had grown to love the slightly musty air, the secluded corner where he could study undisturbed, the rows of old books. He had never enjoyed reading, but during that time he had fallen in love with the excitement of discovery, the beauty of the words and pictures, the faintly scribbled notes of previous readers.

He could still remember his growing sense of awe as he read one book that spoke of a creator who had made everything with a purpose and even now was active, though often quietly and in unspectacular ways. He could remember the exhilarating sense of coherence and meaning this brought to his experience of the world. And over time he had internalized this teaching, his perspective on life being shaped and transformed in its light.

That clarity was what he was reaching for again now. The idea that if God was there, and he created everything, he would ultimately bring justice and establish his way in what he had created. But, more than that, all earthly power existed only to serve the will and purposes of this God. The histories were full of hints of people,

80

with power like his own, always in the background, advising those in authority rather than seeking it, helping commerce and understanding, avoiding warfare. Discovering this had helped shape his ideas of what he, and others like him, should be. It was on this that he and Nehlo had ultimately separated he knew; a belief on what having power meant and how it should be wielded.

There was another reason, though, that he had kept silent. He wrestled with his thoughts, wanting this to be clear, if only to himself. He wanted to offer Nehlo another chance. It felt important to him, for the sake of their old friendship, for his own sense of responsibility at the path Nehlo had taken, and ultimately because if he did not then he would face his creator's justice unprepared, having abused his power so heinously. Tam knew that the people, none more so than the prisoners who had lost so much, wanted to, deserved to, see Nehlo punished, even killed, for his crimes. They would not understand why he wanted to restore him. How could they after suffering so much? Even his sister did not fully agree with him though she understood.

His thoughts turned to Nehlo before everything had changed, before their admittance to the training college, before the great loss that had scarred him irrevocably. Nehlo had rarely spoken about it afterwards and to all outward appearance had recovered from it, but Tam knew that he had felt the loss as a betrayal and had never forgiven. He tried to understand what it would have felt like for Nehlo: the hurt, the confusion, caused by people he had trusted implicitly. It did not excuse what Nehlo had become, but it was part of the story.

Chapter 16

Tam studied the cards spread out in his hand. Not a winning set but okay if he played it right. He glanced around at the others, who were head down, staring intently at their own cards, giving nothing away. He reached down beside the bale he was sitting on and picked up his mug of ale, taking a long gulp before replacing it. Maj placed a card down on the table, a silver knight. He picked up two from the spare pack and slotted them into place in his own set. Tam reached forward and picked up the silver knight, placing it next to the one he already held. His set had improved markedly with that one exchange, but he kept his face set. He caught Nehlo's questioning look, weighing up his own move, before he looked back at his own cards and nonchalantly flicked down a scepter onto the table. The others all groaned; the end had come too soon.

Each boy laid their cards down, face up, mentally calculating wins and losses as they matched up against each other. A few arguments followed as to some finer details before the scores were tallied up and added to the chalked list on the wall. Nehlo was well ahead through some well-timed bluffs but also through aggressive play. Tam, more naturally cautious, was third, but he would come out no poorer than he had gone in. The last two would have to make up Nehlo's winnings; Ben and Tyler looked despondent as they reached for their purses.

Tam leaned back against the taller bales, picking up a handful of nuts and brambles that they had foraged earlier that day. The barn was dimly lit by the single lamp above their heads; his father would not allow more due to the risk of fire. It was warm though after the sunny day, which they had all agreed was a rarity on the first day after school had broken up. They were all used to the slightly musty air, despite the wide door being open to let in a breeze. There was still some daylight left, but it was waning, casting long shadows from the house that they could see through the open door.

"Have you guys settled up your debts?" Maj asked.

Nehlo looked up from counting the pennies that had been handed to him. "Yup. All except this button, which I think you still need," he replied, flicking the button to Ben, who mumbled an apology and placed it in his pocket. "Always enjoyable, playing you two in particular."

"I am sure it is. I will have to do extra chores at home to earn all that back again."

"You can come and do mine. I will pay you with your own money."

The others laughed, but Ben looked like he was considering it before deciding he was better off trusting his dad's payment and oversight.

"How long have you got before you have to head on?" Tyler asked, looking at Tam.

"A few weeks I think," replied Tam. "The term does not start till autumn, but I was told to go to town a bit early to get used to where I will be staying and find my way around."

"Are you keen to be going?" Ben asked, helping himself to the bowl of food before filling up his mug from the jug of ale next to the rickety table they used for cards.

Tam shrugged. "Mostly. I don't really know what to expect. I have never really liked town any time I have been before, but maybe it will be different living there. I will miss home though."

"That all you will miss? Not a certain lass whose name is never to be mentioned?"

Tam blushed slightly as the others grinned at him. "For all the attention she gives me, I might as well be in the town."

"You never know, she might realize what she is missing once you are gone," Nehlo chipped in.

Tam felt the mix of embarrassment and regret that he always had when teased on this. He was the only one who got ribbed about a girl. He did, though, have to reluctantly admit to himself that he was also the only one who had made a particular fool of himself. Not that he had done anything daft, just that he had not done anything at all except walk up to her, lose any sense of what he should say, never mind anything interesting, and walk away again crestfallen.

"I am sure she will miss all your scintillating chat!" added Ben.

"She will get it in all the letters I am planning to write."

"What? You don't mean to do that?"

"Sure. Maybe some poetry with some pressed flowers. I have given it a lot of thought."

"Not enough by the sound of it. You will scare her off all men, never mind yourself! Have a thought for those of us left behind." Maj sounded genuinely worried. Tam laughed, and the others, realizing he was joking, laughed along with him.

"What will the training school be like?" asked Ben, after a few moments silence. He sounded almost in awe.

Tam did not answer for a while, feeling a little uncertain. He did not like the feeling of separation that was already developing between him and the friends he had known all his life. The times where he had sensed movement before it had happened had increased in frequency to the point where he almost had another accident, this time in the fields while working. Nehlo had questioned him about it and that had prompted him to speak to his father. Instead of disbelieving him, his father had listened and a few days later the masters from the college, two men and a woman, had come and spoken to him. They had said it was a rare gift that needed nurturing and training like all skills. Tam had heard of people who could do amazing things as if by magic, though his father had always maintained it was not magic but manipulation of matter, but he had never met or even seen one. He picked at a loose bit of straw on the bale he sat on.

"They said that I would learn how to use the senses that are developing and other skills that go with them. They did not really talk much about what that would involve."

"You also said they would be teaching you a lot about times past and rules and codes and other serious things like that." Tam caught the slight edge in Nehlo's voice and glanced at him, but Nehlo was looking in a bored manner out the open door to the deepening darkness. Tam knew he was keen to go, keen to leave the village, where he had started to feel constrained. He had told Tam that he envied him, that he would love to develop such skills and try his strength, and that he could not understood Tam's worry about leaving and entering a world so different from what they had known.

"And then what happens? After you finish there, I mean?" asked Tyler.

"He becomes a legend like Morgan!" quipped Maj. "Able to leap over buildings, fend off multiple foes bare handed and whistle for the wind."

"And able to smell out hot apple pies from a thousand paces!" added Ben.

Tam laughed with the others. "You have that gift already it would seem." He thought of the stories of Morgan which they had been told as children; he had risen from a small village to become counselor and friend of kings in faraway places. He and Nehlo had often joked about this in the past and it seemed still like a joke for Tam; he was not sure it was for Nehlo any more.

The conversation lapsed for a little, and in the silence they heard approaching footsteps. Marrea popped her head round the door and looked around, slightly shyly but also with obvious interest.

"Father says it is time for you all to finish your game and settle your debts. Though looks like you are all done for the night anyway," she added, noting the empty jug and bowl.

"Okay. We will be in soon," Tam replied. Marrea nodded and turning headed back to the house. Tam noted with a little irritation that his friends all watched her leave a little longer than he would have thought necessary.

"Grab a bale guys," he said, standing and getting their attention. They quickly put back all the bales they had dislodged before separating, Nehlo heading toward Tam's house with him as he was staying overnight. The others walked away together, yelling their goodbyes as they went. Tam did not think about whether there was any particular reason for Nehlo staying as it was something that happened from time to time, though it was an unstated understanding that Nehlo did not want the reverse to happen for reasons that Tam had not delved into. He had sometimes wondered whether his friend was happy at home, but he had never raised it with him. He turned his thoughts to finding the spare pallet and blanket.

Nehlo lay half awake on the pallet in Tam's room. The sun was only just rising, but he could hear Tam's dad moving around, getting a meal ready, and his mum moving much more quietly and humming to herself. He felt rested but lazy to get up, and as there was no movement from Tam in the bed above him, he allowed his head to relax back again. He always slept well when here; better than in his own bed. Maybe it was just the sense of calm and solidity that pervaded Tam's house, in contrast with his own. His thoughts turned to his parents; they always seemed to be on the verge of calamity, usually in relation to money, of which there was never quite enough, but sometimes in relation to a town matter or even their own relationship, but they had never spoken of that in his hearing. They were close enough he reckoned, but for some reason he always felt nervous for them in a way that he never did when around Tam's parents. Everything was haphazard, from mealtimes to paying the rent, though it did have the marginal flip side that they kept very little tabs on what he was doing or when he returned.

Getting restless, he became aware of a hunger ache in his stomach. Rising, he nudged Tam to waken him before pulling on his trousers and washing his face in the bowl of water they had taken up the night before. He waited while Tam roused himself and did the same before following him out to breakfast. They were met by the sound and smell of bacon frying mixed with fresh bread from the oven. Tam's mum smiled at them both when she saw them and beckoned to some seats. Marrea was already there, and Nehlo tried to catch her eye when she glanced at them both, but she had already turned back to the tea she was brewing. Tam's dad came in from outside with some fresh milk. He voiced his good morning to them both but held Nehlo's eye for a moment, measuring him in a way that felt slightly disconcerting before he turned and tipped the milk into a jug. He took his seat and that was the sign for everyone to start.

There was silence for some time as everyone helped themselves to the food and piping hot tea. Tam's mum and dad chatted a bit about the chores for the day. Tam made a sign to Marrea, which Nehlo did not quite see, that made Marrea smile. He studied her for a moment, finding her friendly features even prettier with her smile, which still only dimpled her cheek on one side despite her being now into her teens. She was starting to shape like a woman too, which he could not help himself noticing, even though she was Tam's sister. He looked away, conscious that he was staring.

84

Upon finishing his meal, Tam's father pushed his chair back, looked quickly at his wife, who nodded, and then addressed himself to Nehlo, much to his surprise.

"Nehlo, lad. There is something I must talk with you about when you are ready after your meal." He looked serious, and Nehlo felt a slight apprehension in his stomach that immediately robbed him of his remaining appetite. He put his knife down and looked at Tam's mum to request permission to leave. She nodded at him kindly, but he thought sadly too.

Standing, he followed Tam's father out of the house to a rough bench that leaned up against the wall, where sometimes they sat as a family in the evening to play games or just talk. He had been there once, and although he had not ventured to say much, he had enjoyed the moment. Tam's father motioned for Nehlo to sit and then sat beside him.

"I have a letter for you to read Nehlo. It is from your parents. Before you do though, I want you to know that they are doing what they think is best, for you and for them." He had turned to face Nehlo and forced him by his own presence to hold his gaze. Nehlo nodded glumly, feeling sick while a slight moisture gathered in his eyes, blurring them for a second. He did not want to read the letter. He had no idea what it could contain that they could not say to him later this morning, or any morning.

Taking the letter, he held it loosely, not willing to break the seal. Tam's dad sat beside him, waiting patiently and in that position some moments passed. Numbly, Nehlo realized he had to open it, had to face whatever it contained. He snapped the seal and unfolded the paper, revealing a number of lines of text in his mother's hand. His father's writing was messy, so of course she would have written it.

"Dearest Nehlo,

We love you, our boy, more than anything, and it is for that reason that we want so much more for you than we can give and do not want you to face what we must. We must travel, far afield, to your uncle and his family who moved to Elishadra to build a new life and have been successful there. We must go to him as we have nothing here and what work your father had is no more, and we only have enough to pay our debts and passage. Our journey is full of risk and though there is work at the end of it, we do not know if it will support us all."

Nehlo stopped reading, barely comprehending the words or their meaning. Tears welled up in his eyes and ran down his cheeks despite his efforts to roughly brush them away. A dull ache rose in his chest that seemed to tighten round him, and he had to force himself to take a few shuddering breaths before attempting to go on with what was left of the letter. He could now pick out only a few scattered words and phrases. "We will return for you ... Nathan and Sarah are kind people ... look after you and care for you ... you will learn ... trade ... grow and flourish with them." For a second he did not understand who she referred to before realizing she meant that it was arranged for him to stay at Tam's, work there with Nathan, Tam's father. Suddenly, he felt angry. How long had they been planning this? How could they do this to him? But just as quickly his anger was swallowed up by such a desolation that he felt his weight was too much for him and he must fall and sleep and not wake up again. He felt a heavy arm round his shoulder, pulling him in. He resisted for a moment, but it was too strong. Tears were flowing now in a torrent that he could not stop, and his breathing came in gasps that hardly seemed to bring him any air. He collapsed into Nathan, feeling that he was the only solid thing left in all the world. He did not know how long he stayed like that; time seemed to slow around him as he tried to get his mind to settle on what had just happened, what it might mean. He could not see or hear anything around him apart from the slow movement of Nathan's chest as it rose and fell, the only marker of life moving on.

Slowly, a thought that he needed to check, to confirm for himself what had happened, formed within his mind. He pulled himself away and scrubbed his face roughly with the sleeve of his *jacket. They were alone; he surmised that Sarah had kept Tam and Marrea away. Slowly, he stood, pushing away Nathan's arm more roughly than he meant to. Looking around, he saw to his astonishment that it was still early morning, and the ground was still wet with dew. He walked forward, slowly at first, his limbs feeling strangely alien to him and distant though still under his control. After a few paces he moved more quickly, urgently, suddenly cursing himself for a fool for delaying even those moments. What if they had not left yet? What if they were still there, waiting, giving him one last chance to join them? He did not think about what it would mean to leave his home and friends, only that he did not understand why they could leave him. He forced his legs to move faster, breaking into a run, down the track away from Tam's to the main road along the valley and on to his home. He ran faster and faster, feeling a savage relief in pouring his anger, sadness and pain into his limbs and feeling them strong and powerful again. He wanted to move even faster, to not flag but to run like this all the way, possibly to never stop. Instinctively, he reached out around him, seeking he knew not what to propel him on, trying to summon energy from somewhere. A faint howl, like wind tearing through the barn when he left both doors open, answered him, and he felt himself buoyed up and carried along. His stride lengthened, and his body felt so light that his feet barely seemed to touch the ground. Stunned, he almost lost his balance, but righting it he raced on, his heart hammering inside him. The air whipped by him with such force that he felt he had to snatch at it to breath. His mind felt clear though as if it were slowing down to compensate for the speed he was moving at. There were few people out, but he was aware of those that were turning to stare at him as he pelted past. But he did not care. In the exultation of the energy that carried him, he almost forgot about the letter, but then, almost too quickly, he was at the turning to his home. Reluctantly, he forced himself to slow down and turned into his own track, his legs suddenly heavy again and his thoughts in turmoil.*

Pushing at the door, he walked in and stood in the parlour. The old, familiar range was there, the heavy chest that held all their plates and pans in its place on the other side of the room, and the table in the centre. It looked almost normal, but in a glance he could see that there was no life. No dishes were piled up on the side, no clothes on the pulley, no food hanging over the range, no sounds except those that penetrated from outside with an unusual harshness, as if berating him. He walked slowly from room to room but each drove into him the truth that he could no longer push away: they were gone. He sat on his bed with his back to the wall, pulled his knees up to his chest, wrapped his arms around them and just stared at the wall, his mind blank.

He did not know how long he sat like that, but he became aware of other people moving toward him. He looked up at them dully, recognizing Tam and Marrea. He did not want to look at them properly, to see their pity, hear their empty words, but they just quietly sat down on either side of him and waited with him, Marrea with her hand on his. In the quiet that followed, Nehlo forced himself to think about what had happened to him. He did not doubt that his parents loved him, in their own way, but that made the betrayal he felt worse. He could not understand why they could not have told him, did not recognize that only way they could leave would be without seeing and knowing his hurt. He thought about his previous desire to leave what he felt to be a restrictive environment, but he knew now that those ideas had always been based on him having somewhere to return to, some roots. What did he have now? Who did he have now? Who would stay with him when even his family would not? With those thoughts, he felt something harden within him. He did not look at them, but he could feel Tam and Marrea on either side of him, and he almost resented their closeness, their togetherness.

Eventually, he felt Marrea's hand tighten over his own.

"Nehlo. Come, we must go home. You, with us. Mother and Father are waiting."

He looked at her bleakly. Her earnest gaze gave her a homely look, rather than a pretty one, which in this moment spoke to him about all that he would not now know in his own family. Part of him wanted to run from it, run from them all, but he allowed her to pull him from the bed, Tam following, and walk through the home that he would never step into again.

Chapter 17

The dark clouds and continuously falling rain added to the low mood that Seth had sunk into since the previous night. He was back at home having insisted that he return there the next morning. The lady had dressed his leg tightly and watched him test his weight on it a few times before she reluctantly agreed he could go. He was supposed to wait until Alec or someone else had come to get him, but he had had no desire to wait. He wanted to be back in the familiarity of his own room, where he hoped he could start making sense of what was happening. Once there he had fallen asleep for a while, exhausted from the night before and the painful walk back across the city as he tried to shield from watchful eyes any sign of injury to his leg. He had relaxed his guard only when his door was shut behind him, and he could hear no sound of being followed. The walk had caused the wound to reopen and blood to seep through the bandages. He did not want to remove the dressings that the lady had applied, so he had strapped more on top from the small supply that she had given him. He really should have been more grateful to her, he knew, but he had just wanted to get away and now could not go back, partly because he was not entirely sure which house it was and also because he knew that any attention drawn to it would not be welcome.

His thoughts kept returning to the square, to the look of fear and horror on the face of the man he had killed, the feel of blood on his hands and face, and the lifeless body at his feet. And then to the shock and pain on the face of the wounded and defenceless soldier who had been killed in front of him, the horrible spasm that had run through his body before he had died. Had it been Alec that killed him? He did not want to think it had been or to believe he could be so ruthless, but he knew deep down it was probably him. Seth felt the turmoil in his head reflected in his stomach and limbs, which trembled unless he focused on keeping them still. He did not know what he wanted to do. He was committed to the rebellion, partly through his own choice and desire for things to change, but mainly because Kayla was committed, and he had given his word to her. What he was certain of was that he could not kill again, not unless he or someone he loved was directly in danger. No sooner had he made that realization than a sense of his own weakness assailed him, his own cowardice and willingness to let others bear the burden of taking life. He thought he was willing to risk his life again, so was he a coward for being unable to take a life? His thoughts revolved endlessly as he tried to figure out what he should do. It hadn't even occurred to him that due to his injury there may be no use for him.

He became restless, wanting to know what was happening, but fearful of the possibility that the authorities were looking for him. It was unusually quiet outside, which added to his tension. He tried to eat something, but as soon as the food was on his plate, he felt sick. He got up and tested his leg, finding it to be stiff and sore but able to support him. He paced up and down the room a few times, chafing at the restriction. The low ceiling seemed to be pressing down on him as though it was slowly entrapping him. Grabbing his jacket, he pulled open the door and walked down the stairs.

On stepping out, he was surprised to find that it was almost dark. The air was still heavy, despite the earlier rain, affording him only slight relief from the atmosphere in his room. He pulled his jacket tight, more for the sense of protection it gave him than for warmth, and started walking, keeping close to the side of the road where his features could be hidden. Even so, he felt on edge, any noise causing his heart to race and his ears to strain. His eyes kept moving, searching out spaces that could hide someone, and he resisted the urge to look behind him. His leg hurt, but in some ways it felt a little better now that he was moving, as long as he did not over flex it.

He walked as swiftly as he could, his feet automatically taking him to Kayla's home. He stopped just before reaching it, suddenly concerned that if anyone had followed him, he had led them straight to her. He stayed still for a few moments, listening intently, unsure what to do. Nothing stirred, so he walked up to the door and tapped softly on it. Initially there was no response, but he heard someone approach the other side and then Kayla's voice.

"Who is it?"

"It's me, Seth. Can I come in, just briefly."

The door opened just enough to admit him. Kayla quickly closed and bolted it behind him. The cottage was familiar to him, Kayla having lived there with her father. The door led straight into the kitchen, where Kayla had slept while her father was still alive. One further room lay off from the kitchen and this was now her bedroom. Kayla busied herself making herb tea while Seth sat at the table, feeling tense and unsure. He took the cup, the hot liquid soothing his dry mouth and settling his stomach.

Kayla looked tired, an ugly bruise on her forehead and a gash on the side of her head standing out against the paleness of her skin. She tried a weak smile, which Seth returned, and then she looked at the shuttered window as if struggling to find anything to say. Seth knew what she was feeling; he was bereft of any of the little forms of conversation that would normally cover over these moments.

Eventually, Seth broke the silence.

"How are you?"

Kayla grimaced and motioned to her head. "Hurts a lot. I could not really sleep because of it. I have some salts to use, but they don't really take away the pain. I also feel a bit faint and slow, but apparently that's normal after a knock on the head." She closed her eyes, a spasm of pain crossing her face. After a few moments it settled and she looked up at him, ignoring his concerned look. "How about you?"

"Fine, I think. My leg hurts and keeps bleeding a bit, but I was told it would heal okay if given time."

They were both quiet for a few more moments. Seth watched her but there did not seem to be any more episodes of pain. He wanted to tell her about the man he had killed, that the picture of his face as he died could not be erased from his mind, as he felt he could not keep his thoughts inside anymore. She seemed so much more fragile though that he could not bear to burden her with it. She seemed lost in her own thoughts for a moment before speaking slowly.

"It is strange. All I can remember is charging in and swinging blindly before I must have been hit on the head. The next thing I know I am being carried somewhere and then I was being patched up. I was told that you were protecting me, at the end." As she said it, she looked up at him gratefully.

"I am not sure I could have done much to protect you, truth be told, but thankfully the others had arrived."

They were silent again, though this time it was easier to bear.

"What now?" Seth asked.

"I have no idea. Sleep for now as far as I am concerned. And a lot of hot tea."

Seth smiled and in doing so felt the muscles of his face relax. "Sounds good."

"I have no idea what comes next after that though," she continued, a bit more hurriedly. "I suppose we wait to hear from Alec or one of the others."

"You still want to carry on?"

Seth saw the flare of anger in her eyes, but it was gone quickly. "Yes, I think things are nearing a big push, and we need to see this through." She challenged him with her look and in response he nodded his agreement but did not have the energy to put it into words. After this the conversation turned to other things. They kept it going with a bit of effort, but after a while Kayla was clearly starting to tire. Seth had started to feel a little faint as well, due to the tiredness and strain he thought. He stood too quickly, his bad leg spasmed and he almost fell before catching the table. Kayla looked up at him, concerned.

"Are you going to make it home okay? You can stay if you need to."

Seth considered it for a second, but now he just wanted to get back to his own bed, among his own things. "I will be okay. It eases once I get going."

He walked as normally as possible to the door. She opened it for him and touched his arm briefly as he went through the opening. He heard the door shut firmly behind him and the bolts being drawn. There was a light, misty rain now which added to the poor visibility. He hurried home, his feet given speed by his fear at every turn of being spotted.

A few days later Seth knocked on the door of a house he had been told to report to. His leg still hurt and was stiff, but it had stopped bleeding and most of the swelling had gone down. He was able to walk fairly normally, but he was pretty sure running was beyond him. Still, he was on the mend and was starting to feel his old self again. The memory of what had happened was losing its impact, whether through time or just becoming accustomed to it. He was not sure which, but he was feeling more in control.

The door opened and he was ushered through a narrow hallway to the back of the house. The room he entered contained a table and chairs, and some shelving but was otherwise empty. He circled round the table and looked out the window.

To his surprise the window overlooked the river that coursed through the city and wound its way round the castle where Lord Malzorn lived. He could see the castle walls across the river with the imposing tower beyond. He had never been inside the wall; in fact, he didn't know anyone who had been.

He turned as the door opened again and Alec walked in, followed by two men that he did not know. Alec came toward him with his usual easy confidence and clasped his hand warmly, asking him how he had been and how his leg was. Seth mumbled something in reply, confused suddenly about how he should relate to him and conscious that the other men were watching him. One of them stayed near the entrance, leaning on the wall in the slight shadow, without making any attempt to hide his suspicion. Alec did not refer to him at all but introduced the other man as Owen. Seth shook Owen's hand, noting the appraising look that he was given.

Alec sat in one of the chairs at the table, his legs stretched out in front of him. Owen and Seth sat opposite to him, their backs to the wall and to the other man, which made Seth feel uneasy.

"Alec, what is this about? Why have I been asked to come here?" Seth asked.

Alec looked relaxed, clearly in charge of the situation. "We need your help again. After the other night, I have managed to convince the other cell leaders that we need to make a move now." He waved down the objection that was starting to form on Seth's lips. "The other night showed that we cannot assume we have time on our side as the authorities knew where we would be, and my group and I could easily have been wiped out. We need to attack now and take them down." As he said it, he nodded backward through the window to the castle. Seth looked at the sheer walls rising up from the riverbank and the grim stone tower beyond. He could not see a way to attack that, but Alec again looked unconcerned.

"How?"

"We are working on that. Multiple strikes at the same time in different areas, including across the river, which is where you come in."

Seth looked at him, confused. "I can barely run, what am I going to do?"

"I need someone I can totally trust to guard our escape route should it all go wrong. There is a stair through this house which leads down to the river, where there are small boats moored. We will use them to cross before circling round the base of the wall to an area we know is weaker. The boats will be on ropes, so if needs be they can be pulled across in a hurry. That's it."

Seth considered it for a moment. He knew that it would not be even as remotely simple as Alec made out. He had always had a way of smoothing over the wrinkles in any plan and getting Seth to pitch along for the ride. He did not see how he could refuse though. He wanted to help and was being asked to do relatively little.

"Sure," he replied. Alec stood up immediately and smiled.

"Excellent. Owen here will show you what's what, and he will be sticking with you. Just come when he calls." He crossed the table and clapped a hand onto Seth's shoulder. "Soon, this will all be done, and we can get on with making things fairer round here."

As quickly as he came, he left the room, the other man following on behind, leaving Seth and Owen together at the table. Owen shrugged and motioned for Seth to follow him. They went into a different room, from where stairs led down.

91

At the bottom of the stairs, Owen opened a door and they both stepped out onto a ledge of rock that stretched a few metres into the water with iron rings hammered into it, from which small boats were moored. Seth looked up and down the river and saw similar boats bobbing in the current of the river.

"For fishing mainly," Owen said, and then immediately looked a bit abashed. Seth realized with a start that that was the first thing he had said. He was a bit younger than Seth with a roundish face and wavy hair. He had a quiet, slightly high-pitched voice, which tailed away at the end of his sentence. Seth nodded; he had seen the boats out and about but had not known where they were berthed.

"Are they yours?"

"My family's, yes."

"And you are happy for them to be used for this?"

He shrugged again. "We don't really see that we have any option. Our business has been affected like every other; our best fish going to them for little to nothing leaving the rest to be bought for money we are ashamed to ask for. But that we have to eat like everyone else." He looked up to the castle with a determined look in his face as he spoke. "Folks can only put up with so much."

"And you think this is the way?"

"I don't know that. I do know that we have tried talking and tried bargaining and tried refusing and all that gets you is the cane on your back or worse." He paused to lift his shirt to show lines of scars, which were now fading to brown against his pale skin. He did not seem proud or embarrassed about his scars, just matter of fact as if they were the necessary price that he had had to pay for speaking out of turn. "There will have to be a fight," he stated evenly and with composure.

Seth nodded and turned to study the boats beneath his feet. He had never been on a boat before and did not much fancy going on one now, never mind in the dark. The water looked calm enough, but he knew that the current was strong in the middle. Owen touched his sleeve and motioned for him to return inside.

"I will call on you when we are needed. It will not be this night or the next I am told but be ready after that. Dress warmly too as it may be a long night."

He led him through the house and back out onto the street. With a quick smile he closed the door again and Seth turned and retraced his steps home.

Chapter 18

A light fog had settled on the river, obscuring the view of the castle and giving the air a clammy, dank feel. Seth had dressed warmly, just as Owen had suggested, but the chill was already getting to him. He wore padded gloves but with the fingertips removed so that he could grip properly. The cold taking hold of the exposed fingers was rapidly removing any feeling. The fog deadened the sound around them. Since the boats had left, they had heard little except the movement of the river against the rock. He was not sure how long he and Owen had crouched against the wall of the house next to the river, but he reckoned it must have been about an hour, which now meant it was the quietest part of the night. Certainly long enough for the others to get across the river and get into position. He had grown tired of straining his hearing, finding it only increased the tension he was feeling, and had resolved to just wait and do his best to not think about what was going on. He kept shifting his weight to stop his leg from stiffening up, though not with great success.

He and Owen had hardly spoken since he had arrived. There did not seem any point in talking at the moment. If this night went well, then there would be plenty of time; if it didn't, then the less they saw of each other the better. The house behind them was empty, a precaution Owen had said. It just added to the eerie isolation that he felt, despite Owen being next to him. He had not known just how quiet it could be in a city this big at this time of the night, and a part of him wished he was asleep like everyone else.

He had not known the men and women that had left in the boats, except Alec and the man who had been in the room previously. None had spoken to him, though Alec had given him a thump on the shoulder as he had walked past. They numbered about eight: a small group really, considering what lay ahead of them. Seth did not know anything about the other groups, but from what Alec had said previously, he assumed there were at least three or four other groups, potentially bigger, at other points around the castle, which was guarded by water only on this side.

He nudged Owen, who started at the sudden movement.

"Do you think we would hear anything if there was a battle or fight?"

Owen shrugged. "I don't know. It is not far as the crow flies, but over water and with this fog, I couldn't say for sure."

Seth nodded and lapsed back into silence again. After a few more moments he tensed, a noise coming from the direction of the castle. He turned his head to better hear and saw that Owen had become more alert too. He thought he could make out shouting and the sound of clashing metal but then all too quickly it was silent again. He tried to figure out what that meant. Were they now through the first perimeter and advancing on the castle itself? Was that the last resistance before the castle interior, after which they may not hear anything more? The silence grew even more oppressive and worrying. Now that they had engaged in battle, they faced victory, defeat or a dangerous retreat to the boats.

The moments passed achingly slowly. The lap of the water that should have been soothing was jarring on his senses, which strained to hear any other sounds. The occasional dog barked in the distance, but he could hear nothing from the river. He shifted uncomfortably, his leg becoming sore under him, and then suddenly stiffened as he heard a sound above him. He focused on the house behind him and listened carefully. For a long moment, there was nothing, but then came an unmistakable creak of weight being placed on the wooden stair above them. He motioned silently to Owen, who was still looking outward over the river. He did not see at first, and Seth did not want to make any sound to draw his attention. Slowly, Seth stood from his crouched position, wincing at the rustling noise of his clothing against the wall. Owen turned now, and Seth put his finger to his lips warning him to be silent before pointing at the door that led to the stairs. He now listened and nodded when he too heard another creak, this time much closer, his face suddenly white but resolute. He had a small sword at his side, which he loosened, and Seth did the same. He tried to estimate how many people could be there: perhaps only one or two, judging by the sound. Owen moved quietly to the other side of the door and they both waited, trying to stifle even the sound of their breathing.

There was another period of quiet, and Seth started to feel his hands and face become sore with the tension that was running through them. He willed himself to relax, but the fear and cold made it impossible. He shifted slightly and then the door opened a fraction. He flinched, almost striking out in reflex but stopped himself just in time. He could see Owen sweating slightly, his eyes fixed on the door, sword now raised. But the door stayed as it was. Still they waited, not wanting to give away any advantage.

When it happened, it was so quick that Seth barely had time to react. The door flew open as two soldiers barrelled through, swords raised. They quickly turned as Owen and then Seth moved forward to attack with their own short swords, Owen with more precise movements, Seth with anxious, frantic swings. They tried to push their assailants towards the river but were easily parried. The door was now behind them, and Seth could hear more men coming through it. But he had no chance to turn. It was all he could do to keep the blade of the man in front away from him. With each movement his balance became more uncertain, his movements more ragged and his defence poorer. He knew that there was only ever going to be one result from this. Dimly he saw one of the soldiers behind them drive his sword at Owen, who screamed and fell, the blade digging into his lower back. Fearing the same, Seth swung his blade in wide arcs, circling round, trying to fend off attacks that he could not even see.

Suddenly, he felt himself forced down so quickly that he crashed to the ground, unable to rise. The men attacking him stumbled forward, his sudden movement taking them completely by surprise. As he raised his head, Seth saw a new figure in the doorway advancing on the men, who turned to meet it. The figure was unarmed as far as Seth could tell yet walked forward slowly, almost casually. The men attacked but with slight movements their blades were evaded or deflected in a way that seemed impossible to Seth. With gasps of shock each of the attackers became rigid, with their arms pinned to their sides and their swords clattering to the stone as they then fell to their knees. They tried to call out but couldn't, their breathing now heavy and difficult, their eyes showing fear. The figure ignored them and went straight to Owen, who was lying unmoving. Seth saw the figure feel over the wound in Owen's back before rising again and moving toward him.

Seth started to rise to meet the figure and realized with a start that whatever had been pressing down on him was no longer there and he was able to get to his feet though his legs were weak and unsteady. Once standing, he realized that the figure in front of him was small and slight, and though the face was partially hidden in the dark, he could see that it was a woman.

"Are you hurt?" she asked him, her voice calm and assured.

Seth shook his head, his mouth too dry to talk, his thoughts too chaotic.

"Then help me with your friend. I arrived too late I am afraid. My patchwork on his wound will only last a short time, and he needs urgent help."

Seth stared at her, trying to think, but he was still reeling from the fight, which had only lasted moments. He then remembered the others who may, even now, be trapped and frantically needing his help.

"I can't leave. I have to stay. There are others who may need my help to escape back across the river."

Her sudden look of sympathy unnerved him. "I am sorry. No one will be returning. The attack failed and all of them have been taken."

Seth felt suddenly faint. He grasped the wall behind him, using it to keep himself from swaying. How could it have failed so completely? Who was this woman? How could he trust her? He wanted to shout out, to see if anyone was out there needing his help.

"You have to believe me. I can explain later, but I know that no one has escaped. Your friend will die if we do not get him aid. You can help him, but the others are beyond your aid."

Seth almost welcomed her certainty. He looked at her numbly, trying to gauge whether she told the truth. She did not look away, holding his gaze calmly. Seth looked across the fog-shrouded river, willing the appearance of familiar faces. But the gentle noises of the river pushing against the ledge somehow seemed to confirm the woman's words. He nodded and together they lifted Owen and carried him up the stairs, leaving the men behind. The woman saw him glance back.

"Don't worry. They cannot harm you now. They will be released once we are far enough away for them to be able to do any more harm."

She was clearly stronger than she looked, being able to support Owen more easily than he could. Owen moaned now, and Seth could feel the cold clamminess of the hand that he held.

"Which way?" the woman asked urgently.

Seth tried to work out where they should go. The nearest place he could think of was Simeon's, where Kayla had taken him. He thought he could find it again. He did not know if he would be welcome there, but he could not think of anywhere else. He nodded down the street. They each wrapped an arm around Owen, under his arms, and carried him, trying their best to not jar him while walking as fast as they could. Seth felt the strain in his neck and shoulders, and his leg started to throb before they had even walked half the distance. He gritted his teeth and focused on just walking steadily, one step after another. He attempted to ignore the growing pain, thinking instead of the man he carried and the need to get him to safety. With relief he came upon the doorway and knocked quietly but firmly. After a pause, the door opened slightly. Seth stood where he could be seen, hoping that Simeon, if that was who was there, would recognize him. The door swung further open, and Simeon looked out, glancing at Seth before focusing on the woman. He paused, obviously thinking to himself, before moving back inside and motioning for them to follow. With difficulty they negotiated the door which shut with a reassuringly solid sound behind them.

Once inside, they stopped and turned. Seth started to speak. "I'm sorry to bring this to your door, Sir. I trust you remember me? Kayla's friend."

"I remember you lad. You are right to come here. Follow me."

With that he turned and walked down the corridor. Turning, he entered a room that served as a bedroom, where there was a pallet bed on the floor and a chair to the side. He motioned for the woman to lay Owen down and then left, quickly returning with his wife. She smiled at Seth before looking anxiously to Owen, turning him over gently to inspect his wound.

"What is this?" she asked. "I can see the wound, but I can't touch it."

"That is my doing. I needed to stop the flow of blood as he was dying. I can remove it when you are ready."

Anna gave the woman an appraising look but did not question her further. Simeon returned with water and towels, as well as some linen. Anna sent him away again with instructions to bring some coals and then turned and examined the wound again. Owen was pale and unmoving, even when she touched around the wound, and his breathing was shallow. Quickly she cut the clothing away from him and removed it, taking care not to worsen the wound. She then moved him onto his side, before covering him again with blankets. Seth could now see the wound clearly. It did not look like much, but the blood-stained clothing and waning life in front of him told of the injury inside that he could not see.

Simeon returned with a bucket containing red-hot coals and some water in a pot with steam rising from it. Anna plunged her knife into the coals and held it there for some minutes. She then quickly cleaned it in the boiling water before nodding to the woman. "Now, please." Seth did not see the woman do anything, but the wound suddenly opened up and started bleeding. Anna did not hesitate and carefully fed the knife into the wound, probing until she was sure she had reached its base. She then held it there, steam and some smoke issuing from it alongside the smell of burning flesh. Owen flinched and moaned but did not move. Removing the knife, she repeated the process but did not probe so far. She then did it a third time before she was satisfied. The bleeding reduced now to a trickle from the edge of the wound. Taking some of the linen and some salts from

96

a pouch in her apron, she carefully packed them into the wound, pushing them into the base and applying more and more until the wound was full. She finally wound a longer piece round his body to bind it all into place. Finished, she knelt back on her heels and surveyed her patient.

"I cannot tell what internal damage has been done, but he will not lose any more blood. He may die yet though if the knife pierced anything important, or from what he has suffered already. He will need a lot of care."

"You have done as much as you could." Seth was surprised to hear the woman speak. "You have great skill and compassion."

Anna nodded but the look she gave her husband was troubled. She turned back to Owen and, satisfied that her dressing was going to stay in place, carefully lowered him onto his back. Taking some water, she spooned a little into his mouth. He coughed and swallowed, so she gave him some more. Then she stepped back and motioned for them all to leave the room to allow him to sleep.

Chapter 19

They all stood silently for a while in Simeon and Anna's kitchen. Seth felt tense, and he thought Simeon and his wife were too. Only the woman seemed calm and at ease as she looked around the room with interest. It was a fairly standard kitchen with a rough wooden table and benches, shelving with some pots and pans and some drawers with crockery. There was a small table, where Anna obviously prepared food, and a large bowl near the open fireplace where a welcome fire was burning.

He had not really had a chance to look at the woman properly till now. She was slight and yet strangely substantial, with brown hair tied back from a face that was pleasant rather than beautiful. He would have guessed her to be at least 10 years older than himself. He could not really tell the colour of her eyes, but they held his gaze as she turned to look at him.

Simeon cleared his throat and spoke firmly but not unkindly. "I think, lad, you need to explain what has happened to bring you to our door with that poor man close to death and a stranger in tow."

Seth looked at him, uncertain what to say as he realized he knew very little himself about the night's events. "You are right sir. And I am grateful for you taking us in without any delay, but I can only tell you what happened as far as I know it. I don't actually know who this is," he added, turning to the woman, "but neither of us would be alive, and I would not have been able to get Owen here on my own, without her."

Simeon looked surprised at that and a little suspicious though this softened as Seth told him and Anna what they had been doing and what had happened.

"What happened to Alec and the others?" Anna asked gently in the quiet that followed.

Seth looked down, doubts suddenly assailing him at the decision he had made to leave his post. "I don't know. We heard nothing further from the castle until we were attacked. When this lady rescued us, she told me that the group I was helping had all been captured. With Owen badly injured I did not know what to do. I just felt we had to get him to safety." His voice trailed away as he became conscious of how foolish it sounded to risk so much, and trust someone he did not know, so implicitly.

Simeon had been listening intently but Seth could not tell whether he sympathized with his decision or not. He turned to the woman, his look serious and intense. "What you told Seth, you know this to be true?" When she nodded, he continued. "How can you be sure? What has happened?"

"I saw some of it and learned enough from that to figure out the rest. They were all captured. It was a trap. Soldiers were waiting for them at each of the strike points. They did not have a chance. There was barely even a fight." She looked round and saw their questioning looks. "I have been here for some time, trying to work out what is happening. I did not know everything about the attacks but I had surmised that something was going to happen, so I had been watching and waiting for any sign of it."

Sudden suspicion rose in Seth, and he could see similar ideas on Simeon's face. Anna looking troubled and drawn sat down heavily on one of the benches. The woman read their thinking.

"There was a traitor, yes, but I am not the one you are looking for. I have been watching, learning, trying to figure out what is going on in this city and who is responsible. I have played no part in what has come about except to come to your aid," she said, looking at Seth. "There had to be a traitor." she continued. "They knew exactly when and where to look for your friends and they were there in great numbers. Your friends had no chance and there was nothing I could do."

Seth and Simeon nodded, not ready to believe her but recognizing the possible truth of what she said.

"Who?" Simeon asked.

"I don't know the names of anyone, but there was one of the leaders who was kept apart, who seemed to me to have more of shame than surprise or fear in his countenance. Young, about your age, but taller with darker hair. He led the team coming across the river and up the wall."

Before she had finished, Seth had felt a growing nausea. Of all that had happened, this struck him with such fierceness as to almost rob him of breath and strength. He must have wobbled as the next thing he knew strong hands were holding him and guiding him to a seat on the bench.

"You know him?" the woman asked.

Seth did not feel able to speak so nodded his head glumly. He had no reason to trust this stranger, except that when he looked at her and listened to her, he found it difficult not to believe her. And that made him angry, that he was so easily led and so ready to think the worst of his friend. He tried to think it through himself, but his thoughts would not solidify or allow him to focus. He knew that Alec had convinced the others to mount an attack, but why, if he was the traitor, would his group have been attacked in the square? Unless something had changed since then.

How could it be Alec? He had known him for years, liked and looked up to him for as long and was pretty sure he had been his friend. Was that all lies? His head hurt and his eyes were heavy and damp. He wiped them hurriedly and then a further, even more painful thought smote him.

"Was Kayla there?"

The woman looked confused for a second. "I don't know. There were some women in the group, but I don't know who you mean."

Seth looked pleadingly at Simeon, whose face was grim and serious. "We need to go and find her. To find out at least."

"We will lad but you cannot go anywhere tonight. If what this lady says is true, there will be soldiers everywhere and anyone out this night will be assumed to be part of the plot and will be arrested. There is nothing we can do for her tonight, but we will find out just as soon as we can. I have people who will find out for me."

An objection formed on Seth's lips but then died away as he thought about it. It added another shaft of self-hatred to those already piercing him as he sat there in the warmth and safety of this kitchen while others lay in prison, someone he had grown to like lay dying in another room and Kayla was more than likely in prison too or worse.

Simeon spoke now and Seth listened dully. "How was it that you knew to go to this lad and his friend? How did you know where they would be and that they would need help?"

"Some luck. I heard some orders being given and saw groups of soldiers fan out into the city. I knew there was at least something I could do, so I chose one to follow."

Simeon nodded and lapsed into silence. Anna busied herself now, preparing tea and some bread and warming some soup. She offered it round and all ate. She took some in a bowl and went into the other room to offer some to Owen. Although he had not wanted it, Seth felt the benefit of the food, gaining some strength from it. He felt the woman's eyes on him, studying him. At last she spoke.

"It may not be what you think about your friend. He may have had no choice in what he did."

"Everyone has a choice," Simeon countered, a little harshly.

"That is true, most of the time. But there are some in this land who can bind others to their will, sometimes against their will. It is possible that Alec was bound in this way, that he had no option but to act as he did. He may even have fought against it. From what I can see, you, Seth, were kept relatively safe until the end. Maybe his bonds of friendship were stronger than the bonds that held him."

"How can that be? That someone can be bonded to another's will?"

"I cannot explain it all now, but it is why I am here. My people hold that gift, or curse, depending on how you choose to see it. We do not exercise it in this way, however; we do not bind people against their will. We only guide, and that occasionally. There are codes governing what we do, but one of us, the man you call Nehlo, has broken them, and we believe somehow given this ability to others in return for their loyalty. Such a one is the man who governs this city."

This all sounded nonsense to Seth, but he could see Simeon considering it. He knew more of the city, its workings and peoples than Seth did, so maybe it had connected with something that he knew.

"You know this for sure?"

She nodded. "It is why I am here. I am here to aid someone to try and set things right."

"How?" Seth asked. He could see no way forward now, in this city.

"We have some gifts and skill and knowledge of these things that will aid us, certainly for now."

Seth looked at her disbelievingly. For all he had seen of her skill and strength, she remained just one woman and whoever her friend was, they were just one

100

person too. Nothing they could do would reverse the evil that had come over this place, that even this night had snuffed out the only serious attempt to counteract it that he was aware of. He suddenly felt utterly tired and hopeless. All he wanted was to sleep and then wake to find out that Kayla was okay. Anna came back in at that moment and taking one look at him reproached her husband for not taking better care of him and then took him by the hand to lead him out.

As he was about to leave the room, he turned and looked at the woman.

"Thank you for helping us tonight. I don't know who you are or what to think of what you say, but I owe you my life."

She smiled at him warmly in response.

"What is your name?" he added.

She paused for a second before replying, simply "Marrea."

Seth nodded and turned to leave. A sudden thought occurred to him.

"Were you watching, above the square that night, when my group was ambushed?"

She looked puzzled before shaking her head. Something obviously troubled her about his question, but he was too tired to think about it any further. As he left he heard Simeon and Marrea talking in low voices, but he was no longer interested in what they had to say. He allowed himself to be led by Anna to a small room that contained little more than a bed, where she left him. Tired as he was, his troubled thoughts meant sleep eluded him for a while, till even they were overcome.

Chapter 20

Finn gazed at the small caravan of carts that wound its way along the road. On them were those of the recently freed prisoners who were too weak to walk, which was most, as well as their stores and food. Some of them were able to sit up on the sides, and they looked around warily at the steeply wooded hills on one side, the other side protected by the river. The others were lying down, sleeping. Finn himself was mounted on a horse; he was no great rider but he felt he should be visible to the group, and the added height also gave him a useful vantage point for keeping watch. The soldiers and the stronger of the prisoners walked in a ring formation around the carts with some of the best men ahead in a scouting party and others bringing up the rear. It would take a significant party to challenge his group if they kept together.

It had been two days since they left the camp, having packed up anything they thought useful or valuable. In those two days the unity that had been brought about by Tam had enabled them to make good progress, but it was starting to wane the longer they were away from him, or maybe the further away they were. Finn couldn't decide which. Certainly, more friction had arisen today than had been the norm. Some of it was from among the weaker ones who were only now starting to voice the bitterness that had been pent up for many months. Some though was between the freed and their previous captors as grievances surfaced. Finn was well aware that his authority was only partial and relied somewhat on the goodwill of the soldiers and their ongoing willingness to make amends for what the prisoners had suffered, as well as a lingering sense of the good that Tam had tapped into in them all. So far, their journey had at least been peaceful though he doubted that would continue as they got onto the flatter lands. His plan, as much as he had one, was to continue to Ardvastra, taking whatever detours were necessary to deliver people as close to their home as could realistically be done.

He shifted uncomfortably in the saddle. Thankfully the horse was well trained and responded well to his heavy-handed control of the reins. He would much rather be marching, being well used to being on his feet in his years as a soldier. Maybe, he mused, it was time after this was done to get a proper job and start a family. Maybe start a farm; he had always liked the open air, which was partly why he had never minded the life of a soldier. He was roused from his thoughts by a shout behind him and turning saw Will jogging toward him with Daria walking swiftly behind. Finn stopped his horse and waited for them to catch up. Will already looked stronger and fitter. He was still thin but his cheeks had filled out and the sickly colour had left him. He was popular among all the people, on either side, and had already, with Daria's help, been acting as a peacemaker as tempers frayed. Daria looked at times like a kindly mother, but at other times she could be severe and able to bring order with a few words. Finn was sure he was not the only one who was slightly afraid of meriting her displeasure. She looked elderly, but it was difficult to age any of the prisoners, who were physically worn by the relentless hard toil and deprivation. Daria had undoubtedly been a strong woman, but the slight stoop in her back told of a loss of vigor. Finn acknowledged them both as they came abreast.

"We were wondering whether it would be best to stop soon?" Daria offered. "Some are getting tired, and we will need some time to make sure everyone is properly cared for before night sets in."

Finn nodded. "I was thinking of stopping soon. Folk must be tired, and I don't want to get too close to Halistra, which is up ahead, just in case there is trouble."

"We will pass the word then," Will replied.

They dropped back among the group while Finn looked ahead to a space where the land beside the river widened out. It was a good a space as any, he figured. He worried about stopping for the night as it left them exposed. He needed to be careful with his men. Long days and nights of sleep broken by long periods on watch would quickly take its toll on their alertness and readiness. He thought about asking Will if there were some of the others who could watch. He gave the signal to stop to the group, which wound its way into the clearing. The carts trundled into the centre and his men set up their camps at the perimeter. Some immediately set up campfires and started cooking and boiling water, while others moved into the trees to search for wood and also to observe any areas from which an attack could come. There was a bustle of activity as the prisoners got down from the carts and prepared for the night. Sooner than Finn expected, everyone was settled and eating with bed mats rolled out.

That night passed quietly enough. Those on watch had not seen anything suspicious, and apart from grumbles about the slight rain that had fallen, the group seemed in good spirits as it rolled out. Finn hoped to make good time and, if possible, get past Halistra, though it was unlikely that they could do that without attracting attention. He had gone round and spoken to all his men before they set off, and they seemed to be positively minded. From the way they were talking, it was clear they had taken on the plight of the prisoners as their own, perhaps, like himself, from some sense of their own culpability and need to make amends. What was also evident was that some bonds of friendship were forming among the group, a shared sense of getting through this together, which would stand them in good stead.

As the day stretched toward its midpoint, Finn became aware of more traffic on the road. The valley they were moving through was widening out, and some houses lined the road now and smaller roads led off into large clearings in the trees, where more houses nestled amid small patches of farmed land. The people who were walking moved off the road as they passed but did not speak to them, used as they were to guarded caravans. Finn's eyes hurt a little from squinting ahead through the glare created by the morning light on the wet road and the smoothly flowing river beside them. After their stop for a meal, the road moved a little away from the river, and from here they could see the town walls ahead and the port just before it.

The carts were traveling more closely now with the soldiers drawn in in a tighter perimeter. Finn did not expect trouble, but he wanted the group to present a confidence and purposefulness that would deter any that might come. He had asked the people on the carts to sit up as best they were able, and he was thankful that many of them had started to lose their starved and haunted air. Even so, they were likely to attract attention. As they passed the port, he was surprised to see the lack of activity. Not only the precious stones they carried were shipped here; goods from other parts of the hill country also made their way here by river for transportation into the town and beyond. Normally merchants of every kind, with retinues to match, were found there and it was filled with bustle and noise. This day, one lonely ship was berthed, and the port workers moved around listlessly. It was the same as they came up to the town gates, which were usually guarded and well-maintained. Finn shared a look of surprise with one of his soldiers but said nothing. One of the first things he had learned as a soldier was to adapt to change and ask questions later. Taking the opportunity, the group moved passed the gate and continued along the road until they reached the crossroads before turning north along the other wall of the town.

Once they had travelled on for a couple of miles, Finn signalled a halt. He called for Will and one of his most trusted soldiers. Rob was a tall, broad man with a head of bristly brown hair that was reddish in his beard. He had a fierce look about him when angered but that was rare, and in the main, he was dependable and calm. Finn tasked them with going back to the town, with some of the stones, to barter for food and supplies and also information. The group would carry on for another few miles and set up camp just off the road. He watched as they set off with two of the pack horses, walking quickly so as to be in the town early enough to trade.

Will stood close to the horses, the reins in one hand, the other stroking the horse nearest to him, which had become restless since entering Halistra. On passing through the small shacks that stacked up around the town walls he had been struck by how watchful the people had been, as if they were assessing Rob and himself. It had been unnerving, and he had been glad to escape their gaze upon entering the gates. There were less people on the streets of the town than he would have expected and those that were had, in contrast, paid them no attention, keeping their gaze lowered as they hurried by.

He was standing in the main square, which was enclosed by large buildings and had a covered, raised platform in the middle. On one side of the square were some taverns, outside of which sat soldiers and townspeople, all drinking but with a steely air that somehow spoke of necessity rather than enjoyment. He surreptitiously kept watch on them, as well as the market stalls on the other side. He felt nervous to be exposed like this, an outsider, on his own. Rob had gone to the merchant's guild house to sell the stones Finn had given them, and he had been gone some time. Will felt a tremor start in his hand, and the horse responded by becoming skittish. He dropped his hand to his side, clenching and unclenching his fist in anger at his weakness, willing himself to take back control. He suppressed a desire to turn the horses so that his back would remain to the wall, protected. Fear flitted through him, the same fear and dread he had felt in the mines of being watched, vulnerable, weak and at all times prey to others' whims. He cursed under his breath. He was free from that place now and had no reason to fear, but it was difficult to escape the sense of being under a cold and scrutinizing gaze. A hand clasped his shoulder heavily causing him to jerk round in shock, his heart hammering. With relief he saw it was Rob, who looked at him for a few seconds before picking up the reins to his horse. He spoke without looking at him further. Will appreciated the moment to recover from his shock.

"I have got some coin. Not much, but it should be enough." He paused before going on. "There is something far wrong here. The merchants were barely interested in our stones, and their guild was heavily guarded as if they expected trouble. I managed to get one talking though, and he told me what has happened. The town has no leader and any order seems to be disintegrating. Factions that were suppressed have resurfaced, and there has been some violence."

"What has happened?"

"We will talk once we are out of here. We need to get some supplies and then be gone. I don't like the look of that group at the tavern. I don't recognise the soldiers, but drinking and mixing with townsfolk can only mean they are rudderless, and they could be dangerous."

Will felt his mouth go dry and a prickly feeling run down his back. He itched to turn and look, or to walk swiftly away, but he looked instead at the market stalls. "Let's get what we can. We should separate to do it quickly."

"Yes, but see if you can get any of them chatting. Find out a bit more."

Rob reached into his jacket and pulled out some coins, passing them to Will with a quick gesture. He then turned and sauntered to the stalls, leading his horse, looking to Will as if he was ignorant of any threat. He tried to do the same, but his horse initially baulked, a nervous look in its eye. Talking to it softly he gently led it forward and walked as confidently as he could to the nearest stall.

It was nearly dark when they made it back to the camp. Will felt tired, his legs heavy. He had thought that his body was recovering from the ordeal of the mines, but any undue stress still rendered him weary in a way that was hard to overcome with will alone. His mind was also heavy with the news that they had heard and what it might mean. Thankfully, Finn did not ply them with questions immediately, proffering instead a flagon of ale and some bread and cheese. Will took his gratefully, sitting down heavily on a rough bench taken from one of the carts.

Finn looked at the packs on the horses. "What supplies did you manage to get?"

Rob answered, "Dried meat and fruit, some sorry-looking vegetables, some dried fish. A little milk. Enough for a couple of days we think. We got as much as we could. Things are not great in there, and these stones don't go as far out here as they would in the capital."

Finn seemed to accept that with his usual steadiness. He would know that demand here would not be great, where people needed useful things, not status symbols. "It will do for now, and we will do better the closer we get to Ardvastra.

And what of the town itself? Why the lack of guards at the gate and the lack of activity at the port?"

Will looked to Rob to respond, as he had reported to Rob whatever information he had gleaned from the market. "About ten days ago or so, as far as we could gather, the leader of the town, a man called Tomaz, disappeared and no one knows what happened to him. Since then there has not been any leadership, as by all accounts there is a struggle for his position. From what we could gather, he was not much of a leader and was rarely seen, but he, or at least his presence, must have kept things in check, as I have never seen the town like that before. There has been talk of other people disappearing as well or turning up badly beaten. There is tension everywhere, and it will not take much for things to deteriorate quickly."

Finn looked back towards the town, obviously thinking.

"Does anyone know what happened to this Tomaz?"

"There are lots of rumours but nothing certain. Some of Tomaz' guards are supposed to have said that a man broke into the house where he was staying and abducted him. Some say that he has been killed, but that is not widely believed as far as we could tell. Most think he has been taken away against his will."

Here Will broke in. "Some say, though, that Tomaz fled with this man." Despite his tiredness, he could feel anger beginning to stir within himself. He waited though, allowing Finn some time to put it all together.

"What do you make of it all?"

"It must have been Tam," replied Will, more heatedly than he had intended. The tension and fear in the town had somehow made him more conscious of his own, and he felt it spilling out as he spoke about the town. "It fits with the timing of when he turned up among us and who else would be able to do what has been claimed?"

Finn turned to Rob, who looked a little troubled. "It does make sense that it was Tam who took him, but to what end I do not know. I doubt he planned for all of this mess to happen, whatever his motives were."

"No, but it was pretty obvious it was going to happen," Will interjected hastily and heatedly. He found it difficult to think clearly, and he could feel his weariness eating into his bones. It was hard at this moment to look in a friendly way at any cause of more upheaval and disorder.

"Do you think this Tomaz was bonded to Nehlo, the way that Tam described?" Finn asked.

"Hard to say," Rob replied, "as he was not seen much, and some said he was sick. He may even have been used by the people really in power. That might explain, though, why Tam, if it was Tam, was interested in him."

Finn mused for a second. "I don't think our old master, Stannon, could have fled after Tam had finished with him. There is something different here."

Rob seemed to agree but Will was certain it had been Tam, and he felt his impatience at their slowness to see this.

"From where I sit," Finn continued, "it does not change what we have to do or what has happened to us."

"And does it not change anything for you about Tam?" Will was not certain himself what it might mean, but he felt that it at least cast doubt on Tam's motives and possibly his character. What did they really know about him? How could they trust him without questioning what he was doing?

Finn looked at him before answering. "We don't know it was him and we, you, of all people, have no reason to doubt him or what he has done for us, for all of you."

"For me yes, but for the people in that town who are faced with possible anarchy?"

"Maybe, but even if he was involved in the disappearance of this Tomaz, he did not cause the chaos that followed."

Will felt his tiredness, that had briefly been eclipsed by his anger, sweep over him. He shrugged noncommittally, not able to argue any further. Finn thanked them both and walked back into the camp, leading the two horses, Rob beside him. Will followed more slowly, now just desiring to sleep. He did not know what to think, but doubts about Tam swirled around his head.

Chapter 21

Seth felt the tugging on his arm slowly pulling him from sleep. He looked around in alarm at his surroundings before remembering where he was and recognizing Anna kneeling by his bedside. He still felt tired, and his body was stiff and sore. He had a dull ache in his head and even the low light in the room pierced his eyes painfully. His dreams had slipped from one nightmare to another, of pulling in a boat from the river only to find it empty, of turning away from his comrades on the other shore as they called wildly for him to save them from the soldiers advancing on them, of soldiers encircling Kayla, who cried out to him. He had tried desperately to reach her, but his feet would not move, and the look of betrayal on her face as she was dragged away from him was emblazoned even now in his mind. In all these dreams Alec appeared with the soldiers, a knowing smile playing on his face.

He focused slowly on Anna, who waited patiently beside him with a strange look on her face. He had never really been able to age her before, but now, this close, he could see the lines that marked her years but also seemed to add a kindness to her face. These were creased now as she studied him.

"You must drink something," were her first words.

Seth nodded gratefully and she bustled away, returning soon with some water. The small delay allowed Seth to fully wake and remember all that had happened overnight. He took the water and quickly drank, the first swallows cooling his parched throat.

"And soon I will get water for you to wash with. That will help ease some of the pain I see behind your eyes, though I am afraid that I must tell you something first that will be difficult for you to hear."

She paused to allow him time to prepare himself. Seth just looked at her numbly, fearing the worst.

"Our contacts returned while you slept; it is now past midday, but I did not have a heart to wake you till now as there is nothing you can now do." She looked away, uncertain how to proceed but then focused again. "There has been an announcement from the castle that traitors tried to overthrow the rightful rulers last night but that they were prevented by the bravery of the guard. The announcement concludes that an example will be made of them to show what happens to traitors." She tailed off again. Seth continued to look at her, unable to help her finish. "There will be executions of those thought to be the leaders and the rest will be sentenced to hard labour in the King's mines for the rest of their days. We think Kayla was in their number."

Seth nodded, his heart stopping within him and robbing him of even the anger he should have felt. All that he could feel was the senselessness and hopelessness of it all. Why had they ever thought they could change anything? Why was it not enough to just work and marry and take what they could from life rather than risking it all for something more? His heart ached for all that would now never be between himself and Kayla, all that he had never said or done and now never would. He had heard rumours of the mines and all of them had concluded that no one sent there returned. He felt a pressure on his hand and was surprised to find Anna holding it, a tear in her eye mirroring those flowing from his own. He blinked furiously and fought to control his emotions, but it was some moments before he was able to speak.

"Where is Simeon? Is he okay?"

Anna nodded. "Yes. He has gone to find out more. He said that you must stay here for now as you will be arrested if you are found." She saw the sudden look of panic in his face and understood it correctly. "We have informed your parents that you are okay and we have helped them to hide. They are safe for now."

Seth's look was so full of gratitude that Anna had to turn away for a second. He had not really thought of what might happen to them, and only now did he realize how close he had brought them to ruin with himself. Their lives may never be the same again but at least they were alive and safe. He wanted to just lie down again and sleep till this day ended though he knew that would change nothing.

"How is Owen?"

"Much the same. He is in some discomfort, and his sleep is very disturbed and restless. He has taken a little soup, which is good, and his wounds look clean to my eye. There is nothing more we can do but wait and care for him."

Seth nodded. Anna looked distant for a second before asking, "Alec was with you and Kayla when you came? Will he think of, or tell others about, our establishment if they are looking for more people?"

Sudden fear clutched him. This was tinged with guilt at the risk to which he was exposing these good people. He lowered his head. "He was with us. The Alec I thought I knew would never have betrayed a confidence, but now I don't know. I am sorry I came here; you were the only people I could think of nearby who might shelter us."

He felt Anna's hand beneath his chin lifting his face up so that he was looking directly into her eyes. They were worried but clear. "You have no need to apologize. We are glad that you thought of us, and we are not concerned for ourselves. Our worry is for you and Owen."

"Should we move somewhere else, more secure?"

"Ideally yes, but we cannot move Owen as he is too unwell. We could help you to escape though if that is what you wish?"

Seth thought for a moment, considering what was best. He did not want to put them in any more danger, but he knew he could not run and leave them alone with Owen while Kayla was imprisoned. He looked at her carefully, trying to read her. "I wish to stay but only if you and Simeon are okay with that?"

Anna nodded. "We thought that would be the case, and we are happy to offer our home to you. We will bear what comes together."

"Do you think that what Marrea said is true then? About Alec?"

"There does not seem to be any doubt now. His name has not been included in the list of those condemned. We have to hope for now that Alec either does not think of us or chooses not to reveal what he knows. Whoever Marrea is, she seems to be trustworthy. We spoke at length last night, and if what she says is right, things may not be as bleak as they seem just now." She did not explain further but patted his hand and then stood and bustled out again, returning with a bowl of fresh water and a towel. "Wash, revive yourself a little and when you are ready there is fresh bread and soup to eat in the kitchen."

Seth nodded again and watched as she left and closed the door behind her. He sat for some time, not really thinking about anything, his mind blank before mechanically getting up and washing his face and neck in the cold water. Even with that he felt listless and empty. Thoughts of Kayla washed over him, the fear she must be feeling, the hopelessness. Though they seemed to burn him in his very being, he almost welcomed the pain as it felt real, almost tangible, as if it connected him to her and tethered him to his old life. Eventually he realized he had to get up so he numbly found his way back to the kitchen. Anna was there and she smiled at him before nodding to the bench at the table, where he sat while she ladled out a bowl of soup and cut off a thick slice of bread. He dipped the bread in the soup and tasted it. He knew it would be good but he had no appetite. He forced himself to finish it quietly and declined any more. He leaned back against the wall and watched Anna at her work, preparing vegetables and humming gently to herself, the mundane ordinariness of the sound and movements calming his thoughts.

After a while he heard steps in the hall and Simeon came into the room. He acknowledged Seth before giving his wife a brief kiss. He then sat down, and Anna placed soup and bread in front of him. They both watched him eat, allowing him to finish before he recounted what he knew. The food finished, Simeon got up and poured a measure of spirit into three glasses before sitting down and sliding two of the glasses across. He took a small sip of his own and motioned for Seth to follow suit. Seth took a small sip and felt the benefit of the warmth it left in his mouth and stomach. He took another before setting his glass down on the table. Simeon looked at the golden liquid remaining in his glass for a while before looking up at them both.

"Anna has told you what has happened." It was a statement rather than a question, but Seth nodded anyway.

"You might as well know the worst of it from me then. They have hung six of the people they are calling the ringleaders from the castle walls. I watched them do it and it seemed mercifully quick. They have left the bodies there, as a warning they say."

He stopped and stared again into his glass, turning it round in his hand. Seth did not know what to say or ask and looked to Anna helplessly. She was quiet for a time before asking if he knew who the people were. Simeon did not seem to hear for a while but then looked up suddenly.

"Thomas, Aiden's boy and Lauren who works at the drapers. I did not recognize the others. Kayla was not one of them," he added, looking at them both.

Seth felt a brief moment of relief but then felt the futility as well as the selfishness of that.

"I think Lauren has elderly parents. They will need help."

"I think that is being taken care of." Simeon was silent again for a few moments. "The atmosphere in the city is really tense. There are soldiers milling around every important gate, and the castle is locked down. Most people are staying off the streets for fear of reprisal."

"And what of Marrea?" Anna asked.

"I don't know. We watched the hangings together, but then she said she wanted to find out more and disappeared."

"And this person she spoke of?"

Simeon looked up wearily. "I don't know Anna. What can he do? The city is near uproar, the castle is more heavily guarded than ever before and Lord Malzorn sits up there, untouchable and beyond judgment."

Anna looked like she wanted to respond but decided not to, instead getting up to boil water. She gave a cup of tea to Seth and Simeon, who smiled gratefully, before sitting down and wrapping her hands around her own cup. Simeon turned to Seth.

"You spoke of Alec?"

Seth nodded glumly, feeling a knot of tension settle on him that he doubted would lift. Any moment there could be pounding at the door, the thud of feet, the shouted command and then what? He could expect no better than the fate that awaited the other prisoners. In some ways he almost wanted it compared to this tense yet impotent waiting. Simeon though looked calm.

"You will need to lay low for a while lad. As Anna no doubt said you can stay here. The room is yours for as long as you need it."

Seth thanked them as best he could. He had no idea what he should do and welcomed the chance to not think about anything for a while and to let time and events pass around him.

Chapter 22

Marrea stood at the river's edge with Tam at her side. It was late in the afternoon and the sun was low in the sky, but it still shone clearly on the castle walls where they could see the bodies hanging. Even at this distance they could see the distortion of the faces caused by the hanging as well as the attention of the carrion that had gathered in wheeling crowds. The movement of the bodies in the wind added a further sickening element, a cruel trick to suggest that some life still remained. They both stood silently, watching and thinking. Tam had arrived in the city earlier in the afternoon. Despite the heightened tensions he had easily made it past the guards, who had taken no notice of him once they had looked him up and down and found that he was unarmed. Marrea had been waiting for him with growing concern every day. They had wandered the streets together, listening and watching before being drawn to this spot. They could both feel the fear and suspicion emanating from the people in the streets; the looks were downcast and sullen, the words terse, the mood dejected. Soldiers were concentrated at the major points, in greater numbers than before and their presence felt oppressive, watchful. The better off were staying in their homes, not daring to venture out until they were sure of their safety. Marrea had not seen any violence but the soldiers were tense and she feared would over react if there was further disturbance.

Marrea felt that Tam looked more tired, more fragile than she had seen him before. She was used to her brother looking calm and assured, but now there was a trace of strain in his eyes and across his face. At last Tam shifted and turned to go.

"Do you know somewhere we can go to get some food and rest?" he asked.

She nodded, thinking of Simeon's home. "Yes, friends that I have found. It is not too far from here and is safe."

He turned and half smiled but not enough to relieve the tightness in his features. "Let's get going then."

She hesitated a second before reaching up and touching his face with both hands. He looked at her before assenting, and she probed carefully. She almost recoiled as she sensed the mass of evil pulsing strongly in his mind but steeled herself to maintain the contact. She could feel the walls that he had erected, and they were secure but even so the sense of evil was strongly perceptible. She understood clearly how much of his energy he was having to use to maintain his control over this, to stop it taking over his mind and will, and she shuddered to think about what would happen to him and to this country should that happen. She knew he would not let it happen, but what if he had no choice and it became too much for him? She withdrew carefully from his mind but kept her hands on his face for a moment longer. He gave her a tired but more reassuring smile and gently lifted her hands down. They turned to walk through the street, back the way they had come.

Tam put his spoon back in the bowl and finished the last of the stew before pushing the bowl slightly away and thanking Anna. He became aware that the others had finished eating quite a bit before him and were looking at him expectantly. They were few in number, just Simeon, Seth, Marrea and Anna, and had been largely silent through the meal except for the odd comment relating to the food. He looked at Seth and Simeon; Marrea had told him about them, but now he studied them carefully. They looked tired and defeated, which he could understand given how bleak their situation looked.

"Thank you for welcoming me into your home, Simeon, and for giving me a chance. I will hope to not let you down."

"No thanks needed and it will be us thanking you if you can do anything to change this city. What I don't understand, not meaning to be rude, is what you can do."

Tam smiled as warmly as he could. "I am not sure myself sometimes till I get going. What do you know of the man that you call Malzorn?"

"As much as anyone, I think. He was the head of a mid-level family in the city a few years back. Then the King came, Nehlo I mean, but only for a number of months before returning to the capital, and since then Malzorn has steadily taken control. No one can quite explain how it has happened. One day we were free, but then quietly and in a way of which we were hardly aware, he drew more and more power to himself and his cronies, until here we are, cowed and frightened in our own city."

"And are the guard loyal to him?"

"I think so but most just follow orders like soldiers everywhere."

"And does he have any family?"

"Yes, his wife. The two are usually seen together when they are out."

"And is there anyone else who has any power in the city. Who could challenge him?"

Simeon thought for a bit before shaking his head. "Not for a long time."

"That is usually the way of it. I can take care of Malzorn, though you have to let me do it my way. The problem is that it will not be enough to save this city from itself. Once he is gone, there will be no one in power and that means anything can happen, including rioting and worse."

Simeon and Anna nodded, but Seth was harder to read, his eyes looking down at the table. Anna put a hand on her husband's shoulder. "We have contacts that we can speak to and spread the word asking for calm. From what my husband has been seeing, people are more afraid than angry; they do not have the will left, I think. I understand what you say though. Once the fetters have been removed that fear could turn to anger quickly."

Her husband nodded slowly. Tam could see hope and a sense of purpose reviving in him. "Yes," he added, "we can do that much. And I think it may give folks enough hope to keep going for now, particularly if they are given some sense that change might come."

"And is there anyone that people would accept as a leader, at least temporarily?"

Simeon looked at his wife again for a few seconds. "That is more difficult. We would have to hope that whoever takes over, from what is now the ruling class, will be someone who is fair at least. Anything would be preferable to what is happening now. People would see that and as long as they were promised fair representation later then I think it would work. But what of you? What will you do?"

Tam considered again the difficulty of explaining what he must do. He looked to Marrea, but she just nodded to him in encouragement.

"It is likely that Malzorn is a direct bond servant of Nehlo. By that I mean that he has allowed himself to be bonded to him, to Nehlo's will, in return for certain gifts. Some of the gifts are what you can see: power, influence, wealth. But others you cannot see like the ability to bond others in his turn."

Simeon and Anna nodded. "Marrea spoke of this, and I have had time to think it over. It would make some sense of how he was able to come to power, but I have never heard of such a thing before." Seth looked more distant though, as if not comprehending what was being said, or maybe just not believing. No one spoke for a few moments.

"Can you kill him?" Seth asked quietly, almost in a whisper, so that it took a second for Tam to realize that he had spoken.

"I am afraid that it is not that simple. If I kill him, the bonding returns to its master, who must not know that I am here for now. Neho must be led to believe that all is as he would have it. So, I cannot kill Malzorn without removing the bonding first, and if I do that, I would not have the right to kill him."

"And can we not put him in prison and throw away the key?" Seth countered.

"Not without removing the bonding. He will have the chance to give it up if he wishes, and then he will face whatever justice seems fair to the people of this city. But if he does not give it up, I will be forced to remove it. He is too dangerous, and the taint of the bonding too great, for me to leave it alone. It and others like it are sickening this whole country, and my main focus has to be removing it or there will be no healing."

Simeon and Anna looked thoughtful, but he knew that Seth was not convinced. Tam was not surprised by that; why should Seth trust a word of what he said, particularly as it sounded so alien and odd and didn't provide the answers that he needed or wanted. He may never understand, but in some ways that would not matter as the taint would be dealt with regardless; that much he could do.

Marrea, who was always quick to read the mood of people spoke softly into the silence. "Once Malzorn has been dealt with, others that he has bonded will be freed. We will know then whether Alec was acting of his own will or not. And we will have a chance then to free the people that were recently imprisoned."

Tam looked at her gratefully and nodded. Her words seemed to connect with Seth, who looked a little bit more engaged.

"But how will you do it?" asked Simeon.

114

"I don't know yet. I assume I will find him in the castle, so I will go there and see what happens." As he spoke he smiled and, for a brief moment, he felt youthful and energized. He caught Marrea's eye and knew that she could see it in him, but then her confidence turned to worry and he remembered the bondings in his mind, leaching power from him all the time; how much he could not tell, and would not fully know until he was tested. But from that moment, whatever his condition, there would be no turning back.

The conversation fell to planning of sorts. Tam wanted to know as much information as they could give him about the guards at the castle, where they would be, what their movements were likely to be as well as what may be the best way in. He was undecided whether it would be possible with so many guards to sneak in and out, as he had done before, or whether a more direct approach would be needed. It was agreed that the attack would happen in two days to allow time for Tam to rest and for Anna and Simeon to disseminate the information through their contacts.

Tam was woken by Marrea shaking his shoulder. He oriented himself immediately and looked at his sister.

"It is Owen. The lad who was stabbed. Anna thinks he has taken a turn for the worse. He is in obvious pain and lying still. Are you able to help?"

"You know my skill in healing is limited."

"Better than mine, and I have warned her that you may not be able to help. But the boy will die if nothing is done."

Tam rose from his bed and followed her. The room he entered was warm and dimly lit by a couple of candles. He could see Owen lying on the pallet, his face pale with a sheen of sweat over it. He was obviously in pain but lying rigid with his breathing shallow. He did not move when Tam and Marrea entered, but Anna came to meet them from where she knelt at his side. She took Tam's hands in hers.

"Can you do anything for him? He seems to be getting worse, and I have nothing more to offer him." She looked tired and pale, having obviously been up all night caring for him, and her eyes expressed her desperation.

Tam held her hands for a moment and looked in her eyes. He felt heavy and uncertain. Could he do anything? But he had to at least try. He knelt next to Owen and studied him. Barely a young man, he had not yet broadened out, and he looked frail and weak. His eyes were open but not focusing, and his breathing was shallow but regular. Tam felt his heart which was beating but fast, too fast. His head was hot but his hands when Tam felt for them were cold and clammy. His stomach was hard but every touch and movement of it seemed to cause more pain to spasm through him.

Tam hung his head for a second. He knew that Owen was near death. He gently probed him with his senses and felt the leak of air and fluid where there should have been none. He thought for a second before deciding that the sword must have pierced Owen's bowel and the leak was poisoning him, his ability to fight it ebbing away. He focused on the leak and probed around it, feeling for the severed tissues. Gently he drew them together, using the air that was already there. He felt the tissue come together but then start to pull away again. The swelling caused by the trauma was forcing the tissues apart. As he worked he could feel the

115

bondings pulsing and pushing in his own mind, yearning to dominate, to overpower and subdue. He concentrated two ways, one on keeping the bondings at bay and the other on the fingerbreadth of tissue that was frayed and slipping from his grasp, threatening to reopen the incision that was drawing life away from the man in front of him. He focused in on that little area, losing sense of his surroundings, and gently wove intricate threads of air that kneaded the tissues of the bowel together. He then bound them round with fatty tissue to seal the patch he had created. He became more aware as he did so of the bondings, clawing at him, dangerously close to breaking free, and he knew that if they did he would not have the strength to resist. He probed again but this time could feel no leak. Tam quickly drew his focus onto the bondings, rebuilding layer upon layer of wall around them and forcing them back into the recesses of his mind. He then sat back on his heels, breathing heavily, suddenly aware of feeling cold and his damp shirt sticking to him. His own heart was beating fast, and it took some moments for him to calm himself. He knew he had come close to being overcome, and it scared him. How could he hope to fight on and add to this burden? He could not relax his guard for even a moment and the focus that needed was becoming an effort. He took some deep breaths, trying to calm his thoughts and heart. Once sure that he was safe, he turned again to Owen. He looked no different. His breathing was still shallow and the sheen of sweat had not lifted. He was teetering on the edge of death. Tam stood slowly and stiffly.

"I have done what I can. There was a leak in his stomach, which I have sealed as best I can. But the infection is still there, and I do not know if he has the strength to fight it."

Anna nodded. "You have given him a chance. I will help him take it if he can."

Tam marvelled at this woman with her simple strength and obdurate will. "He needs rest and his fever taken down. He is not to get food, only water. Boiled and cooled would be best if possible. It is important that it is only water until he has healed inside."

Anna nodded again before kneeling down by her patient, who seemed to feel her cool hand upon his forehead, as he stirred ever so slightly. Marrea touched Tam's arm and smiled as he moved to leave the room. As he neared the door, he saw Seth standing, watching. Tam could see him considering and weighing, but before he could acknowledge him, he had turned and gone.

Chapter 23

As he walked up the road to the castle, Tam thought over the discussion again. It had been a last-minute decision spurred by the announcement of a feast to celebrate the crushing of the rebellion, which also had the purpose of demonstrating the ruler's power and control. Many of the most important people in the city had been invited and no one turned down such an invitation. It would be full of people and guards and, most importantly, Malzorn himself was guaranteed to be there.

It was late in the afternoon but a few hours of daylight remained. Tam was not totally sure why he had decided to attack during daylight hours rather than at night, which had been his original plan. By day there would be more guards and no chance of being unseen. Maybe that was it; he was tired of doing things in secret, of hiding what he was doing like a thief in the night. After this, he knew that he would have to go to Ardvastra to face Nehlo, an encounter that he did not know if he had the strength to win or even survive. Maybe this uncertainty contributed to what might be a decision lacking poise and deliberation. Maybe he just wanted to publicly show resistance to what was happening here and throughout this land. Whatever the ultimate reason, he had reasoned with himself that his task was no harder during the day than it was at night and the presence of many guests might even aid him.

The road was largely empty, the feast having started some hours before. The road rose up a gradual slope toward the gates, which were still open but guarded by two soldiers on either side and likely more within. Tam carried a wooden staff that he had found in Simeon's house. It was comfortable and balanced in his hand with a reassuring weight. Otherwise, he was unarmed, and as it was hot for the time of year, he was dressed in his loose-fitting travel clothes. He walked calmly and slowly up the hill, aware of the scrutiny of the guards as he approached. He was a source of obvious curiosity for them as he was clearly not a guest, nor was he a merchant or servant, and everyone else in the city knew to stay away at this time.

Despite his air of calm, Tam was concentrating hard. With Marrea's help he had walled off the bondings within his mind so that they felt distant and their pulse weak. That allowed him to push his senses out, probing the castle for any sign of a similar bonding, that taint that was so hideous to him and yet which drew him as fever drew the cool balming hand of Anna to the lad he had left in her care at the edge of death. His senses were alive to any movement or threat, and with the bondings at their weakest for some weeks, he felt vigorous and full of purpose and energy, every ripple and movement of air around him being felt and assessed without requiring thought.

As he neared the gate, he saw the guards give each other a bemused look and then move to block his path. He could sense four more in the guardhouse to the side of the gate and a further two on the other just inside the wall. He was already aware of more on the walls. Once inside it would be more difficult as the castle was full of people, with all the guests and extra servants, in addition to the normal castle staff. He did not even pause to break stride or engage them. He pinned them to the gate posts one on either side, wrapping their arms and legs together with tight threads of air and forcing their own shirts into their mouths as gags. They were helpless within a second, their eyes following him in fear as he moved nearer. In the same instant, he drove a blast of wind through the small window slit in the guardhouse, slamming the door shut and blocking it from the outside before the soldiers inside had a chance to give startled yells. With a thin tendril of air, he locked it tight, noting with satisfaction that their hammering was barely audible through the thick wood.

The sound of the door shutting had alerted the two other guards inside the wall. They came round into the entrance, swords sweeping up from their scabbards. Tam moved swiftly forward to meet them. He could sense the movement of their blades as the air split in advance of them and, with slight movements of his own, he moved between them and then used their loss of balance as they over swung to force them down onto the ground on their stomachs, the breath whipping from them as they landed hard. In the second of quiet that followed, Tam bound their hands, as he had the others, and pinned them to their sides. It had taken seconds and throughout he had kept probing, searching ahead, conserving his energy for what would come. He walked on through the gate and into the open square beyond, aware now that he was a target from all sides but also aware that soon he could be lost in the crowds.

Once inside the square, he kept an even pace but looked around keenly to get his bearings. A number of carriages with fine horses and liveried servants were waiting patiently, close to the castle inner walls and the inner gate that led to the central enclosure and tower. What Tam took to be stable buildings lined this wall and all were well-kept and well-made, though he noted absently that they were a defensive weakness, should the castle ever be overrun by enemies, as they offered purchase on the inner wall. Castle staff moved around busily, talking to the servants while offering them and the horses they tended food and water. Some guards stood apart, but they were more intent on the serving girls than on keeping watch, and no noise alerted them to the now unguarded gate. Tam was among the throng of people in a few more steps. He did not pause but kept walking toward the inner gate. He received a few glances, but no one questioned him or saw anything amiss. As he neared the gate, he saw two sentries on either side, and he sensed two more on the far side. They were alert, however, and attentive, intent on preventing any of those in the outer court from getting in.

When he was within a few feet of the guards, they became aware of him approaching and raised their weapons, their legs and body immediately in a fighting stance. One held out his hand, raising it to get Tam to stop, but instead he picked up his pace and ran lightly forward, ignoring their shouts and the heads turning toward him. Just as he felt the blades sweeping through in a diagonal cutting arc from both sides, he buffeted them to the side with weaves of air and rammed his staff into first one and then into the other guard, who were both caught off balance. They fell forward almost in one motion, blades clattering to the floor, and Tam dodged between them. As he passed them, he brought the staff back down onto their heads, and they fell motionless but breathing on the ground.

Once through he did not hesitate but struck the nearest guard heavily on his arm as he attempted to release his blade and then brought his staff up, knocking the guard's head back and against the wall. Feeling a blade approach from behind, he swivelled lightly out of its path, deflecting it slightly so it did not pierce the fallen soldier. Tam's staff swung round and landed on the guard's shoulder, which Tam felt dislocate beneath the force of the blow. The soldier went white with pain, but Tam's next blow across his head robbed him of consciousness. Now through the gates, Tam drew a blast of air towards himself to ram shut both gates and then lifted the great beam into place across them to shut out the soldiers beyond.

Tam turned and looked around quickly. There was a thick mass of men and women in the enclosure, all obviously wealthy, judging by their fine tunics and robes. They all held drinks and had been chatting in small groups, but those nearest to Tam had fallen silent and watched him intently, unsure of what to do. A ripple of quiet swept through the group as they quickly became aware that something untoward was happening. He could see the large door of the keep some fifty paces away and the great hall beyond, from where all these people had spilled out after the meal. Inside he could see some others milling around, but he was not interested in them. He probed again for the bonding and found that he could now sense it faintly ahead of him. He heard shouts above him as soldiers on the walls became alert to him and started to react. None of the guests confronted him, and he could sense their fear and uncertainty. He started forward purposefully again, holding his staff up as if to part the people in front of him, but they needed no bidding to move out of his way. He felt the air splitting rapidly around him as arrows flew directly toward him from behind and both sides. Without breaking stride or even looking, he sensed their rapid approach and tilted back and then forward to allow them to slam harmlessly into the ground. As he moved forward at a run, he felt more arrows being released from all around. Summoning air from the keep to himself, he swirled it round and round himself as he ran. The crowd clutched at their clothes and staggered as the air pushed past them. Round Tam all they could see was a whirl of dust caught up by the wind as it circled around him and each arrow being deflected from its mark by the vortex and being ploughed into the earth at his feet. The ground behind him was pierced with arrows as he made the safety of the door and crossed inside, releasing the air to cause it to slam the great door behind him as more arrows thudded into it.

The people inside the hall scattered at his approach, down any corridor they could find. Their panic hindered the soldiers who were trying to come into the hall, allowing Tam to get part way across the hall before the first entered. He could sense the bonding above him now and knew that he had to move quickly as Malzorn would also now be aware of him. Air whistled in through all the windows

119

at his command and he channelled it at the tables and chairs, upending them and barrelling them across the room. They slammed into the soldiers who were just entering, crushing them against the walls or forcing them back down the hallways. Tam ran to the far end of the hall and up the steep stairs, passing frightened servants, who cowered as he passed them. Boosting his speed with a channel of air behind him and some under his feet, he almost flew up the remaining flights until he was at the top. Taking that same air he smashed it into the door ahead of him, which flew open and crashed loudly off the wall on the other side.

He paused now and stilled himself before entering, not entirely sure what would meet him. Probing ahead he realized that there were four people in the room, one of whom must be Malzorn as the bonding this close was like an overwhelming stench to him. He forced himself to walk forward and through the threshold, realizing as he did so that he must be in the main bedchamber. Before him were two soldiers in simple garb, armed with short swords and knives. Behind them, standing by the bed was a middle-aged man, slightly balding but with strong eyes and a stern expression on his face, and next to him a woman, whom Tam assumed was his wife, of younger years, whose face was striking in its beauty and hauteur. At a word from Malzorn, the two soldiers moved slowly forward. Tam noted their purposeful movement as they separated and came at him from both sides. The light in the air faded a little, the candles flickering as he drew the air around him. He felt the movements as the swords plunged forward from different angles to evade his defence. He deflected one with his staff, which he whirled round to crack off the top of the blade, causing it to tumble to the ground. The other he deflected with his arm, which was cushioned with the air that swirled around it in an invisible band. Whirling quickly he spun his staff round, deflecting the knife that flew at him, and smashed the staff with a sickening thud on the side of the soldier's head, who then sank to the floor.

Suddenly, as the remaining soldier attacked again, Tam felt the pressure around him building as air pressed in on him so heavily that it almost seemed as if the walls were falling in upon him. He struggled to move his arms and legs, feeling now like they were moving through a thick liquid rather than normal air. His attacker had no such difficulty, and Tam saw the blade move swiftly toward him as he struggled to bend out of its way. At the last moment he focused hard and pushed with all his might against the pressure, forcing it out away from himself with such power that the walls themselves buckled momentarily and the glass in the pictures on the walls shattered. The remaining soldier flew outward in the blast, smashing against the wall to lie slumped and still on the floor.

Tam cast around with his senses and felt the evil of the bonding. Malzorn and his wife had fallen but now stood close together, eyeing him warily but without any apparent fear. He paused, unsure how to proceed now that he was facing them. Tam could not tell definitively who was bonded to Nehlo. He did not want to harm anyone unnecessarily and targeting the wrong person would leave him vulnerable. He felt the pressure building again and the air thickening around his arm and throat, and at the same time, he felt his breathing become laboured, such that he had to forcefully suck the air in to get enough. He was about to push back when he felt a second attack, this time focusing on the walls in his mind that he had built up around Nehlo's bondings. He sensed some of those walls splinter and crack and the bonding start to snake through and immediately begin searching and scrabbling for a foothold in his mind. Panic started to rise in Tam, a feeling that he had only rarely encountered, but now it threatened to overwhelm him as his defences crumbled and his lungs strained for any air to fill them. As his concentration started to slip, the attacks increased in ferocity and the tainted pulse of the bonding throbbed forcefully in his mind. He was dimly aware of his staff slipping out of his hand as he sank to his knees, his hands flat on the cold stones, his vision starting to go black.

Chapter 24

Marrea circled round the castle walls. She felt relieved to be acting after the days of watching, waiting and talking. She was usually quick to see what needed to be done and used to making her own decisions, but she was shaken by her fears for Tam, and what he was bearing, and that made her unsure. He had been a constant presence through her life, and they took it for granted that they would support each other. She was afraid now, because she felt that she was not able to help him in what he had to endure. Moving quickly and purposefully now eased her fears. She was followed by Seth, who had insisted on coming when he had heard her plan. They had followed her brother at a distance and watched him enter the castle. She could still sense him inside, moving his way forward toward the keep. She used the momentary confusion and distraction of the guards to assess the wall before choosing her entry point. Channelling a little air to aid her, she pulled herself up with her hands, her feet finding purchase on some of the small gaps in the stone wall. She moved swiftly and lightly up the wall, reaching the top in moments. She lay there for a second, looking around. The wall itself was four paces thick at the top and regularly patrolled by the soldiers. There were none at this point. Marrea could see them gathered further on, focusing on Tam as he ran toward the keep. She knelt and unwound the rope that she carried around her waist. Bound up in this were short wooden batons that she had roughly carved out of heavy oak, and which she felt would suffice for weapons. She liked their relative lightness and the flexibility they allowed her to move quickly, strike accurately and incapacitate but not kill an opponent. She lowered the rope over the wall and braced her feet against the ledge as Seth pulled himself up. Once Seth had reached the top, Marrea picked up the batons, and motioning for him to follow, they both ran crouched over. Two guards on their side of the wall turned at their approach, but Marrea did not slacken her pace and quickly bound them with bands of air before pushing them face down on the walkway. When they drew parallel to the gate into the inner enclosure, Marrea spotted a sheltered area on the ground in the inner courtyard, and grabbing Seth by the hand, she jumped, ignoring the gasp of surprise and suppressed cry that he gave at leaping out from a wall many meters high. She channelled air to cushion their landing, holding Seth up as he stumbled forward. She looked out from behind the shed where they stood and watched the nobles running in confusion, calling to their servants to bring their horses and carriages, though Tam was now nowhere to be seen. The gate to the outer enclosure had been opened, but the melee had impeded the soldiers from forming into any cohesive unit. She could see the captains trying to bring them together and clear the crowds. The door to the keep was closed, and she could see arrows sticking out from it and a few soldiers pushing to gain access.

She and Seth followed the wall round to the side of the keep and then down a slight slope to the lower levels. From what Simeon had learned, the prisoners were kept in a dungeon whose access was below the main keep. Moving slowly, Marrea could sense two guards who had kept to their post outside a thick, heavy door. It was difficult to be sure with all the confusion, but she did not feel that there were other guards near. Knowing she had little time before order was restored, she ran forward, her batons raised in her hands. The guards were alert and ready for attack with their blades already drawn. They immediately turned to face her and separated slightly to allow themselves room to move, simultaneously raising their swords. One feinted with a low blow before angling upward, and the other brought his blade carving through at the level of her chest. Her momentum should have carried her straight into the attack, but she sensed the air splitting around the blades and slid to a halt, tilting back from her waist and away from the blades. Taking advantage of their outstretched arms, she struck both on the wrists hard with her batons, causing them to drop their swords. Barely pausing for thought, she wrapped their feet and hands in bonds of air before lowering them to the ground. Their eyes were wide open with fear and fixed on Marrea, who motioned for Seth to gag them both. He cut some lengths of cloth from their coats and hesitantly stuffed it into their mouths. Ignoring the guards now, Marrea turned to look at the door, aware of Seth standing now just behind her. She studied it for a second, sensing where the weaknesses might lie. It was well-made but, like every door, was weakest around the hinges and the lock. She focused on the lock, working on the mechanism with little tendrils of air, and then felt it click open. A further gust of air pushed the door inward to slam against the wall to the surprise of two guards seated at a table playing cards with a grimy lamp their only light. She bound their arms swiftly with bands of air before tipping their chairs over to leave them scrabbling on the ground on their sides.

Marrea peered into the dark jail, seeing dimly a door at the end of the corridor, where it turned to the right. There was a dampness to the air, which felt cold, and she could smell excrement and sweat so strongly that she had to suppress a feeling of nausea. Suddenly, she sensed a strange emotion from Tam that was also unusually strong for her to be able to feel at this distance. She had not sensed it from him before, and it caused her heart to race and her stomach to clench inside her with fear. She looked up at the stone ceiling above her, in the direction of the keep where she knew he was. She ached to join him, but she had sworn to him that she would not. She knew that not only did he want to keep her away from danger but that he also needed her to complete this task. She realized, with a heavy heart, that she would have to trust him to come through whatever struggle he was in and concentrate on the work in front of her.

Seth rose from gagging the two guards. He felt disoriented by the speed of their ingress into the castle and had barely managed to keep up with Marrea. He watched as she somehow unlocked the door and pushed it open, using the few moments of respite to catch his breath. What Marrea could do was incomprehensible to Seth, and he struggled to marshal his thoughts. Marrea dealt quickly with the guards inside, but then she stopped, looking up, a worried look on her face. Seth stepped closer, suddenly afraid. He thought of Kayla though, somewhere in the darkness, and he forced himself to step inside, the stench and cold assailing him.

He looked back at Marrea, who motioned for him to go on, as she turned to guard the entrance. He took a second to let his eyes adjust before picking up the lamp and venturing forward. He could hear people up ahead, some talking in low voices, others moaning or crying. He reached the end of the corridor and peered into the room through a small window cut out of the door. Inside he saw a small room and in the feeble light afforded by the lamp, he could see only the outline of three or four people lying on the floor close together. There was no bed or furniture, only what looked like dirty straw on the floor. One looked up at the window, drawn by the light, but he did not recognize them. Biting down his anger at their desperate condition, Seth concentrated himself on the task in hand. He felt along the door and found that the key was in the lock. Turning it, he opened the heavy door and took a pace forward into the cell. Faces turned away, hiding their eyes, and two of the people shrank back in obvious fear. He had not expected this and suddenly felt unsure how to rouse them. He turned to a woman who seemed less cowed.

"I am here to try and get you out of here," he said, his voice sounding weak in the darkness. "But I don't know how much time we have, so please come with me." He felt sudden desperation that they might not listen to him and that more guards would come before he could find Kayla. He shone the weak lamp into each face, feeling callous as he turned away from each in disappointment. He started to leave but felt a slight touch on his arm. Looking back, he saw the woman struggle to her feet and reach down to help someone else. Seth had to trust that the rest would follow, and he continued down the corridor, finding three more cells like the first, each with even more people crammed into them. He could hear some of the prisoners shuffling slowly out of their cells towards the entrance, but with each passing moment, he felt anxious and scared that Kayla may not even be here.

He opened the last cell and entered with almost a feeling of futility. The people inside had heard the noise of the others leaving. They were standing, facing him, wary that this was a cruel trick. He scanned them quickly before his eyes alighted on Kayla. Her face was downcast, covered with grime, and swelling almost closed her left eye. He walked over to her and went to hug her, but she flinched and drew back, scared. He waited, trying to be patient, to allow her time to see him truly. She looked up slowly, and he saw her recognition grow, the fearful look on her face being replaced by an almost pitiful hope. Slowly, she reached forward and touched his hand, almost as if testing that he was real. He took the hand and held it gently, not having any words to say. Seth became aware of the other prisoners leaving slowly. He had a sudden pang of fear that they would all be found and trapped.

"Kayla." He stopped, not knowing what to say. She tried to speak, but her voice was hoarse. She squeezed his hand and nodded. Turning, he led her out of the cell, following the rest as they walked slowly back along the corridor. Reaching the entrance of the dungeon, they each stopped, the brightness of the late afternoon blinding them, and some cried out in fear. Slowly, they all stumbled out and stood huddled together. Seth stepped out, leading Kayla. Marrea gave him a warm smile before quickly scanning around. He saw her start, and he followed her gaze to find a tall man with dark hair walking towards them.

Seth felt sickness claw at him, his heart suddenly hammering on his chest. He had not anticipated coming face to face with Alec. A mix of emotions flooded through him and suddenly his legs felt weak. He had wanted to confront Alec, drive home to him the misery his actions had caused, but now the bitterness of betrayal and his anger swelled so strongly within him that he felt overwhelmed. He was no longer aware of the group of prisoners and even the pressure of Kayla's hand seemed distant. He released it and walked mechanically towards Alec, who had stopped. Even in his confusion, Seth could perceive Alec's uncertain air.

Seth stopped a few paces from Alec. Part of him was keenly conscious that he needed to flee with Marrea, Kayla and the others, that at any moment guards could appear and they would all be trapped, but he needed to understand why Alec had betrayed them. He stared at Alec, hardly recognizing his friend in the man before him who could not lift his eyes from the ground and who seemed to have shrunk in size. Seth wanted to shout at him, to vent his rage, but violent words would not come. Seeing Alec brought to the fore all that had been lost, the breaking of friendships and lives, and he just felt tired. Anger seemed pointless.

He became aware of shouting from the keep and the need to run. He turned to go, but Alec looked up, pleadingly.

Seth looked at him, almost pityingly. "Why, Alec? We were your friends," he said, almost in a whisper.

Alec flinched, tears forming in his eyes. "I had to. Malzorn's people had my mother and my sister. They somehow knew that I was involved, so they took them and hurt them." He paused for a moment. "I tried to protect you and Kayla, but they would not stop hurting them till I had told them almost everything I knew. What would you have done in my place?"

Seth felt the question pierce him. What would he have done? He had found that he was not as strong as he had thought, that he was not as brave or as determined as people needed to be in a time of rebellion. Would he have resisted? He did not know. But he could not trust Alec again, and this made him feel almost desolate, as if something of the meaning of friendship had been tarnished forever. He turned and walked back to the group but felt an urgent tug on his arm. He turned sharply, suddenly scared, pulling his arm away and raising his other hand to strike. Alec stepped back, a look of horror on his face, his hands now raised in supplication.

Seth lowered his arm slowly, feeling ashamed and confused. Alec looked behind himself and spoke quickly. "The castle grounds are going to be full of guards very soon. They have secured the courtyard already. If you want to get them all out, you need to listen to me."

Seth just wanted to run, to start moving but he forced himself to listen.

"You don't trust me now, I know, but I want to help. There is a gate at the bottom of the slope. It is small, barely anyone knows of it, but you can escape that way. You will need to hurry."

Seth thought quickly. He knew that Alec would be right about the courtyard but heading down the slope meant that if he was lying now, they would be trapped. Marrea could likely escape but probably not with them all. Alec did not wait for him to respond though. He turned and walked slowly back up towards the keep, his head down. Seth watched him for a second before making his decision.

"We have to go back this way," Seth advised Marrea on his return.

Marrea did not question him about whether they could trust Alec but simply nodded and motioned everyone to follow. They moved as swiftly as they could, the stronger supporting the weaker, until they reached the outer wall and found the small gate, barely wide enough to take two men abreast. Seth pulled up the heavy bar that lay across it and swung the gate inwards. Looking out, he saw a steep slope leading down to the river on their left. In the other direction he could see this portion of the city spreading out. There was a narrow path, which wound its way down the hill, and although it was steep, it looked secure. Marrea held the gate and Seth led the way, holding Kayla's hand, as one by one the prisoners moved through. The descent seemed painfully slow and at each moment Seth felt they would be discovered and recaptured. At the bottom of the hill, the relative safety of the narrow streets seemed to spur the escapees on and soon only Seth, Kayla and Marrea remained.

Seth itched to leave, to get back to Simeon's with Kayla. Marrea stalled though, her gaze back up at the castle wall above them, her face showing concern.

"Is Tam still in there?" he asked quietly.

"I am not sure," Marrea admitted. "He was definitely there before we entered the prison, and he was in trouble. But I don't know what happened." She tried to make a brave smile but was unable to.

"Can we help him?"

"No. He would not want that. If he has been taken, then we would not succeed where he has failed. And if he is still fighting, we would only be a distraction. No, I must hope that he is okay. I will know soon enough."

Seth discerned Marrea's love and fear, and he felt a sudden stirring of warmth towards her and her brother. He realized, with some shame, that he had only ever been sceptical of them and their motives, even when following Marrea into the castle. Surely, they had shown they were worth his trust, and even more? "We must hope," he said softly, correcting her. "I was a fool to doubt you both. I know better now."

Marrea smiled, more warmly, though her gaze went quickly back to the castle. "You must go now. You have a long walk ahead of you to get back to Simeon's. I will wait here to see if I can be of any assistance. Tam and I will meet you there, I am sure."

Seth felt keenly aware of the need to get Kayla to a place of rest and safety. He turned to lead her through the narrow streets but stopped before the corner. Looking back he saw Marrea's solitary figure, deep in thought before walking back up the hill and into the castle grounds through the gate from which they had just come.

Chapter 25

Finn stood at the rear of their small caravan, looking back along the wide valley. They had gone a further day's travel from Halistra along the well-paved and maintained main road, one of the main arteries of the country. They had made better progress as the prisoners strength improved. With progress had come a certain amount of good cheer, so the atmosphere when they had stopped for the night the previous day was much lighter than it had been. But Finn remained alert to the dangers and had insisted that they not camp until they had reached a raised area, just off the main road, that he felt offered them some degree of protection.

Rob stood next to him, his face inscrutable as he followed Finn's gaze. The news about Halistra had disquieted Finn, so he had asked Rob to take up the rearguard for most of the day, a good hundred paces behind the rest. From long experience, Finn had learned to respond to disagreeable reports and not just brush them aside, and also to trust his senses. It was Rob who had alerted him to the force of men that followed them at a steady distance, neither catching up with them nor falling back, the way that wolves might track a herd. Even now they had stopped, just within sight. Finn could just see the dark outline of the group in the distance. His eyes strained to identify details of their strength and intent.

"How many do you think?"

Rob scratched his beard while he considered the question. "From what I can see at least sixty men, and I think most if not all are armed and about a quarter have horses."

"So about twice our number. Do you think they mean us harm?"

"I think so. Our stones may have attracted some unwanted attention, and we make easy prey for violent gangs."

"We could possibly defend ourselves, but any loss would be a regret. Do you think they would settle for some of the stones, if they had anything to sell?"

"I doubt it. In my experience, people like the ones I think are following us always want everything they can get their hands on and always think there is more to get than there is."

Finn turned to look at Rob. "So, prepare for a fight then."

"Yes," responded Rob in a matter-of-fact voice. He had been a soldier for a number of years and the thought did not faze him. It worried Finn a little though, as he needed to consider how to defend the weakest while making the best use of his trained soldiers.

"We will need anyone who is able to be armed and ready. Ask Will to help you."

Rob touched his forehead in brief salute and then turned to walk back toward the rest of the camp. Finn stayed for a few moments looking back to the group that followed them. They had been lucky to get this far without more attention, but in some ways that made it harder now as he had almost started to think they could get everyone home. Perhaps by as soon as this night that would no longer be possible.

The light-hearted mood of the previous evening had vanished by the time Will and Rob had finished their survey and the carts had been arranged in a defensive circle. The possibility of an impending attack had cast a pall of gloom and anxiety over the group. Finn doubted whether anyone would get sleep tonight; he certainly did not expect any. He had placed the most vulnerable and weak in the centre of the ringed carts and sentries at the weak points between the carts. They were going to work shifts keeping the watch with clear instructions on who to wake at the first sign of anything suspicious. They were on a slight rise so had a commanding view of the area around them, and as long as the moon stayed out, they would be able to detect anyone coming from a reasonable distance. He still worried that they were outnumbered and had too many who were untrained and untested.

The night was long and cold. Finn spent most of it going from sentry to sentry, keeping them awake and alert and ensuring that they slept when they should. The night passed uneventfully, but by morning light Finn was bone tired and his muscles ached from the cold and the tension. One of the prisoners brought him some hot tea and bread, which he ate gratefully, and as the camp was being dismantled, he managed to grab an hour's sleep. Rob brought the news that their hunters were still there, at a safe distance back.

As they set off again, the strain of the previous night broke out in small irritations and arguments. Finn stopped them early that day, again on a slight rise and in the same defensive posture as the previous night. The group had kept pace with them all day, though this time riders had moved closer toward them and had been unashamedly observing them. Everyone was conscious of the watchful presence following them, and the tension in the group was growing. Finn felt it too and knew that if something didn't happen soon, he would struggle to hold the group together.

Sunrise broke another long and weary night of watching. No attack had come that night either. All through the night it was difficult not to be conscious of a menacing presence somewhere out there in the darkness, stalking, pacing, biding its time. It was a weary group that packed up the camp for another day on the road.

Will and Daria approached him just after they had set off.

"Folks are wondering what we are planning to do about that group," Will started.

"What do you mean?" Finn asked, unsure where this was leading.

"We mean, should we not deal with them now, before they run us ragged with worry and tiredness?" pitched in Daria.

"I have thought of it more than once, but it would be a disaster. They would see us coming and outnumber us. I am hoping they will realize that we are not the easy prey they thought we were."

"And if that does not work?"

"Well we will need to ensure we are ready for whatever may happen. And we keep moving as every day moves us further from their homes and closer to Ardvastra."

Will looked like he wanted to argue, but Daria cut him off with a look. She nodded curtly. "We will do our bit when the time comes." Finn watched as they both walked away, Daria in the lead now, her gait purposeful. She was strong. Finn had no doubt she would do anything that was needed.

The day was long and throughout it all Finn worried. They were now in the flat plains below the hills that led to Ardvastra, and there was little cover or raised ground to rely on. On either side of the road were wide, open grassy spaces and then further away the fertile fields of the plain, which were well-kept by the many scattered farming households in this area. On a different day he would love to have lingered to enjoy the different colours of crops nearing harvest. Instead, he kept everyone moving until the light had almost faded in the hope of finding a haven, but none had appeared. Finn was now so tired after two nights of little sleep that he was starting to struggle to keep his thoughts in order and more than once he had drifted asleep in the saddle as his horse plodded on. Finn knew from experience that if battle came to them, he would have adrenaline enough to drive off the tiredness, but he worried about the others in the group without his training.

They set up camp as on the previous two nights, but he ensured that the circle was tighter as they had no protection on any side. That left two carts in the centre, under which the weakest sheltered. Every soldier slept with his sword by his side, and those who could handle a bow were stationed at each gap between the carts. The night crept by, and as he walked around, he was aware of the restlessness in the camp. Most were ostensibly asleep, but from the amount of movement and sound, he knew there was little true rest being had.

As the night wore on, Finn felt as if he was floating in tiredness. Eventually, he sat with his back to a cart and closed his eyes and rubbed his forehead, trying to ease the tension that seemed to reside there. A shout suddenly roused him. With a pounding heart, he gripped his sword and sprang to his feet, weariness gone. Suddenly, there was noise everywhere as the prisoners in the centre of the camp woke and started shouting and screaming. For a moment he was unsure where to go as it seemed they were being attacked from both sides. He ran to the nearest cart and peered out. At first he could not see anything, but then he saw them, not fifty paces away, some on horseback and some on foot, and all armed. Slowed for a moment by the sudden alarm in the camp, the dark figures regained their pace, encouraged forward by one who was clearly their leader. Arrows flew now and thudded into the carts. Some flew over the carts on their perimeter and with sudden cries of pain two of the prisoners gripped their stomachs, arrows embedded deep within them. Cursing, Finn ran back to them and dragged them behind a cart that was in the centre of their camp, where he stood and watched as the others ran for cover. His men now released their arrows and Finn watched in satisfaction as three of the approaching figures fell. His satisfaction was short-lived

129

as the assailants now running quickly covered half the distance to the camp. More arrows flew from the defendants and more of the attackers fell, but they were too many. Drawing his sword, he saw all the men and women around him who were armed do likewise, and bellowing his defiance, he turned to face the coming charge.

Chapter 26

Tam thought rapidly and feverishly. He used the hardness of the stone to anchor himself to something substantial. He could not fail now; to do so would be to undo all that he had achieved. Worse, it would mean all the problems that he had unleashed would be for nothing. He sought desperately to hold in his mind belief in a creator God, who was good and purposeful, who acted to reconcile. This belief gave him strength and conviction. But doubts crowded in. Why, if there was a creator, was this perversion of his gifts, this evil being allowed to triumph? The certainties that he had based his life upon suddenly seemed inconstant and fragile, unable to take the weight of his questions and fear. Where was this God now? Tam had committed himself to using his gift in service to others because of his belief in this God, but now, facing his sternest test, God seemed absent or powerless to help. And if that were true it made a mockery of his life, of his beliefs. He could feel the malevolence of the attack, the suffocating pressure that strove to crush life from him, but there was also the attack from within, the pulsing evil of the bonding that sickened him and threatened to control him. Under the overwhelming strain on his body and mind and the surge of doubt, he felt a sudden despair that he might die here, might fail, and then, if it was all false, there would be nothing. But a small part of him could not accept that the life within him, that he saw all around him, that he had grown to wonder at would end in nothing. He had to believe there was a loving purpose behind all of this. Tam clung desperately to this conviction as his last defence and would not let them be swept away.

He closed his eyes and focused again, ignoring the burning in his lungs. He did not fight back against the attacks but quietened everything in his mind, recalling all that he had ever been taught, all the skill he had refined over the years and all the strength that, despite his doubts, he knew deep down he had been given. Tam shouted out in his mind to the creator, willing him to listen, to act, to honour his belief. He reached out with his senses, feeling the thickness of the air around him, the pressure bearing down on him. He strove to reach beyond that, to drive his way through the growing darkness. Suddenly, he could feel the air outside, the space, lightness, moisture and life it contained, the heat and light from the sun, the grain of the stone around and above him, the cool water of the river below in its constant movement. In doing so, he connected with it all in ways that he had never done before. With growing wonder he saw, in its vitality, beauty and order, the evidence of the creator's design. And once again he was awed by the gift and responsibility that he had been given to harness this to serve. He reached out and drew into himself what he could only think of as the life of it all.

He opened his eyes to find light splitting through the windows and the cracks in the walls so that the area where he stood was suffused with light and warmth. Tam drew the air in hungrily and felt his strength and focus return to him. He planted his feet firmly, and feeling through his shoes the strength of the stone, he drove himself upwards, tightly grasping his staff in his hand. The bondings in his mind retreated, cowering away from the light and life into the darkest recesses again, and would have fled were they not constrained and imprisoned there. The suffocating pressure from Malzorn and his wife retreated until he felt it snap and he was released completely.

Tam turned his attention to Malzorn and his wife, who had both collapsed, pale and sweating on the floor. They slumped now before him, their strength spent, their confidence and pride gone. As he looked at them, he saw their blindness to the deception that they had been under, to the hollowness of their gain and to the awful cost others had paid. He knew that he had come as much to release them as to remove their yoke from the people. In studying them, though, he saw that they were not the same. Malzorn looked haunted, desperate, as if trapped. A thought flitted into Tam's mind that he had seen this before, and it took him a moment to remember that Tomaz had been this way before he had set him free. Malzorn's wife was very different, her face even now registering anger and calculating hatred.

He spoke quietly, but in the stillness, his voice was clear and carried to them. "I know your master and I know the hold that he has over you. If you want to be free from him, I can help."

As he spoke, Malzorn looked at his wife, questioningly, almost pleadingly and then looked back at Tam. His wife did not return the look however and had regained some of her composure.

"I will remove the bonding, as I cannot allow his influence to continue. You cannot be allowed to continue to carry out his will with impunity in this city. I only offer you the choice to give it up freely, to renounce your way of living and to go a different way, a harder way for sure but a better way."

Tam was aware of their every movement, and he could feel the evil of the bonding within them, twisting and turning, and seeking to even now bend them to its will and attack. He could also feel, however, slight resistance to the bonding in Malzorn. Tam kept his focus strong and his pressure on them relentless. He could hear shouting from the bottom of the stairs and knew that he did not have much time. The woman heard it too and a slight smile flickered across her face.

"You must decide now. I cannot remove it by force without hurting you, possibly in ways that you will not recover from. Please don't make me do it." Tam was surprised by the pleading in his voice and realized how sick he was of drawing this evil into himself like this, but he could see no other way. He made his decision.

Moving forward, he bound the woman with cords of air tightly so that she could not move. He then focused his full attention on Malzorn, who, without looking at his wife, bowed his head before Tam and allowed him to place his hands upon it. Reaching out, Tam once again felt the sickening taint. Pushing down his revulsion, he drew it into himself. He could feel Malzorn pushing it away with an initially weak effort but then, as he felt it leave him, with stronger and stronger desire, holding Tam's hands to his head as he did so. The bonding crossed to Tam, who almost fell forward under the additional burden, his mind trying desperately to wall it off before it overcame him, unable to keep his focus on anything else or to maintain the flows of air that held the woman. Out of the corner of his eye he saw her move and reach for a knife, draw it back and plunge it toward him, but he was powerless to move or stop it, the internal battle consuming all his strength. He desperately fought to erect the barriers in his mind, layer by painstaking layer as in slow motion the knife moved closer. He knew he was not going to manage it in time, that the next moments were going to be his last, but he pressed on. Just as the wall was completed, he felt the blow, not to his chest but to his side, and he fell sideways landing heavily on the floor, gasping, reeling under the shock and pain. It took him a moment to realize that he had not been stabbed, that there was a struggle beside him. Malzorn had knocked him over and now wrestled with his wife, seeking to tear the knife free from her grasp. He was stronger than her, but she inched the knife closer to his neck, driven by rage and the bonding in her mind, wanting only to be free to strike again at Tam. Malzorn strained and, just before the knife plunged into his neck, pulled her arm down and twisted, throwing her off and onto the ground beside him. Only in that moment did both he and Tam see that the knife had cut deeply into her thigh and blood was coursing out. She scrabbled back onto her hands and feet, the movement causing even more blood to pour from the wound, and she started to totter. Tam rose to approach her, but she waved him away, a crazed look in her eye, and Tam knew that Nehlo would never let her go, that she had allied herself too far to return or to take his aid, even now when her life ebbed from her.

After a few short seconds she weakened and her movement stopped. Her husband approached her, a look of utter misery and distress on his face. He bent to her and held her close, whispering to her. His searching hands found hers and held them tight. As she died, he let out a moan of grief that pierced through Tam, but above this, he heard and felt the bonding shriek and return to its master. He rose, as pounding started on the thick wooden door at the entrance. The man looked up briefly and stared at him with such confusion that Tam almost wept as he was unable to help him now make sense of what had happened.

"You go now to Nehlo?" His voice was strained and coarse.

Tam held his gaze for a second before nodding wearily.

"Go then."

With that he turned back to his wife and bent his face to hers. Tam walked slowly and heavily to the window and climbed onto the sill. He stood for a second, looking down at the long drop below before stepping out and allowing himself to fall.

Marrea's attention had not wavered. She felt the struggle in her brother and saw him stand at the window, despite the distance. She saw him plummet to the ground and knew that he did not have the strength to break his fall sufficiently. She ran toward him, and as she did so, she drew air from all around her, feeling it whip in from every direction, causing windows and doors to clatter and loose objects to fly through the air. Disregarding this, Marrea drove the air under Tam,

133

cushioning his fall. He still landed awkwardly and almost fell, but she caught him and helped him regain his balance before guiding him toward the gate. She could hear men shouting from above, calling for guards, and as she looked down the hill, the gate seemed a long way. Initially, Tam seemed weak and moved sluggishly. Marrea matched his pace, but she was tense and had to resist the urge to make him move faster. Once he had started though, he gained strength and was able to run slowly alongside her. They moved, painfully slowly, towards the gate. Now Marrea could hear shouts of pursuit behind them, and every moment she anticipated the splitting of air behind them as arrows sped toward them. They kept moving, as fast as Tam was able, till they had reached the gate and almost fallen through the narrow opening. Marrea pulled the gate shut behind them and sealed it with weaves of air, feeling a sense of relief at the solid barrier between them and the approaching guards. They then slipped and stumbled down the hill, not bothering with the path but careering straight down, barely managing to stay on their feet. At the bottom Marrea stopped, uncertain where to go. At that moment she heard a call and saw Seth and Kayla beckoning her forward. Half pulling and half lifting Tam, she ran forwards and followed them.

In the capital, Ardvastra, Nehlo felt the bonding return to him and knew for certain that his servant was dead. How she had died he was unable to tell, but it could not have been an accident. He cared little for the woman, only what she did for him and what it meant for him that she had died. He had not feared attack for many years, but if someone had killed her, they had either caught her unaware or they had power to match hers. That could be a threat to him. He sent his people out into the city to his spies, the ones he had bought and the ones he had manipulated, and his thoughts now intently focused on identifying and neutralizing any challenge.

Chapter 27

Finn braced himself, tiredness forgotten for the moment and raised his sword. He yelled at the men nearest him to stand their ground; it was crucial that they maintained their defence at the perimeter and funnelled the attackers into areas where their superior numbers would not count for so much. Their assailants were all running as fast as they could, their weapons raised, their faces visible now and their yells audible above the noises in the camp. For a brief second, Finn wondered how he had come to be here, standing between men intent on bloodshed and these people, whose cries of distress or pleas for help he would have simply ignored even a few days earlier. Their attackers slowed, each picking their point at which to attack, wary of getting in each other's way. Finn parried the first sword thrust but felt himself pushed back despite desperately trying to hold the line. The narrow space between the carts constrained the assault, however, and regaining his foothold, Finn crouched to swing low, feeling his own blade catch just below the knees. The man fell forward, his legs giving way beneath him, and Finn followed him with a downward stab into the base of the neck. He did not pause but pulled his sword free in time to face the next man clambering through the gap. He could not look around him now and had to trust that everyone would hold their positions. Finn drove forward, seeking to push his assailant back. With small, smooth movements of his sword, he broke through the man's defences. The man tried to move back but the pressure from behind of men pushing forward made it impossible. Finn barrelled into him, using his free hand to slip his knife free before driving it into the man's midriff and pushing him back as hard as he could, causing him and the man behind him to fall backward.

As he sheathed his knife he risked a moment to check their position. The prisoners were huddled in groups, some sheltering under the carts in the centre of the enclosure. Many were too scared to even look up and shrunk back from the melee around them. In some areas his guards were had pressed but so far they held firm at the ring of carts. Finn could see bodies lying on the ground, but he could not tell at a glance whether they were friend or foe. He had armed some of the fitter prisoners with long, strong, sharpened branches. They now stood uncertainly in the centre, overwhelmed and unsure of what to do. Finn yelled to get their attention and pointed to the weakest areas where he felt that the defence might fall. Seeing Daria nod, her face set in determination, he did not stop to watch and see what happened. Finn turned again to the gap in front of him through which two men were advancing, clambering over their fallen comrade. Finn used their momentary lack of balance to charge forward with broad swinging strokes of his sword before abruptly changing tack at the last moment and striking with a deep thrust. The man in front had moved to block the strike he thought was coming, and Finn's blade passed under his defence and caught him on the top of his leg. As he staggered back, he grasped hold of Finn, dragging him out of the protection provided by the carts. Feeling a moment of panic, Finn wrenched his sword out with all his might, causing the wound in the man's leg to rip open. The movement left Finn exposed for a second as he struggled to get control of his balance and his sword. He was too late though and felt the punch of the blade cutting into his arm, rendering it useless, and his sword fell from him. The man raised his sword again to strike down, and Finn desperately raised his arm to meet it.

The blow never came. Suddenly, the man fell back with an arrow embedded deep in his chest, the blood already soaking the shirt around it. He looked surprised more than pained as he fell, his hands clutching his chest. Finn did not stop to see where the arrow had come from and quickly moved back to the relative safety of the enclosure. Arms pulled him in and some of the prisoners moved to block the gap that he had left. He pressed down hard on the gash in his arm to try and staunch the flow. He fought to focus and saw that the attackers had been driven away from the enclosure. He could see some men and women on the ground, some moving, some not, but around each there were others tending them. Finn turned and stumbled to the perimeter again and looked out. Bodies lay everywhere, arrows protruding from them. Those still alive were in full flight, desperately trying to distance themselves from the arrows that sped down with deadly accuracy. Finn could not see who was firing the arrows, and at that moment he did not care. He sank down onto the ground, leaning his back on the nearest cart, his legs suddenly feeling weak from nights without sleep and the loss of blood, and allowed his eyes to close for a second. The next thing he felt was someone holding a cup of water to his lips, which he drank from greedily, and then pain in his arm as his wound was bound tightly.

Finn struggled to his feet, willing strength back into his muscles. On standing up he had to lean briefly on the cart as he was assailed by dizziness. He moved slowly through the camp, noting with real sadness some of his men and women who had been killed. They had already been laid side by side by the prisoners. One of the dead was Daria. Her usually stern face bore a look of surprise and pain, and her hands still rested on the wound in her chest where the blade had pierced her. Will sat nearby, his back to a wagon wheel, staring at her, his face blank. Despite his years as a soldier, Finn had never understood death, the sudden removal of the person from the body, and it seemed even more alien now, so horribly and deeply wrong and unnecessary. A mix of sadness and anger filled him, and he silently cursed the men who had thought only of their own gain and not of the harm they would render. He could see that the injured were being tended as much as their meagre supplies allowed, so he turned his attention to the perimeter again. His remaining people still stood guard, too well trained to assume that the lull meant the end of the fighting. He walked round, sharing brief words with each of them and commending them for standing their ground. He saw with amazement that they had stood firm throughout their perimeter though the price had been high with the loss of eight good soldiers and four of their charges.

"Captain."

He turned to face the guard, who touched his forehead in a small salute.

"There is someone approaching."

In the early light of morning, Finn saw a slender woman walking toward them carrying a bow by her side, with an empty quiver slung over her shoulder and a sheathed sword strapped to her waist. She held her other hand up and stopped twenty paces from him. Finn walked out into the open so that she could see him. They looked at each other for a few moments. She held his gaze confidently but not aggressively. Her hold on her bow and her movement spoke of her comfort with her weapons. Her dark brown hair was tied back to reveal a handsome rather than pretty face.

"I think that we owe you some thanks," Finn started, "but I saw many arrows and from more than one direction. Where are the others?"

She smiled before answering. "You were holding your own from what I could see. You needn't fear us. I have come alone so that you did not feel we were a threat to you. My men are ensuring that your attackers do not return."

Finn reflected on all this for a moment before speaking again. "How did you happen to be here just at this moment and why intervene in a fight that was not your own?"

She looked down for a second, obviously considering her answer. "As to the first part, that is easy. We have been tailing both you and the other group for the last two days as we could see that they were intent on causing trouble. As to the why, let's just say that we have been released from harm ourselves and would not now willingly pass by others facing the same."

She slowly moved closer so Finn did the same until they were within a few paces of each other and could speak more easily. Up close, he saw that she was a little older than he had thought, though still in young womanhood. Her eyes were brown and clear and her gaze direct but a little wary.

"Where do you head?"

"North to the capital. Where do you go with this strange group?"

"The same. We have some who are ill and frail as well as many injured among us that we are seeking to return to their homes." He was not sure why he spoke so freely but something in her manner made him want to tell her. "How many men do you have?"

"Twelve men and women are with me though they are not really mine. We travel together, and I suppose I lead where that is required, but we all have the same goal."

"And what is that?"

She thought for a second again before answering softly. "To be honest, we don't know exactly. We each feel a drawing to help a man who helped us, but more than that I can't say." She laughed, slightly embarrassed by her own words.

It was Finn's turn to consider things. There was no reason to think that the man she spoke of was Tam, but events and people did seem to swirl around him.

"Was the man you speak of called Tam?" he asked tentatively, almost reluctantly.

She looked at him in astonishment, her eyes conveying her smile. "Yes, have you met him?"

"He is the reason I am here looking after this lot and getting stabbed," Finn answered gruffly.

"From my experience, he has that effect," she replied. "Tell me, how did you meet."

"In time," Finn responded. "First, let me tend to my people. Will you join us?"

A low whistle answered his question. The woman turned and waved behind her. "Is it okay if my party come along? We are pretty self-sufficient and won't be a drain on you. The extra guards might deter any other groups from attacking you."

Finn felt unsure, but he had to trust them; they had almost certainly saved them all, and he itched to learn more about her connection to Tam, to find out more about that man and why he was upending everything around him.

"Yes. First, we will tend to our injured and dead, then we will eat and talk. My name is Finn."

"Mine is Zoe," she replied before turning and walking back to meet the rest of her party, who had started to gather. Finn watched her go for a few moments before going back into the camp.

By the evening, the two groups had melded together. The day had been given to burying the dead, venerating their sacrifice and tending the wounded, but then their thoughts had to turn to their own survival and freedom. And over shared food, wine and stories, their spirits had risen. Finn had listened to the tale being told and retold of the battle that day, and with each telling, the fighting grew fiercer, the injuries greater and the rescue more peremptory. The actual events became hazy so that eventually everyone had a story they could tell of something they had done.

Later in the night Finn sat next to Zoe on a rough bench and listened to her story, which was both different and similar to his own. They had both been set adrift by Tam, untethered from their previous lives, with their only goal the shared one of seeing a particular journey through. What followed, neither knew.

Will sat apart from the others. He could not join them in celebrating their survival. In the darkness his mind kept returning to the battle. He could still remember the feeling of panic coursing through him, the confusion all around, the thought that death could come at any moment and he was not prepared for it. He felt his legs tremble and stamped them angrily into the ground to distract himself. He heard again the yell from Finn, and he pictured Daria moving to where Finn had pointed, her stride determined. He had followed reluctantly but with this movement had come a reassuring sense of taking back control of what happened to him. He could still feel the wooden spear gripped in his hand, its weight cumbersome and unnatural to him. His arms almost enacted the thrusting motion with which he had stabbed blindly forward, again and again, not sure of what he was hitting, only willing himself to keep going, to keep their attackers at bay. Beside him, Daria had laboured, her face pale but determined. He could not remember exactly how someone had got past their spears, but as they tired and their defence weakened, an attacker had darted through. He was too close for their wooden spears to be of any use, and Will had been helpless to block the sword that pierced Daria. He rubbed his eyes, not wanting to see again the blade sinking in, the look of shock and fear that flashed over Daria, emotions he had never before seen in her in such intensity, despite all they had endured. She seemed to visibly change before him. Will had dropped his spear and caught her as she fell, in that moment not caring what happened to him. He had been only dimly aware of one of Finn's men taking their place and fending off their attacker.

Will could not determine how he felt. Daria was not family, not even a friend as such. She had been too strong, too self-reliant for that. She had been a constant presence, and he felt angry that she had survived so much and now, within days of reaching home, her life had been snatched away. How could that happen? Was there to be no justice or relief? He knew that she had lived in Ardvastra, but he did not know her family, did not know who to speak to of her. His thoughts turned to his own family. He hardly dared to think of them normally, trying to keep busy in the camp to keep his hopes and fears at bay. Were they still there? Would they be able to love him still? Would he be able to return to them and be as he had been before, a loving father and husband? Would he have changed too much? Somehow, the loss of Daria made everything even more uncertain.

Chapter 28

"Tam, what do you feel would have been the correct advice to give given everything you have heard?"

With an effort Tam roused himself from the somnolence that had been slowly enveloping him and looked, in what he hoped was a respectful manner, at their tutor, who stared at him from under thick eyebrows that gave an added severity to his stony face. In his mind he went back over the last things he had heard, but he could not be sure when he had drifted off. Glancing quickly around the room, he could see that it was clear to his fellow students that he had been mentally absent for some time as they were all watching with interest, some with more than a hint of mirth. Some of them would love to see him humiliated, he knew. All he could remember of the lesson was that the situation had become difficult when Lucas had started listening to a small faction who sought to seal off their city from outsiders.

He cleared his throat, hoping that his voice would work as his mouth felt strangely dry. "I would seek to show the mutual benefits of the limited movement of people."

"Hmm. And if he did not listen to this and continued on the path of entrenchment?"

Tam thought quickly. Old Hardy was a difficult one to second guess, and he could be severe if you unwittingly stepped over one of the lines of what he regarded as good conduct. "I would bide my time and seek to keep highlighting the effects of his decision."

"Highlighting or convincing?"

Tam blinked in surprise at the directness of the question. He knew he was being pressed due to his inattention. "Highlighting, Sir. I do not feel this would merit more."

Hardy studied him for a second. Tam held the intense gaze though he would rather have looked anywhere else, and he suddenly felt an irritation in his back. The room was strangely quiet, waiting to see which way Hardy would go. Eventually he turned on his heel and moved back to the centre of the floor which the chairs were grouped round. "Good. Maybe though you will find my next topic of more interest to you. Morgan is often a hero for you country folk."

Tam slumped back into his chair feeling more drained than he should. Marrea seated beside him gave him a supportive smile and Neblo grinned at him with a look that said he had lucked out. He was seated on the second row of chairs, which banked up steeply behind him in a semi-circle around the speaker's lectern. The design allowed everyone present to have a clear view of the speaker and to hear every word. In years gone past this great space would have been filled with students like them but now there were maybe only twenty and all at different stages of training. All were gathered for these lessons with Hardy that focused on practical dilemmas or politicking as Neblo called it. Often Tam found it interesting. It somehow resonated with him more than the physical training of his other classes, but today he had struggled to concentrate. He forced himself to sit up again and attend to what Hardy was saying as he really was interested in Morgan, having heard so many tales of his exploits over the years.

"I want you to forget everything you think you know about Morgan. He was no hero. He came close to destroying everything that was built over the decades before him in these halls, and he is the reason our numbers are now so pitifully small and we struggle to keep the presence we have in corridors where before we would have been esteemed and sought after." Hardy stopped and looked round the room sure of the impact of his words; every eye was upon him now. Tam's mind raced back through all the stories he had heard with the slightly sickening feeling that came with the disorientation of discovering that cherished certainties and heroes were not quite what they had appeared.

Hardy spoke for a long time, but Tam caught every word, and from the silence in the room and the absence of the usual rustling and fidgeting, he assumed that his peers were as transfixed as he was. By the time Hardy had finished, Tam was reeling. He had only known snippets of stories that had been passed between villages, and from those, he had, like all boys, built a picture of the man behind them, embellished further by his own imagination, till he towered over all other men. As Hardy had been speaking, that tower had come crashing down, and with it some of his own certainty about right and wrong. If a man like Morgan could do such terrible things, surely anyone could? How near he had come to destroying everything of value for what? His own power and legacy? His own sense of what was right for the world, no matter the cost? How had he been allowed to get so far? Why was he not stopped and why had he not himself realized where he was headed and what the outcome would be? How could the stories be so wrong? The questions crowded into his mind, demanding answers.

Tam looked up at Hardy, who was surveying the room, gauging the effect of what he had said. After a few moments Hardy rapped on the table before him, startling them all.

"Few know what you now know. The decision to make it thus was made shortly after Morgan's final defeat. Instead, over the years, stories have been circulated that paint him in a very different light and over time the truth of what happened has been forgotten. If it had not been, those of us with power would not be trusted anywhere. But do not be in any doubt. What I have just told you is the true history of Morgan chronicled at the time, and the texts are kept here so that we remember what is possible if we abuse the power given to us by the Almighty."

Again he stopped, ensuring that everyone present had heard and registered his words. "We will talk on this some more once you have all had time to consider it. For now you are dismissed." He then walked from the room.

Everyone sat for a few moments in stunned silence before slowly drawing together their paper and pencils. Tam looked at Marrea and Nehlo, who both seemed deep in thought. Nudging them he rose stiffly and heavily and followed the others out into the courtyard. Groups of students dotted the courtyard, some sitting on the grass in the middle and some on the low walls that surrounded the courtyard and separated the path on the perimeter from the well-kept grass. Turning, Tam led Marrea and Nehlo to their favourite spot, from where they could just see the steep hill that lay beyond the confines of the city and beyond which, two days walk away, lay their own village. On the other side, the land beyond the college walls sloped down, terraced by flat-roofed houses until it reached the plain that bordered the glistening sea beyond. Boats of many sizes lay anchored within the mighty walls of the harbour, which was just visible from where they sat. Carried by the wind sweeping off the sea, the call of the seabirds that whirled above the fish markets beside the harbour was faintly audible.

All the groups were in close conversation. Some were friends of Tam's, but he wondered how deep the bonds went. He and Nehlo had struggled to build much relationship with those born into a life different from theirs, one of city dwelling and relative wealth. He had been relieved when

141

Marrea had joined them a year earlier, and it was really through her more easygoing nature that they had got to know any of the others.

"What do you make of what old Hardy was saying?" Nehlo asked quietly while looking out over the wall to the hill beyond.

Tam thought for a moment. "I suppose we never really knew much about Morgan, just what we were told, and we never questioned that. Why would we?"

Marrea, who had been lying down with her eyes closed sat up and straightened her top. "I was just thinking about what we were told back home and really it was not much. I think we invented most of the rest as it was exciting to think of someone like us doing so much and having such gifts."

Nehlo nodded in agreement. "Hardy was using Morgan as a warning to us all not to use our gifts to assume power or authority, as if what he did was inherently evil. But I don't know if it was." He tailed off, still looking past them both.

Tam started, his mind reaching to catch up with Nehlo. He had only really thought about whether what they had been told was true or not, and if it was, it had seemed clear to him that Morgan's actions, painful as it was for him to admit it, were wrong. He analysed again in his mind what Hardy had said, sifting the possible facts from interpretation.

"But many died because of what he did and possibly many more since then," Marrea replied, getting in just before Tam had formulated his own thinking.

"Yes, I get that, of course," Nehlo responded quickly, his face flushing with what looked to Tam like anger before he paused and gathered himself. "But people have always died as a result of what our Counselors do, and maybe less would if either we did nothing or maybe if Morgan had been successful."

Tam wondered if he heard an edge in Nehlo's voice when he used what would be their future title once they completed their training. "So leave people to make choices without guidance and possibly enough knowledge, or take over completely? Are those the best options you see?"

"I don't know. I just don't think it is as clear as old Hardy made it seem. Maybe he wasn't so bad. Maybe he just wanted to do what he thought was right. Maybe he was best placed with all his training and experience to decide what was right for people."

"Surely it is best to teach and guide but then ultimately for people to make their own decisions, for good or ill?" Marrea followed up quietly.

"But that is never the case really, is it? Someone is always in power, and as far as I can see from what we have learned since coming here, very few earn the right to it or have the talent to merit the role." He sounded tired and resigned all of a sudden. "The most we can hope for is to advise and watch as others make a mess of things. Maybe Morgan got tired of doing that."

"Maybe. But they were the vows he took, to only use his gift to serve others, never for his own gain, and to guide those in power but never to take power for himself. These vows are the only thing that assure rulers they can trust counsellors and without that trust we have no purpose or role. He had no right to grow weary of his vows, no right to assume power that he had vowed to always forgo."

"That is straight from old Hardy. We don't need to just accept everything he says."

Marrea flushed, clearly embarrassed at Nehlo's slightly contemptuous tone. Nehlo shook his head as if to clear his thoughts before turning with his palms raised to them both.

"Sorry, I did not mean to say that. We have often enough debated things Hardy has told us, and I know you don't just swallow it all whole. It is just that sometimes I feel we are being moulded into believing in something that I for one am not sure about, but there seems to be no way of questioning it or turning back without quitting.

142

Tam studied Nehlo, thinking hard. They had always backed each other, and as far as he was concerned, they always would, but he could feel distance developing between them. Tam was drawn to the vision that the college presented to them; it seemed to give him a certainty about the world and his place in it. He had been happy with his family, had never really thought about leaving until his gift had become apparent and he had recognized the responsibility that came with it. The vow they had taken was important to him, and though he questioned some of the actions of the counselors they learned about and the staff at the college, he found himself wanting to be part of that long history, checkered though it may be. He had sensed before now his friend's growing frustration but had not linked it to the college itself, more to the lack of acceptance from their fellow students.

He glanced around, seeing that the courtyard was emptying. He felt slightly chilled, partly through sitting on the ground and partly by the cooler air of late afternoon. "Come on, let's go down to Molly's and see if she has any soup and bread left that we could wheedle out of her. I am feeling a bit chilled."

Nehlo nodded quickly, clearly glad to end this conversation. Marrea stood and picked up her pack. "Okay, but I said I would meet someone I met in town, but I could just ask her to come along as well. I will see you there."

Tam and Nehlo nodded before grasping their own packs, which they dropped off in their room in the college on the upper floor of the building on the other side of the courtyard. On the way out of the college grounds, Tam caught some looks from their fellow students, but he shrugged them off as being their usual patronizing manner toward them both.

Nehlo followed Tam out the gate of the college, immediately leaning forward to meet the cool wind that funnelled through the narrow streets. The houses on either side were single story with smooth white walls and flat roofs, which on a calm day the owners would sit out on to enjoy the sunshine and the view of the sea. Now, as evening approached, there was little thought of that; instead, shutters were being closed and people were hurrying past with their jackets pulled tight.

Despite the wind, they walked at a steady pace. Nehlo was glad to get out of the confines of the college and into the streets of the city, which he enjoyed walking through. Somehow, he felt more at ease here than he had during his years of living in Tam's home, despite the kindness of Tam's parents. He liked the mix of nooks and alleys and how they would round a corner and be able to see the sea beyond. He also liked the relative anonymity and the ability to just disappear and lose himself.

They entered a small square that contained a market during the day. Toward evening two of the houses facing the square converted into ale houses with seating outside and in. Some people were already there, huddled over jugs of ale, conversing quietly. After glancing round, Tam and Nehlo made to walk across the ground which was marked by wheel ruts, market stands and the passage of people. At that moment Nehlo felt a slight pressure behind him and ducked reflexively. He saw Tam stumble forward beside him with a short cry. Looking round quickly he saw the jug that had hit Tam lying on the ground behind him and the one that had narrowly missed him lying a few feet away. He reached out to help Tam up, whose face was pale with shock, before looking quickly around. At the far side of the square, he saw some of the local men staring at them in surprise. Then he saw a group looking at them contemptuously, their clothing identifying them as of a higher class, and he recognized two of their fellow students from the college in their midst. Nehlo looked them over, thinking quickly. He felt Tam pull on his sleeve, urging him to walk away. Looking quickly at him and seeing him recovered but still shaken, he pushed down the urge to smash the look from their faces and turned to follow.

143

"You country thick skins, what makes you think you can make it as one of us?" taunted one. Nehlo stiffened and almost turned, but Tam shook his head and whispered, "Leave it."

"Orphan, you should not seek to rise any higher than the hovel where your parents left you!"

Nehlo stopped, stung and angry but also feeling a clenching in his stomach. He was not sure how they knew about his parents. The only people he had told about them were the college supervisors as they had requested the information before allowing him to join. Beside him Tam had also stopped, his face betraying his anger. Nehlo turned back to find the group advancing toward them and felt rather than saw Tam join him. At a quick count there were six, including two from the college. As they moved forward, they drew short clubs from their cloaks, holding them by their sides.

"We could run yet," Nehlo murmured, "and save ourselves a beating."

Tam looked around quickly, indicating to Nehlo two others approaching from the other side who could cut off their route out of the square. He smiled ruefully. "I think that moment has passed. Better now in the open, I think. If we move fast, we could do some damage and then maybe they will think twice."

At that moment the group fanned out in an arc to come at them from different sides.

"Things just got a bit trickier."

Tam nodded his agreement, the two of them instinctively backing away till they could sense the walls of the courtyard protecting their backs.

Nehlo reached out, feeling for something that would work as a weapon, and his hands fell on a rolling pin that had been left out on the table of what had obviously been the bakery stall. He held it up to Tam and shrugged slightly. Tam looked around quickly but all he could find were two of the long wooden spoons used to stir the pot. He held them up in front of him, trying to look determined and certain. Nehlo suppressed a smile and turned back, feeling the weight of the rolling pin, which was surprisingly heavy.

"We don't want any trouble. Why don't we buy you a drink and then head on to where we were going?" Nehlo could hear Tam trying to put some friendliness into his tone.

"You have no part with us. We would not want a drink from you and only you leaving this city and college completely would be enough for us. You should never have been admitted and today we heard what happens when your like are trusted with anything more than a plough or shovel."

Nehlo looked narrowly at Tielvo, the speaker and their peer at the college. He did not look angry, just disdainful and slightly frustrated, as he might if dealing with an errant dog. For a brief second Nehlo felt ashamed of his background, his parents, his clothes and wished himself anywhere but there, facing this man. Then anger took over as he realized that he would never be accepted, even were he to succeed in his training; he would always be seen as a servant, beneath even their anger, valued only for his gifts and knowledge, his usefulness, like a well-made tool or good milking cow is to a farmer. Maybe this was what Morgan had realized. He glanced at Tam and saw anger and tension in the set lines of his friend's normally placid face. He gripped his rolling pin tightly, glaring at the advancing men, who clearly expected little resistance.

"Remember the barn dance from home?"

Tam nodded, without turning his head.

"Okay, how about we do it now? Keep moving, they will not expect the changes of direction, and we might just make it out of here with our heads intact."

Tam nodded again. "Sure, but you had better let me take the woman's part. You trip over often enough even doing our part."

Nehlo grimaced but agreed.

"Now?" Tam breathed softly.

144

"Now. Let's knock some country dirt into these arrogant fools."

Nehlo moved forward and stepped to the side. He felt Tam move into place with his back to him, facing outward. Lightly they danced forward, stepping sideways. Nehlo caught a look of surprised amusement on the face of one of the local men before they both swung sharply round in unison, causing their opponents to veer back involuntarily before closing in again. Nehlo and Tam kept moving in unison, their makeshift weapons raised. Nehlo parried one attack and ducked under a wild swing that he felt rather than saw coming. Just in time he felt Tam duck under the same blow. Grasping his rolling pin firmly at one end he thrust it out, punching it into one assailant's midriff before swinging round and connecting another blow with someone's arm. Then everything became a blur of continuous movement as they weaved around, following the steps of the well-known country dance while defending and attacking desperately, inflicting blows but unable to disable anyone for long. Nehlo could hear Tam's breathing becoming faster and more ragged, and his own legs and chest were burning with the effort. The sweat dripped down his face and into his eyes, but he did not dare to pause to clear it as the attacks kept coming, seemingly now driven by frustrated rage.

At last there was a brief respite as they circled round to one side of the square and their attackers drew back. Nehlo leaned down, attempting to get his breathing under control.

"We need to get out of here or we are going to get pummelled," Tam said softly, between gasps of breath.

Nehlo nodded, looking around him for a means of escape, but the first thing he saw was Tielvo with a look of slight amusement on his face. He had obviously not taken part so far; his clothing was unruffled and clean and his skin unblemished by sweat or dust. Before he could stop himself, Nehlo rushed at Tielvo, the desire to topple him into the dirt overwhelming any tiredness or fear. He felt the first blows splitting the air in front of him and to the side but twisting slightly and arcing round he evaded them, hearing, as if from a distance, Tam's voice calling him back. Parrying another blow, he swung right and then left, feeling the hard wood crack onto bone and tissue. He drew nearer to Tielvo, seeing with satisfaction that his look had changed to one of alarm, before a sharp pain lanced through his knee, causing him to stumble and fall, and almost lose his grip on the rolling pin, which was wet with his sweat. Another blow hit his back, forcing him down further, despite his mind yelling at his body to get up and keep moving. A reflex caused him to duck his head, and he felt a heavy wooden stick passing closely by. As he ducked, he caught one last look at Tielvo and saw with resentment the contempt return as he stepped back from the fray. Nehlo gasped as a kick caught him on the side, almost tipping him over, but he grimaced and resisted the movement, drawing his legs and arms up to protect himself. He heard a shout that he recognized to be Tam's and wanted to warn him away but was too weak to move and help. He watched as Tam fought desperately, but despite the flurry of movement, his attacks were weak and each blow with the spoons did little damage. Nehlo felt sick with fatigue and pain but mostly with the shame of lying there, unable to defend himself against those whom he now hated with such strength that somehow it set like stone within him. He heard another shout and saw Marrea approach, her face filled with such anger and steely determination that he felt he had never known her until this moment. She tossed a staff to her brother and without another sound mounted such a ferocious attack with short staffs in each hand that all the men were driven back. Nehlo saw Tam grasp the staff for a second and weigh it in his hands before swinging it fore and aft in short arcs and then suddenly turn and thrust it forward. Nehlo watched men fall with grim satisfaction, some holding their heads, others bent double. A whistle sounded from somewhere, piercing through the fray. Tielvo immediately moved away, drawing his cloak around him and the others followed, some limping or walking weakly. One man lay on the ground near Nehlo, his

145

head bleeding. He felt a touch on his shoulder and looked up to see Tam staring down at him, his face bruised and grimed with muck and sweat.

"Can you stand? That is the watch. They will be here in a moment, and we will be liable for all of this."

Nehlo nodded though he was not sure he could stand at all. He took the hand that Tam proffered and used it to drag himself up, wincing sharply at the pain in his knee and chest. Tam gave him the staff to lean on and he half walked, was half carried across the square and out into the streets beyond. He was dimly aware of others following, but they walked on till they thought they had put enough distance between them and the square. Nehlo sank down gratefully against the wall, enjoying the cool of it on his aching back, his mouth parched and sore while every part of him yelled out for relief.

Looking up he saw Tam hug Marrea, who then pulled back for a second to examine his face and head with her gaze and hands. Satisfied she looked at Nehlo, and he saw that she meant to do the same for him, but he waved her away gruffly, not wanting to see her concern or feel a pity that would deepen his shame and anger. She nodded briefly, looking disappointed, but then turned to greet another woman that Nehlo realized had been following them.

"This is not quite what I had in mind for the evening, but this is my friend, who I wanted you both to meet. That is, if she still wants to get to know two boneheads who can't seem to avoid getting into brawls."

"And need you to rescue them it would seem."

Nehlo saw Tam look up at the sound of the rich voice and stare intently at the woman behind his sister. She held his gaze, almost laughingly, before Marrea gave her brother a thump on the arm.

"This is my idiot of a brother Tam, and this is Nehlo my near brother. This is my new friend Theresa."

Nehlo wanted to laugh at Tam, who obviously could not pull his gaze away from Theresa, but he realized there was no laughter in him anymore. A deep anger had displaced it and any other emotion that would not help fuel his rage. Anger at Tielvo and all he represented, anger at a college that preached so much about principles but failed to act accordingly toward himself and Tam, and anger at Tam, who seemed to be embracing the college and all it stood for, despite its blatant flaws. Anger at his parents and, strongest of all, anger at himself for being humiliated by his enemies. Nehlo vowed that never again would he be in that position. He managed a bleak smile before closing his eyes as a sudden flash of pain in his head reminded him that he felt terrible.

Chapter 29

Marrea knelt holding Owen's hand, feeling the slight but weakening pressure that he exerted. Earlier in the night he had become distressed, and Anna had called for her. Together they had soothed him with comforting words and caresses, holding cold cloths to his forehead to ease his fever. Anna had crushed some herbs and put them under his gum, and they rested there, easing his distress. He had been quiet since then, but his breathing was ragged, and apart from periodic twitching, he lay still. Anna knelt at the other side of the bed, her gaze fixed upon his pale face, which did not now register any response or acknowledgment of their presence. Marrea felt certain he was dying, the fever now overcoming his reserves and laying waste to his weakened body. They stayed, taking the place of his mother, who could not come to him. Anna and Simeon were not even sure that his parents knew where he was or that he was nearing death. As the hours passed, she tended him as best she could, guided by Anna's knowledge and intuition. She watched his breathing become slower and felt his hands become colder until eventually there was no return of pressure. She held his hand until long after his last breath had left him and his eyes had become blank and unseeing. Eventually, Anna stirred and stood, slowly and painfully, her face looking worn and tired. Motioning to Marrea, they tended him one final time, cleaning and dressing him so that he looked as loved in death as he had been in life.

She looked at him one last time now that their vigil was over. She thought back to that night and remonstrated with herself for not moving sooner; he would be still alive if she had not been so cautious. She felt partly responsible for his death and her guilt mixed with sadness for his parents. She had never wanted children, content in her role as counselor and aunty to Tam's growing children. Her thoughts turned to them now, and she felt a catch in her throat as a tear sprung to her eye. She wiped it away quickly and took a few breaths, smiling sadly to Anna before turning and leaving the room quietly.

The mood the next day was sober. Everyone felt Owen's death. It was almost as if the success of everything had hinged on whether he would live or die; his death was the marker determining whether it had all been worth it. Those who had been freed from jail were now in safe houses throughout the city, which was awash with rumour. No one knew quite what had happened in the castle except those in the room, but everyone knew that change was coming. But Owen would not see it.

Simeon had been bringing in news each day. The most immediate response to the events at the castle had been a restriction of movement throughout the city. Armed guards were stationed at all the major intersections, and after the business of the day, no one was allowed out of their homes. The talk was that her ladyship had died, but there was no sadness at her passing. Most had never had any dealings with her at all, and those who had had feared her rather than respected her. Her husband lived, they said, and was going to take full control. The other nobles waited and maneuvered, and the people tried to live and work and eat and sleep. Restricted in movement, they contemplated the change that was coming. They hoped for better things to come but change, they kept reminding each other, was not always good.

Marrea sat at one end of the table with Tam and Simeon on one side and Seth and Angie opposite to them. Anna was pale and tired, having been up all night and frequently the previous night; she had insisted that she would rather keep busy and sleep at the normal time, so they had let her prepare the evening meal, and she now sat at the other end of the table. Marrea looked quickly at Tam, who was also tired despite it being the third night since their attack on the castle. She knew that he had not slept well, the image of the dying woman and the agonized husband returning to him when he closed his eyes. He had also started to fear the taints in his mind, which pulsed strongly. He did not think they would overcome him in his sleep, but the worry of it stopped him from truly resting. Marrea was concerned for him, fearing he would not be able to keep the bonds at bay, yet fearing also what lay ahead of them. She did not often pray, her faith being less sure than her brother's, but now she silently asked the Creator to strengthen him. The others round the table fared better, though they too bore the mark of the strain of recent events and the ongoing uncertainty.

Eventually, Simeon raised his hand.

"To Owen," he said simply, and brought his hand down heavily onto the rough wooden table.

Marrea raised her hand with the others and the table vibrated to the strong blows that fell on it as they said Owen's name. There was a deep, contrasting silence for a moment as each reflected, their eyes downcast. Simeon stood and replenished their glasses with weak ale, allowing everyone to speak of other things.

"What news from the city today?" Tam asked Simeon quietly.

"Much the same. Things carry on. People I speak to are hopeful of positive change but scared to hope for too much. It all depends on who now leads the city."

"Any news from the castle?" ventured Marrea.

"Just that Malzorn lives. It may be that he will cling to power." As he spoke, he looked at Tam, seeking to gauge his response.

Tam returned the look for a second before lowering his head and speaking slowly. "I don't know if he will or not, but if he does, he will be a different man. I know that for a certainty." He had already explained what had happened that day and what it took to reject Nehlo's bonding. "He may be your best option at present, until things settle down."

Simeon grunted. He obviously struggled with the thought that the person who had been the source of so much harm could change to such an extent that he be allowed to stay in power, even if he miraculously now started to work for the good

148

of the people he had once suppressed. She understood their fears and questions, but from what she understood of the bondings and what she had gleaned from her brief contact with the ones in Tam's mind, she was confident that Tam was right.

"What of you and Marrea?" Seth asked. Marrea had noted the change in Seth since the castle. He was no longer suspicious, though he was questioning, uncertain even.

Tam shared a look with her before replying.

"We need to move on to the capital. As soon as possible now. Nehlo will know something has happened and will now have time to prepare. I need to face him before that gets any harder."

"And can you defeat him or kill him?" Kayla asked. She had been hardened by her experience and her anger often surfaced. Seth was a softening presence, but he was only just starting to learn how best to help her.

Marrea could see Tam trying to be gentle with her. "I honestly don't know. I certainly used to be his equal."

"More than that," she broke in, suddenly wanting them to understand what her brother was, or at least had been, capable of.

"But a lot has changed since then for both him and me," Tam continued after only a slight hesitation.

"You are too bloody soft!" Kayla spat out, her anger overcoming her. "You had a chance to kill that bastard in the castle and you did not take it and you will not have the strength to kill Nehlo, even if you get that far. We are wasting our time with you."

Marrea's hand tightened on her glass, her anger stirred. She wanted to speak, but her brother motioned slightly with his hand to forestall her. With difficulty she loosened her grip and forced herself to be calm. Kayla's words hung in the air, no one knowing what to say in response. Seth looked apologetic but not clearly in disagreement with what she had said. Anna and Simeon looked pensive, not wanting to see more bitterness and division. Her first anger settling, Marrea now felt pain and embarrassment for Tam. He looked down at his glass for a long moment before speaking.

"I understand what you say, and you may be right in some ways. But I believe showing mercy ultimately leads to healing and less of this pain that you are seeing around you now. But I know that my words are weak and that you cannot see the truth of what I say. My only answer is that everyone, you, me, even Nehlo, needs at least the chance to turn around and change when they have gone the wrong way. Lord Malzorn took his, and I must respect that."

Simeon and Anna looked thoughtful, but Kayla snorted in anger. "You have no right to say that. You do not know what he has done and the harm he and all like him have caused. They do not deserve any of your mercy." As she spoke, she allowed her final word to be filled with as much disgust as she could summon. "It is weakness, not mercy, to never execute judgment where it is needed."

Tam stood suddenly and leaned forward, his hands flat on the table. His voice was hard and penetrating, beating down Kayla's fury, who cowered back involuntarily. His sudden anger shocked Marrea, catching her off guard.

"You say weakness! You do not know of what you speak, and you have no idea the extent of my anger and sadness at all that Nehlo has done. But that can't remove the need for mercy or what else is there? Only cycles of discord and violence."

Tam stayed standing for a moment, seeming to loom over them all. Taking a deep breath, he lifted his hands off the table and sat slowly but his eyes remained focused, his face tense. Marrea could see him trying to control his emotions before he spoke again and when he did so, his voice was more quiet but still firm.

"And mercy now does not mean he will never face justice for what he has done."

Kayla stared at him for a long moment, as if seeing him for the first time, before turning abruptly and walking from the room. Seth sat for a second, clearly torn, but eventually stood and followed her, casting a confused look back at Tam and Marrea as he left. Simeon and Anna both kept their seats. A long silence followed. It was Anna who broke it by standing and bustling around in the kitchen, making tea and tidying away some dishes, which allowed for the discussion to turn again to the task in hand.

"When do you plan to leave?" Simeon asked quietly.

"It is best that we leave in the morning. We can slip out of the city when all the workers in the fields and villages leave."

Simeon nodded. "We will make sure you have provision for the journey. You have horses?"

"Outside the city, hopefully still safe."

"Good, we will make some packs for you. If you go out the west gate, it will be easier I think. I can show you the way."

Tam thanked him, but Simeon waved this away.

"I don't know what will happen here once you are gone but there is the possibility of change for the better now, which we did not have but days ago. I know that you mean well and that you will do what you think is right when you get to the capital. I just pray that whatever that is, it turns out right for the rest of us."

With that, he got up to help Anna. Marrea and Tam also rose and went downstairs to the room that normally served as Simeon's drinking house. It stood empty now, Simeon having closed it until some form of normality returned to the city. Marrea wanted to talk to her brother, to find out the truth about how he fared; an outburst like she had just seen was so unlike him that she almost felt afraid. But Tam spoke first.

"I am sorry Sister, but I cannot talk now. I know that there is much for us to discuss, and we will talk on the way."

Marrea nodded reluctantly and gave him a brief hug. The discussion around the table had gone on well into the night, and Marrea was weary. Two pallets had been laid out in the room for her and Tam, but sleep did not come quickly to her. She kept turning over in her mind all that had happened. She wished she could leave, go home and take Tam with her, but she knew that was impossible. They had to go forward, but she had never felt so weak or unable to meet the task they faced. They were committed now by more than their own purpose; too much had changed and too many lives had been affected for them to be able to turn back now. They had to succeed but the thought kept recurring that the cost she and Tam might ultimately have to pay would be too great to bear.

150

The next morning they rose and packed in silence. They travelled light with only their cloaks, cooking utensils and a set of spare clothes in their packs, so this did not take long. On moving through the house, they found Simeon and Anna waiting for them in the kitchen. Anna had prepared hot food with hot water and honey to drink, which they took gratefully before making their departure. Anna gave them both a warm hug, while Simeon waited at the door. Neither Seth or Kayla were there, which pained Marrea.

They walked briskly through the city streets with Simeon leading the way. It was busy despite the early hour with people going to their work outside the city or to the bigger houses in the city itself. As they traversed the city, Simeon reported the news filtering through of Malzorn regaining control and ordering the lifting of restrictions and the return of the guards to their barracks. He was inviting anyone with a grievance to tell it to new special commissioners that he was installing in each area of the city. Few trusted him though and most reckoned it to be a trick. If he genuinely meant to heal the wounds of the past, building the requisite trust was going to take time. They passed a few of the guards who had been left on patrol, but they paid them no attention amid the flow of people moving toward the western gate. As they neared it, Simeon slowed, unsure how to take his leave. Tam reached out his hand, which was grasped and held tightly for a second. Then Simeon turned and gave Marrea a brief but warm hug. No words passed between them, but just as they were about to leave, they heard Simeon's name being shouted. Turning they saw Seth running toward them, carrying a staff in his hand and a pack on his back.

"Sorry, I meant to catch you at Simeon's, but Anna said you had come this way. I have something to give you both. They are not much, but I worked on them all last night so they would be ready."

He handed Tam the staff, which he took and held lightly in his hands. Made of hard wood, it had been turned beautifully by Seth to allow for a thinner area at the centre, where it would be gripped, and for perfect weighting and balance. Each end of the stick had been covered in brass, and etched into the handle area were the words, "All that I have to give."

"It is a rich gift. It will be a support to me, and I will treasure it." Tam reached over and gripped Seth's arm tightly with his hand.

Seth nodded, his eyes a little moist. He then reached into his pack and brought out two smaller staffs, once again turned from hard wood. Marrea took them and held them for a second in each hand, appreciating their weight and balance. Each narrowed at one end to form a handle, perfectly fit for her hand, and was engraved with the same message. She slipped them into her own pack and gave Seth a hug, which initially caught him by surprise but which he then returned.

"Thank you. I know Kayla can't see it now, but she will come to see what you are trying to do. And I will never forget what you did for her and us."

Marrea smiled and saw Tam do the same. They both turned and walked toward the gate. In the crowd pressing through the gate there was nothing to distinguish them to the cursory glance of the guards. Soon they were outside the walls and walking round the city towards where Tam had left his horse some days before.

Chapter 30

The flat fertile plains had fallen far behind them over the past three days of travel as they climbed into the hills. Ahead of them, in the distance, the jagged outline of a mountain range rose up into the sky. These marked the boundary of their small country. Finn had never been to the mountains, and he suddenly felt a yearning to explore their vast expanse and take in the cold, pure air. He had never met anyone who had been into them, and as far as he knew, no one lived there. Having borne the responsibility of this group for many days now, he felt ready to break out and be on his own. Just then his gaze fell on Zoe, and he allowed it to linger for a moment, watching the serious face, her eyes betraying a sadness that often came over her in unguarded moments. He looked away quickly in case she happened to see him staring and wondered how in such a short space of time he could find himself thinking so much about someone. Would she come with him when this was all done? His contact with women outside the guards was limited; he knew she liked him well enough, but he was pretty sure his feelings for her were a lot stronger than that.

The road wound its way slowly up toward the narrow valley that led to Ardvastra. The land was rocky, but patches of land had somehow been cleared in places to create the small farms that had grown up along the road. The group had reduced to about half its original number as one by one the former prisoners returned to their homes, which had now come within reach. Most of them were fit enough to walk the short distances to their homesteads or their villages. Finn had done what he could for them now, but he still felt the anxiety and uncertainty of their not knowing if their families were still there. Some of his guards had gone with them, having formed attachments along the way. No one wanted to continue as a guard or soldier now, and for most, the capital held only the threat of being recognized and reconscripted or arrested for a deserter. The rest of the group needed to get to their homes in the capital and that was where he felt pulled to go as well, much like Zoe and her men.

He had thought over what he might do when they finally made it to Ardvastra. He had no family there, or anywhere that he knew of. The guards had been his life for so long that it was difficult to imagine what life beyond looked like. For the first time in many years, he was not sure what to do. Since Tam had turned everything upside down, he had just taken the steps in front of him that seemed right at the time but soon, for better or ill, there would be no clear path and he would have to make a new life. The thought filled him with a mixture of excitement and anxiety, and he wondered again what Zoe's plans might be when this was all over. "Fool," Finn muttered to himself and gripped the reins a little tighter as if to discipline his errant thoughts. They were not going to reach the valley today, so he started to look for somewhere suitable to make camp.

Later that evening, Finn joined Zoe's group seated near their fire. He had already been round his men and the rest of the group. He had started to genuinely care for them, and he wondered if this was what it was like to be a leader; to hurt if they were hurt and to want the best for them, almost like a parent. Zoe smiled up at him as he approached and made room for him in the circle. He sat with them for a while, listening to the banter flowing back and forth and enjoying just being there and not having to talk. When he got up to leave to check on the guards he had posted, he realized that he had been in contact with Zoe the whole time and she had not moved away. She turned as he rose, and he met her gaze and for a second found himself looking at her intently before he remembered where he was and pulled himself away with a slightly embarrassed smile. He did not look back as he walked away, so he did not see if she watched him or not.

At mid-morning the next day they entered the valley. It was about a hundred paces wide with steep, almost vertical sides that looked like they had been chiselled out of the hill. Where the rock face ended high above them, the hill sloped upwards, covered with trees. It had always been the first and best defence of Ardvastra, easily defended at either end by a small, determined guard and by arrow fire descending from above on any attacking force that made it through the valley entrance. Finn always felt exposed going through it and had to resist the urge to hurry the group. It took the rest of the morning for them to reach the far side of the valley, where it suddenly opened out to reveal the immense open plain that lay between them and the city.

As they left the confines of the valley, the small group stopped to survey the scene in front of them. It felt to Finn that he had not been here for a long time, but it could not have been more than a few months. Each time before, he had been marching as part of a troop, and either through discipline or fatigue, he had never stopped to enjoy what was before him now. The ground fell gently away from them to the shores of a large lake that stretched all the way to the city, which could just be seen in the distance. Beyond the city, the mountains climbed steeply, their snow-crowned tops just visible, while those in the far distance stood shrouded in clouds. On either side of the lake, the ground was tilled and tended. The different crops formed a patchwork of vibrant colours that contrasted with the deep blue of the lake. Houses belonging to the field laborers dotted the landscape and some boats could be seen on the water. Beyond the fields, the sides of the valley rose steeply into tree-covered hills to give the impression of a landscape isolated from the rest of the world. Protected as it was on all sides, the city had never been taken by force of arms; it had only ever fallen to internal dissent.

At the bottom of the slope, a road wound round each side of the lake. These were well kept and busy with people and the occasional troop of soldiers. At many places the roads bridged the streams that fell down off the hillside into the lake and supplied the fertile land that fed much of the city. They made good time now, a notable feeling of excitement building in them all as the end of their journey, and

153

for many their torment, drew closer. They would not, however, reach the city before the day ended, so Finn drew them to a halt on a flat, untended area, and they made camp. They could see the city walls now and beyond them the city itself rising up the hill. It nestled into the lower slopes of the mountains which seemed to gather the buildings together, at this distance the roofs almost touching in a dense mass, punctuated by towers, the low sun glinting off the domes of the more expensive houses. The imposing tower of the castle at the furthermost reaches overlooked it all but was disappearing now in the low light into the mountain beyond. That night, the talk was all about family, friends and homes that had not been seen for many months or even years. Those who had been imprisoned did not know what they were going to find, and Finn felt worried at what it would be like for them if their hopes of family waiting for them were to be dashed after so much suffering. The mood was bright and cheerful though and many a toast went round and many a plan made about what they would do when they saw the first sight of home.

Before the camp retired for the night, Finn went round to each of the prisoners. He counselled them to slip away when they came close to an area that they recognized, but if they should find that nothing awaited them and they had nowhere else to turn, he suggested an inn where he would be staying. He had no idea what he would do if many came, but he did not have the heart to take them this far and leave them friendless now.

The next day as they neared the wide-open gates of the city and Finn saw the guards, he had a sudden pang of fear that word would have reached the city of what had happened at the mines and that they were walking into a trap. He had mulled over this frequently on their journey and had decided the risk of them being recognized or even searched for was low, and for many of them there was no real alternative. Now though, when the moment had come, he wondered at the folly of thinking they could just walk back into the city where they had either served as soldiers or been arrested as enemies. He looked round reflexively for Zoe, but by agreement she and her men were entering separately and in ones and twos so as not to attract attention. He looked quickly round the group that he was in but despite his sudden fears, he could see that there was nothing different to mark them out from the many others that entered and left in the middle of the morning. Finn knew that the gates were closed only if word came from the valley of impending attack and that had not happened within living memory, so the guards were relaxed in their attitude and barely paid any attention to the mass of people passing by them. Finn rode on and the carts trundled along behind him, and before he knew it, they were inside the city walls and going up the main road toward the centre.

The main thoroughfare was broad, well paved and swept clean. On either side were tall buildings, all built of the light-pink rock that was particular to the city and its environs. They were well cared for, and each, with shutters coloured differently from the other, gave a sense of vibrant individuality. Along the wide road were stalls selling everything that travellers could want after a long journey. The sudden noise of people shouting and selling was momentarily disorienting, but Finn quickly settled into its familiarity and the pleasure of a homecoming. A little further in, the number of sellers thinned and the street was lined with trees. The nobility lived here, and Finn could see the domes and spires of their homes and the main castle rising up at the rear of the city, near its highest point.

He turned away from that, however, and took to the narrower streets. From these came the sounds of normal business and family life as shops and sellers gave way to homes and tradesmen's workplaces. Tall buildings still lined the roads, and it was not unusual for each three or four story house to be home to a number of different families. It was much darker in these streets, which were in permanent shadow and without the warmth of the sun's rays. The smell of cooking and people living in close proximity struggled to escape the close confines, and often the streets were lined with rubbish. Children and animals ran around, most thin, poorly and scruffy, but their liveliness helped dissipate his own fears. He dismounted and, leading his horse, made his way slowly through the city, keeping to the side roads and alleys, not stopping or looking back as the remaining members of the group slipped away to their homes. He had made his goodbyes the previous night. He need not have taken this precaution, however, as no one paid them any attention and here, in a city this big and populous, it was easy to disappear and become anonymous. Now that he was in these familiar streets, he wondered if he could also just disappear, find a part of the city away from the soldiers and the nobility, learn a trade and just live out a simple life. No doubt he could, but he was not sure that Tam was finished with him yet or whether he had finished with Tam. And then there was the question of Zoe, but he tried not to think about this as it complicated and confused the future even more. The inn that he had chosen was well away from the main streets, and by the time he reached it, he was tired and footsore. Of the group, only four of his own guards remained, all with long-standing service like himself and without anywhere better to go. They all went inside, but Finn carried on a bit further to a trader that he had heard about. He had grown fond of the horse, but he had no means to keep it in the city and it brought attention to him. It was a fine animal, though now showing the mark of many days on the road without proper attention. He bargained hard and got something close to a reasonable sum. As he slipped the bags from the saddle that contained his share of the stones, he spoke to it and it nuzzled him. After the long march and all the partings, the seeming forlornness of the animal as he walked away was almost too much for him.

He nodded at the bartender when he walked into the inn. He knew him well from previous trips to the capital, and more importantly, he knew that he was a discrete man, if somewhat garrulous on first acquaintance. He took a table at the far end of the bar with his back to the wall, where he could see the door. The bartender came up to him with a large jug of ale and some bread and cheese, which he placed on the table with a smile and some chatter that Finn paid little attention to. It was the kind of place where the choice of food was limited, but the ale was cool and the bread still warm from the oven. Finn enjoyed it after the days on the road with much coarser fare. As he ate, he watched Rob and Keiron at the bar, talking loudly with some people they had met. He did not worry that they would say anything untoward; they had been with him long enough and he trusted their good sense.

As he finished his meal, Zoe walked in, followed by her men. She looked around and, on spotting him, walked over, her men moving toward the vacant tables nearby.

155

She smiled at him as she sat beside him. "Nice place."

Finn shrugged. "My kind of place. Out of the way, clean enough."

"You alone?"

Finn shook his head and nodded toward the bar, where Rob and Keiron were still engaged in conversation. "I think most folks have got home, but I will stay here for a day or two to make sure."

He was aware of her turning to look at him, but he kept his gaze on the door. "I think you have done enough for them. What next for you?"

Finn thought for a second before answering. "Not sure. I think Tam will turn up here soon enough, and I want to be here when he does. And then ...," he tailed off, suddenly conscious of all the thoughts that he had been having about her. He felt his face redden and looked down, not sure what to do with his embarrassment. When he looked up, Zoe was looking round the bar, giving no hint that she had been aware of his discomfort.

Just then the door opened again, and Will pushed his way in. Finn looked at him in surprise and sudden sadness. There could only be one reason for his arrival. On seeing him, Will walked over, his eyes fixed on Finn's, unconscious of those around him. When he reached the table, he stood, suddenly uncertain, the hope that had sustained him till now having given way to grief. He sat down heavily and put his head in his hands. No one spoke. Finn reached out a hand and placed it on Will's shoulder.

"No one. None of my family was there." His voice broke as he talked, and he wept quietly into his hands. Finn squeezed his shoulder, waiting.

"Was anyone there?"

Will looked up, his eyes wet. "Another family, people I did not know. They said my wife and children left over a year ago and that they have not seen them since. I asked around but no one knows where they went."

He again went silent, his gaze on the table, but the tears did not return. Finn looked at Zoe, whose face mirrored Will's own sadness.

"Does your wife have any family that she might have gone to?" she asked softly. "Or any friends?"

Will looked up and thought for a second. "Her family live at a great distance and she never really spoke of them, so I don't think she would have gone there. And the only friends we had were where we lived, and they have not seen her."

He lapsed back into silence. The noise in the bar seemed very distant as Finn looked at him. He had been through so much and now, finally, this looked like it was going to break him. Finn could not think of anything to say or do, so he and Zoe just sat with him, so that he was not alone in his despair.

Chapter 31

Marrea watched Tam as he ate. They had chosen to climb the hill and move away from the lake, and from where they sat they could just see the outline of some of the laborers' cottages beneath them and smoke curling upward from the rooftops. They could also see some of the lights from Ardvastra, half a morning's walk ahead of them.

Tam was tired, but he had taken care to not overtly show it as they walked and rode together over the last few days. By unspoken consensus, they had not spoken at all about what lay ahead or about what had happened before. They had initially enjoyed tales about Tam's children, laughed together about their own childhood and spoken fondly of his wife Theresa. Marrea had no family, but she was such a constant part of Tam's family that she very much viewed them as her own, and the feeling was mutual. She had played a part, many years before, in introducing Tam to his wife and had rejoiced with them at the birth of each child. She had nursed many a sore knee and bruised head as their children grew and been a source of counsel when they started to approach adulthood. But these memories had stirred in Tam a sadness that he had been unable to hide, and the conversation had gradually stilled. His usual energy had left him, and Marrea knew it was the constant effort of keeping the bondings at bay, of preventing their takeover of his personality. She shuddered to think what would happen if he fell under Nehlo's control, but she trusted him to manage his burden; he had always found the reserves before, and she was confident he would again. She just worried about what it was costing him to do so, and she hoped fervently that he would be able to withstand what was ahead of him. He looked thinner, his eyes a little more sunken, his skin a little greyer, his form more stooped; much of it was very slightly marked but obvious to her eyes. He was silent as he ate, and his gaze repeatedly turned to the city in the distance. Deep in his own thoughts, the look on his face gave Marrea more disquiet than usual. She got up and put a little more wood on the small fire that they had made to ward off the chill of the night air. He looked up as she moved and smiled at her, and then laughed a little as he saw her quizzical and concerned expression.

"I am okay Marr. I just feel a bit heavy about what lies ahead."

She nodded but did not answer. She knew that he wanted to explain and that he would, in his own time and way. He looked at the fire for a moment, his hands outstretched to enjoy its warmth.

"I feel the weight of these bondings in my mind all the time now, and it feels that if I even relax my concentration for a second, they will consume me." A stab of worry pierced her, which he saw but waved away. "It is fine for now. I can contain them. The question is what happens when I meet Nehlo."

He paused and looked at her for a second before turning back to look into the fire again. Marrea felt tense, not wanting to hear what he had to say but knowing she had to.

"Is there no other way?"

"It is why we are here; to try and bring him home. Or at least offer him the chance. And we have a chance to undo some of the injustice and suffering he has inflicted on these people."

"I know, but what can you say that will convince him? He has gone so far and changed so much. There can be little remorse or regret, surely?"

Tam shook his head slowly. "I don't know. It is so long since I have seen him, and all that I hear and see makes me think that this is bound to fail and is folly to even try, but maybe second chances are always offered a bit naively?"

"Will he even know you?"

"Have I aged that much sister? In truth, I don't know. I look different with the years and then this changes me a bit," he answered, stroking the rough beard that had grown up over the weeks. "That may be test enough of whether there is any of our old friend still there or whether he is too far gone down the path he chose."

"And will you tell him who you are?"

Tam was silent for a few moments before answering. "I don't know. If it will help, maybe. Part of me thinks it is better if I don't; it has been so long, and our last parting was cold. It may make him less likely to listen."

Marrea pondered this for a few moments. She could not imagine Nehlo failing to recognize her brother, but she had come to accept that he was very different from the boy and man she had known. It seemed that the bitterness and hurt, which had already begun when she had known him well, had deepened over the years and had now taken too strong a hold.

"But surely he will be able to sense your ability or even his bondings?"

"Not if you help me to hide them. You have always been good at that. That is maybe a good reason I can't reveal myself to him as he would look hard to find my ability, and then he would surely find it, and his bondings, no matter how hard I try to mask them. Then he will know the threat he faces and will react to defend himself by almost certainly lashing out. Then any hope of reconciliation will be broken. Conversely, if he finds nothing when he searches, he will never believe it is me no matter what I say. I don't think he will search too assiduously if I go to him with my power veiled and my identity unclear. He could never understand why we did not vaunt our power more. I think that is one of the things that ultimately drove him away."

"And what then? If he doesn't know you and doesn't want to change?" She asked softly, but she was not prepared for his response. Tam slumped slightly, his head dropping but his hands and shoulders tightening, making him seem somehow smaller than normal. He breathed deeply, struggling to master his emotions. When he finally turned to her, his face was contorted by such pain, fear and remorse that she almost shrank back from him. Instead, she reached forward and gripped his hand, feeling with relief the return of pressure.

158

"I can't fight him Marr." His voice was strained, and he almost gasped the words out. "I can't as I don't have the strength to keep these bondings at bay and defeat him as well. I have known this since I was at the mines, where someone much less powerful than him almost bested me." He smiled weakly, painfully.

Marrea did not want to ask the obvious next question, fearing that even in the asking it would make the event more certain, so it hung between them, teasing them both mercilessly. She gripped his hand even more fiercely.

At last he spoke again, his voice less strained but more resigned and quiet. "I have been starting to understand that he has invested much of his power in these bondings, in an almost tangible, physical way. He took a risk in doing so, dividing his power in this way, as it must have left him weaker, more exposed. He could not have expected someone to take the bondings, and he ensured that they, and the power they contained, would return to him if the bearer was killed." He fell silent for a moment and stared intently into the fire. When he spoke again, his voice came slowly and with effort. "I think if the bondings die, the power they contain could die with them. Maybe all of his power to bind people, but that might be hoping for too much."

"But there is no way for us to destroy the bondings?" It was more than a question, almost a plea. Marrea gulped down a sob that rose suddenly and almost overwhelmed her. "The only way would be for you..." She could not say the words, the thought was too painful.

Tam nodded, understanding her unspoken words. "It may be the only way Marr, the only way to scourge away this evil. There might be another way though, that I can't see at the moment. We can figure it out together. How I hate this evil and what it does to people. I would do much to get rid of it."

"Surely someone can defeat him? If we get help. Maybe none of this needs to happen?" Her voice was so quiet and weak that she was unsure she had even spoken aloud, but Tam shook his head in response.

"I don't think anyone is strong enough, and it may cost many lives. He has gone so far. And I still hope that I can convince Nehlo to return with us. Others may not give him that chance. You know what they thought of him, even from the start. He may wish to return; he may be sick of this life that he has fashioned, though that seems unlikely."

As he spoke, he looked at her beseechingly, his normally resolute features almost fragile and weak, and she saw a father tasting the bitterness of possibly not seeing his sons grow into the men they would become, and a husband feeling the embrace that was never meant to be the last. She loved him then more strongly than she thought possible, and she ached for him in almost equal measure. After a long pause he spoke again, his voice more measured, his features more resolute and circumspect.

"I have been thinking a lot these last few days. I have had so much to be thankful for; more than anyone could expect really. Certainly, more than I ever expected back when we were kids. And the more I think of it, the more I feel for Nehlo, despite all he has done and become. Do you remember? Every step he took seemed to meet with difficulty and life just never seemed to give him anything. Maybe I would have done the same as him, been the same, were it not for the good things the Almighty has given me. I don't think it means he should not face justice if he does not seek clemency, but I think we must give him a chance."

Marrea thought back over their life with Nehlo, recognizing the truth in what her brother said. She remembered his hurt, so often masked in proud distance, and his growing questioning and mistrust of everything they learned and, ultimately, of the people around him. And where growing knowledge had led to faith and purpose for Tam, Nehlo's growing scepticism had led to disillusionment and ultimately to separation.

"I can see that but following what you believe now is leading you full circle, back to Nehlo and possibly to one of you not..." Her throat caught, stifling her words. She took some breaths before continuing. "How can that be right for you, serving as you have all these years?"

Tam did not answer immediately but nodded thoughtfully. "Back in the tower, I was close to death and somehow at that moment it all made sense. Life, the creator, these gifts we have been given, the knowledge that I had a task to finish, that I was not meant to die there. But more than these things, I have come to understand that some evil cannot be defeated by strength of arms, or even through negotiation, but only by sacrifice. I suppose like the flower's bloom dying away each season to make way for new growth the following year, sometimes there has to be loss to allow for greater gain." He fingered the writing on his staff, tracing again the words 'All that I have to give.'. "Seth helped me to see this, and Owen too."

Marrea nodded, slowly. She could feel some understanding building in her, but when she tried to grasp it and fit it more concretely in her mind, it eluded her. She wondered what she would do in his place. Would her belief in a creator who valued service over strength, sacrifice over dominion, stand up in the face of this? It made her evaluate where she stood and realize that she was uncertain. She wanted to believe that service and sacrifice could break the cycle of evil, as it gave purpose and meaning to what others had suffered and what she and Tam might have to endure, but what if it was not true? Would Tam's sacrifice then be worthless? She knew, though, that Tam was resolute in following this path wherever it now led and whatever the cost, and just as clearly, she knew that she would do all she could to help him.

The next day, they stayed where they were, in view of the city but far from the noise and bustle of the people moving to and from it. Under Marrea's tutelage, Tam practiced inverting and submerging his power deep in his subconscious to try and completely hide it. At the same time, he pushed the bondings back, confining them with walls of his power, so that he was unable to sense their tainted pulse anymore, even when he searched for them. In doing so, however, he had to relinquish the use of his power, which would allow the bondings to the surface once more. Marrea probed his mind from time to time until she was satisfied that she could no longer sense any power in him. In part he was relieved as the loss of his power, and the unfamiliar sense of vulnerability that accompanied this, was mitigated by the relief of freedom from the taint, and he felt a wholeness that he had not felt for a long time. With that came a renewed sense of calm and resolve.

Chapter 32

Tam welcomed the breeze although the air it carried was still hot, even after the sun had set and the last of the light was fading. The small ferry that carried him drifted along with the current, the oarsmen content to rest a little at the end of a long and tiring day and to let the boat just glide along rather than strain at their oars. The smell of animal and human waste that rose off the river's edge in the heat combined with the richer smells of spices and meat, that lingered still from the cooking of evening meals in the homes that clustered by the banks, to create a sensation that caught at his throat in a slightly unpleasant way and made him wish even more keenly for the cool, open spaces of his home. In the low light, he could see the banks were busy with people washing their dishes and clothes, and sometimes themselves, in the slightly murky water. The noise of constant chatter interspersed with the laughter and shouting of children, who splashed around near their parents. A constant stream of boats moved up and down the river, carrying those able to pay for their passage and so able to avoid the intense heat and dirt of the streets.

He felt tired but his mind was alert, taking in the scene around him. It seemed like a long time since he had hugged his wife and baby son, but it was not more than six months. His assignment to promote the role of the counselors had turned out easier than expected, and he was returning with an invitation for one of them to become the permanent guide to the elders of the Lakelands who had prior to this kept themselves separate from the events around them. He felt satisfied with his work, confident that the advice he had given was sound and for the benefit of that slightly wild but dignified people. Now he was heading home, and he could not wait to see and hold his wife and see the changes that must have come in his son. He just had this one last visit, to see his friend, before he could give vent to his desire to return home.

Tam stepped lightly from the ferry onto the wooden wharf. He adjusted the pack on his back and the cloak he wore and waved his thanks to the crew, who were busy making the small craft secure. Grasping his staff, he walked up the bank, his feet sticking slightly in the wet earth before he reached the dusty road that lead away from the river. Small one roomed dwellings, made mostly of wood and dried earth with dried clumps of grasses for a roof, lined each side of the road. All around were people, the younger cooking and cleaning, the older just sitting and watching everyone passing by. As he moved further into the city, the road became wider, and the homes changed to clay brick with slatted roofs. Less people thronged the walkway, but he could see lights in the windows, and through the open doors, he could smell food being cooked and hear the noise of family life. A further period of brisk walking brought him near to the centre of the city, where he could see the domes of the palace against the darkening sky lit from below by hundreds of lights, casting them in an ethereal form as the lights shifted and danced. Here the road was paved, though still dirty, and the houses were set back from the road behind walls and gardens.

Walking up to the gates of the palace, he proffered the seal of counselors and was allowed through after a cursory check showed that he had no weapons. He entered a garden of walkways lined with small trees with rough bark. They bore clumps of small fruit among their broad leaves, and small monkeys chattered in their branches. The lights dotted around the garden made it feel even hotter, almost oppressive. Tam wished he could remove his cloak, which hung heavy on him, but that was not seen as acceptable in the palace, so he loosened it as much as he could. He climbed the steps to the large door, which was open but flanked by guards, who at his approach stepped forward with their spears held ready. He held out his seal once again and, after a short moment, entered the palace.

Inside he found himself at the back of a crowd. All were dressed in long robes of light material that looked wonderfully cool to Tam. They faced the front, where there was a raised area with benches along both sides, and at their head, at the furthest distance from the crowd, a cushioned seat, upon which sat the Ruler. He looked pensive, his slightly puffy cheeks shining a little, and his eyes darted between the various people who vied to be heard. The noise was overwhelming at first, but as Tam became accustomed to it, he could distinguish different voices shouting across the room, some placating, others angry. He tried to catch what was being said, but the meaning eluded him in the chaos of noise and accents that were new to his ear. The mood of the people around him was becoming restive with muttering and movement of feet adding to an already tense atmosphere. Tam thought about leaving again; he had no official business to conduct, and whatever was happening, it was of no immediate concern to him. He made to turn to the door but stopped suddenly, his heart racing and his senses suddenly alive and alert. He could feel someone exerting power. It could only be Nehlo, unless the college had sent another counselor. The shouting at the front of the room stopped, and with it the crowd near him stilled, straining to see and hear what was happening.

Tam leaned forward, looking for Nehlo. He saw someone come forward and talk to the Ruler, but in the gloom behind the ruling seat, he could not make out their features. He felt a slight pulse of power and saw the Ruler nod his head in approval. Then Nehlo stepped forward. Tam had not seen him for three years since their time of training together had come to an end and Nehlo had accepted this posting, much to Tam's surprise. On talking it through, he had understood that Nehlo had just wanted to be away from the college, to leave the tension and belittling that he felt all the time. Nehlo looked much the same but for barely perceptible changes that gave Tam a strange sense of unease. Nehlo's tall, broad frame had always been imposing, but it now seemed to exude an air of dominance, and his face seemed harder somehow. Almost cruel Tam thought for a brief second before feeling ashamed of himself and banishing the idea as ridiculous.

Nehlo spoke softly, but his voice seemed to carry through the room. "Your Ruler has listened to all your points and counter points. He has weighed them all up and has decided."

There was a murmur at that. Tam knew that among this people the Ruler was only the head among supposed equals. He felt Nehlo was treading on dangerous ground.

Nehlo paused and looked around the room slowly. No one met his eye and gradually the murmuring ceased. "He has decided," he repeated with emphasis, his voice still quiet and smooth, "to award the land and all its yield to the hill clans."

There was a brief silence before shouting erupted all around him. Some people near Tam turned away in disgust.

Tam looked at Nehlo to see how he would react. He saw a smile briefly play across his lips before sensing power surge around him again. Tam felt pressure building round his head and in his ears and all the sounds became muffled. Caught by surprise, he did not react before hearing Nehlo's voice, sounding soft and as if through a fog, yet reverberating loudly in his mind.

162

"Your Ruler has spoken. The lands will go to the hill clans. You will accept this as you should and pledge your fealty to the Seat."

With an effort, Tam pushed back and reasserted his own control. He saw a brief look of puzzlement on Nehlo's face, who looked round searchingly before their eyes met. Tam was not sure what the initial look conveyed. Was it anger, resentment, fear or embarrassment? It was gone in a second to be replaced by a tight smile. Looking round, Tam saw looks of acquiescence and heads being lowered toward the Seat, and the Ruler accepting them with a look of slight boredom. Nehlo stood until all had done so and then turned and disappeared behind the Seat. Immediately the pressure lifted and normal chatter resumed, but Tam could not hear any dissent or anger. He could hardly comprehend what he had just witnessed, nor could he imagine what Nehlo's reasoning could be for breaking their vows so blatantly and wilfully. Feeling a little lightheaded and sick, he turned and left the hall.

Tam was suddenly glad of his cloak. The evening air was warm and less stifling now, but a chilled feeling coursed through him that he knew was due to worry. He heard a voice calling his name and turned to see Nehlo approaching, a grin on his face, holding out his arms. Tam wondered if he saw some wariness behind the smile which he had not seen before.

"I am so glad to see you. You gave me a shock when I saw you in there."

Tam returned the strong clasp of the wrist. He was confused at the greeting, as if nothing was amiss. He managed a smile. "I am on my way home. I was passing only a day's south of here and thought it would be good to see you. We rarely get the chance now that you have hidden yourself out here."

Nehlo gave him a close look, his smile suddenly becoming strained. "It is far, I know, but I am better here than in Toravaig. Here I am useful, but back there, I am nobody. But enough. Have you eaten? Where are you staying?"

Tam was not sure if he was hungry or not. He had not eaten for hours, but his stomach was clenched tight and rebelled against the thought of food. He shook his head though. "No, I have not eaten. It would be good to eat together and exchange our stories."

"You will have many, I am sure. And how is your lovely wife?"

Tam smiled more warmly. As he spoke of Theresa his wife, his small steading and his son, he felt some of the tension ease away from him, so that by the time they reached an inn, he was ready for food and tucked into the stew with relish. It was hot with spices, and before he knew it, he had to remove his cloak. Nehlo laughed at him with something of his old nature and raised his pint of ale.

"You get used to it after a while. It helps to drink along with it though."

Tam nodded and took some gulps of ale, which was somehow cold despite the warm environment. The two together really was good, and he finished off the plate. He nodded his thanks to the boy who came to clear up the plates and then sat, looking into the tankard of ale, aware that he now had to raise what he had seen with Nehlo. He did not know how to begin, and he could feel his heart beating faster in anticipation of an almost certain confrontation. He wished he had not been there, had just passed by and remained oblivious to Nehlo's actions. Had he done so, even now he would be that bit closer to home rather than facing the prospect of bringing the judgment of the college and their order onto his best and possibly only true friend. Should he? The question disturbed him. What did they owe the college really? Nehlo was right; neither of them were valued or truly accepted, and they were still regarded as interlopers despite their years of training and work. Who would know or care if he just forgot about what he had witnessed, and they just passed the time sharing their experiences? Maybe Nehlo was helping here? How could he know to the contrary, having just arrived and being ignorant of all the *negotiations and possible difficulties that had gone before this evening's meeting? Tam could not see his way clearly. Nehlo was silent as well, and Tam wondered whether his thoughts were similar, but glancing up he saw a slightly sardonic smile play across his strong features, almost like a challenge.*

Tam gathered his thoughts and his resolve. "We need to talk about what happened this eve," he said quietly but firmly.

"Not here," replied Nehlo simply, looking around at the packed inn and standing in a fluid motion. He led the way out of the inn and along the streets, which were dark now and almost empty. Walking swiftly, they passed through the gate in the walls and into the gardens of the meeting hall. Crossing it, but avoiding the paths, Nehlo opened another gate in the far wall, which led down some steps to a stream that was flanked by trees. It was cooler and quiet, except for the gentle movement of the water and the soft noise of insects. Nehlo sat on one of the steps and picked a leaf, which he pulled apart and threw into the water a few feet away. Tam sat next to him looking into the gloom above the stream, where he could make out the trees looming over the far side, glad that they were not facing each other for what must now be said.

"What happened?" He asked quietly, almost to the night.

"You experienced it. You know what happened."

"Why though? Why break all our rules? You know what that means for you? And for us all eventually?"

"Whose rules?" Nehlo sounded suddenly angry, but he checked himself. "You know I always questioned them and that the vow was taken at the start, before I knew more and better. They are not my rules, and they need not be yours. Those fools at the college only follow them when it suits them."

"You don't know that. And even were that the case, it wouldn't justify what you just did."

"What did I do? Got a rabble to agree on something for once, something that might just be for their benefit."

"Theirs? Or yours?"

As soon as the words were spoken, Tam knew he had made a mistake and wished them unsaid. They created a chasm between them that seemed to be almost palpably pushing them apart. Had he meant that? He desperately wanted to say something that would make amends or show that he did not question his friend's motives.

"I'm sorry. I did not mean that." He wondered whether he had spoken aloud, so little were the words able to penetrate the gulf between them. A heavy silence followed.

"You did, even at some small level." Tam could not tell whether Nehlo was angry, surprised or, worse, broken hearted.

"Nehlo, please. What am I to think when I come here to see you and instead find you manipulating decisions like that?"

"You could have trusted me."

"But it is not about trust. Even the best of us don't know what is right for people; that is why we guide only once we have weighed people's thoughts and motives. We don't decide. Morgan himself started out good."

"And who is to say he would have ended badly? We only have old Hardy's word on that, which counts for very little with me. What if he actually knew what was best, was sick of conflict and argument, sick of fools making decisions for people below them by dint of birth, not merit. Here there has been stagnation for generations as they feud and argue blindly."

"How do you know what you decide will be any better for them? Can you see what repercussions there might be? And will you be the one to carry the responsibility of that when it happens?"

164

"It cannot be worse, and I at least have no bias and no favour to seek that might cloud my judgment. And as for taking responsibility, I have always stood to meet what comes. Anything else is cowardly talk."

Nehlo's certainty unsettled Tam; it rocked his own belief in their vows. He had seen enough now in his travels and work to know the right of what Nehlo said. So often bad decisions spawned worse effects for the powerless. Who was he supporting when he helped guide those in power? How could he be sure that the decisions he helped others make were good and wise? But … a thought tugged at him, then grew in intensity. He could not be sure that everything worked out for the best. But he, Nehlo, and others like them, had to be responsible with the gifts they had been given. Ultimately, using their gift to serve, rather than lead by force, had to be better. Otherwise only power and strength would determine everything and this, he knew, led to more conflict and suffering. Feeling more certainty, he turned back to Nehlo.

"I know that you have never stepped back from a fray when you were in the right." He paused for a moment, remembering Nehlo's words about Hardy, his distrust of everything their college tutors had told them. He sought to bring some separation between himself and their tutors, to try and reach common ground with Nehlo. "But you know me too, that my mind is not so easily swayed as to just swallow what Hardy says."

Nehlo was silent, but Tam thought he saw a slight nod from the corner of his vision.

"I have wrestled with these things, to try and find some certainty, something to guide me. Why can we do what we do? Why was anyone ever given this ability, and who determined what it was for? And the only thing I come back to is the beginning. That there is a creator God who is good and that he meant these gifts to be used for good, to serve others as that alone can break down barriers and heal enmity. And I believe everyone is accountable ultimately to the creator, and we, with our gifts, are even more so."

The words almost sounded silly as he gave them quietly to the darkness enveloping them both but in his heart he believed them to be true. Nehlo was quiet for a few moments.

"You still believe that? In a creator, a higher power?"

Tam nodded. "Yes, I have to."

"I can't. I see and feel nothing of a creator. And if he gave this gift, why give it to someone like Tielvo? A spineless, arrogant fool?"

"I don't know. But where else did it come from? And when you harness the air around you, do you not feel something of the power in creation and wonder where that came from?"

"I feel the power and marvel that I can manipulate it and use it, but I do not question further. It is a tool as many other things are. For the use of the one who wields it."

"But that is the point. A tool can be used for good or ill and that is why the boundaries are there. To prevent us using it badly, even if our intent is good."

"Awful things happen either way. And I have experienced enough of them. I have as much chance as any of making good decisions and then at least decisions are made, rather than endless argument that circles around without ever answering real need. Surely your Almighty would be happy with that?"

Tam noted the slight mocking in Nehlo's tone. His friend seemed harder, more intense and less reasonable than he had ever known him. Somehow, this did not shock him as it should; he had seen glimpses of it when Nehlo lost his parents, when he realized the college would never accept him. Tam suddenly felt afraid. Not of Nehlo, but of what it all might mean and what Nehlo might become. With his certainty of purpose and conviction of being in the right, would he ever stop from continuing down a path that could lead to greater and greater wrong?

"Not if the means used were not what he wanted. I think He sees more clearly than us what all the mess means. I don't know why good and bad can result from what we do, I just know that

I think it right that we guide and serve but don't rule, as He means us to. I would not trust myself to do anything more."

"Are we so wrong inside that we cannot trust ourselves to make decisions at least as well as others?"

"I sometimes wonder. I only know my own thoughts and actions, some of which I am not proud of."

Nehlo gave him a questioning look. Tam felt himself colour and stared straight ahead to avoid meeting his eye. He had spoken truthfully, though he knew it sounded insincere.

"And yet you are willing to judge me? You know everything that has happened to me, and you have experienced none of it."

Nehlo's tone was suddenly resentful and angry. Tam felt his own quick anger rise.

"I don't judge you, only your actions tonight, and I question where they will lead. What other option do I have?"

"To leave well alone."

"I wish I had. I could have been happily on my way home, not here with …"

"With what? Or who?"

"This problem."

"There is no problem unless you chose to make it so."

"Of course there is." Tam realized he was shouting in angry frustration but could not help it. "Can I just walk away knowing what you are doing here? Would that be right?"

"Right? There is no such thing." Nehlo's voice was raised in response. "You are either my friend or you are against me like the rest."

Tam felt a coldness suddenly clutch his heart. Had it come to this? Would he have to choose, here and now between his friend and what he had decided to give his life to? A fog seemed to close round him, disabling his thoughts, not letting him work out a way through this.

"I am not against you. I am afraid for you and where this path will lead."

"You of all people know that I loathe sympathy or worry of that sort."

"What then? I cannot leave you here and do nothing. I can't."

"You won't, you mean. So you will take your tales to the college and let them do what they have always wanted and cast me out. And I will lose what position I have built here."

Tam felt pressure building in his mind and looked sharply at Nehlo, who was staring straight ahead. Was he trying to manipulate him? Tam could not be sure and once again he felt fearful. This was not the Nehlo he knew, who would have protected him to the end. He was different, harder, more self-absorbed. Tam focused hard and pushed back against the pressure, feeling his mind clearing. Nehlo turned, his eyes hard.

"I will not allow that to happen." Nehlo's voice had gone eerily quiet. Tam felt an urge to stand and back away, but he resisted it and stayed seated, though he was now tense and fully alert.

"I would hate to see you before the college. But neither can I do nothing. Why don't you leave here? Start again. Promise to abide by our vows and rules. And my home will always be open to you." Tam could hear his voice breaking a little. He hugged his knees, a tight feeling in his throat. Nehlo was silent for what seemed like a long time.

"We can no longer be friends, I think. We will always disagree on this, and I do not want you to be my enemy. I will leave here, but I cannot promise more than that. You will have to accept that, or you can report me to the college and leave me to their justice." The last word was heavy with sarcasm and bitterness, though he had initially started talking with resignation in his voice.

166

Tam felt a tear prick his eye as a deep sadness sank through him to his core. His limbs felt heavy and wooden, his breathing somehow harder. What would become of Nehlo? Tam had his wife and child, his family, his role. He was conscious of how alone Nehlo was, how embittered. And Tam felt he was judging and abandoning his friend when he most needed his aid, but he could not see how he could both help his friend and also stay true to what he now saw as his calling. He almost mourned the day he had been granted a gift that he had never wanted, which had set his and Nehlo's life on such different paths. But he could not relent. Nor could he find the words to respond, so he sat in the silence that settled like a shroud over their friendship.

Nehlo sat in his room, looking out the window into the gloom. He could make out rooftops here and there in the pale, low light of the moon. Some flickering, smaller lights also came from houses scattered randomly through the city, where others must also be awake for reasons he could not surmise. He felt cold, a deep penetrating coldness that would not respond to the cloaks he had put on since returning from his meeting with Tam. He glanced at the cold embers in the firepit at the side of the room and felt an irrational anger that they were providing no warmth. He thought for a second and then reached out with his mind, searching for anyone that he could manipulate. Finding someone he assumed to be a servant who was not in deep sleep, he commanded them to bring wood for a fire. A few minutes later, someone knocked and entered carrying tinder and coals with a lit brier. He noted with slight relish the resentment on the face of the man, who looked tired and careworn. Nehlo realized that he did not care what the man thought of him, and once the fire was lit and burning well, he dismissed him with a brief flick of his hand.

Nehlo pulled his chair close to the fire and stared into its depths. He felt the heat rising up to him, but it failed to eradicate the cold inside. He thought back over everything that had been said with Tam and the final silent betrayal. He wondered now why he had thought Tam would take his part, would fight for their friendship before his commitment to the college. A bitterness rose within him that felt like gall in his stomach; after all they had been through together, after all that Tam knew of what he had endured. Nehlo felt utterly alone. He thought of Marrea, whom he had not seen for the years he had been resident here. He wondered what she thought of him, but a nagging voice, that demanded to be listened to, assailed him, convincing him that she would side with Tam, that she always had, that he was only important to her as Tam's friend and nothing more. With an effort he pushed his thoughts of her away and embraced his aloneness. What need had he of others when he could command anything and it would be done?

He thought of his resolve. He would keep it. He would leave this place and not return. But he would find somewhere else, somewhere he was not known. And he would start again, except this time he would have no reservations, no lingering ties to the vows that he had rejected in theory many years ago and now fully renounced. It strengthened him to make these decisions, to feel that he was keeping his side of a bargain despite it being so tilted against him, and having done so, he felt that he did not owe anything to anybody. There was no almighty being that he had to justify himself before, no friendships that he had to honour, no rules that bound him. He embraced the warmth of the fire and the cold in his core, desiring both and using both the sense of what the world could give him, and his rejection of the need for others, to feed his strengthening sense of purpose. He would leave, and he would never again be subject to anyone.

His thoughts turned to where he would go. Somewhere far enough that he would be free of the college and its interference until he was too powerful to heed their influence, and yet near enough that they would hear and know and be troubled and angry. He wanted them to see his rise and feel their impotence. And part of him wanted Tam to hear of it. He was surprised to feel such venom toward his friend, such bitterness. He realized that part of him wanted Tam to feel the burden of whatever he did next, to feel responsible, as Nehlo knew he would, and to be conflicted, *even pained by it. He did not try to push these thoughts away but rather fed and nurtured them until what once had been hurt grew to enmity, a hatred almost as strong as his love had once been.*

There was only one place that he could go. One place that had been on his thoughts as a focus of yearning but also hatred ever since his parents had left him those many years ago. He resolved to go to Elishadra and there live and rule.

Chapter 33

"We can get him in easy enough but what then?" hissed Cox, his thin face leaning over the table that separated them. He was flanked by two of his men, whom Finn did not know, and as expected there had not been any introductions.

Finn looked at him through the smoky air of the inn's bar. It was quite busy, but most were at the bar. The tables nearby were taken up by what remained of his men, eating their dinner. They looked sufficiently distasteful to dissuade any of the bar's regulars from approaching. In truth Finn did not really know the answer to the question, but neither did he really need to know. Zoe sat beside him on the bench with their backs to the wall, but by agreement she had remained silent during the meeting.

"Tam will take it from there. He has said that all he needs from us is to get him through the outer guard and into the main residences."

"On his own?"

Finn noted the scepticism and did not blame him. He had known Cox for a long time; they had served together in the guard before he had left, suddenly. Cox had never told him why he had gone but Finn had later learned that his parents had lost their business and their home after falling out of favour with Nehlo. Cox had gone with them when they had been forced to leave Ardvastra, but Finn did not know how they had lived. Cox had returned when his parents had died four years later and since then he had gone into private security looking after the homes and businesses of the rich. Business was good now by all accounts, but he knew that Cox still nursed a deep hatred of Nehlo. He was not sure this would be enough, though, to take the risk of losing everything on a man he had never met before this night, on the witness of an old friend in circumstances rather hard to explain.

"No, there are a couple of volunteers who want to go with him. He did not want them to, but they insisted." This troubled him, particularly as one of the volunteers was Will. He had remained shut off and distant ever since the night he had discovered his family had gone. He was eating and drinking, but Finn was pretty sure he was not looking after himself in other ways, and he barely engaged with the people around him who tried to relieve his burden. The only interest Finn had seen him display was when they had spoken about Tam going into the castle, and he had insisted, with animation that Finn had not seen in him before, that he be allowed to go along. Finn worried that the desire for vengeance drove him, or, worse, an eagerness to put himself in a situation where death might easily find him. He put it out of his mind for the moment to concentrate on Cox.

"Tam will be fine. As I said, he has particular skills that will get him in and out again more easily than if he had a hundred men at his back."

Cox cast a quick look to the corner where Tam sat, seemingly unaware that they were talking about him. Finn followed his gaze. Tam was eating, talking to his sister, and in the dim light of the inn, he looked a bit thinner and paler and less ... . He struggled to find the word to describe the impression that Tam had made on him when they first met. Maybe alive was it; someone who just brimmed with life. But Tam now looked as if life had taken its toll. Finn did not understand why, and Tam had said little to enlighten him. And yet Tam's steady conviction in his ability to do what was needed had superseded any concerns Finn might have had about his seeming frailty. He was not entirely sure how Tam and his sister had found them, but he had walked into the inn yesterday and straight up to him. That should have been unnerving but strangely wasn't. He had kind of figured that whatever Tam had done to them all back at the mine, some trace of it still remained and could be sensed by him. He could see Cox weighing Tam up, looking for anything that might show evidence of particular strengths or gifts, but if the expression he wore when he turned back to Finn was anything to go by, he had clearly found little to convince himself.

"Have rumours not reached Ardvastra then of what has been happening?"

"Aye, the news spread fast about a revolt of sorts that happened in Harran, but I heard that it was crushed. My clients were all worried about it spreading here, though that seemed unlikely. There have been rumours more recently about an attack in Harran on Malzorn himself, and that his wife was killed, but they are not widely spoken of. People are rightly a bit cautious about listening to rumours too closely. And none mention Tam."

Finn nodded but left him to draw his own conclusions. They remained quiet for a few moments before Cox spoke again.

"If, and it is a big if, I agree to this, I need to know what he plans to do. I can't risk getting someone caught and this linking back to me, which it would, if I don't have any idea what he means to do and whether it might be worth it to me."

Finn nodded again but did not answer immediately. This was a more difficult question than it seemed. He knew from what Tam had said to him that he hoped to speak with Nehlo, convince him to leave with him and never to return. He was aware of how that would sound to a pragmatic man like Cox, so he hesitated to state it. But, equally, he could not say that Tam intended to kill Nehlo even if he failed to convince him to leave.

"He has assured me that, whatever happens, Nehlo's hold over this city and land will be weakened to a point where he will be vulnerable, perhaps enough for him to have to disappear of his own accord, but certainly weakened to a point where he can no longer rule with impunity or maintain his influence in every facet of life. Maybe even to the point where a challenge might arise against him to take over.

"And you can't be more specific than that? You are asking a lot my friend. And, if as you say, Nehlo is neutered and can be shifted or better still removed completely, what then? I hear of chaos in Halistra. That your man's doing?" He did not wait for an answer, however, before continuing. "My business is good but would be near impossible to maintain if the city descends into chaos."

Finn acknowledged this. "It has been different in other places. Tam is not purporting to be able to sort out all the problems we face or will face, but he can remove the one thing that is getting in the way of true change. That's what he has done before. He does try to steer things a little in the aftermath, but people must then choose what kind of place they want to live in."

Cox smiled, his thin face warming a little. "I am not used to this kind of language from you. You have changed into quite a passionate agitator for change, something I never saw in you before."

"People change," he replied gruffly.

Finn felt Zoe shift slightly at this. He did not turn to look at her though. He had to keep focused on the man in front of him who was the only person he knew and trusted to get Tam to where he needed to be without significant risk or bloodshed.

"Except Nehlo, I would wager!"

Finn's smile in response was tight lipped. "Maybe. From what I have seen Tam do, though, I think we need to give him the chance. Each man and woman here is ready to back him, if needs be in battle."

Cox looked around the small group of Finn's men, some of whom he knew of, and then let his eyes linger for a second on Zoe, who returned his gaze steadily. Finn could sense that she was tense although she looked relaxed.

"Okay," he said, eventually. "But just Tam and one other to guard his back, and someone I know and trust will get him in." He waved down the protest that was starting on Finn's lips. "Just one. If it is as you say and he can handle himself, then having a couple extra men will not make any difference, but it may make it harder to get him in in the first place."

Finn could see the logic in that, but he did not like it. He thought for a second but could see that Cox had made up his mind and was readying himself to leave. He reached out his hand, which Cox grasped tightly. "Okay. Tomorrow night?"

"I will send for him. Just him and one other mind."

"Agreed. The rest of us might stage a small show elsewhere though."

"The less I know the better. I will keep my side."

With that he stood and, followed by his two men, left the inn. Finn stretched his shoulders back to release the tension that had been building in them and leaned back against the wall. He felt nervous all of a sudden, as if he had made a major decision that committed them all to something that was now irrevocably and awfully fixed. Zoe squeezed his hand, noting his sudden apprehension.

"You have done what was asked of you. Tam wants this to happen."

"It feels more like I have helped lay a trap for him that he will not escape."

"I think this is where he always felt his path would lead. He knows what lies ahead and the dangers he faces, and he seems reconciled to that."

Finn nodded but the knot in his stomach did not ease.

171

Chapter 34

Finn glanced at Zoe before knocking on the door. They were standing in the dark hallway outside the room that Tam had taken for lodging. It was at the top of the inn, and they could hear the wind whistling through the gaps in the roof above them, sweeping away any heat that had risen up from the bar below. He was not sure why they had been asked to come and see Tam and judging from Zoe's return look she had not been told either. A soft voice beckoned them in, so he opened the door for Zoe and then followed her in, closing the door behind him.

Inside, Tam was sitting on the only chair, next to a small window which looked out across the neighbouring houses toward the castle. Despite the late afternoon sun, the room was dimly lit and chilly. There was a low bed against one wall and a table against the other, upon which Tam had placed his small kit bag. He smiled as they entered and gestured for them both to sit on the bed. He looked tired but less troubled than he had been when they had last met.

"Thank you for coming. I wouldn't have asked, but that I wanted to ask you both something important."

"We are happy to come. But are you well? You look tired." Zoe looked concerned but Tam looked at her with his steady gaze and smiled gently.

"I am fine. I don't sleep as well as I used to, but otherwise I am well." Zoe nodded but did not look convinced.

"What is it you wanted to ask us?" Finn moved things on as he felt that Tam did not want to focus on himself.

"Something that is really close to my heart. I know I can trust you both. Tonight, I will go to meet Nehlo. I understand that Will can't be convinced to stay behind?"

Finn marvelled at how calm Tam looked when the very mention of what he intended made him feel as if he had no strength in his limbs. "I have spoken to him, and he is adamant he must go with you. He says he has nothing left to live for now and wants at least to help you in this. He used to work in the castle sometimes, and he says he can help you negotiate it. He knows that you may not be able to protect him once you are in, and he accepts that. He denies it, but I worry that he just wants revenge for what has happened to him and that he will be killed seeking it."

Tam nodded slowly. "I would rather he did not come as I may not be coming back, and I would not want him to waste his life needlessly. But if this is what he feels he needs to do, I will not try to stop him."

He stood and looked out the window, not speaking for a few moments. Finn and Zoe waited quietly as obviously he had something else more important to ask them. "You have both met my sister Marrea?" he asked quietly, before turning from the window to see their response. "Aside from my family, she is the most important person to me. If I fail, she will want to finish what I have been unable to do, and she will need help. Can I ask that you and the men and women that are under your command stay with her and aid her?"

Finn looked over at Zoe and could see his apprehension mirrored on her face. "We have accepted that we cannot go to face Nehlo with you, though we would wish to."

"I know, but you can't help me with what I have to do as I am going to try and convince Nehlo to come with me. If I succeed, then I will be fine, but if not then your force of arms alone will not aid me and you will be lost. But even if I don't succeed, Nehlo will still be weakened, and Marrea will try to force him to yield. That is when having greater numbers may help. With your support, she will have a greater chance of success."

Questions arose in Finn's mind again. Why did Tam have to give Nehlo a chance? Why would he not fight him? Why would Nehlo be weaker if Tam failed, thereby allowing Marrea to prevail? He sensed though that Tam did not want to or was unable to explain, and he did not want to press him.

"Perhaps I could come with you, in place of Will I mean?" Zoe's voice was tight and constrained and her suggestion caught Finn by surprise. "I can guard your back much more effectively. Surely you will have a better chance of success or escape with me. Will is a good man, but he is no soldier."

Tam started to reply but then stopped and turned away for a moment. Finn wondered if he saw film of tears in Tam's eyes but when he turned back again, he was composed. "I value your offer more than I can say and truth be told I would feel some security with you by my side. But it would only lead to you being caught or worse."

"Why cannot I take that risk, like Will? The weeks after you left us showed me that I could not rebuild my life in Fraebost. No one, bar John and Katie, ever trusted me. Nor did I deserve their trust. I want to take responsibility for what I have done and to help you rid Elishadra of the evil that ensnared me."

Finn could see the resolve in Zoe's gaze and for a moment, Tam looked uncertain. He paused and looked out of the window towards the castle. Finn felt a tightness in his throat as a sudden fear swept through him that Tam would say yes. He realized that he did not want her to accompany Tam, that it was taking too great a risk and that he feared losing her. When Tam turned back again, Finn could see that he had reached a decision.

"I think I understand you Zoe, but I must refuse." His tone was gentle but firm. Finn let out a long breath, feeling relieved but then a little guilty as he saw how deflated Zoe looked. "It is because you are so trust-worthy and so capable that I ask you to help my sister. Will is coming with me as he feels he must, and I cannot dissuade him. You must trust me now, though. You cannot help me with force, but you can help my sister should I fail. Hers may yet be the heavier burden,

173

and you will ease mine if I know that you share it with her as much as you are able."

"And will she accept our help?" Finn interjected. Zoe flashed him a look that showed her disappointment that he had given in so easily. He had been listening to them closely, however, and could recognize when someone's mind was wholly decided and firm. Tam would not waver and the pragmatic soldier in Finn accepted his request as a command, whether he liked it or not.

A smile broke through the concern on Tam's face. "I doubt it. But I ask you to give it to her nonetheless."

Finn snorted, suddenly amused despite himself. "So you are as bad as each other, and you have landed me in a right mess."

"Knowing my sister, I am afraid so."

"Right then. Deal with what's in front of you I always say. Which is why, Zoe, you have to deal with Marrea."

She choked back an angry retort when she saw the mischief in his eyes. She shrugged, not happy, but with no route to take her discontent.

"Will you eat with us this evening?"

"I am not sure. I may not have the stomach for it," Tam replied, his smile now betraying a little apprehension. This small show of frailty brought a sudden rush of emotion to Finn that surprised him. To cover it he rose and reached out, grasping Tam's forearm strongly and felt the pressure returned. He held it for a few moments before turning to leave. Zoe stood after him and went toward Tam. Reaching up she cupped his face in her hands and looked at him closely, before gently kissing his cheek and walking passed Finn out of the room. She stopped in the corridor and waited for him to shut the door.

"Are we just going to do what he says and leave him to go to Nehlo on his own, with no support?"

Finn took her arm and steered her further down the corridor. "I think we must, but that doesn't mean we do nothing to help him."

In the room Tam still stood where they had left him. His hand went to his cheek where he could still feel the softness of the kiss. He could feel tears welling up in his eyes as his thoughts turned to his wife and the softness of her womanly touch as he left, which he had not thought then may be his last and now doubted he would feel again. He sat down heavily, his strength suddenly failing him, and put his head in his hands. He indulged himself for a moment, allowing his emotions to carry him further into his memories till he almost enjoyed the pain of them. But then he forced his eyes open and looked out once more at the castle and pushed the memories and emotions back to focus on what was in front of him and what he had to do.

Chapter 35

Will and Tam moved quickly so as not to lose sight of the boy who ran in front of them, whose energy spilled out into little jumps and erratic movements. He had appeared at the inn just as it was closing for the night and had asked for Tam. The boy had said little except that they were to follow him without any delay. Will and Tam had already eaten what they could, so they just had to pick up their weapons, in Tam's case his new staff and in Will's a short sword, before a hurried leave-taking. Despite the time he had spent with his sister on their journey, somehow that last farewell had felt rushed, abrupt, as if leaving so much more to be said. He had not wanted to upset her and he wondered now whether he had been warm enough. She would understand, he knew. It was dark and the streets were largely empty save for some men on their way home, most after more drinks than they could properly handle. Some gave them an uneasy look as they jogged past but no one challenged them or followed after them. A slight rain exacerbated the cold, which had intensified in the few hours since the sun had set. The damp soaked into Tam and drove the warmth from his hands. They followed the boy through the narrow streets, skirting round the castle to approach it from another direction, Tam assumed. Eventually the boy slowed to a walk, put his hands in his pockets and whistled a low tune. In response a man stepped out from the darkness of a side alley and beckoned them to join him. Only when they were in the confines of the alley could Tam make out his face and determine that it was Cox himself. He motioned for them to be silent while he kept a watch out into the street for some time. Obviously satisfied that they had not been followed, he turned back to them and produced a strained smile.

"Nice night for it."

Tam shrugged. "I was expecting one of your men."

"Wanted to do this myself. I trust my men, but if what Finn says about you is true, I would rather see you into the castle myself. Don't worry, I scouted this route out myself, so I know it well."

He turned and looked out into the street again before motioning for them to follow him. Very little of the light from the moon penetrated through the misty rain, so Will and Tam kept close to Cox as he moved up the narrow street. After walking quickly through a number of streets, they finally stopped at a dead end. A wall stood before them, at least the height of four of the houses that leaned up against it. It was to one of these that Cox led them before climbing deftly up and onto the flat roof. Tam and Will followed him as silently as they could. Cox quickly moved off again, leading them over the roofs, which were joined together apart from the occasional small pathway that they could jump over. Cox kept close to the wall, sometimes testing the way ahead with his feet before committing himself. Tam could not hear or see anything except the roofs ahead of them and the grey bulk of the wall rising above them, its smooth surface glistening slightly in the damp night air. Occasionally Cox ran his hand over the wall, but what he was feeling for he didn't say. Eventually though he slowed and examined the wall more closely. Moving forward a few more paces he stopped again and then reached up and worked with his hand on the wall above his head until he pulled free a small rock, leaving a well-worn small hole. Once he had done this he sat on the roof, leaned his back against the wall and took out a small flask, from which he took a long draft. Tam and Will crouched down next to him, accepting the flask when he offered it to them and enjoying the warmth of the strong, thick brew.

"What now?" Will asked quietly.

"Now we wait."

Water dripped into Finn's eyes. A light rain had been falling ever since he had taken up position. He could not see any of the rest of his party, but he knew they were out there, in alleyways along the broad street that led to the main castle gates. It was dark, with very few people on the street; the doors to most homes were shut tight and only a little light leaked out from the shuttered windows. Straining, he heard the sound of approaching horses, and he reflexively reached for the sword at his side, loosening it ever so slightly from its hold. Looking out, he could see them being ridden by two guards, whom he assumed to be officers, with two more guards walking behind. Gritting his teeth and hoping his men were actually out there, he stepped out of the alley and directly into the way of the horses. They were trained to keep moving, but their riders pulled on the reigns by reflex and stopped a few paces before him. Before the guards could react, the rest of Finn's men spilled out from the alleyways behind them, quickly and silently encircling them with drawn swords. Two nocked arrows, aiming them at the two officers.

Finn held up his hand. "We do not intend harm to you or your men, but we will not hesitate to do so if you do not do what we say."

Both men looked around them, angry but weighing up their options. They had been caught totally unawares on a routine patrol. Their gaze settled for a second on the drawn bows before the one whom Finn assumed to be more senior nodded.

"Dismount then. We are going to secure you. You will be released in the morning."

A few moments later, dressed in the officer's uniform, Finn quickly took his place on one of the horses. He glanced over at Rob, who was sitting uneasily on the horse next to him. Two of his other men had donned the uniforms of the remaining guards and stood ready behind them. No doors had opened. People had either remained oblivious to what had taken place or chosen to remain so. With what he hoped was a reassuring nod, Finn nudged his horse forward and rode slowly along the street. Two of his remaining men had stayed with the guards, and the rest had fanned out through the alleys to their next positions.

176

Marrea tried to calm her thoughts but found it impossible. She could not believe that those last moments with her brother might be her last. She had not said enough, focused enough, as the details, even now, seemed less definite; the moment was so fleeting and then he had to leave. She had wanted to go with him, to protect him in his frailty, but she knew that was not what he wanted or what she had to do. She could not sense him at all now, as his power was inverted and hidden; she knew she should be glad about that as it would help him when he faced Nehlo, but she was so used to knowing where he was and that he was okay, that it almost felt like he had been taken from her already. She stood up and started to pace the floor, the movement helping to calm her a little and to focus her thoughts. She had to be ready to move. Tam had said that she would know when to strike, and there was much to do before that.

Zoe leaned against the door frame, watching Marrea pace up and down. Zoe could feel a deep knot of tension, but outwardly she looked calm and her thoughts were clear, except for the odd moment when she wondered where Finn was and whether he was okay. She was still a bit amused, or possibly confused, by how much he was in her thoughts. He was older than her and certainly not attractive in the way of men she had known in the past, but she was drawn to him, to his sincerity and quiet loyalty. She sometimes even wondered, when this was all over, whether they could start a home together. She had never wanted that before, had seen it as a trap, but now she craved predictable routine and someone by her side who would not reject or manipulate her. Finn was such a man, and she loved him for it. But they both had to get through this night and that depended on Tam and, possibly, if what he said was true, on Marrea.

Tam looked up as Cox stood slowly and stashed away his flask into his coat. The rain had stopped, but the damp and cold remained. He had struggled to focus his thoughts on anything as they flitted between his family, his sister and what lay ahead of him. He was relieved to get moving again before he lost the certainty that he needed to keep going. Both he and Will kept their hands tucked under their arms for warmth. Cox motioned upward, indicating it was time to move, without any explanation for their wait. He then reached up and gripped the small hand hold he had released in the wall and pulled himself up, using his feet to scrabble up the wall. His other hand reached up and found purchase just above and with a grunt he hauled himself higher, his toes finding little areas to dig into and support some of his weight. He made slow progress for a few moments. The noise of his efforts and of his boots scraping on the wall seemed dangerously loud to Tam and Will waiting below. Once his feet had reached the original hole, however, the climbing became easier and they could see Cox move more swiftly.

Tam nodded to Will who stepped up to the wall. Tam knelt, however, and placed his hands on his knee. Will stood on his hand and Tam boosted him up. Will's hands searched ahead of him until they found the first handhold. Will pulled himself up as Tam pushed from below and saw him reach out for another hold. Digging his hand into it, Will pulled, his feet scrabbling until one found a secure hold in the first hole. He stopped for a moment, panting slightly, before reaching up again. Tam watched as he now moved more quickly and easily after Cox.

Tam looked back around him, considering for a moment. He did not know what Cox had been waiting for and could sense nothing to indicate the reason for their movement now. He had no option though, but to trust the man who was rapidly disappearing into the dark night sky above him. He used his scarf to sling his staff to his back. Reaching up, he grabbed the handhold and pulled himself up, finding himself unused to the natural weight of his body without his power to wield air to aid him. His other hand found the next hole, and he hung there for a few heartbeats. He then focused hard and reached up swiftly to the next hold, pulling purposefully until he gained the next hold and could feel for the holes with his feet.

On cresting the wall, he found Cox and Will waiting for him, lying on their stomachs on the walkway at the top. Slipping down beside them, he looked around. He could see the lights of guard posts dotted around the wall, and inside the grounds he could make out the buildings of the castle. Cox moved along the wall, keeping low, and they followed him until he reached a narrow stairway that led to the ground. They were now nearer one of the guard posts, and they could hear laughter and loud talking from inside. They quickly descended the steps and stood for a few moments, backs against the wall, waiting to see if there was any movement. Tam allowed himself to reach out gently with his senses, but he almost did not need to; Nehlo's power emanated strongly, and Tam could point to his exact location with little effort.

"Our entry is that little door on the outer building," Cox whispered. "It will be open and remain so for the night." "I have arranged it," he added in response to their questioning looks.

Looking round one last time, he ran half crouched over the open ground until he reached the closest wall, against which he flattened himself and was almost immediately lost to view. Will cast a look at Tam, shrugged and ran forward but stumbled almost immediately and fell. Tam flinched, his heart suddenly racing. He focused above them, listening for any noise and heard a sound on the wall; one of the guards had come out and now stood almost directly over them as he relieved himself into the space below. Will had not noticed him and started to rise, his foot scrabbling on the ground as he moved forward. A sliver of anxiety knifed through Tam; being spotted this early would make his task impossible. He imagined the guard quiet and still, seeking out the source of the noise. Will would have been invisible had he lain still but his movement could easily attract attention. Tam heard the man above shout something and turn to move back to the guard post. He could not see Cox or Will to warn them, and he could not move until he was sure the guard had returned to the relative warmth of his post. For a long moment he listened intently before a sudden noise from further round the castle broke the silence, followed by the sound of shouting and running feet. The door of the guard house on the wall above opened and the guards poured out, moving away from Tam towards the noise. Tam took a deep breath and crept forward slowly, trusting that the attention of the guards was elsewhere for the moment and would stay so if he avoided sudden movement or sound. Every moment he expected to hear a shout or to feel the sharp thudding pain of an arrow in his back. As he moved forward and got further from the wall, he quickened his pace until he could see Cox beckoning him forward. He ran the remaining short distance to the wall and leaned against it, surprised by how shaken he had been by the threat of being discovered.

They stayed where they were for a few moments, watching as torches blazed into light on the wall and men moved rapidly along it to the other side of the castle. Tam had no idea what was happening, but had it been a few moments later he was sure the guard would have come down and found Will. Cox motioned to them before creeping round the base of the building. He reached the door and tested it gently. Tam stayed his hand for a second and probed through. Sensing no one on the other side, he nodded to Cox, who gave him a quick, appraising look before opening the door softly and stepping inside.

Finn and Rob rode slowly with what Finn hoped was confidence toward the main gate. His two men walked smartly behind them, their posture tense. The wall rose high above them. The main gate was closed, leaving just the inner gate open, which was wide enough to take two horses abreast but little more. The two guards on the gate straightened as they approached, but on seeing their own, they relaxed and stood aside. One saluted sharply and Finn returned it as they rode by, careful to keep his face hidden and tucked into his jacket, which would seem normal given the cold and damp. Beyond the gate the road turned sharply left and wound its way round between the outer wall and another smaller wall on the inside. Finn urged his mount to turn and start up the slight incline, the hooves clattering dully off the wet cobbles.

As they moved along the road, the guards turned their attention back to the gate. Finn nodded to the two men behind him who turned and drew short blades silently. They moved behind the guards, using one hand to cover their mouths and drug them back, the other to hold the blade to their throats, before pulling them to the ground. Finn dismounted quickly and gave the reins to Rob. He walked to the gate and waved his hand twice. Men emerged from the surrounding streets and ran quickly to the gate. Within moments two of them were dressed in the guard's uniforms and took up position at the gate, the guards seated, legs and arms trussed but blanketed against the cold, their backs to the inner wall.

Finn mounted his horse and rode forward, up the slope which was lit at intervals by burning lamps. The remaining men at his disposal numbered ten in total, four of his own, whom he trusted completely, and six of Zoe's, whom he would have to trust. He rode up the middle of the wide street, trying to ignore the walls on either side, Rob at his side and the two of his men dressed in guard's uniforms behind him. The other men moved quietly along the side of the wall, keeping to the deep shadows. They approached the inner gate, which was closed, but a smaller door within it opened at their approach.

One of the guards looked through and quickly scanned them.

"You know the rules. Dismount before you come through to this area. Then come and report to the guardhouse."

Finn hesitated, uncertain. They could not go into the lit guardhouse, as they would almost certainly be recognized as imposters. If they went through that gate, there was no turning back; they might be trapped beyond it. The decision weighed heavily on him, not for himself but for the men who followed him. Would he be leading them to their deaths? He glanced at Rob, and the men behind him who were waiting expectantly, ready. The guard, who had been speaking to someone

179

behind him, turned back to them, a look of annoyance on his face at the delay. Finn pushed his doubts aside. They were all soldiers, trained to take these risks and follow where others lead. He must lead now.

Finn spurred his horse forward and ducked as it plunged through the doorway, knocking aside the guard who had no time to react. He heard a shout as Rob followed him, but as he cleared the gate Rob's horse stumbled, the sudden movement unseating him and he fell heavily to the side. Rob's horse, freed but startled, neighed shrilly and bolted across the courtyard inside. Finn cursed and turned to see his two other men through the gate but grappling with guards as more spilled out of the guard post to the side of the gate. They struggled to hold their ground before the gate, to keep it open long enough for the rest of their party to come through. Finn slipped off his horse and moved to engage the guards nearest to him, his sword rising to deflect blows. One of the men slipped on the greasy stone and Finn did not hesitate to smash the flat of his blade across his head as he fell, whipping it sideways. The man landed with a sickening crack and lay still, some blood leaking onto the stone. The other guard steadied himself and approached more carefully, but Finn did not have time to spare as he could see Rob struggling to rise and more guards approaching. He threw his blade at the man in front who parried it awkwardly, surprised, and in the same moment Finn barrelled into him, his shoulder driving up into his stomach and chest. Finn fell heavily but the wind was knocked from his assailant who gasped for breath, his sword clattering to the ground.

Rising, Finn picked up his sword and saw with relief that the doorway in the gate was still open, and his men were moving through. His relief was transient, however, as they were outnumbered and in a few moments more would arrive. He yelled and charged forward, flanked by men on either side. He had insisted that they not shed blood wantonly, but as he crashed into the guard nearest him with his blade stabbing forward, the thought occurred to him briefly that nothing was ever the way anyone wanted in battle. He grappled with the man, blades clashing until a low blow cut through and pierced his side. Finn yanked the blade across, feeling it tear flesh and the man fell, clutching his ruined side.

Sweating and out of breath, Finn could feel men jostling him on either side and all he could hear was the frantic noises of men fighting and dying. He saw two of his men fall and more guards spilling round to outflank their small group, who backed toward each other in a defensive circle. He really had thought that they would get further than this, that they would at least play a small part in what happened tonight, but that seemed impossible now. He raised his sword again and with a small sigh of resignation prepared to meet the coming assault.

Chapter 36

Cox led the way into what seemed to be a storeroom. They threaded their way through dusty barrels and crates, which were piled high around them. At the far end of the room, he stopped at another door, listening for a few moments before turning to Tam with a slight grimace and beckoning him forward. Tam probed ahead carefully, not wanting to upset the balance he had created in his own defences by exerting himself too far. He could not detect anyone in the near vicinity, so he nodded to Cox, who opened the door softly and peered through the crack before closing the door gently again.

"This is as far as I go. If you go down the corridor outside, it will lead to the ground floor of the main building, and from what I understand, Will can take you from there."

Will nodded, though he looked far from certain.

"If you don't mind, I will not wait for your return. Whatever happened outside has meant the guards are distracted for now and my route out is easier. That may not last."

"I understand and don't want you to wait. I can't be sure your wait would not be in vain anyway." Tam passed his staff into his left hand and reached out to grip Cox's wrist with his free hand. Cox looked surprised and a little abashed before returning the pressure and then turning to retrace his steps through the storeroom.

Tam opened the door carefully again and looked through. A dimly lit corridor at a slight incline led off to his right with doors, possibly leading into other storerooms, punctuating it at intervals. He could not see or sense anyone, but without the use of his power, he felt strangely exposed and fragile. Suppressing a mild sense of rising discomfort, he slipped through the door and walked slowly down the corridor, straining to hear for any noises ahead. Will followed and they reached the end of the corridor without incident. Ahead of them was a larger door, which by its weight and size Tam surmised to be the original door to the Keep. He tested the handle; it moved freely and easily, but he paused before opening it.

"Do you know where we go from here?" he asked Will quietly.

"Not for certain, but I will once we get further in and I start to recognize things. It has been a few years as you know."

"Okay. You ready?"

Will nodded but his face looked pale, and even in the dim light, Tam could see a faint sheen of sweat. He could not go back with him now and did not have time to delve any further, but it did nothing to ease his disquiet. He gripped his staff tightly, feeling the reassuring weight and sturdiness as well as the engraved writing, and pulled at the door. It was set into thick stone walls but opened with a disconcertingly loud squeal. He paused for a second and, hearing nothing further, stepped through.

A large room opened before him, with a wooden floor and, in the middle, a long wooden table lined with benches on either side. A cooking range was at one side of the room, where the remains of a fire smouldered and some pans hung on the wall above it. At the far end an opening led to some steps that climbed upward. They skirted round the table and passed noiselessly up the stone steps and into a wide corridor with a tall high ceiling. The floor held no furniture but the pictures and tapestries on the walls gave the area a regal appearance. A large door was on their left and windows lined that side of the wall, though the darkness gave nothing away of what lay beyond them. They could hear, however, shouting from outside and the ring of metal striking metal. Tam surmised what might be happening with sadness, but there was nothing he could do to help even if his friends were the cause of the disturbance. Much better that he press on and use what time they had given him. The castle still seemed quiet. Will stopped for a second, pondering, before eventually pointing to a door on the right about midway down the corridor. Tam nodded and moved quicker now, sure that it was only a matter of moments before guards appeared. He paused at the door but sensed nothing beyond except the presence of Nehlo, growing stronger now. The bondings within him stirred slightly, responding to the flicker of trepidation as his thoughts involuntarily leapt forward to the coming encounter with Nehlo. Forcing himself to focus on the steps in front of him, he opened the door carefully and with his staff at the ready moved through it.

He stood still for a few seconds, just inside the room, to get his bearings. He could hear only the quiet tread of Will behind him. A large oval room stood before them, with wooden paneling on the walls and chairs lining the periphery. He looked back at Will, who indicated toward the left-hand door of two on the far side of the room. Tam turned and walked slowly forward, for some reason uncertain and nervous. As he reached the middle of the room, he became aware that Will was not with him and turned to see him still at the doorway, a strange look of despair and hopelessness on his face.

"I'm sorry Tam," he uttered, barely louder than a whisper, yet still conveying the strain in it. "You have no chance of succeeding, and you are only making things worse. Nothing can bring my family back, and there is nothing you or anyone else can do."

With a sudden lurch, Tam heard the doors at the far end of the room burst open. Guards poured in, weapons drawn. More barrelled past Will, who stood motionless as they surged passed him, his eyes fixed on Tam and tears streaking down his cheeks. Just as the swell of guards blocked him from Tam's view, he turned and left the room, closing the door behind him.

The only thing that saved them in the first assault was the sheer number of attackers, who in the confusion of the moment impeded each other, allowing

Finn's small group to knit closely together and repel them without further loss of life. Finn looked around desperately in the slight lull for some way out or weak point but could see none. Their only option was to have something solid at their backs. The guard post stood twenty paces away, but they had to get there together, or all would be lost. Shouting as loudly as he could, he instructed them to keep together and move towards it. He yelled the order to march, and as one they stepped as swiftly as they could, keeping in time with each other. As they moved, they kept their weapons raised, their eyes darting back and forth, their alertness preventing any opportunistic attack. Still, their movement seemed painfully slow to Finn, who could see the guards rallying and hear orders ringing out.

When they were still at least ten paces away, the second attack came: fewer men but with more purpose and intensity. They advanced quickly but with balance, not overreaching but picking their points, stabbing forward, cutting low. All thought of attack or retreat was lost in the need to parry and parry again, while keeping their position and not breaking the tenuous circle that kept their foe from attacking their rear and kept them alive. Sweat dripped down Finn's face, and he could feel the strength draining from him and his reactions dulling as time after time he deflected blows. But even so, the number of strikes started to tell in the blood oozing from at least two cuts that had pierced deeply. He saw someone stumble; Rob, he thought frantically, was too weak and exhausted, was rising too slowly. Powerless to prevent it, Finn saw with rising horror a sword break through Rob's defences and drive deep into his chest. Where he fell, space appeared in the line, which, if the guards could use to split them up, would take with it whatever slender chance of survival remained.

It took Finn a moment longer than it might normally to sense that their attackers had not broken through the gap in their defences, and that they had delayed when they should have driven home their advantage. His experience took over, and he steered his remaining men back, back, back, using their remaining energy to carve a path through the guards, until they were against the wall, protected finally on one side. He could see now that the attention of the guards had shifted to their rear, where he could hear some confused shouting and the sound of fighting. Then the massed group of guards suddenly seemed to give way before a swiftly moving attack, and the attackers broke through to the open ground before him. Finn's heart leaped as he saw Zoe at the front, her face set and determined. She did not acknowledge them but turned immediately to protect the flank of her group as they came through, Marrea in their midst.

Once they were all through, they moved back and formed a protective ring around Finn and his men, who sagged in relief. Some would have fallen were it not for the wall at their back. Zoe's eyes glanced at Finn for a moment before she turned to face the guards, who hung back now, suddenly uncertain but knowing that they still had their quarry within their grasp. The losses they had suffered showed in their wariness. An order suddenly rippled through their ranks, and they moved back to allow room for men carrying bows to move through. They quickly took up position, nocked arrows and drew them back, the strings taught, each picking a target they could not miss at this range.

Finn started to move. He would not stand and be killed like an animal. He felt around him the others stir to follow him, some barely able to move but still alert enough to know that death was moments away. He saw Marrea say something to

Zoe, who reached out an arm to stop him moving and shoved him back with surprising strength. Marrea moved her hand toward the thick door of the guard post a few paces to their left, which inched open wide enough for a man to slip through. The men started to move toward it just as the order to fire bellowed out and the arrows were released. Finn let out an involuntary yell and braced himself for the thud of the impact.

None came. Marrea had stepped out in front of them all. She stood calmly facing the barrage. Finn watched in astonishment as the arrows thudded into a wall that he could not see, just in front of her. Zoe yelled something at him that he did not understand, but it broke through his shock and he stumbled the few paces to the door and lunged through. Once the last men were through, Zoe followed and then Marrea, who pulled the door shut before Zoe hauled down the thick block of wood that secured it. Arrows struck the far side ineffectually.

Tam crouched down, his staff in both hands, waiting. He tested the defences he had erected around the bondings and found them to be secure. His own power was hidden and he could not use it for fear of Nehlo discovering him too early, or losing control of the bondings. But he could still use his senses and speed. The guards descended on him from all directions, their swords stabbing forward. He sensed the movements subconsciously and reacted without thinking. He swung the staff with small precise movements, batting away multiple strikes, his body twisting and turning to let others slide past. The first wave deflected, he exploded into attack, his staff swirling and striking in powerful blows with point and side. Each strike connected with joint or throat, head or neck, so with each a man fell. He did not pause to allow them to recover and mount a second attack. He sprang forward into the nearest group, who recoiled away from him and that gave him a fraction of a moment. He crouched low and in punching blows up and down he struck punishing blows into knees and hips, feeling them crack beneath the weight of the wood and his own strength. Each fell, incapacitated.

Spinning round, he fended off a short stabbing blow into his back and brought the other end of his staff down on his assailant's head, grimacing as it cracked the helmet and splintered the skull below. He could not pause for a second as more guards approached him and still more spilled into the room. Knife blades whistled through the air toward him. His staff moved so quickly that it became a blur, deflecting the knives as they flew, directing most into the walls and floor around him, but some hit advancing guards and pierced their limbs; one of the guards staggered back with blood arcing from a knife wound to his neck.

Tam took in the room with a glance. Men lay all around him, some groaning and some motionless. The air was hot with the number of men and the effort of battle, and he could feel the sweat running down him. A thin layer of slick liquid covered the floor. Devastating as he had been, there were still at least twenty men standing in the room, most of whom were fresh to the fray. Wariness marked their movements though, now that they could see what he was capable of. They advanced more slowly, careful to give each other room to move and swing. Two bore blades with longer hilts, negating the advantage of his staff's reach. He knew that he could not defeat them all, not restrained as he was, yet he could not see any other way out. He had always known that reaching Nehlo was going to be difficult, but he had not counted on being trapped in this way. He thought of Will and the look on his face as he had left; a look that spoke of Will's own suffering even as he had brought ruin upon Tam. It absolved him of some of the anger Tam felt, leaving mainly regret that it had come to this.

The approaching men darted at him from all sides to strike before quickly retreating. Tam countered each attack but could see that they hoped to tire him into making a mistake and letting his guard falter, which it would in time. Swatting aside the longer blade, he moved within its reach, and dealt a deep blow into the attacker's stomach, forcing the wind from him and driving him back. Spinning he rounded on the next, his staff striking quickly, beating the man back before landing a heavy blow onto the side of his head. More men took their place, however, and he found himself just managing to keep them at bay, his staff and body moving endlessly and seamlessly to parry and dodge the strikes from all around.

Eventually his speed slowed a fraction and a blade crept through, catching him on his upper arm and drawing blood, which seeped into his top and down his arm. Another blade caught him on his side, piercing him before he managed to twist away. The sword had gone deep and his movement had wrenched his body free in such a way as to widen the cut and increase the blood flow. He staggered back, unable to staunch the flow on danger of losing control of his staff. He looked around again for any hope of a way out but could see none through the men advancing on him. His eyes lingered for a moment on one at the back, who had not yet been part of the battle but had stood aloof. He parried yet more thrusts and swings but, with each movement, the flow of blood increased and his defence weakened. A cut he had sensed but had been unable to deflect sliced through his leg behind his knee and immediately he fell, the power in his leg gone. He swung his staff wide from the floor, in a desperate attempt to keep them back as he strove to regain his feet. When he did so, his leg was unable to bear his weight, so he stood on the other, his staff held wearily before him. A powerful blow from the side took the staff from his hands, and he was unable to stop it clattering to the floor beneath him, from where he could not stoop to recover it.

Summoning his remaining strength, he directed his thoughts into the man he supposed was the leader. Putting every ounce of his authority behind them, he forced his thoughts through, strengthening the man's resolve to take him to Nehlo. He then fell and knelt on the floor, his strength spent, his breathing coming in gasps. His head reeled from the loss of blood and the violent exertion. There was a pause, the guards obviously uncertain how to proceed now that he was defenceless. They were not killers in cold blood but trained to fight and kill only where needed. The order to kill did not come. Instead, the man spoke some words that Tam did not hear. He did not look up but crouched still further as the flat of the blades rained down on him, followed by pommels thudding into his already weakened body, battering any remaining resistance from him until eventually darkness took him.

The guard post was dimly lit with lanterns on the walls. There was a table up against one wall with some chairs and a bench against the other. Above the bench hung racks for weapons. A couple of bunks were attached one above the other onto the wall at the back. Finn sat in one of the chairs, his men collapsing on the bench and bunks, glad of the rest. Zoe's men moved quickly to tend to the wounded, using old material scattered around the room to bind up wounds inexpertly but sufficiently to slow blood flow and give some relief. There was also water to distribute and the remnants of some food, which were gratefully taken.

Zoe stood at a small slit in the wall next to the door, enough to see out but with only a limited view of what was happening. They could hear little, the post being built of the same thick stone as the walls it was part of.

Marrea turned from the door, where she had been standing, with a resigned look on her face.

"What is happening?" Finn asked Zoe, drawing her gaze toward him.

"Nothing that I can see. The guards are there, but they are not advancing. We can't get out and they can't get in without significant loss of life, so they are doing nothing at present. They don't need to do anything. We have bought ourselves a little extra time, that is all." Zoe looked frustrated, turning to look at Marrea more than once as she spoke.

"No, we did what we needed to do, and we shall see what happens," replied Marrea to the implied criticism. "We are safe for now."

"Until they starve or smoke us out!" someone voiced from the back. Finn did not know who had spoken, but he could not disagree with the sentiment.

"That may happen but not tonight, and a lot can happen in the few hours left of this night." Marrea looked more settled now, more herself again, the brief look of resignation gone from her face and replaced once again with calm.

"What now then?" Finn asked.

"All we can do is wait. We cannot break free from here the way things are. It is up to my brother now, and I have never known him to fail when he has set his mind to something. We must be ready to act when he gives us the opportunity."

186

Chapter 37

Tam stood, supported on either side by a guard. His hands were manacled, but his wounds had been roughly bound, including his knee, which was splinted and could bear a little weight. He was so weak, though, that he would have fallen but for the arms of the guards propping him up. He was only dimly aware of his surroundings as bruising to his eyes had swollen them half shut and light brought searing pain to his head. He could see, though, that they stood waiting outside a large door and that guards surrounded him on all sides. His mouth was dry and sore. Motioning to one of the guards, he asked for some water. The man looked at him for a moment before his eyes registered a flicker of pity. Unhooking his water bottle, he poured a little into Tam's mouth, easing his discomfort for a few moments.

At some unseen signal, the door opened, and Tam found himself being dragged into a large and brightly lit room, with lanterns around the walls. The light flickered off the clear marble floor, bringing sharp spasms of pain behind his eyes. At the far end there was a raised dais with an open fire, before which stood a large, ornate chair. Men and women stood in a ring around the room. Their heads were bowed, and they were still, yet each was armed and stood as if in readiness for combat at any moment. On the large chair, sat Nehlo. Tam recognized him immediately, mainly through the tainted power that emanated from him, but also from the striking resemblance that he still bore to the man he had known many years before. He was still handsome, though in a hard, angular way, but his lips, thin and permanently lifted in a slight sneer, betrayed his capacity for cruelty. His hair was dark, his frame tall and muscular, though he had little need of physical strength now. He had always, as long as Tam had known him, prided himself on his strength even as his power had grown in other ways.

Nehlo looked up when they entered the room, his gaze listless and showing only passing interest. He motioned to the lead guard, who stepped forward, his head bowed.

"The would-be assassin, my Lord."

"The traitor was trustworthy then," Nehlo mused, half to himself. His voice was low and softer than expected. Different to how Tam remembered it. A soothing voice, almost. Tam thought of Will again. He thought that Will had always questioned what Tam was doing, that he had been unable to see past the chaos that followed Tam's actions. And then his grief at the loss of his family had been all that he could feel or see, and Tam had not had the capacity to reach out to him. He did not blame Will; he had not fully known what he had done when handing Tam over. The guard did not speak but inclined his head still further. "Any losses?"

"Many injured, my Lord. Some have died. If I may say, my Lord, had we not had him enclosed and with large numbers, he may not have been captured. He was armed only with this staff."

Nehlo showed a flash of interest. Not in the deaths but in the apparent strength and skill of the man before him. He handled the staff, which had been presented to him, spinning it slowly, feeling its weight and balance before running his fingers over the inscription in the handle. Tam kept his gaze fixed on the floor in front of him but was aware of Nehlo considering him for a long moment. Eventually, Nehlo motioned to the guards, who pulled him forward and dropped him to the floor on his hands and knees. He felt the cold marble beneath his hands, countering the heat he could feel coursing through him as a result of all his injuries. He felt weak in a way that he had never before experienced, without the power to even get himself on his feet, never mind defend himself. He had never felt so exposed and helpless, so at the mercy of another as he did now. For a brief moment, he felt anger rising, at himself for being so trusting and stupid, at the hopelessness of his position, at this worthless country that he had come to aid. His anger lasted only for a second, however, as deep in his heart he had known it would ultimately come to this, to weakness and to a meeting between Nehlo and himself. This way he was no threat, there would be no contest and little chance that Nehlo would recognize him. He knew that, weakened as he was, he could not hope to beat Nehlo and making himself known would only result in the bondings being found and restored to their master. Then, if Nehlo would not return with him, they would have achieved nothing for all the chaos and loss they had unleashed. He focused inward, ensuring his power was still undetectable, inverted and barricading away the bondings, so that even he could not feel their taint.

Nehlo dismissed the guards, leaving just his attendants behind. Once they had left, the room was silent save for the rhythmic rasping noise of Tam's laboured breathing. Nehlo stood for a moment and placed the staff carefully on the floor of the dais, in front of Tam.

"Why did you want to kill me?" he asked eventually, his soft voice belying the threat behind his words.

Tam, exhausted and bearing wounds throughout his body, struggled to think. A response did not come to him quickly. He had not come with the intent of killing Nehlo, not if it could have been avoided. Now, that would be impossible for him.

"Not to kill you. To help you," he answered, his voice dry and weak.

"You came here to help me?" Tam could hear the derision through the soft, half-spoken words. Nehlo turned and walked to the fire, holding out his hands to it. After a few moments he turned back to face Tam, walking toward him as he spoke.

"Why would I need your help? What help could you hope to give me?"

Tam did not respond. Every breath hurt and required an effort for which he did not really have the energy. His arms could barely take the weight that he was placing on them, and he struggled to keep them locked and rigid. If they bent, he was sure he would fall, and he did not want to show such weakness, even now. Suddenly, Nehlo, with a sweep of his foot, pulled Tam's hands away from him. Tam's face crashed off the hard marble as he fell forward, unable to control or break his fall. He felt his nose break and blood pour from it, and the bitter taste of blood filled his mouth where his teeth had pierced his lower lip. Tears rose unbidden to his eyes from the trauma to his nose, and his vision clouded for a second before he blinked them away. He lay still for a second panting, before drawing his arms painfully toward him and forcing his arms to lift him back into a kneeling position. The strain was almost too much for him, though, and for a long moment he was unable to process anything around him as he focused on regaining his breath and calming the spasms that shook through his muscles. It helped him to feel the hard marble beneath his hands, to centre himself on something real and solid when his own life was so frail and tenuous. Looking down at the marble, he forced his mind to go blank, to ignore the pain that coursed through him and the panic threatening to overwhelm him.

His thoughts calmer, Tam felt the sheer emptiness of the man before him. The lack of meaning and worth except that which power gave him, the vast need and insatiable desire to be more than he was, and more than those around him. And he felt the fear and insecurity of a man who, despite all his power, had to lash out wantonly at a shackled and beaten man at his feet. The cruelty of a man who would so blithely cause pain and sweep away the last vestiges of another's dignity. Tam felt pity rising up within him; a real, tangible, deep pity for his old friend before him, so totally lost now within the vacuity and cruelty of the world he had fashioned. In some small measure, Tam saw the rightness of his being here, the rightness of offering even this violent man a chance for redemption. Slowly, he raised his head, wanting to look Nehlo in the eye and talk to him as an equal. Their gaze met. Tam held it for a long moment. For the first time since he had been dragged before Nehlo, he felt that he had some degree of control, that he had chosen this mantle of weakness by bearing the bondings, that there was purpose and meaning to his weakness and to this meeting with his old friend. He saw the quick rise of anger in Nehlo and tensed, expecting him to lash out, but then Nehlo controlled himself with considerable effort. Nehlo looked toward his attendants, who stood unmoving and impassive. When he turned back, he looked closely at Tam again, who could almost feel the effort that it took to meet his gaze.

Tam tried to speak, but his mouth was so dry that it took a few moments to get his words out, and when it came, his voice was hoarse and soft. He saw Nehlo lean closer to hear him.

"How has it come to this? What has become of you?" he asked with sadness. Nehlo flinched and moved back a fraction, his eyes registering his confusion. Tam saw him look intently at him, searching for something, and he felt Nehlo probe him, looking for power. He wondered for a moment if his old friend was starting to recognize him, to remember his past, but after a few moments Nehlo regained his composure, and his voice, when he spoke, was quiet and smooth.

"Who are you? Why have you really come here?"

Tam ignored the first question. "I have told you the truth. I am here to try to right some of the wrongs that you have done and to help you."

"I have done nothing wrong. And what help can you offer me? You cannot even help yourself."

189

"I can offer you a way back. It is not too late."

"A way back?"

"To a meaningful life, to acceptance, to healing rather than harm. To the right and good way before our maker. You would have to renounce your power, but it has only brought you and others misery and loneliness. Harm and suffering follow in your wake, but judgment stalks you." Tam spoke quickly, as energetically as he could, sensing that in these moments he may be able to connect with Nehlo. He saw what he hoped was a glimmer of interest, maybe even desire, cross Nehlo's face, but it quickly disappeared, and his face hardened again.

"Renounce power? Only the weak and powerless think of this as a good thing. I don't believe in your god. I can do what I will, without any fear of the judgment you speak of."

Tam strove for an answer, but his fatigue made it almost impossible to think. To alleviate the pain of normal breathing, his breaths came shallow and fast, and he was feeling increasingly lightheaded. He shifted on his trembling hands to try and keep himself alert and to ease the burning ache. Nehlo too was quiet for a moment, his eyes downcast. Tam heard him start to speak, softly but clearly, and he forced himself to focus.

"There is no meaning to life without power. I have no desire to give that up for the paltry things you have spoken of."

A sudden spike of anger fuelled Tam, enabling him to raise his head and look directly at Nehlo. He started speaking before he had properly formulated his thoughts, the words coming from him in a torrent. "You understand little of what is happening and even less of the judgment that awaits you. You have abused the power the Creator gave you and trampled on the laws which he wove into the world. You cannot be allowed to carry on as you are; you are causing too much harm and suffering." He paused, out of breath, before continuing more slowly and gently. "Whatever happens to me, your power will be broken, but it does not have to be this way. I offer you again the chance to come with me, to leave this country, to let it heal before it is too late for you. There is still mercy for you."

Tam saw Nehlo flinch at the word mercy, saw his anger flare again. It was such a divisive word and sentiment; to some it meant a new chance and life, to others the yoke of weakness and servitude. With a horrible clarity, he saw his mistake in using it with Nehlo, but it was all that he had to offer. And it was everything that Nehlo needed. He saw Nehlo glance at one of his attendants with a look of uncertainty that was quickly followed by such hideous rage that Tam felt a sudden lurch of fear. He watched, helpless, as Nehlo suddenly turned, and his power surged in him. With a sliver of compressed air as sharp as the finest blade, he bore down on the attendant, stabbing down savagely. Tam could see the fear and pain in the man's eyes as he fell, unable to cry out, with hands clutching feebly at his neck. He realized now that all the attendants must be bonded to Nehlo as none moved, or even flinched, in response to their master's wrath. Sickened and saddened, he turned away as the man slumped, lifeless, to the ground, his blood coursing onto the marble floor. When finished Nehlo returned to him, his breathing a little ragged but his rage assuaged for the moment.

"I have no use for mercy."

Tam now knew that Nehlo would not turn, would not change; he did not see his need, did not want to see it and could not envisage his own downfall. His head sagged. A sudden pain lanced through his chest and back, catching his breathing and almost causing him to fall to the floor, and he knew he would not be able to get up again. He had no more fight in him and nothing more to give. He knew now that he would die here, his task incomplete. Had he been a fool? He thought briefly of releasing his burden, of regaining his power, unfettered and complete, and even in his weakened state fighting instead of submitting. But then, if he lost, all would be in vain as the bondings and the power they contained would return to Nehlo. But if he died here, now, and the bondings died with him, then some of Nehlo's power would die too, and his sister would have a chance.

His sister. He thought of her and her trust in him as well as her constant, easy companionship. He then thought of his wife and family. He would never see his children in their prime as adults, never see what they achieved or meet their wives and children. He would never grow old, as he had promised, with Theresa, his kind and loving wife whom he had loved since first meeting her. A deep, deep sadness filled him to the point where he could feel nothing else, no fear or anger, just sadness, a surge of feeling that connected him with those he loved but also threatened to overwhelm him. He was vaguely aware of Nehlo approaching him, of his arms raised above his head. He fought to keep his thoughts under control, despite the fear now coursing through him. He knew from the teachings that those who served the Creator went to him in death, and he clung to that belief now. The bondings within him scrabbled to be free. He fought with them desperately, using all his remaining strength of will to hold them in, to trap them in himself until the very end.

He felt the sudden stab of the razor-sharp blade of air as it knifed through him. His breathing collapsed with an awful lurch, his heart hammering out his life blood, and a sudden panic welled up as cold and darkness gathered around him. He felt himself starting to fall forward, unable to lift or even feel his arms as the darkness rose to meet him. So cold and empty. He could sense the bondings breaking free and was powerless to stop them. But then, just at the edge of his consciousness, he felt something else. A newness coming to subsume him, a brightness challenging the darkness that dragged him down. A brightness that eviscerated the bondings in an instant. A brightness that, somehow, he knew. And at the last it welcomed him.

Chapter 38

It was strangely quiet in the guard post. Finn's remaining men had fallen asleep, partly through exhaustion, but also partly to be ready for whatever exertions lay ahead. They lay on the floor or on the bunks at the back of the room. Zoe's men were awake but quiet, listening to try and glean some knowledge of what was happening outside. The awareness that their retreat had bought them only a few moments of respite dissipated any desire to talk. Zoe remained standing at the door, looking through the small slit. She had been silent since reporting that the guards outside had formed a perimeter and had no immediate intent to attack. Finn chafed at the uncertainty and waiting. He looked at Marrea, who sat on the floor near the door, her eyes closed. She had barely stirred from this position since they had entered the post, moving only to accept a small drink of water. Her staffs lay across her knees and periodically she ran her hands along them, seeming to gain comfort from the texture of the wood. Finn wondered where the staffs had come from; he had glimpsed writing etched onto the handles but had not been able to make it out. Marrea looked peaceful, but he could see tension in her shoulders and a faint paleness in her face. His own wound throbbed slightly, but the bleeding had been arrested by a rough dressing. He had eaten and drunk a little water and now did his best to ignore the ache and fatigue in his muscles.

After what seemed like a long time, Zoe moved away from the door and approached him.

"I think something is happening outside," she half whispered to him. "More men have arrived, and they are carrying a heavy trunk. There are also some braziers. They mean to either batter the door down or smoke us out. Either way, we do not have long."

Finn nodded, thinking. They did not have many options. They could stay where they were and fight it out if the guards tried to take the post by force; a fight that would end in their death for little real gain. But if they decided to burn or smoke them out, there was very little they could do.

"What do you think?"

Zoe looked at him, her gaze surprisingly soft for the gravity of their situation. "We have to get out of here now."

"I agree. But we may not get very far."

"Maybe not. But better than waiting for death in here. We have had a chance to regroup, patch our wounds, rest our limbs. And we have Marrea."

On the mention of Marrea's name, they both turned and looked at her. There was no mistaking it now; she looked pale, her breathing rapid and a faint sheen of sweat lay on her forehead. Zoe started toward her, but something about the way Marrea looked made Finn hold her back.

"I will ready my men, if you do the same for yours. We will lead when the time comes, and your men will need to protect our rear."

"And Marrea?"

Zoe shrugged. "I don't know. We will just have to be ready."

"And, if we make it through their perimeter, are we heading out of the castle or further in? To make it into the castle we will need to keep moving, no matter what. And we will likely have no means of retreat."

Zoe looked at him carefully, reading him. "Marrea needs to go and find her brother or finish what he started, and we have sworn we will help her make it. But the more injured of your men may not have the strength to go further."

"I will give my men the option, but they will want to finish this. They have come too far to back out now."

Finn reached out his hand and grasped hers, which felt warm and strong. He held it for a moment, looking at her before she turned and moved toward her men. Finn roused his group. Once fully alert, he explained in terse sentences what was happening and what they were planning. Looking round he saw resignation but also a shared sense that it was better to take their lives in their own hands, rather than wait to be trapped with no chance of escape or even fight. They readied themselves as best they could. On testing, the bows hanging on the guardroom wall turned out to be well cared for. Quickly stringing them and filling quivers with arrows, they passed them round, each placing it on their backs so that in the flight out they would not get in the way.

Finn returned to the front of the post and peered out of the slit. He could make out some men but the range of view limited his ability to get a clear picture of the positioning and number of the guards; once out in the open they would just have to deal with whatever came at them. Turning he saw Zoe bend down and speak to Marrea, who watched her closely, listening, before nodding and replying. She took some water and then stood, suddenly alert and purposeful, her staffs clutched tightly now.

Zoe and Marrea moved to the door and stood ready. In the silent moment before the coming explosion of action, Finn strained to hear what was happening outside. As he listened, he became aware of a growing clamour, of men shouting, but not in the crisp way of the giving and receiving of orders. Rather, voices seemed raised in anger and dissent. The noise grew, interspersed now with the sound of men running and the occasional clash of swords. Zoe looked out of the slit before turning to speak quickly to Marrea. She looked back at Finn, seeking his assurance that now was their time to move. He nodded slowly, keeping his eyes on her before turning to his men and giving the signal. One of Zoe's men lifted the block of wood that kept the door in place. Zoe pushed open the door and stepped through, with Marrea close behind.

Will did not know how long had passed since he had closed the door, shutting Tam out of his world, shutting out the view of him surrounded by enemies with no route of retreat. He could not, however, shut out the look in Tam's eyes when he realized he had been betrayed, and that look burned in his mind. More than once he had stopped to grip his head, his eyes closed, trying to force his mind to focus on something else, but still it returned. He had wandered aimlessly through the castle, meeting no one and not caring which way he turned. He had nothing now, with his family gone and no way to return to Finn and the released prisoners, who would quickly realize what he had done and would despise him for it.

He kept returning to his decision. It had seemed the only thing that he could do. It had all seemed so hopeless since his family had disappeared. But even before that he had doubted Tam; chaos, disorder and even suffering seemed to frequently follow in Tam's wake. And then there was Tam's noticeable weakening. With each passing day, he had seemed less able, more fragile. Tam seemed certain to fail, and then everything would be worse, particularly for anyone who had joined him.

There was more. He forced himself to think through his motives. Everything had been such a blur since his hopes of seeing his family had been decimated but, forcing himself to examine it now, he saw that he had wanted to make this decision. He had felt such pain that he had wanted to lash out at anyone who he could connect to the misery that was threatening to overwhelm him, and at that moment he had hated Tam with an almost visceral intensity. He did not know exactly why. Perhaps it was Tam's sense of purpose that had caused his hatred to grow; it had stung like vinegar on his wounds in the midst of his own chaos. So Will had made his decision. But now that he had betrayed Tam, Will's justifications seemed frail and false, and he could not quiet the voice in his head screaming how worthless he was. It was not lost on him that he had betrayed the one person supposedly able to topple Nehlo, the very person who had directly or indirectly led to the loss of years of his own life and the loss of his family. Now, as the cold reality of what he had done forced itself on him, he felt a crushing sense of self-reproach and self-disgust.

He leaned against the wall, feeling weak and faint, his heart pounding. He closed his eyes but felt himself swaying as if he was going to fall, so he fixed his gaze on the floor, willing himself to stay upright. He stumbled forward, his hand tracing the wall, his mind reeling until he came to a floor-length window set into the thick wall. Slumping, he sat beside the window with his back to the cold wall and his knees drawn up to his chest. Leaning his forehead on the window, he stared out, seeking solace in the sky, which was just lightening with the first hint of the morning sun.

Despite Finn's experience, he struggled to understand what was happening around them. They had been unchallenged on leaving the guardhouse. Guards filled the open area, but they were listless and confused, with some walking aimlessly, others seated in groups, and still others lying on the ground, obviously injured. There must have been fighting, but Finn could not comprehend why that would have happened. At that moment, though, the reason did not matter. Zoe had not hesitated to push on as fast as she could, trusting the others to follow her. The challenge when it came was half-hearted and wilted quickly before the speed and ferocity of Zoe's advance. Before many more moments had passed, they were at the wall of the main keep and had started circling it, looking for the entrance. Finn kept looking back, confused by the lack of any cohesive pursuit or attack but still alert to danger.

Nehlo walked away from Tam's fallen body without another thought. He did not know why he had felt any hesitation about killing him, but now that it was done, he did not dwell on it any further. Killing him had shown the man's weakness and the emptiness of his words.

It took him a few moments to realize that something was very wrong. He stopped abruptly and looked around him. There was no one else in the wide corridor that led to the reception room. It was silent, but that was not unusual as no one spoke in Nehlo's presence unless he wanted them to. The absence of people, though, was strikingly unusual. Normally, a throng of people waited on him. They should be there, some could not, in fact, be absent. It took a second for that to fully hit him. People bound to him should not be able to move without his sanction, yet they were not here. And even those not bound to him, yet dependent on him in other ways, would normally be there for a multitude of reasons. How had this happened? For the first time in many years, a sliver of doubt ran through him and something that he had to admit was fear pierced him. He stood for a second, analysing this, suddenly uncertain about what to do. He thought deeply, considering all the people he had seen over the last few days, trying to work out who might be a threat to him, who he might have misjudged but no one seemed any more than they had appeared. He probed around him, seeking anyone with power but felt nothing. In the stillness, noise reached up to him from the square below. On walking to the window and looking down, he could see men moving in the low light of the early morning, but even at this distance, he could see that the order that he insisted on and craved was gone. Enraged, he turned and strode away.

On circling around the keep wall, they came to the wide steps that arced up to the main door. Here they met some guards who fought with resolve. Ultimately though they were outnumbered and outclassed by Zoe and her men, who quickly overwhelmed them. Marrea and Zoe raced up the steps, Zoe motioning for her men to fan out around the top, facing outward. Finn's men spread out in front of them, pulled their bows from their backs, nocked arrows and stood, ready to fire. Looking back, Marrea could see guards gathering but, without anyone to lead or direct them, they stood uncertainly, unnerved by the line of drawn bows which were held steady and purposefully. She noted them automatically, trying to keep her thoughts focused on what lay ahead. She had been relieved to be moving forward, worry about Tam coursing through her when they had been holed up in the guard house.

Zoe pushed on the door, but it did not move. She motioned to Finn, who came alongside her and pushed with her. But the door remained firmly shut. Quickly, they both scanned it for any weaknesses, but there were none. Marrea turned to the door and examined it for a few moments.

"I can open it, but then Nehlo will likely sense me when we are this close, and we will lose any element of surprise that hiding my power brings. I am not sure I am strong enough to defeat him without that."

"But if we can't open it, we will die here. Eventually someone will take charge of those men, and then it is only a matter of time."

Marrea looked around her, suddenly uncertain. She could sense Nehlo above them, and she knew that he was enraged by something. She could feel the strength of his power coursing through the anger, and she knew that she needed every advantage she could glean, including the small one of surprise. She was fairly sure that he would not be able to sense her unless she revealed herself to him, but what good was that if they were to die here, before ever facing him? She waited though, willing for something to happen. As if in response to her wishes, she heard a scraping sound on the other side of the door, which suddenly loosened enough to allow Zoe and Finn to push it open. They held it ajar, ushering everyone in, and then pulled it shut after them.

Will had stared out of the window for some moments before becoming aware of the clamour beneath him. In the dim morning light, he could make out men moving, and the sound of voices raised and fighting. He stared out, trying to make sense of it and then saw a group moving more purposefully than the others. He saw it burst through the men milling around and move as a unit toward the keep. He lost sight of them as they passed beneath him but then saw them again as they moved out from the wall toward the steps to the main door. At the rear he could make out men, obviously acting as a rear guard with their faces turned backward, and among them he recognized Finn.

A sick feeling smote him, and he turned his head away, unable to look down on the group, now understanding who they were and what they were trying to do. He could hardly bear to look in case someone saw him and recognized him, impossible as that was from where he sat. But he was also drawn to watch, to make sure that they made it. He saw them clash with armed guards at the base of the steps, quickly overwhelm them and then move to the top of the steps. He could hardly believe that they were going to make it, but then he saw them stop, unable to progress, and he realized that the heavy door was closed. Surely they had means with which to open it, but as the seconds ticked by, he saw that they remained on the steps. Guards had started gathering, not threatening, yet with growing intent. He could not just sit there and watch his friends being cut down, so Will rose and ran, uncaring of the noise that he made as every second might mean their loss and he could not add that to the searing pain of his betrayal. He barrelled past some servants, the first up for their morning duties, and careered into the main entrance hall, where only a short time before he had been with Tam. He didn't pause to consider the absence of the guards. Reaching the door, he heaved at the heavy wooden bar, fixed tight within its brackets. For a second he thought that he would not be strong enough, and despair almost brought tears to his eyes. Focusing as hard as he could, he fought the bar upward, and inch by inch it rose until it swung out and the door loosened. Straight away it was pushed open, and Zoe and Finn almost fell through, quickly followed by Marrea. They held the door open as the rest of their group filed through and then the door slammed shut and, for a moment, all was quiet.

Marrea leaned against the wall. She looked at Will, but he kept his head down, standing a little away from the group, which was organizing itself quickly to move further into the castle. It took her a second to remember that he had been with Tam and was now alone. She had feared the worst already and this confirmed it, but she dared not give thought to this as she might be overwhelmed just when she needed to be in control. She focused, trying to sense Nehlo's position, and with a shock realized that he was close and moving toward them. She quelled a feeling of panic and turned to Zoe.

"He is coming," she said, simply.

Zoe darted a look around the room before returning to look at Marrea. "You are sure?"

Marrea nodded. "I think so. He is certainly moving closer, quickly." She motioned toward the far side of the room, where there were a number of doors. "One of those but I cannot say which for sure."

"What do you suggest?"

"I cannot protect you all, but I will try. You need your men to spread out, to protect themselves as best they can. Those with bows may be able to help me if I weaken, but they need to be careful as their arrows could easily be a weapon Nehlo can use against them."

Zoe nodded again, looking tense but thoughtful. Marrea marvelled at how someone so relatively young compared to her could appear so calm. She wanted to ensure that whatever faith they were putting in her was rewarded. She watched as the men fanned out to the edges of the room, testing their bows but leaving their arrows in their sheaths. They searched for nooks to lean into and kept clear of the windows and doors. Zoe and Finn stayed near her, and for a moment she wanted to ask them to move away as well, but they looked resolute, and in truth she valued their proximity and needed the encouragement of their presence. She breathed deeply, calming her mind and heart, allowing her senses to reach out and feel the ground beneath her and the air around her with all its textures and constant movement. Extending her senses further, she felt deeply conscious of the great expanse outside, its many parts already warming in the energy of the sun's first rays. Whatever had happened to Tam, she knew that he would not have failed, and that no matter what Nehlo appeared to be, he had been robbed of some of his power.

Nehlo stalked the corridors, his rage emanating from him and scattering the small number of servants who were up at this time. As he walked, he cast his senses ahead of him, but although he could feel people within and without the castle, none had any power or were any real threat to him. He still could not understand what had happened, and that lack of clarity and control fuelled his anger. He did not know what he planned to do, but he cared for no one and was ready to lash out mercilessly if any stood in his way.

He approached the main entrance way but did not stop to open the doors, instead blasting them open with the strong gusts of air that swirled around him. On entering the wide room, though, he stopped abruptly. Immediately across from him stood a woman, slight of build and stature, but even at this distance she looked familiar. She did not move at his entrance, which surprised him. A plain woman and an older man stood just behind her, and though they flinched when they saw him, they stood firm. Nehlo looked around the room and saw, almost with cold amusement, men spread out around the edges, obviously afraid but unmoving. The pause was momentary and in it he realized that they were there waiting for him, ready for him. He almost laughed at their temerity, but his anger was too strong to allow even this false levity to escape him.

Marrea felt Nehlo's approach, but now that he was here, she did not fear him anymore. As the door flew open, she felt the full force of his anger and power. But she felt ready to face him, no matter what happened. She stared at him, hardly recognizing the man she had known so long ago and had respected, though had never been able to love. With his height and breadth, he was as physically impressive as he had always been, but now a sinister confidence marked his bearing. She could see the contempt and coldness that almost radiated from him as he surveyed the room, his eyes lingering on her for a second before seemingly dismissing her. Instinctively, she felt him reach out to manipulate the air in multiple different areas, and she readied herself to respond.

Chapter 39

Without moving, Nehlo targeted each of the people around the room, excepting the slight woman in front of him. Something about her was familiar, and he wanted to know before he killed her as he needed to understand what had happened and would explore any possible link. He manipulated the air around each person, working in multiple different areas at once, pulling it from them and condensing it in a band that tightened around their throats. Nehlo watched as they gasped and their hands reached up to their necks, and their faces registered the shock that always overtook people when they scrabbled for air that would come. He liked to watch as they desperately struggled against a power they could not see or understand and as they clung frantically to life even as it ebbed away from them. Their colour changed, their faces turned a strange mix of blue and red as they were simultaneously engorged with blood and yet starved of the oxygen it normally carried. Some weakened quickly, their hands dropping and legs sagging beneath them; others fought on longer though nothing could save them. The older man and the plain women kneeled, with their eyes fixed on the woman between them. And then, the impossible happened. Nehlo felt his control slip and then crumble, and the air wrested from him. Throughout the room, he heard gasps as air was sucked back into lungs that had almost breathed their last. Some lay on the floor, too weak to stand, their chests heaving in pained relief. His eyes darted to the woman in front of him. She looked pale but resolute, and power emanated from her. How had she hidden it from him? Who was she? She did not strike out at him but instead studied him, her pale eyes almost glistening.

Marrea had taken time to work out what Nehlo had done and how to combat it. Fearing that she would be too late, she gently manipulated the air around each of her people, almost like untying a knot. She felt the extent of Nehlo's raw power and did not try to overpower him, instead seeking to guide and mould air in multiple different ways. She studied Nehlo now, seeing his momentary confusion before his eyes rested on her and any hope of remaining hidden disappeared.

"Who are you?" His voice was colder than she remembered, but it retained a beguiling smoothness of tone.

"Don't you recognize me? Look closer."

"You are familiar." He paused, studying her before quietly continuing. "Yes, the mercy bearer. You look like him." He paused again, looking round the room, his gaze settling on Will, who shrank back from it. A sardonic smile twisted his lips. "The traitor. It all becomes clear."

Marrea's calm faltered momentarily as she looked at Will, seeing in his reaction the truth of what Nehlo said. She knew now for certain that Tam was dead. She could not sense him anywhere, and the lack of his presence left a deep void that threatened to overwhelm her. She had borne the sorrow of knowing that he might die, but now the hard and unyielding finality of death struck her forcefully, almost robbing her of her senses. Her eyes misted over, before recalling all that they had spoken of, all that he had meant to achieve, even at the cost of his life, and all that now depended on her completing what he had begun. She forced her sadness and grief to the back of her mind to be dwelled on later, if time and life allowed. Marrea's eyes flashed as she focused again on the man in front of her.

Nehlo, too, had been momentarily preoccupied as he searched his memory. "You are very like him, could almost be family. The whelp who offered me mercy while kneeling in weakness at my feet."

"He was my brother," she replied, quietly but clearly with a hint of pride in her voice.

"Was. You know he is dead then. Without even a fight."

She felt the compassion of her companions as they turned to her, but she kept her gaze fixed on Nehlo.

"I know it."

"And yet, how can you be his sister," he mused, almost to himself. "You are strong. He was nothing."

"You still don't see what is happening here?" Marrea almost wept at her brother's sacrifice, to try and guide and redeem this man only for him, even now, to be oblivious of the chance he had been offered and its cost. "You are so blind."

Nehlo started, obviously nettled. Colour monetarily flashed through his face and eyes.

"Nothing is hidden from me. He was a nobody, as are you, even with your power. He could not harm me or turn me, and you will find that you cannot either."

"You knew us both once, loved us I believe. I am Marrea. And Tam is the man you have just rejected and killed."

She spoke the words firmly but with an inescapable tone of sadness. The effect on Nehlo was immediate. He stepped back, and his hands reached for the wall behind him. His head dropped for a moment as far-distant memories surged back, rocking and unsteadying him. Loss and sadness, sometimes humiliation that even now burned, but also friendship, loyalty and camaraderie. Was it possible? Could that man have been Tam? He shuddered as the thought ripped through him, the emotions that followed in its wake leaving him weaker and more vulnerable than he could ever remember. But then other memories arose, ones he often returned to. Of misunderstanding and betrayal, of rejection and the ending of a friendship that he had believed to be lifelong. Years of steeling himself against any weakness could not be so easily torn down and he felt, with a mixture of relief and savage pride, his sense of power and resolute authority return.

"You, I could believe to be Marrea, though you have changed. The other could not have been Tam; he was weaker than even these poor fools who follow you."

"Did you know me or sense my power before I revealed myself?"

200

Again, he hesitated, suddenly unsure when faced with this truth. "He could not have hidden it from me. I searched him and would have known. And at the last would even he have not resisted, knowing to do nothing was his death? It is not possible!"

"You did not sense his power because he used it to hide the filthy bonds he had taken upon himself. Bonds that you had used to enslave this people. But he spoke the truth. He did not come to harm you but to offer you a way back. But he knew too that if you did not take his offer and instead took his life, you would bring ruin upon yourself. And so you have done. And yet, it is still not too late."

Nehlo glanced around him, his lips curling into a sneer. "And this, this is my ruin? He died for nothing, if this is all that I face. And you have never had it in you to kill."

"And those you bound to you? Where are they now? Could it be that they have been released and are no longer under your control? How could that be unless my brother released them through dying. Your control, such as it was, is over. You will never again be able to bond this people; that much at least my brother has done. And I suspect some of your power died with him in those bonds, but we will only know that if it comes to a testing between us. That does not have to be. We came to offer you a new beginning, the possibility of redemption. You do not need to face this destruction."

Nehlo faltered; the words hit home. She could not possibly know about his attendants. He cast his senses out but could not detect any people bonded to him, near or far. He had never trusted or loved any of these people, but they had been a form of support or protection, and he suddenly felt exposed without them, alone. The feeling made him angry with himself and with the woman who provoked it. Had he not striven to remove any need for others, to be strong and independent? And he had become stronger than any.

"You offer me return? And you think that by coming yourself that I will desire it and accept it?"

"We hoped that there was enough memory of our friendship for you to listen to our plea."

"I did not even recognize your weakling brother and cared nothing for his empty words."

"Would you have heeded him if you had known? Would you be willing to make amends for the harm you have done? If not, then there is nothing left for you. You cannot continue as you are, and both Tam and I knew that it might come to this."

"To what, little sister?"

She looked down for a second before lifting her head and looking at him directly, her eyes clear and unblinking. "To your end. You must choose, Nehlo. I cannot leave here with you in place. I will fight and best you if I must, but you can choose to come with me. That much I am clear about, and you should not doubt my will in this."

Nehlo met her gaze but could not laugh as he intended to. He could see her intent and did not doubt it. He did not fear her though; long ago he had seen to it that he outstripped them all, ensuring that no one could defeat him. He did not feel anything for her. In his detachment any link with her or the past was empty and meaningless. She was now just an obstacle to overcome. Focusing on her, he concentrated all his power in drawing air to himself from all directions, disregarding the consequences. A terrible roaring noise filled the room with windows shattering loudly and doors crashing open as air hurtled into the room towards Nehlo. Channelling it all onto Marrea, he bore down on her, the pressure forcing her to her knees with her hands flat on the stone floor. Blood dripped onto the floor from her nose and eyes. She felt as though her body was being crushed under the pressure. She could not breathe with her chest wrapped tightly in an iron-like band. She sank further, her arms buckling beneath her.

Focused as Nehlo was, he did not see the woman at Marrea's side raise her hand. He did not see the men around the room who had sought shelter from the onslaught of wind, rise and nock arrows to their bows. Her hand fell and a torrent of arrows were released, racing toward him from every side, their flight ragged in the tumult but most going where directed. At the last moment he felt them split the air that remained around him, and instinctively he redirected some of the air from Marrea and encircled himself in it. The arrows slowed in the denser air, stilling in mid-flight to hang suspended around him. More arrows followed the first but again they could not penetrate to him. He prepared his counterstrike.

Marrea felt the lightening of the pressure that had been crushing her. She rose slowly to her knees, her body weak but her mind clear. She could see the maelstrom around Nehlo and could sense the power holding it at bay. She focused as hard as she could and ripped the control of the air from his grasp. She then turned it in on him, buffeting him with winds that ripped his breath away and threatened to tear the very flesh from him. She did not relent, however, and heard Zoe cry out beside her. More arrows fired, and though most missed their mark in the tumult of wind, one flew true and pierced Nehlo high in the chest, throwing him back and causing him to fall to the ground. Marrea forced the air down on him with even greater force now, crushing his chest and causing the blood to flow strongly from his wound. At the last, when she felt he could not sustain it any longer, she stopped. She sagged to the ground, almost spent but unwilling to strike the last, fatal blow.

Chapter 40

All was quiet for a few moments. Zoe's men approached Nehlo cautiously, their bows raised, arrows ready. He seemed lifeless but for the blood still staining his shirt and the slight movement of his chest. Zoe reached down to help Marrea, but she waved her away and stood on her own, though with evident struggle. Once on her feet, she wavered unsteadily. Finn looked around, not believing that it could be over, so suddenly and with so little loss of life. He had no idea what they were to do now with Nehlo, never mind with the city and country if his reign was truly over. He sensed that Marrea could have killed him in that moment, but for some reason she had relented. He respected her decision but thought ruefully that it left them with a difficulty that was not easily overcome. He did not doubt that Nehlo would regain at least some of his power if left alive, and he could not fathom how they could contain him when that happened. This, though, was not his responsibility; he had completed the task set before him, and decisions would now have to be taken by people much more influential and knowledgeable than him. That farm, maybe with Zoe by his side, was the limit of his ambition now.

Beside him, he realized that Marrea had become tense and watchful although Nehlo had not moved. Then Finn saw Marrea suddenly clutch her side as a shard of glass pierced her and embedded itself. Fresh blood flowed quickly from the wound. She gasped and fell to her knees, both hands now soaked in blood. A sharp pain pierced his own low back and touching there he felt the warmth of his own blood and the sharp edge of more glass. With horror, he now saw shards of glass from the smashed windows flying through the room, too many and moving too fast to be able to avoid. They sliced and stabbed into the men all around him and where there had been quiet, suddenly there was cries of pain and panic. As he stumbled back toward the wall, he saw Nehlo rise, a look of hatred and fury on his pale face as well as something more, the imperious look of the victor surveying those who had had the temerity to challenge him. Finn felt fear buffet him in ways that he had not experienced before. There was nothing any of them could do against such power and such will to destroy. They were all going to die.

Nehlo's voice, harsh and grating now with none of the smoothness of before, carried over the chaos. "You should have killed me when you had the chance, but you were too weak. You will not have another."

Marrea did not answer him but instead bowed her head. She felt nothing now but regret and sadness. Her brother was gone and had sacrificed himself for nothing. She was going to die here too, in a foreign land, away from his family, which she loved as her own. She knew that they would never recover from the loss of them both. There was no one to challenge Nehlo now or stand between him and them; she could barely stand and knew that her life was ebbing away from her wounds even before Nehlo attacked again.

Nehlo stood and looked around the room at the devastation he had wrought. He saw with cold satisfaction the wounds he had inflicted, the pain and suffering he had caused. He exulted in it, that having been brought so low, even to his weakest point, he had overcome and they were all subject to him. He left them to die, in their frailty and pain, knowing they were no threat to him.

He turned to look at Marrea. He saw with disdain that she had knelt, her head down, unable to offer any more resistance. At that moment he saw how far he had come, how far he had truly surpassed them; Tam, Marrea, anyone else his people chose to send, but he knew there would be no others. They would not dare. He realized then that he had always had a lingering sense of dread that he might not be strong enough, that when they came they would defeat him and bind him, and that he had prepared all this time to avoid that humiliation. In defeating the best they could send, he finally felt released from this subjugation; there was no end to his power now, to what he could achieve and who he could dominate. He considered saving Marrea so she would witness his assent but preferred to watch her crawl for these final moments of her life. She was the last connection to his people, and he felt nothing but a savage satisfaction as he watched it die.

Marrea looked around the room, feeling the pain of all the men and women there. All had been struck and were lying or kneeling on the floor, clutching helplessly at bleeding wounds. They had followed her, but she could not defend them now. Zoe had collapsed, a shard of glass having sliced her neck. Finn was by her side, trying desperately to staunch the flow of blood while his own ran freely. Marrea reached out desperately to try and plug the wounds with flows of air but felt herself repelled by Nehlo. She felt bleak, cold despair start to seep over her, threatening to drown out any other sense.

And yet.

Her brother had died so that Nehlo would be weakened, so that she would be able to defeat him. Tam had robbed him of some of his power, maybe even much of it, and Nehlo may not yet have come to understand that. Tam had known that she would have to finish what they had started together, and he would not have left her here unless he believed that she could do it. His love was as fierce as her own and he had never let her down or left her to face such harm before, and she did not believe that he would have done so now. She thought also of his faith, his certainty that they were here to serve the Creator and that He would not let them fail. Tam had been willing to die for that belief. The extent of that sacrifice and the belief that underpinned it suddenly hit home. And with that came the certainty that she too was the Creator's servant, equipped by Him for this purpose.

She knelt on the ground, her head down and her eyes closed. The sounds of the suffering around her receded as she felt the blossoming of hope within her, the growth of confidence in the capacity she had been given to defeat this evil and complete what her brother had begun. But her fears and doubts fought back, her physical weakness assailed her and the taunts of Nehlo resounded in her mind. Marrea focused hard, pushing away the doubts, and searched for the strength to rise again and face him; he was not what he seemed, and she was more than he knew.

Finn was on his knees, leaning over Zoe, desperately trying to staunch the flow of blood from her neck with his hands. He could feel his own blood oozing from him, but he fought to keep his strength from failing, to focus on keeping the pressure on her neck to stop her life draining away from her. She was horribly pale, with a slight sheen of cold sweat on her skin. He almost cried at the futility of it all; why was he here watching someone die who had become dear to him, seeking to defeat someone so much more powerful than any of them, even Tam? Why could he just not have walked away, with or without Zoe? He had done enough, more than enough, getting those prisoners home. He owed no one anything.

In the edge of his vision, he became aware of Marrea on her knees. He turned to look at her in fear, expecting the worst. He watched as she bent her head, her hands flat on the stone and her eyes closed tight, almost straining to keep them shut. He could not guess at the suffering she was enduring with the loss of her brother and now this end to all their efforts. Despite this he saw the tension in her eyes ease, a new resolve grow in her face, and a new strength surge into arms which had weakened. Somehow this lifted him and gave him hope. Considering her suffering brought to his mind Tam and what he had said about his sister. Maybe this was not the end.

Marrea kept her head down and her eyes closed so she could keep her new-found focus. She reached round behind her and drew her short staffs from the pouch on her back. With one in each hand, she knelt a few moments longer, feeling the finely fashioned wood with the engrained message, "All I have to give." She thought of Owen, dying in a stranger's home, of Kayla, bitter and hardened by her experience, of Seth, trusting in her and Tam despite everything he had seen, and Finn and Zoe. And she thought of her brother, dying defenceless so that his burden would die with him and so that she could stand here with a chance to succeed.

Nehlo watched Marrea reach behind her and draw out some sticks of wood. He almost laughed at how puny they looked in her hands and how pathetic she looked in thinking that she could challenge him armed only with them. But Marrea gripped them tightly and pushed up from the floor with her hands before her legs found their strength, and having stood, she lifted her head to look directly at him. The sadness in her look was heavy in its potency and almost unbearable, even to him, robbing him of the cruel joy he had forged in his sense of dominance.

Marrea saw that for a brief second Nehlo seemed ill at ease. With her staffs in front of her, she reached out as far as she could and drew to herself all the air she could. Buoyed by the energy that flowed to her, the sound of air rushing toward her from all around seemed as a song to her soul and with the greatest artistry and skill she crafted it to her purposes. Before Nehlo could react, she sent it in multiple directions to all who had followed her, binding their wounds to staunch the blood loss, ensuring that she could focus entirely on Nehlo. She drew the air back to herself, feeling the energy coursing around and through her.

"You still seek to overcome me? Have you not learned from your failure, from your brother's failure?"

Marrea looked at those standing around the room, tense and watchful. Nehlo's words made her think again of Tam and the recognition that she would not see him alive again pierced her with almost physical pain. His loss, however, strengthened her resolve and brought home to her how lost Nehlo was, standing alone, with no ties of family or friendship to rely on, no faith in his creator to anchor him. And now rejecting the only thing that could redeem him. With a voice that was low and wrought with regret she replied, "You were our best friend, our brother. We shared so much. And now there is just enmity between us. I wish it was not so, that Tam had succeeded in convincing you, that even now you would relent and return with me. But if that is not to be, I am ready to end it this time."

The words and Marrea's emotion pierced Nehlo in a way that he had not expected. Images flashed before him, unbidden. Playing in the woods as a child, the camaraderie of close friendships. A warm and loving second home, when he had been at his lowest after the loss of his parents. Marrea's look of gratitude as he pulled her from the river. The images were fragmentary and hazy, however, as if recalled from a different life, someone else's life. They seemed disconnected from him, devoid of meaning. Nehlo only now saw the world in terrible monochrome clarity: power or weakness, dominion or servitude. These were the only choices, and he would never relinquish power. He hardened his heart, remembering how he hated what Tam and Marrea believed, the weakness inherent in serving and guiding where they could lead and force others to follow as he had done. He hated Marrea at that moment so strongly that it drove all other thought or emotion from him.

Summoning air to himself, he fashioned it to sharp points, driving them with venom at Marrea. She felt their approach and using the bank of air around her pushed Zoe and Finn aside before swivelling and tilting to avoid the razor-sharp blasts, which flew past her and embedded deep into the wall behind. Nehlo swept forward, his hands raised, directing the air into a blade that he could move as fast as his wrists could turn. He rained down blows on Marrea, flicking and twisting, each blow seeming light and momentary in his movement but landing heavily. Marrea reinforced her staffs with bindings of air allowing her to block the strikes, feeling and sensing them rather than seeing them. Enraged, Nehlo reached out further and lifted more fragments of glass, and drove them at Marrea, while he continued to press with strikes of his own. She leaped back momentarily from the fray and cocooned herself in a blanket of compressed air. The glass ripped into it but did not penetrate through to her flesh.

Nehlo stepped back, breathing heavily. He felt the wound on his chest, which he had bound together but had now reopened and oozed blood. He shook off the weariness creeping into his limbs and stood still, concentrating for a moment. He

206

looked upward, seeking something before turning back to Marrea, a calculating look upon his face.

Marrea suddenly felt a lurch of fear. Nehlo moved toward her again, his hands curled around the base of his blade of air. Just before he engaged with her, Marrea felt movement above her and sensed air seeping around the massive wooden beams in the roof above them, pulling at the joints and loosening them. She only had a second to consider this, however, as Nehlo moved forward, seeking to drive her back with stabs and feints that she just managed to parry, though she had to give ground. With a horrible groaning noise, the first beam loosened at one end and tilted precariously downward, showering them all in dust as the flat stone above it loosened. She thought feverishly as she felt him direct more and more air into the roof while simultaneously probing her defences for weakness. Finally, the beam fell, swinging down in an awesome arc to crash onto the floor, and after it a hail of stones, some small but many large and heavy enough to crush them all. Nehlo redirected his flow of air to form an impenetrable cushion over himself so that the rocks were pushed away from him before falling heavily to the floor. Marrea cried out and in desperation threw her own air outward, above her people. In that moment she could not deflect the sharp strike of air that punched through her jacket into her side, with blood quickly staining its path.

Finn felt himself pushed back toward the doorway by an invisible force as Nehlo approached Marrea. Seeing that, the other men inched round to join them, keeping close to the walls. Marrea twisted and turned to ward off unseen blows, and he watched mesmerized as she and Nehlo clashed, the silence belying the ferocity of the movements and intent. They separated for a brief moment, and then he heard a loud creaking above his head and looking up saw movement in the great beams above followed by a shower of dust. He looked quickly around, seeking escape for his men, but most of them remained weak from their wounds. Zoe, too, lay on the ground, too weak to stand unaided. He shouted a warning and started to drag Zoe toward the door. She tried to help, pushing with her feet, and he saw the others moving painfully slowly with them just as the beam above started to move with a grating sound that rapidly rose in pitch, before the free end crashed to the floor with a sound that reverberated under their feet. Shouts of confusion and fear erupted all around him as everyone rushed to the main door through the dust that had been thrown up by the stones starting to fall among them. Half stumbling, half dragging Zoe, Finn moved as quickly as he could, not daring to look up or back, hunching his back against the expected crushing weight of stone. Panting he reached the door and pulled Zoe through before turning back and reaching out his hands to the others who fell through, exhausted and disoriented. Only on looking back did he see the stones falling onto an invisible barrier above their heads, before they slid ponderously down to crash into a growing pile on the inner part of the room. He looked at Marrea. She sat with her back to the wall, looking pale but resolute as Nehlo approached with his hands poised in front of him.

Finn felt something being thrust into his hand and looked down to see a bow with an arrow already nocked. Stepping back through the door he composed himself, drew back as far as he could, aimed at Nehlo, who was only twenty paces away, and released the arrow.

Marrea stumbled back, the sharp pain in her side almost making her lose control of the air she had banked up between her retreating people and the stones that fell from the roof. She was dimly aware of Nehlo approaching again, but she could not move to avoid him or avert the blow that was coming. She slumped down on the floor, leaning against the wall for support just as she saw that everyone had made it to the door. She turned again to Nehlo, summoning her last reserves of strength to fight one last time.

She felt an arrow split the air flying true to Nehlo. She saw that he was aware of it too and had bolstered the air on that side to deflect it. He drove forward, his hands thrusting the blade of air toward her chest. Marrea pulled the air away from above her head and reaching for the arrow, created a funnel of air that guided it round Nehlo's defence. She moulded a sharp gust of air behind it, speeding its flight and causing it to punch into his shoulder, throwing his upper body to the side. A look of shock appeared on his face as his blow was pushed wide of where Marrea sat. In almost the same motion Marrea reached out and wrestled from him the bank of air above his head and pushed him away before drawing it all toward her and wrapping it around herself. The stones and a further beam fell as she sat, crouched under her invisible shield, and watched sadly as Nehlo staggered away from her, his hands raised up almost pathetically before a heavy rock smashed into his shoulder, spinning him away from her and knocking him to the ground. He lay, unable to move as a great weight of stones bore down on him.

Chapter 41

Finn and some of the less injured cleared a way through to Marrea, fearing the worst after the roof had collapsed. They found her, still seated with her back to the wall, surrounded by dust and the mass of broken stones. She clutched her side which still bled slowly and needed help to stand and walk slowly out of the now ruined room. Once outside Finn saw the castle guard standing back, staring in shock at the shattered remains of the entrance. The confusion of the night, which had seen the attack at the gates and subsequent chaos as bondings had been lifted, was still evident. The castle guard gathered in ragged lines, looking for guidance toward the small group around Marrea, who stood weak and vulnerable at the top of the steps. Finn saw Marrea look at him expectantly, and turning he saw a look of encouragement on Zoe's pale face. He stepped forward, unsure of what to say that would explain what had happened. Then he realized that the time for explanations would come later. He stood straight and tall.

"Tonight has seen the end of a tyranny." His voice was strong and clear and driven through with authority. "Spread the word. Nehlo's rule is over, and a new day has come. It is up to us now which path to choose. But heed me in this. There has been much harm and distrust over the last years and there are many who are broken and will be fearful still. Let our new start be judged on how we look after the most vulnerable, the weakest among us and how we heal the rifts that have so scarred us."

He stopped, unsure. He did not know why he had felt able to command them in this way, but he had suddenly felt that it was right for him to do so. There was movement in the first rank of soldiers, and for a second he thought they were lining up to attack. But then they stood sharply to attention, the rows behind following suit till they all stood silent and waiting. Finn looked at the men around him on the step, half expecting them to look amused, but they too looked at him expectantly. He felt a light touch on his side and then Zoe's hand was in his. She gently steered him down the steps to the waiting soldiers. Some of the captains stepped forward and saluted. Finn hesitated, unwilling to take command. Then he looked out to the city, which needed order and safety, and beyond that to the country they had just walked through, which needed healing. Someone had to make a start until proper authorities could be established.

Marrea watched as Finn walked with Zoe toward the soldiers. Her side ached and she felt so tired it was difficult to remember everything that had happened. She had succeeded but she felt no elation. They had wanted to return with Nehlo, restore him to what he had been among them but instead she had been forced to kill him, something which she knew would always haunt her. Only now could she start to think about what had happened to Tam, to consider a life without him. A life to be lived but one that would always be touched by the shadow of death, by his absence. She saw Will standing a little way off. His whole body spoke of his shame and misery, and it so smote her heart that she felt compassion for him, despite what he had done to Tam and to her. She caught his eye and held it for a long moment.

Will stood a little apart from the others with his back pressed against the wall. Its coldness leached into him and spread throughout his body. He did not know what to think or where to look. All around him he could see men and women coming to some realization of what had happened, and he could see a lightness to them that was savagely contrasted by the darkness of self-hatred and self-disgust in his own mind.

He could still see the look in Marrea's eyes when told that he had betrayed Tam. She had looked at him with such sadness that even now it made him want to weep. He had seen her again briefly when she had stepped from the ruins, and he had felt none of the judgment from her that he knew he deserved, none of the hatred that he felt for himself. She had looked at him, her eyes tearful but warm, which had lashed him more than a thousand recriminations.

He sank to the ground, his head in his hands. He knew that Marrea offered an acceptance that promised, amazingly, to never hark back to what had gone before. It must be a trick. It could not be true. He deserved only rejection and scorn. How could it be that she could give this to the betrayer of her brother? He hated himself, so how could someone accept him like this? The more he thought about it, the more absurd it sounded, the more impossible it became and the darker everything seemed to him. He could not bear to lift his head up to see the brightness of the new day. Darkness was what he sought, to disappear and submerge into, to hide in.

And yet. A little chink of light seeped into his darkness, where only self-hatred dwelled. Was there a chance for him after all? Would others accept him as she had? Could they? As soon as the possibility had arisen, he could no longer look with longing at death or some other form of oblivion. What if he could start again? He had lost everything: years of his life, his family, his friends and his sense of self, but a very small part of him yearned for life and that part latched onto the hope that Marrea held out and would not let go.

Marrea sat up on the bed, refreshed though it was still early in the day. On the day of Nehlo's death, she and the others had had their wounds tended and then eaten a meal, during which there was very little conversation. Marrea had been too full of different emotions to be able to talk and everyone had taken their lead from her. Afterwards she had spent time ensuring that Tam's body was properly cared for before she found the room that had been prepared for her. She had slept the rest of that day and into the next. Finn and Zoe were beside her now. They both looked tired. Zoe remained weakened by her wound and loss of blood. Her wound, dressed with multiple layers of linen which she touched cautiously, would heal with time. Finn's wound had been less severe, but he had been up late, organizing the castle guard and staff and speaking to the many people who had come, most in hope but some, who seemed to see authority resting in his hands, to assert their claims for the future. They had agreed, however, on a period of mourning for those that had died and for all that people had lost before discussions could begin about what would come next. He looked strained but resolute and Marrea knew that he would do his best to set things right in his own forthright, simple way.

Zoe had been sitting quietly on the side of the bed, and she now turned as if to say something but hesitated. Marrea smiled at her, taking her hand in her own.

"Why must you leave so soon? You are tired still."

Marrea squeezed her hand before answering. "I yearn to see my near sister, Tam's wife, and her children. They need to know of their loss and receive Tam back to them for the burial. I feel I cannot properly grieve myself until that time."

"I understand, but neither you nor Tam will receive the recognition or the thanks that is due you as it is still too soon for people to understand. A few more days will allow you to rest and for the story to be told."

"That is for the best. People like me are meant to be in the background, aiding but not leading. Nehlo broke that trust, but we must start to build it up again. I will only be a distraction to those who will be tasked with rebuilding, including you both. I know you will do it well and I will hear about it from my home country and rejoice with you."

A few tears spilled from Zoe's eyes, which she hastily rubbed away. Finn looked emotional as well, and he turned away for a moment.

"Well, if it must be, that is that," he said gruffly. "But how will you travel and how will you manage with Tam's body?"

"I will manage," Marrea smiled. "But I will need a horse and a cart to lay him in. I can travel quickly, and we will be safe. Talking of this has made me even more certain that I long to be home as soon as possible."

"You shall have the best horse I can muster. In fact, I will find you the horse that managed to carry me all the way here; it was a fine animal, and I would love you to keep it to remember us by."

"Thank you."

Marrea reached out and took his hand as well. She held both firmly for a few moments before releasing them with a warm smile.

Before the middle of the day, Finn had recovered his horse and procured a good cart. He and Zoe ensured that the bags on the saddle and in the cart stored plenty of provisions, and they had carefully laid Tam's coffin in the back, surrounded by straw to keep it safe and covered by some blankets. Marrea then bound it, sealing and preserving it for the journey home. These simple preparations made, Marrea hugged them both tightly before leading her horse away from the keep, down between the walls to the outer gate. There, waiting for her, were the men and women who had followed Finn and Zoe and who had been with her at the last. They formed a tunnel, their weapons raised in salute as she walked through before looking back momentarily. Passers-by turned to stare at her as she led her simple horse and cart away from the castle but then went on their way. As she walked down the streets, fewer heads turned and by the time she left the city confines she attracted no attention at all.

Printed in Great Britain
by Amazon

24180055R00126